Tickled Pink

Other books by Debby Mayne

Sweet Baklava

The Class Reunion Series

Pretty Is as Pretty Does

Bless Her Heart

Tickled Pink

The Class Reunion Series

Book 3

Debby Mayne

Tickled Pink

ISBN-13: 978-1-4267-3362-8

Published by Abingdon Press, P.O. Box 801, Nashville, TN 37202

www.abingdonpress.com

Published in association with the Hartline Literary Agency.

Library of Congress Cataloging-in-Publication Data

Mayne, Debby.
Tickled pink / Debby Mayne.
pages cm. — (The Class Reunion Series ; Book 3)
ISBN 978-1-4267-3362-8 (binding—paper / trade pbk. : alk. paper) 1. Class reunions—Fiction. I. Title.
PS3563.A963877T53 2013
813'.54—dc23

2013009062

Printed in the United States of America

1 2 3 4 5 6 7 8 9 10 / 18 17 16 15 14 13

I'm dedicating this book to my pals
Cherie Burbach, Julie Pollitt, Sandie Bricker,
Rhonda Gibson, Paige Dooly,
Debra Collins, Trish Perry, Loree Lough,
and Beth Teller.
Y'all are some of the coolest ladies ever!

Acknowledgments

Thanks to my agent, Tamela Hancock Murray, for believing in me and being my biggest cheerleader. I can't imagine this journey without you.

Thanks also to the fabulous team at Abingdon, including Ramona Richards, Pamela Clements, Susan Cornell, Cat Hoort, and everyone else who has had anything to do with the Class Reunion series.

Happy are those who find wisdom,
and those who gain understanding.
Her profit is better than silver,
and her gain better than gold.

Proverbs 3:13-14

1
Priscilla Slater

Laura and Pete Moss are happy to announce
Piney Point High School's
20-year reunion
on June 15, 2013, at 7:00 PM
in the brand-new Piney Point Community Center
Multipurpose Room.
Attire: Casual
RSVP: Laura or Pete Moss 601-555-1515
Note: There will be no preparty.

As soon as the microwave dings, I grab a pot holder and pull out the plastic tray with steam rising from the corner where I've vented the cellophane. I place it on the counter, lean over it, and inhale, trying to imagine it being a nutritious, home-cooked meal. But all I smell is preservative-laced gravy. Maybe I should go back to my old nightly salad from a bag.

I take a bite of the tasteless food and glance down at my twenty-year-reunion invitation before looking out my condo window at the Atlantic Ocean. Things sure have changed for me over the past five years. Not only have I become a household name among TV retail shoppers who desire to have the coveted Southern-woman big hair, I own townhomes and condos in several places along the path of my chain of hair salons. Sometimes I forget to thank the Lord for all my wonderful blessings, so I squeeze my eyes shut and send up a prayer of gratitude.

Ten minutes later the plastic tray is empty, and now I'm faced with nothing but a mountain of paperwork. You'd think that with all I've acquired over the past thirteen years I'd be on top of the world, kicking up my feet, celebrating my immense success. *In my dreams.*

Don't get me wrong. I'm grateful that I've managed to accomplish so much. But there are times when certain aspects of a simple life in my hometown of Piney Point, Mississippi, appeals to me. Then I come to my senses.

I've never been one of those girls whose dreams consisted of getting married, having children, and settling for whatever came my way. Instead, I went after whatever I wanted with the focus and tenacity of a shark, until I got it. Then I set my sights on something else. Besides, after experiencing the realization that my parents' marriage wasn't what it appeared to be, I know that my image of *home* is just window dressing that disguises harsh realities. But that doesn't stop some of the longing for a more *normal* life, whatever that is.

It takes me all of thirty seconds to clean my sparkling chrome-and-black kitchen before I pick up the class reunion invitation on my way back to the tone-on-tone white and ivory living room. A smile plays on my lips as a brief image of one of Pete and Laura's children in one of my homes flits through my mind, and then I grimace. No telling what they'd do to my perfectly ordered life. Thoughts like that should make me happy I don't have children, but lately . . . well, it's simply not happening, so what's the point of wondering what could've been. All the "what ifs" in the world won't change a thing. And besides, this is what I've wanted all my adult life, so I order myself to stop with those thoughts and get back to the task at hand. I have less than a week to list and send the features and benefits of my newly updated hair volumizing system that includes everything a girl needs to have the Ms. Prissy Big Hair style. The TV Network Shopping Channel has me on their regular schedule now, so even that has become so routine I can turn most of the preliminary work over to my long-time assistant, Mandy. But I need something relaxing to do right now, so I sit down with my laptop and tap out my list as I half-watch the second most dysfunctional family I've ever seen holler at each other on TV. I wonder if they do that when the cameras aren't rolling. Too bad the network doesn't know about Laura and Pete Moss's family, or they'd likely be filming in Piney Point rather than LA.

Five years ago, Bonnie Sue, the third of Laura's four children, got busted shoplifting a skirt from La Boutique in Hattiesburg. When I offered to go back to the store with Bonnie Sue, Laura accepted without a moment's hesitation, glad for the support in spite of the fact that she's never even pretended to like me. On the way to the shop, we stopped off at the post office, where I was stunned by the fact that the preteen girl was embarrassed to be seen with me. However, her tune quickly changed when the manager of the store immediately forgave her because of my slight celebrity status. I'm not sure what lesson Bonnie Sue learned that day, but I'm afraid my plan might have backfired if she came away with the idea that someone famous can get away with anything. Now Bonnie e-mails and texts me constantly, wanting advice on how to become a superstar. I've told her more than once to find her own passion, set goals, and work hard. Too bad her passion is for people to be in awe of her existence. In the last text I got from her, she wanted to know whether she should go to LA or New York after she graduates and which place would make her more famous. I need to talk to her mother before giving her advice, so I still haven't gotten back with her.

The features and benefits of my product line are basically the same, only reworded to prevent sounding redundant. I'm about to click *Send* when my phone rings. It's Laura.

"I was just thinking about you," I tell her.

"Why are you answering your own phone?"

"Huh?"

"I thought famous people hired folks to answer their phone."

I've heard that Laura Moss has grown into her own skin, but from what I can tell, that maturity ends when I'm involved. "So what do you need?"

"Just wanted to find out if you're coming to the reunion."

"Yes, I'll be there."

"Are you . . . will you be bringing Tim?"

I suspect that's the purpose of the call, since my good friend, former ardent admirer, and favorite beauty supply salesman, Tim Puckett, has not just attended the previous class reunions with me, he's singlehandedly moved mountains to make sure things ran smoothly. I don't know what Laura would have done without Tim.

"I haven't spoken with him in a few weeks, but I can ask."

"Can you let me know what he says?" I detect a hint of desperation in her voice.

"Why don't you call him?" I say.

Laura snickers. "I don't have the same clout you have. In case you haven't figured it out, that boy will still do anything you want him to."

"Seems he takes orders from you quite well, Laura." I have a hard time keeping the snarkiness from my voice. This woman brings out the worst in me, which is one excellent reason I don't need to stay on the phone with her any longer than necessary.

"Just let me know what he says, okay? Oh, and while you're at it, ask if he can come a week early."

"I'll see what I can do."

After I hang up, I have to take a couple deep breaths to calm down. Ever since I started building my business empire, I've managed to stay calm enough to buy and open nearly a hundred hair salons, including a couple that are full-service day spas. I'm one of the regulars on TVNS with a line of products that sell out every single time I'm on air. But one short conversation with Laura sends me into a dither that takes hours to recover from.

I get up and go to the kitchen for a glass of water, and my phone rings again. This time it's Tim.

"Have you gotten your invitation yet?"

By now, I'm used to the fact that Tim gets my class news before me. He's super connected through my Piney Point salon, which has turned into Prissy's Cut 'n Curl and Ice Factory Day Spa. After Sheila and Chester confronted me about how we'd outgrown our old location, I made it my mission to find a better place. The historic Ice Factory had potential, so when I had the electricity turned on for the inspection, rodent-chewed wires caused a fire. I wound up paying more for the vacant lot than I would have if the building had been salvageable. But then I saved money on building from scratch rather than renovating to historical society regulations.

"Priscilla?" His voice has softened to practically a whisper. "Are you still there?"

"Um, yeah. I got the invitation. So do you want to go with me again? I mean, I can totally understand if you can't, considering how busy you are with your new position and all."

He laughs. "I've been regional sales manager for three years, so I can handle it. Besides, I'm due for some time off."

"If you don't mind wasting it on my class reunion, I'd love for you to attend as my guest."

"You sure know how to sweet talk a guy, Priscilla. I'd be delighted to escort you to your class reunion. And I'll get there a week early to help Laura."

"Good. That was my next question. I'll need to call her and let her know."

"Tell you what," he says. "I'll call her to save the extra step. No point in everything going through you . . . that is, unless you want to be the middleman—er, woman."

"No, that's fine. Please feel free to call her. I'm sure she'll have plenty for you to do."

Again, he laughs. "Yeah, I'd pretty much bet my next paycheck on that." He clears his throat. "Not that I'm a bettin' man or anything. I don't want you to think—"

"No, I know what you're saying. Thanks, Tim."

"Just makin' sure. Let me know if you need anything else. I'll be back in Jackson in a few days. Mind if I stop by and take you to breakfast?"

"Sounds good." My phone beeps, letting me know I have another call. "It was great talking to you, Tim. Gotta run."

I click over to the next call. It's my mother, and she doesn't even bother with a greeting.

"When are you arriving for your reunion?"

"I haven't had much of a chance to think about it, with the TV work and all."

I hear a low grunt, reminding me that my mother disapproves of my chosen career, in spite of my success. "You know you're welcome to stay here, but I'll need to know when to plan on your arrival."

"Probably a week or two, depending on what all Laura needs from me."

"You'll have to give me an exact date, or I can't guarantee your room will be ready."

Rather than ask why I have to worry about my old room being ready since I'm the only person who ever stays in it, I agree to let her know. "If it's not convenient, I can stay in a hotel. I really don't mind."

"Don't be ridiculous, Priscilla. How would it look for me to let my only child stay in a hotel?"

"I guess it wouldn't look good." I pause. "How's Dad? Have you spoken to him lately?"

"Don't go getting the notion that your father and I will ever get back together. Our divorce has been final a good two years, and we've been separated for six. There's—"

"No, Mother, I don't have any such notion. I was just asking a simple question."

"Are you getting smart with me, Priscilla? Because if you are, I want you to know that even though you're a big shot on that silly network, you're still my daughter."

My breath is ragged as I slowly inhale. "No, I just wondered if you've talked to Dad."

"My answer is no, and I don't intend to talk to him as long as he continues to see that bimbo he's been dating."

I shudder. The very thought of either of my parents dating other people seems so wrong. They're my parents. They made it through more than thirty years of marriage, so why couldn't they have worked things out? Of course, I don't ask Mother that because now I realize it's not all her fault.

"Call as soon as you know when you're coming so I can have Teresa get your room ready."

After we hang up, I lift my laptop, but before I strike the first key, my phone rings again. I glance at the caller ID and see that it's Mandy.

"Yes, I know about the reunion, and no, I don't know when I'm going to Piney Point."

"Whoa. What's got you in such a snit? I was just calling to see if you needed help with the features and benefits."

"Sorry, Mandy. I just got off the phone with Mother."

"Oh, no wonder. Anything I can do?"

"Just keep things running smoothly like you always do."

"Oh, Vanessa just hired a new hairdresser. Will you be comin' back to Jackson before the reunion so you can meet her?"

I pull up the calendar on my computer. "Looks like I might have a little time, so yes, I can slip in for a day or two."

"Maybe while you're here you can do something with my hair. Ever since you let Rosemary transfer to Raleigh, my color hasn't been right."

"I'll see what I can do." I hang up, lean back on the couch, and close my eyes. I've managed to get everything I thought I wanted, but now I don't have time to enjoy any of it.

2
Laura Moss

Some nitwit left the milk out, and I think I know just who that is. Ever since Bubba signed up for the Army, you'd think he'd done saved the planet from aliens or somethin'. He's too big for his britches, and he's not about to lower himself to put stuff away. I won't admit this to a single solitary soul, but I'll be glad when he goes off to boot camp. Then I'll be countin' the days 'til the rest of the young'uns are old enough to get out on their own. I mean, I love all four of 'em, but enough's enough. It's time to enjoy life with my new husband.

Oh, I'm still married to Pete, but since the last reunion when our four little angels went on a joyride while we were supposed to be enjoyin' ourselves with our former classmates, Pete has turned over a new leaf. He finally takes responsibility for his drinkin', and he's joined AA 'cause they make him accountable. I always figured I'd eventually nag him straight, but according to his sponsor, I was as big of an enabler as he'd ever seen. Who'da thought just because I tried to make him comfortable and brought him a garbage can when he was tossin' his cookies, I was just makin' matters worse?

I glance up at the clock and mentally calculate how long I have to fix supper. Seems like as the young'uns get older time goes by faster.

"Mama!" I hear Bonnie Sue holler from the top of the stairs. "Telephone!"

"I didn't even hear it ring." I wipe my hands on the kitchen towel and turn to pick up the phone, but it's not where it's supposed to be. "Bonnie Sue, come down here right now and bring me back the phone!"

"You come here and get it," she says.

My blood starts to simmer. "Do what I say right this minute, young lady. You have no business smartin' off at me just 'cause you're about to be a junior."

The slow thumping sound as she trudges down the stairs grates my nerves to no end. I suck in a deep breath and try to slowly let it out, but it doesn't work, so I stomp to the foot of the stairs and glare at Bonnie Sue who is still standing on the second to last step, holding the phone out with a sarcastic smirk on her face. "I told Lucy I'd call her right back, so don't take too long." She paused. "You could give me my cell phone back, and you can talk as long as you want."

"Keep sassin' me like that, young lady, and you won't be gettin' your phone back 'til you can pay your own bills." I grab the house phone from her and lift it to my ear, givin' her the meanest mama look I can manage the entire time. She rolls her eyes, making me want to yank her by the hair and toss her across the room, but as with all my thoughts of child abuse, I don't act on it, and she knows I won't.

As soon as I speak into the phone, my mother's husband, who I refuse to call my stepfather after he called my cookin' pig slop, started half talking, half sobbing. "Your mama . . . she's . . . I don't know if she's gonna make it . . . Laura . . . "

I go numb. "Randy, where are you? Where's Mama?"

"I'm at the hospital. They're tryin' to save her right now."

"I'll be right there." I holler for Bonnie Sue to come down.

She appears at the top of the stairs, takes one look at my face, and gasps. "What happened?"

"I don't know yet. That was Randy callin' from the hospital. Somethin' awful has happened to your grandma." I turn and start toward the kitchen before I remember my pocketbook is upstairs in my room. "Bonnie Sue, fetch my pocketbook and bring it down here, will ya?"

She doesn't waste another minute before doing as I say, but when she hands me my bag, she tips her head. "What about supper?"

Now it's my turn to roll my eyes. "Fix it yourself, Miss Smarty-Pants. I'm leavin' now." And then I turn and make good on my word.

As I back out of the driveway, I punch Randy's number on my cell phone, but he doesn't answer. All kinds of scenarios play out in my mind, and by the time I get to the hospital parking lot, I've come to the conclusion that I'm about to be an orphan. Daddy passed away two years ago, and I'm still convinced his retired ROTC wife is responsible, but I have no proof. It's just that whenever I was with them, somethin' didn't seem right. And she didn't even cry a single tear at his funeral.

I park as close as I can to the emergency room entrance. Randy is standin' outside under the awning waitin' for me, his eyes rimmed in red, his skin looking all gaunt and sickly.

"Where's Mama?"

He points his thumb over his shoulder. "She had a heart attack, Laura. A real bad one."

I might not know much about medicine, but I don't think I've ever heard of a heart attack that wasn't bad. "Will she be okay?"

"I don't know . . . wasn't sure at first, but now . . . " He slowly shakes his head. "We was just sittin' there watchin' our shows on TV, and she started shakin' and sweatin' all over. I thought she was laughin' 'til I took a good look at her face. Laura, it was the scariest thing I ever seen."

I hold up my hand to stop him and save myself from hearing the gory details of Mama's heart attack. "Let's go inside and see about her, okay?"

He nods. With shaky motions, I put my arm around his scrawny shoulders and lead him back inside. Somewhere along the way, Randy "Save-a-Lot" Elmore has become frail. But now, as I see how much he cares about Mama, he also seems like more of a man.

The lady at the desk sees us and holds up a finger. "The doctor was looking for you, Mr. Elmore. Let me get one of the nurses to come get you. Is that your daughter?"

Randy starts to shake his head, but I speak up. "Yes, I'm the daughter."

Minutes later, Randy and I are following the nurse down the hall and into a small room with a desk and not much else. "Have a seat. The doctor will be right with you."

"I thought we were gonna see Mama."

Randy looks at me with sad eyes. "You haven't never watched those doctor shows on TV, have ya?"

Before I have a chance to answer, a middle-aged man with a tired look in his eyes enters the room and closes the door. The air suddenly seems very still, making my pulse beat faster.

"Mrs. Elmore is a very lucky woman. She suffered a massive heart attack that could have killed her if you hadn't acted quickly."

Randy squirms a bit until he's sitting up a little straighter, while I look at him with more respect than I've ever felt for him before. "I don't wanna lose my wife. Me and her's soul mates."

"Is she . . . " I glance at Randy, then turn to face the doctor. "Will she make it?"

"We've got her stabilized, but it's still too early to tell." He goes on to tell us about some procedures he needs to perform while Randy and I sit and listen. The more the doctor talks, the more worried I get. Finally, the doctor ends his talk with, "If you don't have any more questions, I need to get back in there and prep for surgery."

"Do what you gotta do, Doc," Randy says. "Just make sure I get my wife back."

"I'll do what I can." The doctor stands to leave but pauses at the door. "You can wait here until you're ready to go back to the waiting room."

After he leaves, I turn to Randy. "Thank you so much, Randy."

He gives me a puzzled look. "For what?"

"For being there for Mama."

"I love your mama. I know me and you ain't always been on the best of terms, but I'd do anything for the woman who turned my life around and made it worth livin'."

Knowing Randy as I do, that's about the sweetest thing he could have said. I place my hand on his arm. "When's the last time you had something to eat?"

He frowns at me and shakes his head. "I can't go thinkin' about food at a time like this, Laura. But if you're hungry, I understand. Why don't you go on down to the cafeteria and grab a bite to eat?"

"Nah, that's okay. I'll stay with you."

"They have a snack machine in the waiting room."

"I'll just get something there then."

Four packs of overpriced peanut butter crackers later, I'm sittin' next to Randy, listening to stories about the things he and Mama like to do together—fish, dance, go antiquing, take long drives, and eat out.

"When do you have time to work?"

"You should know better than that, Laura. I was sittin' right there next to your mama last year when she told you I done retired."

"Oh." I fidget with the hem of my shirt as I think about all that's been goin' on in my life, and how I'm always so anxious to get off the phone when Mama calls. "Oh yeah, that's right. I forgot."

He offers a slight grin of understanding and pats my arm. "That's all right, Laura. I understand. You got your hands full with Pete bein' on the sauce and actin' like one of the kids."

"Pete's been sober for a while now," I say with satisfaction. "He's goin' to AA." I make a silent vow to stay in better touch with Mama and Randy. They shoulda known Pete wasn't drinkin' anymore.

Randy lifts his eyebrows. "Good for him. I told your mama I thought there was a good man in there somewhere."

I wonder if that's when Mama started backing off on her rants about how I shouldn't put up with Pete's shenanigans. For a while I got daily calls from her tellin' me I deserve better than that. When she stopped, I was too relieved to find out why I stopped hearing from her. Randy keeps moving up the ladder to my heart.

He points to my pocketbook. "Speakin' of Pete, why don't you give him a call and let him know what's goin' on? I'm sure him and the kids is worried sick about you."

3
Tim Puckett

I get to the door of Priscilla's Jackson corporate office and pause. When Uncle Hugh, who owns the company I work for, made me regional sales manager, he said he wanted me to continue calling on Priscilla's salons, since they now represent near 'bout half his business and we have a good rapport.

Only problem is I don't feel like facin' Mandy after the last time we went out. Me and her was steppin' out on a regular basis, and she started thinkin' we was more than just really good friends. I near 'bout fell over when she came right out and proposed. I know it's wrong, but when I first asked Mandy out on a date, I was hopin' to make Priscilla jealous. No way did I think Mandy would get all hung up on me and start stalkin' me the way she did. No matter where I went after hours, if I was in Jackson, I could pretty much count on runnin' into her. And I have no idea how she can type so fast on her itty-bitty phone keyboard. She can send more text messages in a minute than I can read, and that's exactly what she did on our dates.

After taking a deep breath, I turn the handle and shove the door open. The receptionist—can't remember what her name is, but there's no point since the Cut 'n Curl's corporate office front desk seems to have a revolvin' door—smiles at me. "Mandy's busy, but I'm sure she'll wanna see you."

"No, that's okay. I just came to pick up the order."

The girl squirms around, opening and closing drawers, pretending to look for something, before slamming the top drawer shut. "Sorry, but I think Vanessa has it down in the salon. Why don't you have a seat, and I'll call her to come up."

"That's not necessary. I can go down there myself." I pause at the door. "Tell Mandy I said hey and I'm sorry I missed her."

I'm barely inside the salon when I hear a breathless Mandy behind me. "Hey, Tim."

I turn around in time to see her straightening her blouse. A trickle of sweat makes its way down her forehead, but she's givin' me her desperate smile. I wish I'd insisted on havin' her e-mail the order in instead of agreein' to stop by to pick it up.

Just like a superhero come to save the day, Vanessa appears from around the corner. "Hey, Tim. What can I do for you?"

"Get on back to your station, Vanessa," Mandy orders. "I can talk to Tim."

Vanessa lifts one eyebrow and looks at me without budging. Ever since Vanessa took over when Rosemary transferred to one of the Raleigh Cut 'n Curls, there's been a power play between Vanessa and Mandy. Priscilla has always said that Vanessa is in charge at the salon, and Mandy is the business manager, so I feel justified in speakin' up.

"Sorry, Mandy, but I really need to talk to Vanessa."

She folds her arms and pouts. "Then why did you come up to the office in the first place?"

"Because that's what I've always done." I make a mental note to change my habit that started when Priscilla only had three salons, and all orders came through her. Now that she's turned the company into a major chain, and each salon is thriving, she has the managers ordering for their individual salons. Maybe if

I park in the customer parking lot and slip into the salon real nice and quiet, I'll be able to avoid runnin' into Mandy.

"Mandy, honey, I'm sure you have better things to do with your time than stand down here"—Vanessa walks over to the door, opens it, and turns to face Mandy—"but I appreciate you tryin' to help."

I look everywhere but at Mandy. This whole situation is embarrassin', but I can't buckle, or I'll never be able to get away from her.

Once Mandy's gone, Vanessa turns to me. "What can I do for ya, sweetie?"

Vanessa's one of them women who calls everyone *sweetie* or *darlin'*, so I don't feel uncomfortable in the least. "I'm here for your order."

"Let me get it. Want somethin' cold to drink?"

"What kind a sody pop you got?"

She spouts off a variety of drink flavors, and just when I think she's done, she mentions my favorite. Cream soda. I smile, and she gives me the thumbs up. "Priscilla told me to always make sure I have cream soda 'cause that's what you like."

"Priscilla said that?" I feel warm all the way to my toes just hearin' that Priscilla thinks enough of me to make sure they keep cream soda in their break-room fridge.

"Yup. And she also said you like peanut-butter crackers but not the orange ones." She pauses. "Want me to bring you a pack of them too?"

"Sounds good." I feel like royalty now.

Vanessa comes back with a can of cream soda, a pack of peanut butter malt crackers, and an order as thick as any I ever seen. "We're out of a lot of stuff," she says. "Every time Priscilla has a show on TVNS, business picks up like wildfire."

"I bet folks is hopin' to catch a glimpse of her," I say as I pop the top on the can.

"I s'pect you're right." Vanessa glances over her shoulder and turns back to me. "I best be gettin' back to my client's color job, or her hair might wind up lookin' like she stuck her finger in a light socket."

I head out to my car with a briefcase full of an order that'll bring in enough money to feed a small village, peanut butter cracker crumbs on my lapel, and a half can of sody pop. All the way home, I think about where I am in life and how I got here.

The other salesmen who work for my uncle all wish they could have one client like Priscilla, but I just happened to be in the right place at the right time. Some folks call me lucky, but I'm inclined to agree with Priscilla—the Lord had a reason for bringin' us into each other's lives. What we disagree on is why. She says she'd never do business with a pushy salesman she can't trust, and I have the right sales style for her. I think maybe the Lord wants us together as more than hair salon owner and beauty product salesman. Sometimes I think me and her's on the same page, but then somethin' happens, like her old boyfriend Maurice showin' up or some other such thing, and I realize we're not even lookin' at the same book.

Years ago, both Mama and Uncle Hugh thought Priscilla might come to her senses, so I should just hang in there. But lately, they've been tellin' me to move on and look for a girl who appreciates what a fine husband I'd make. Mama wants grandbabies. Uncle Hugh just wants me to be happy. I'm not closed to meetin' some girl and settlin' down, but only 'cause I haven't found one yet who makes me tingle all the way to my toenails like Priscilla Slater does.

Shortly after I fax the order to Uncle Hugh's office, my phone rings. "Good job on the order, Tim."

"I didn't do nothin'. Just picked up the order, that's all. It was already filled out when I got there."

His voice booms as he laughs. I can picture him leanin' and tiltin' his chair on the back two legs, with Aunt Tammy fussin' and fumin', sayin' he's gonna break the chair and then his hip. "Tim, you and I both know that it took years to establish a relationship with Priscilla, so you did do more than just pick up the order, only not today. And that leads me to the reason for my call. How'd you like to move up to the Big Apple?"

"Huh?"

He laughs again. "Tammy and I have been talkin' about retiring and moving back to Mississippi to our fishing camp cabin in Vancleave."

"So what would I do in New York?"

"I need someone to take over the business, and I can't think of a better person for the job than you."

Now I'm all choked up. When I try to talk, nothin' comes out but a squeak.

"I realize I sprung that on you mighty fast. Think about it, Tim. Tammy and I aren't getting any younger, and we'd like to do it in the next few months. You'd have to come up and learn the business beforehand."

"I'm honored, Uncle Hugh. When do you wanna know my answer?"

"Take your time. Just tell me what you wanna do in the next week or so."

"The next week?"

"Yeah. Like I said, take your time. You don't have to give me your answer right now."

"Is . . . is this a secret?"

"Not exactly a secret, but I'd appreciate if you didn't tell everyone you run into."

"How about—?"

"Your mama knows, and if you wanna talk to Priscilla, I reckon that'll be okay 'cause she obviously trusts you as much as I do. And I don't see her gettin' all mouthy and blabbing to the world of beauty if you tell her it's not public knowledge yet."

After I hang up, I'm still numb with shock. I totally didn't see this one comin'. Uncle Hugh is still pretty young, but I get that he works hard, and he needs to kick back. The most shocking thing is that he trusts me to run the company he's been buildin' ever since he and Aunt Tammy first got married.

I call Mama, and she squeals into the phone before I have a chance to open my mouth. "In spite of the fact he comes from bad blood, your uncle is a smart man."

Uncle Hugh is my daddy's brother, and I think he hired me to make up for the fact that my own daddy up and took off not long after I was born. Me and Mama moved into Granny's house, so I was raised by a couple of doting women. That prepared me for bein' in the beauty business. I understand and appreciate some of the finer points of females.

"So when will you be movin' up to New York?"

"I haven't made my decision yet."

"What?" Her voice screeches. "Don't you go and be an ingrate. Your uncle is offerin' you the opportunity to make somethin' of yourself."

"Mama, I think I've already done that. I'm very happy living in Jackson and doin' what I do."

"It's that Priscilla girl, ain't it?"

"Well . . . "

"That's what I was afraid might happen. Now you listen to me, Timothy Jefferson Puckett. Priscilla has her heart and mind set on one thing, and that's buildin' her business empire. You've sat around long enough, waitin' for her to fall in love with you and settle down. I'm already thinkin' that I won't never be a granny."

"Mama—"

"Honey, I don't wanna put pressure on you, but you sure don't need to look a gift horse in the mouth. Your uncle is presentin' you with the opportunity to start fresh in a high-power job that will bring you more money than you'll ever make in Mississippi."

"It's not about the money. You know I'm doin' just fine where I am."

"That's one of your problems, Tim, and as much as I hate to say it, I'm afraid you might get that from your daddy. He was always satisfied with things just the way they was. I used to tell him he needed to always reach for the stars and never be satisfied until he grabs one of 'em."

"You used to say that to Daddy?"

"Yeah, and he always told me to stop naggin' him about makin' more money and gettin' a bigger job."

I feel like someone done kicked me in the head. This is the first I ever heard this, and I don't think I like the sound of it. I always thought he up and left for no reason.

"Mama, I need to go now."

"At least think about Hugh's offer. Jobs like this don't come along every day."

"I know. And they don't grow on trees neither."

"Are you gettin' smart with me, Tim? 'Cause if you are, you're never too old for me to wash your mouth out with soap."

After hangin' up, I feel like someone done slugged me in the gut. Merely the suggestion of soap brings back the taste of the bath bar she used to shove into my mouth and scrape along the edge of my teeth when I said somethin' she didn't like.

4
Trudy Baynard

In spite of what the regional manager says, bigger is not more beautiful on some women—although I have to admit she looks fabulous even though she wears women's sizes. I've learned that not everyone should be skinny, and she's one of them. I, on the other hand, don't carry extra weight very well.

Back in the day, when I had my figure under control, people stared at me in awe. Now I rarely get more than a quick glance, and the only comments people make are about my complexion, which I've managed to keep mostly wrinkle free. And that's only 'cause I've gone for preventive Botox treatments. Yeah, I know, it's superficial, but most of my life all I've had going for me is my looks, and that's a hard thing to let go of.

My invitation to the twenty-year class reunion arrived last week, and I'm trying to decide if it's something I want to put myself through again. The ten-year reunion was a disaster because I went with a mission of getting my ex-husband, Michael, to love me again, and I passed out at the worst possible time, proving how pathetic I was and showing everyone I went to school with that I didn't deserve to lick Michael's shoes. Well, at least that's what I thought at the time. Then at the fifteen-year reunion, he's the one who came out being way more pitiful since everyone knew he'd gotten the senator's daughter pregnant. I've never been so happy since we split up as I was when I looked at his face and saw regret. Even now I smile when I remember how he's sufferin' for all he put me through.

But then my smile fades when I think about my thunder thighs that no amount of shape wear can hide. Mama got me started wearing Spanx five years ago, and now I'm addicted and won't leave my apartment without them. Since I work in fashion for one of the biggest department store chains in the country, I have to wear the latest styles with sizes that don't go higher than the next one up from where I am now. That worries me. I never saw myself getting this big, and I have absolutely no excuses besides the fact that I eat out for almost every meal since I'm on the road more than I'm home. Even my sisters who both have kids are smaller than me.

If I hear one more person say, "You look good for your age, Trudy," or, "It's normal for a woman to put on a few extra pounds when she gets older," I think I'll scream.

For the past five years, I've been the department store's regional training director for high-end women's apparel, and I've let my boss know I'm interested in moving up. My personal life might be sad, but professionally, I'm at the top of my game—somethin' I never saw for myself when I was younger. Those were the days of beauty pageants, homecoming court, and prancing around as half of the Michael-and-Trudy royalty team. Why I ever thought that would last is beyond me. When I look at my high-school yearbooks, I wonder if anyone else has noticed that I don't smile as big or as often, even though deep down I'm much happier now than I was then.

Mama tells me I really shouldn't worry about attending the reunion and maybe I should stay home, since people will talk about how I've changed. She's right. I have changed, but as I keep remindin' myself, mostly for the good. While Mama's looking at my expanding thighs and businesslike actions, thinking I'm becoming an old maid, I feel like I can command more real honest-to-goodness respect from folks who don't give a flyin' flip about how people look. I still care about looks, but at least now, I understand girls like Laura. Last time I saw her she had hips that make mine look downright skinny. Granted that was about three years ago when I ran into her as she was coming out of Olson's Department Store looking dejected because she couldn't find anything cute. At least that's what she told me. I suspect she couldn't find anything that fit.

People have finally quit asking me about Michael, now that he's married to Jenna, who was already pregnant and showing when they tied the knot. Jenna flaunts their baby all over town, but rarely is Michael with them. I can't help but pity the poor girl, who will never have the emotional or physical support of an overgrown boy who was never taught how to be a real man. Things came way too easy for him in his early years. But now he's payin' big time.

I wonder if Michael will be at the reunion. His father-in-law is still Piney Point's senator, and I've heard that Michael is constantly on his toes, trying to stay in the senator's good graces. That actually gives me a chuckle. In the past, everyone else was always bowing to Michael, trying to get his favor. Turnabout sure is miserable, and nothing will make me happier—forgive me, Lord—than to see Michael suffer like I had to suffer after he kicked me to the curb for his flavor-of-the-month bimbo. Looks like the last laugh is on him, poor little spoiled, washed-up brat.

Am I bitter? You bet! Any woman in my shoes would be. But beneath all that bitterness is the strength of a woman who will do anything to prove herself.

Now that I've thought about it, yeah, I'll go to the reunion. It'll be fun to see everyone again. Well, everyone except Hank, who was all googly-eyed over me, but I couldn't manage to fall for him, no matter how hard I tried. At least I've heard he's involved with someone else, so I won't have to worry about him hanging on me all night—even if he still has that crush on me that started back in high school.

I call the phone number on the invitation to RSVP, and Pete answers. "Is Laura there?"

"Just a minute." Without even bothering to cover the mouthpiece, I hear him holler, "Laura, are you up there? Someone wants to talk to you."

"Who is it?" I hear her holler back.

"How should I know?"

"Didn't you bother looking before you answered?" The sound of Laura's voice as it gets closer to the phone is irritatin' as ever, but at least I don't have to live with her. Pete does. I hear her exasperated breath as she picks up the extension. "Hey, Trudy. Whatcha want?"

"I'm calling to RSVP about the reunion. I'll be there."

"Are you bringin' anyone?"

I think for a couple of seconds. "I'm not sure yet."

"You do realize that both Michael and Hank are likely to be there, right?"

I don't know why she thinks that matters, but I don't say that to her. "I'm well aware of that."

"Let me know if you decide to bring someone. You can call up 'til a day before. We're having it catered like last time, and I don't wanna run out of food."

"Okay. What's happening on Friday night? Will there be a bonfire?"

"We're plannin' on it."

A blanket of silence falls over the line.

"Anything else?"

I clear my throat. "No, that'll be it. Thanks, Laura. See you there."

"Oh, Trudy . . . "

"Yes?"

Laura clears her throat. "I just want you to know that you made the right decision to leave Michael. He's turned out to be one hot mess."

I don't correct her about the decision to leave being Michael's, not mine. And I want to hear what she thinks about Michael . . . not that I really care or that it matters, but out of curiosity.

"A hot mess?"

"Yeah, he's put on about fifty pounds around his gut, and instead of shaving his head once his hair started fallin' out, he's doin' a comb-over. And last time I saw him, he looked like he hadn't had a bath in days."

I try not to smile, but I can't help it. Now I know I've made the right decision to go to the reunion. I can't wait to see Michael, now that he's *falling into disrepair* as he so arrogantly puts it when he sees women letting themselves go.

"If you need anything, call me," I say. I'm sure she knows I don't really mean it, but at least offering my assistance seems like the right thing to do.

"Will do." *Click*. No *see ya later*, no *good-bye*. Well she's never had the advantage of social etiquette lessons from a mama who cares about makin' impressions, so I suppose I shouldn't be surprised.

Next, I call Mama and let her know I'll be in town for the reunion. "I thought I told you not to worry about attendin'." She lowers her voice as though she's worried someone will hear. "Michael and that wretched little wife of his will probably be there. I don't want my daughter involved in a . . . scene."

"Don't worry, Mama, there won't be a scene . . . at least not one that I start."

"Did you know that her own daddy don't even like talkin' about her? Why last time he went campaignin', he didn't—"

"Tell me all about it when I get there. I really have to run now."

The longer I'm away from Piney Point the more Mama's gossip annoys me. I never realized how much she stuck her nose into other people's business until after I left. Even though I can't say I'm unhappy about Michael's woes since he brought 'em all on himself, talkin' about it seems like a huge waste of time.

Before I head out the next morning, I call my boss, Sandy, and tell her I want to take some time off for the reunion. "I'll make sure everything is in order before I take off, and I can be reached if someone needs me."

"Sounds good, Trudy, but I have something I'd like to discuss with you."

"Now?"

"Um . . . can you work a meeting into your schedule on short notice?" The tone of Sandy's voice is different and makes me very uncomfortable.

"Sure. Just say when."

"Tomorrow would be great."

I have an appointment with the manager of the formal department in one of the Atlanta stores, but based on the sound of Sandy's voice, I figure it's best to reschedule and see what she wants. "No problem."

"Good. See you around one-ish?"

After I get off the phone with Sandy, I call and reschedule my appointment. Then I look up the flight schedule on my cell phone and make the decision I'm better off driving than paying the high prices on last-minute flights, which means I'll need to pack and leave now if I want to appear fresh and ready for a meeting when I get there. I'm used to a grueling schedule, and at the moment, it's a blessing that'll keep me from pondering and worrying about the reunion.

I flip on the TV in my bedroom to watch while I toss a few things into a suitcase. The news is so depressing, I press the channel button on the remote until a familiar face pops up on the screen. There's Priscilla Slater hawking her hair products. She's one of the few people who actually looks better now than she did back in high school. I stand there in amazement as I see how comfortable and smooth she looks on camera. Maybe I should give her a call and find out if she's going to the reunion. It'll be nice to have someone to talk to—someone who understands that there is life outside of Piney Point, Mississippi.

5
Celeste Boudreaux Shackleford

Most folks' last words are things like "Don't forget to count your blessings" or "Remember to go to church every Sunday," but not Mama's. The doctor had just left her hospital room when she looked me in the eye, bent her pointer finger, and whispered, "Get closer, Celeste. I need to tell you somethin'."

I leaned over her hospital bed and tried real hard not to breathe in on account of her bein' so sickly and all. "Whatcha want, Mama?" I ask.

"I thought I better tell you I'm leavin' you a rich woman. After I'm gone, you need to go talk to my lawyer and make sure you protect yourself."

Naturally, I assumed Mama's fever was messin' with her thinkin', so I just shook my head, took her by the hand, and smiled down at her. "I'll be just fine, Mama. I don't have to protect myself."

"I—" She stopped, took a deep breath, and shuddered before closing her eyes and exhaling for the last time.

Mama had told her doctor she didn't want no one resuscitatin' her 'cause she was ready to meet the Lord, so we honored her wishes. Her passin' wasn't no surprise either on account of her bein' sick for so long. Jimmy was at work, but I knew he'd be right there with me when I needed him.

The next few days was crazy busy with funeral preparations and all the stuff that needed doin'. Then Mama's attorney called.

"I know you're grieving, Celeste, but we've got this will to take care of, so whenever you're ready, come on down to my office and see me."

Once I got there, I still didn't believe it. "I'm what?" I didn't even bother tryin' to hide my shock.

"You're a millionaire."

So Mama did know what she was sayin'. Well I'll be. After all that scrimpin' and savin', she's gone, and here I am a rich woman. Mama had stock in some of the finest companies, and now it was all mine.

Three months later, me and Jimmy was tryin' to decide whether to stay in Piney Point or move to a bigger city to get away from folks who was sayin' he only married me for my money. Me and Jimmy pondered and discussed the advantages and disadvantages of movin' 'til we was blue in the face. We finally decided we'd go somewhere different, and if we didn't like it, we'd come back. I always had a hankerin' for livin' close to the beach, so we found us a nice place in Biloxi. We been gone three years now, and I don't ever see us movin' back to Piney Point.

Now I'm tryin' to decide whether or not we should go to the twenty-year reunion. When the invitation arrives, I don't even have to open the envelope to know what it is since I been lookin' at the calendar, wonderin' when I'd hear from Laura about helpin' her. Looks like she don't want my help, which don't surprise me. Laura always has liked bein' in control, and she might be afraid I'll try to take over, which is hilarious 'cause I have no desire to have all the pressure of bein' in charge of our entire graduatin' class havin' fun.

I put away the groceries and start supper. Ever since Jimmy started his very own security service, he's been comin' home starved half to death. I smile as I think about how his pride has made him way more successful than anyone ever would have imagined.

After we moved away from Piney Point, he couldn't find a decent job as a security officer like he had back home. Every day he came home depressed and feelin' like a failure. After I had enough of his moanin' and groanin', I challenged him to take some of Mama's money and start his own company. He balked at first, but finally he agreed to borry the money as long as I agreed he could pay it back on account of he don't want no one to think he's a freeloader. We're married, so in my eyes, what's mine is his and what's his is mine, but I think there's some sort of masculinity thing goin' on with him.

Once he started his business, I seen a side to Jimmy I never knew existed. He was real careful about who he hired and where he spent the money. And I was really floored when he come home and said he joined the Chamber of Commerce. A year after he opened the doors of Shackleford Security, he done paid back Mama's brokerage account, and we been livin' offa the salary he pays his self.

I stopped lookin' for a job once I seen how successful my husband was. At first, he said he wanted me to find somethin' to do, but now I think he's just fine havin' me home cookin' and cleanin' and washin' his laundry. I even meet him for lunch sometimes when he has time to go out.

Shortly after I put the potatoes in the oven, I hear the car door slam in the carport. Less than a minute later, Jimmy flings open the door, a cake-eatin' grin spreadin' his face all wide and makin' his eyes crinkle. That look always makes me go all goose-bumpy.

"Hey, Celeste, you'll never guess what happened today."

"Did you land the Dozier account?"

"Even better." He sweeps me into his arms and gives me a great big bear hug. "The Doziers signed the contract and introduced me to the Millers, who say they're not happy with their security company, and they're lookin' for a new one."

The Doziers own a new home construction company in Biloxi, and the Millers own most of the land the Doziers build on. "That's great, honey. I'm proud of you." I wipe my hands on the kitchen towel and pick up the invitation. "The class reunion invitation came today. We need to book our room at the hotel if we're goin'."

Jimmy stops dead in his track on the way to the table, turns, and gives me a look that brings back a lot of bad memories. "I don't know about that. Haven't we done enough with them people already?"

"We don't have to do anything . . . just show up." Now I realize I really wanna go, if for no other reason but to show off my husband's success.

He ambles over to the table, sits down, and hangs his head. "You know what everyone will say, don't you?"

I go over to my husband and place my hands on his shoulders. "They'll say I have the smartest husband in the whole entire world."

"You know better than that, Celeste."

Unfortunately, I'm afraid I do. No one will ever see Jimmy as more than the flunky security guard he used to be . . . or me as the ugly ducklin' turned pretty.

Throughout supper, I listen to my husband talk about his plans for hiring new personnel for the two companies who are about to sign with him. He pauses and gives me his thoughtful look. "But y'a know, I better not hire too many folks what with the economy bein' what it is and the Doziers and Millers bein' so closely connected. If one leaves, the other one prob'ly will too." He taps his fork on the edge of his plate. "I'll get them to sign a contract for a year and have my lawyer look it over before I hire anyone."

A fresh wave of pride fills me from my head all the way down to my toes. Jimmy never leaves anything to chance. His smart business moves has bought us a nice house in a good school district—just in case we decide to have young'uns. But I have to admit seein' Laura and Pete's brats makes me think we might never do it.

"So you really wanna go to the reunion? If it's that important . . . " Jimmy asks, yanking me back to the conversation.

"Um . . . " I look at him and shrug. "I'd kinda like to go. We haven't seen none of our old classmates since we had our weddin'."

Jimmy smiles, and I start laughing. Me and him ran off and got married right before the last reunion. When I found out Laura was hurt on account of she wanted to be my maid of honor, we had a weddin' that Laura quickly threw together at the church. It was sorta gaudy, but Laura really wanted to wear sequins, and she made me a big ol' honkin' bouquet, and since we was doin' it for her, I said, "Fine, do whatever you wanna do." Even Mama came to see me walk down the aisle. That was before she took sick.

"Okay, we'll go, but I can't be on the committee." Jimmy gives me one of them looks that near 'bout melts my toenail polish. "I have too much work to do here."

"Maybe we can just take a couple days off," I say in the sweetest voice I can manage.

Jimmy grins, winks, and places his hand over mine. "I want you to be happy, Celeste. You surprised me and turned out to be the best wife a man can have, and you deserve it."

I know that Jimmy had his doubts when we was datin' . . . and even after we first got married. But once we got comfortable, his whole entire attitude changed, and he fell into his husband role like he'd been doin' it all his life.

"Why don't you bring some of your business cards and hand 'em out like some of the others do?" I ask.

"I doubt I'll get much business in Piney Point."

"That don't really matter, does it?" I tilt my head toward Jimmy and give him my flirty-eye look.

He pushes back from the table and pats his lap. "C'mere, Celeste. I wanna hold you."

We cuddle at the kitchen table before I clean up the kitchen. Jimmy moseys on into the den to watch TV while I stack the dishes in the dishwasher and think about the reunion. I done had my biggest makeover before the ten-year party. Now I plan to stroll in wearin' one of my fancy outfits from the expensive department store that I still have a hard time shoppin' in. I was born bein' thrifty on account of Mama never lettin' on we had a dime to spare. Maybe I'll check Goodwill first. Recyclin' has been the trend with the economy bein' down, and everyone wantin' to go green. Besides, no one has to know.

6
Priscilla

Trudy's call comes from out of the blue, and she actually sounds like she's gotten her act together since the last reunion. Her voice has a professional quality, and she comes across as a sincerely caring person. Clearly she's matured, and I know this might sound cynical, but I wonder how much of what I'm hearing is an act she's learned and how much of it is real.

"You and I are so much alike, Priscilla."

I nearly choke. "Yeah? How so?"

"We're both businesswomen who know what we want, and we're not afraid to go after it."

That's not exactly how I've always thought of Trudy, but I don't tell her that. "By the way, congratulations on your corporate success."

"Thank you, Priscilla, and same to you. I'm so happy for you and all you've managed to accomplish." Since when has Trudy ever cared about anyone besides herself?

Okay, there I go sounding judgmental. As I get older, I'm afraid I'm seeing and hearing more of my mother. That's so not what I want. Now I realize that deep down, Mother is a good person, but she tends to judge everyone and everything in her world, and I don't want to be that way.

"Here's what I was thinking. You and I can go out to dinner before the party, and we can arrive a little bit after it starts so we won't have to deal with all that awkwardness in the beginning."

"Oh, sorry, but Tim will be with me, and Laura is counting on him to help with the preparations."

"Oh." She sounds disappointed but only for a few seconds. "Maybe I can pitch in and help too."

"Are you sure you want to do that?" I don't think I've ever seen Trudy pitching in for anything that required manual labor. "It usually involves hanging decorations and helping the caterer put things where Laura wants them . . . and sometimes moving them several times until she's happy."

Trudy sucks in a breath. "I can do that, as long as I don't have to lift anything heavy or do anything that'll mess up my outfit."

Whew! Now she sounds like the Trudy I've always known. "Tim usually gets all the tough jobs, but he doesn't seem to mind."

"So what's in this for Tim?"

"He's made friends with all the people on the committee, and I think he likes feeling needed."

"Too bad I don't have a Tim in my life," Trudy says. "He's not only helpful, he's real cute."

"Yes, he's very cute."

"I know it's none of my business, Priscilla, but I've been wondering something for a while . . . "

"What's that?"

"Tim is cute, and he obviously likes you in spite of the fact that you're a professional woman. Why don't you and him . . . I mean, you know, it seems like . . . um, you're not getting any younger . . . "

I laugh. "Are you asking why Tim and I aren't a couple?" It doesn't seem so funny anymore, but I'm not sure why I feel that way.

"Yes, I suppose I am." Trudy pauses. "But it's really none of my business, so never mind. I'm sorry I asked."

"That's okay. I like Tim, but he and I are such good friends I don't want to ruin what we have."

"Sounds like the chemistry just isn't there," Trudy says. "I reckon I better run. Looking forward to seeing you in Piney Point."

I hang up and rock back on my heels. If someone had told me back in high school that I'd even be invited to hang out with Trudy, I would have told them they were hallucinating. Trudy was the homecoming and prom queen, and I was voted Most Likely to Succeed. The only times those two paths ever crossed were in articles in the school paper and during end-of-the-year awards ceremonies.

My life has been pretty much a steady progression to where I am now, while Trudy's has taken so many detours I'm surprised she has any idea where she is at any given time. And I have to hand it to her. She's managed to take all the bumps and dips without faltering too long. Even after she passed out at the ten-year reunion, she got up, dusted herself off, and got right back out there to find her way. I'm happy for her—that she's discovered a side of herself she obviously never knew existed before Michael dumped her. He's the one who's spiraled downward, and no one seems surprised or upset.

Thoughts of Michael lead to memories of my own high school crush on Maurice, the other cocaptain of Piney Point High School's football team. During the ten-year reunion, Maurice managed to get my heart beating faster when he acted interested in me. I'm ashamed to admit I fell for it so hard I ditched Tim the next day. At least I came to my senses when his motives became obvious. And Tim was a good enough friend to accept my apology without so much as an I-told-you-so. But I still hate the fact that I hurt him. I'm usually not that kind of girl, and to think that I did what I did . . . well, it sort of makes me sick to my stomach.

Then seeing Didi Holcomb with Maurice at the fifteen-year reunion didn't faze me in the least. Didi had always felt competitive with me, and she resented the fact that my grade-point average was a tenth of a point higher than hers, so she wound up being salutatorian. As valedictorian, I got to make the class speech, while she sat next to me and seethed. She went on to medical school after getting her undergraduate degree, and I dropped out my first semester at Ole Miss to go to beauty school. I can only imagine how that made her feel.

I'm sure Didi felt like she'd pulled one over on me when Maurice proposed to her. From what I've heard, he sweet-talked her out of her savings to ramp up his business, and she moved her medical practice to Hattiesburg to be closer to him. Last I heard they still aren't married, and she's growing more impatient by the day. For such a smart woman she sure is clueless about Maurice.

Tim and I are meeting for dinner at my favorite restaurant on Fifth Avenue in an hour, so I quickly finish getting ready. I like to walk when I'm in the city, so I slip out of my heels and into a pair of comfortable ballet flats.

As I exit the hotel on Times Square and head in the direction of the restaurant, I look around at all the people who lead lives completely different from mine, yet they still have the same basic emotional needs—to be accepted by some, loved by others, and tolerated by the rest. Not one mentally healthy person I know wants to be a complete social outcast, but so many of us are too afraid to do what it takes to ensure the balance we need. I for one have been guilty of holding people at arm's length, simply to make sure no one gets in my way of achieving my goals. And here I am, exactly where I've wanted to be all my adult life. But I still have people who care about me, right? What a silly question. Of course I do. Mother and Dad will always love me, even though they're no longer together. Then there's Mandy, who has my back at the office. Sheila, the manager of the Piney Point salon, respects me, and Chester, who's been one of the hairdressers there forever, appreciates the fact that I always listen to him. Then there are the other hairdressers and managers, like Vanessa, Rosemary, and . . . well the list goes on and on.

I glance over at a couple leaning against the stone building, holding hands, gazing into each other's eyes, and I feel a tinge of something I can't quite put my finger on. It's not jealousy. It's more of a feeling that I might never have what they have and that I'm missing something. Hmm. Maybe that is jealousy. And it's ridiculous. I would be willing to bet neither of those people has the kind of professional status or respect I have. They don't appear to be well-to-do, if their attire is any indication. The guy's shoes look rather worn, and the woman's handbag is of the discount store variety.

They both look up at me and smile. I nervously grin back and avert my gaze so they won't think I'm . . . Well, what *am* I doing?

"Priscilla!"

I turn around at the sound of my name and see Tim standing beside a cab he obviously just got out of. "Hey, there, Tim. Looks like we're both early."

"I knew you would be." He hands the driver some money and holds up his hand, indicating to keep the change. "So how'd your airing go?"

"We sold so many big-hair systems it looks like we might have another sellout. You should have seen us."

Tim winks and chuckles. "I did. Priscilla, you looked so pretty standin' there holdin' up that new device while the show host . . . what's her name?"

"Felicity."

"With you demonstratin' the device, and Felicity sprayin' and combin', there's no stoppin' you."

We walk the last few steps toward the restaurant and stop at the door. "Tim, you've been wonderful about everything, and I have to give you credit for some of my success."

"Nope." He shakes his head as he holds the door open for me. "I can't . . . I won't take credit for one single solitary ounce of your success. You done . . . er, I mean did it all by yourself."

"You've always been there for me, though."

The host leads us to a table, and we sit down to order our drinks. After the server leaves, Tim leans back in his chair, still grinning. Then it dawns on me that he's itching to say something. He has some news of his own to share.

"Do tell," I say.

"Tell what?" The smile on his face turns playful.

"What is going on? Why are you absolutely beaming?"

He makes a silly face. "Can't I just be happy to sit at a table for a meal with one of my favorite people in the entire world?"

"Yes, of course you can, but I've known you a long time, and I can tell something else is going on with you."

"Oh, all right. I might as well tell you now instead of later. Uncle Hugh is turnin' his entire business over to me . . . that is, if I want it."

I study Tim's face and try to figure out what he really wants. He's smiling, but he's always been such a happy person who is able to put a positive spin on almost anything.

"Well? Do you plan to accept his offer?"

He lifts his water glass, takes a sip, and slowly puts it back on the table before looking directly at me. "All depends."

7
Tim

I know I should prob'ly jump on Uncle Hugh's job offer, but I'm not so sure it's right for me. Now that I'm older and a tad wiser, I understand some things that escaped me when I was younger, like why Uncle Hugh insisted I finish college. Mama got a little ticked that he didn't put me in a management position right away, but at least he offered me a job as a salesman after I got my degree. That was one of the best moves he could have made, but I doubt even he realized just how good it was at the time. How could he have known that assigning me the territory that includes Piney Point, Mississippi, would be the start of something big and beautiful with the most successful hairdresser the South has ever known?

Priscilla snaps her fingers in front of my face. "Earth to Tim, are you there?"

I catch a whiff of her citrus-spice perfume that nearly knocks me to my knees every time I smell it. "Yeah." I laugh.

"So are you going to take the offer or not?" She leans toward me, and I catch another whiff of her perfume.

I close my eyes for as long as I think I can get away with it and open them to find her staring at me. "I'm still so shocked by the offer I don't know yet."

"When do you have to decide?"

"Soon." I lift my water glass again, but she puts her hand on my arm and firmly holds it in place.

"Don't let this opportunity slip away, Tim. You're a very smart man and good at what you do."

"That's what worries me. I'm good at what I'm doin' now, but what if I take on more than I can chew by runnin' the whole entire company?" I'm not about to admit that my biggest fear is managing all the sales folks and lettin' them down.

"I've never seen you like this, Tim." Her expression changes.

Uh-oh. Now I've disappointed my favorite girl. "I'm sure I'll be just fine."

"Yes, I know you will. All you have to do is look at what you've done with your territory since you started with the company. You managed to double the profit in your area in the first year, and then—"

"Quadruple," I correct her.

She holds out her hands. "Okay, so that proves what I'm saying."

"That's just sales, Priscilla. Runnin' the company is a lot more than that. I have to manage all the sales teams, make sure their salons get their orders, organize product lines, and—"

"How is that any different from what you've done with all my class reunions?" Her lips twitch into a crooked smile that sets my heart to beatin' ninety-to-nothin'.

"I don't get what you're sayin'."

"Look at it this way, Tim. You've stepped in and helped Laura finalize every class reunion since the tenth. If it weren't for you, we would've been standing around looking at each other waiting for entertainment that might or might not show up, staring at an empty food table, and maybe even been run off the property for not getting a permit for the bonfire during the tenth."

"Well . . . " I think back over the things I done for Laura Moss. "That's true, but I'm sure someone would've stepped up."

"Like who?" She shrugs. "I can't think of anyone. And now you've become one of the most important guests at every one of my class reunions."

That does make me feel real good, but I also know it's dangerous 'cause I don't think it can last, since I never even stepped foot in Piney Point High School until ten years ago. "You make some good points, Priscilla. I'll have to consider 'em while I make my decision."

She reaches for the menu. "That's all anyone can ask. I'm starving. Did you see the board with today's specials?"

"Braised beef tips." I rarely miss anything related to food—particularly when I'm this hungry.

"See? We were talking when we walked in, and you still managed to see the board. You don't miss much, Tim, which is another reason why I think you'll be a wonderful CEO."

"Priscilla, you sure do know how to sweet talk a guy."

The sound of her laughter goes all through me—in a good way. Whenever I'm down, all I have to do is call her up and say somethin' . . . anything, and she'll laugh. It don't even have to be funny for her to find the humor in it.

"But it's gonna be hard if I decide to take the job 'cause I'll have to move up here, and in case you haven't noticed, I'm not exactly a city boy."

Priscilla's smile fades, and she gives me one of her serious get-down-to-business looks. "You're not any kind of a boy, Tim. You're a man who can tackle whatever you need to in order to get the job done."

All but one thing, and that's to get her to fall in love with me. Lord knows I've tried. But her focus has always been on her career—except for that brief time when Maurice distracted her—and by now I've accepted that she's not ever gonna want me to be the man she settles down with.

"Enough talk about me," I say to lighten the mood. "I saw you on air, and you looked mighty fine."

She tries to hide a smile, but it don't work. "Did you see when Felicity spilled that conditioner all over the tray?"

"Well, yeah, but that didn't seem to hurt sales none." I see her flinch, so I correct myself. "It didn't hurt her sales *any*."

"True. But Felicity was upset, and when they went to B-roll so we could clean it up, Felicity fussed at the set stylist."

"Why would she go and do something like that?"

Priscilla shrugs. "I like Felicity and all, but she doesn't ever like to take the blame for anything going wrong on the set."

"But I bet she takes credit for stuff goin' right, don't she?"

"You got that right, but to be fair to her, the TV business is tough, and everyone is stressed all the time. I'm just glad they had enough B-roll footage to cover the time it took to clean up."

"Yeah, you was wonderin' why they needed all that scientific information." I sit up all proud. "And I'm glad I was able to get it for you."

I see Priscilla glancin' away all nervouslike, so I turn and catch some middle-aged woman leaning over and gawkin' at us out of the corner of my eye. When I look directly at her, she snaps back and pretends she's mindin' her own business.

"Don't look now, but I think one of your fans might be in the restaurant."

Priscilla gives me one of her frustrated looks. "I know. She's been staring for quite some time."

The woman's eyes bulge as she openly stares right at us. I lift a hand and wiggle my fingers in a wave.

She takes that as an invitation to hop right outta her seat and sidle up to our table. Her mouth opens as she looks back and forth between me and Priscilla. "Oh my gosh, I totally can't believe I'm actually standing here beside Ms. Prissy and Brad Pitt."

I nearly choke on my iced tea. "Um . . . "

Priscilla looks like she's ready to fall off her seat, she's so amused. "And what's your name?" she asks the woman, her lips twitching like she wants to crack up.

"My name's Beth Fay Swanson. Oh my, no one's gonna believe this back home. Can I take your picture?" Without waiting for an answer, she snaps a shot and grins at us. "Ooh, this is good."

Priscilla pulls one of the empty chairs toward her and pats the seat. "Why don't you have a seat and let"—she glances at me and winks—"let *Brad* take our picture."

The woman's eyebrows shoot up. "You and me? Is that okay . . . ?" She turns to me. "I mean do you mind?"

I stand up and take the camera she's thrust toward me. "Naw, I don't mind at all."

Right after I snap the picture, she grabs the camera and glares at me. "You're not Brad Pitt."

"Never said I was, ma'am."

"Then who are you?"

Before I have a chance to answer, Priscilla leans forward on her elbows, like she's gettin' all chummy with the strange woman and whispers, "His name's Tim, and he's a big shot at one of the finest hair product companies in the entire country. But it's a secret, okay?" She narrows her eyes and leans even closer to the woman. "We don't want the paparazzi to come after us."

The woman nods and looks all serious as she straightens up and backs away. "Paparazzi? Oh . . . " She scurries back to her table, lookin' for all the world like she's ready to jump outta her skin.

As soon as she's out of earshot, I turn to Priscilla. "You're good."

She curls her fingers toward herself, blows on them, and rubs them on her collar. "Don't I know it?"

"Don't look now, but our new friend is shootin' loads of pictures of us . . . one after another."

"I don't think we can stop her." She shrugs. "But what does it matter anyway? A few pictures from a fan can't hurt, can they?"

The rest of the night we chat about this and that, from her next trip to New York to what I'll do with my territory if I wind up takin' the job. As we speak, I see why Priscilla has been so successful. She has a way of analyzin' the whats, whys, and wherefores of what makes things work, givin' me another thing to admire about her.

After supper, I walk her back to her hotel. There's lots of folks out takin' advantage of the nice weather and all the stuff there is to do in Times Square. We stand and talk outside her hotel before she looks down at her watch.

"I had a wonderful time, Tim, but I need to go get some sleep."

I nod. "Yep. Tomorrow comes mighty early."

After she goes inside, I stand and look around at what just might wind up bein' my hometown soon. It sure is a far cry from any place I ever lived in Mississippi. A cab pulls up to the curb in front of me.

I lift a finger, and when he nods, I hop inside, and we take off. As we head toward the Staten Island Ferry, a queasy feelin' comes over me. I love visitin' the big city and hangin' out with

Uncle Hugh and Aunt Tammy, but the thought of livin' here? That's a whole 'nother story.

The next mornin' I have a cup of coffee with Aunt Tammy and head on over to the office to spend a little more time with Uncle Hugh before going back to Mississippi. When I arrive, he surprises me with a slap on the back and the biggest cake-eatin' grin I ever seen.

"Tim, my boy, you're a natural for this job."

"Wha—?"

That's when I notice he's shakin' a newspaper in my face. There on the cover is a picture of me and Priscilla sittin' at the restaurant, lookin' like we was in love . . . or something.

"Where did that come from?"

"One of the assistants brought it in. You sure do know how to make a splash when you come to town. Do you realize that this one little picture is responsible for our phones ringing off the hook?" He points to the eight-line phone that's all lit up. "Just look at what you've created."

"All 'cause of that one little picture? How can that be? Some girl spotted Priscilla last night, but she thought I was Brad Pitt."

He belts out a deep belly laugh. "Yeah, I know. I just read all about it. Apparently, she went straight to the tabloid and told them all about her celebrity spotting."

I rub the back of my neck and try to figure out if this is a good thing. From the way Uncle Hugh is actin', I would say it is. But I'm not used to havin' my mug broadcast all over the place.

"The Ms. Prissy Big Hair phenomenon is taking over the US Canada, and Great Britain." He sits down and gestures toward the chair on the other side of his desk. "Now that people know she was having a . . . business dinner with Tim, the big shot at one of the finest hair product companies, we're on the international map."

"Well, I'll be." Priscilla planted an idea in that woman's head, but I had no idea this kinda thing would happen.

"So you gotta take me up on my offer, but after this, I'm thinking I might need to stick around just a little while longer to help you deal with the business exploding so fast."

"Yeah," I say. "That would probably be a very good idea." I'm sorta numb, so I'm not sure what all I'm sayin' or implyin'.

One of Uncle Hugh's assistants appears at the door. "Sorry to bother you, Mr. Puckett, but there's a woman from ABC on line three."

8
Priscilla

I'm finally back in Jackson, after a very long trip from New York, with flight attendants giving me strange looks and fellow passengers snickering. After being on TVNS for a while, I'm used to double takes, but this is different. It's almost as though people know some deep dark secret about me.

As I make my way to baggage claim, I turn on my cell phone and see that I have half a dozen messages—all from Tim. Uh-oh.

I punch *Call Back* from his message, and he answers right away. "Honestly, Priscilla, I had nothing to do with that article."

"What article?"

"You haven't seen it?"

"No, I haven't. I don't even know what you're talking about."

He makes a whistling sound as he exhales between his teeth that are obviously clenched from whatever is bothering him. "There's an article . . . in *Famous People News* . . . "

"C'mon, Tim. What's going on?" Some woman walks past me snickering, giving me a thumbs-up. The man beside her tugs her away from me, but right behind her is another woman gawking and shaking her head. "People have been acting really strange today."

"Want me to read it to you?"

"I'm not sure." I've reached the baggage carousel, and I see my luggage coming toward me. "Can I call you back in a few minutes?"

"Sure, but don't talk to anyone before you do."

I let out a nervous laugh. "Whatever that newspaper printed, Tim, just remember that most people don't believe a word of it."

"Call me back as soon as you can."

After I disconnect the call, I drop the phone into my handbag, walk up to the carousel, and tug the suitcase off the belt. Some man comes toward me looking like he wants to help, but the woman beside him yanks his arm, and he comes to an abrupt halt.

I didn't want to leave my car in long-term parking, so I have to get a cab to take me home. Once I'm settled in the backseat, I punch in Tim's number again, and he answers immediately.

"Can you talk now?"

"Yes." I smooth my skirt and take a deep breath. "So what's got you all worked up."

"Apparently, we're involved in a steamy relationship that started when my company supplied you with the magical product that pulled your struggling business from the gutter."

"What?" Tim is such a jokester, but this isn't funny—not when it comes to my business that I've worked so hard to build over so many years.

"*Famous People News* had that and so much more to say about me 'n you."

I see the cab driver looking at me in the rearview mirror, so I scoot as close to the window as the seatbelt will allow, getting out of his line of vision. "That explains a lot of what's been happening today." I tell him all about people's reactions to me at the airport and on the plane.

"I hope you know I had nothing to do with it," Tim says.

"Of course, I know that. So are you upset?"

He chuckles. "I haven't had time to get upset. Ever since that article appeared, orders have poured in, and I'm juggling the supplier, sales reps, and . . . "

"And what, Tim?"

"ABC called. They want to do a piece on *Good Morning America*." He pauses to catch a breath. "And I just got off the phone with someone from CBS. They're interested in something for *Entertainment Tonight*."

My throat constricts. "Oh my."

"You can say that again. Priscilla, I've had to deal with all kinds of crazy stuff, but this takes the cake. I never seen this one coming."

"Same here."

"But you've always known you wanted to be a celebrity. That's never been something I've even thought of for myself."

I bristle. "Tim, that's not true. I've never thought about becoming a celebrity."

"Um, Priscilla, for as long as I can remember, you've talked about bein' on TVNS."

"Not for the celebrity status. I just wanted to get my products into the hands of as many women as possible, and that seemed the best way to do it."

"C'mon, Priscilla, you're a smart woman. When you appear on TV, you become a celebrity. That's the way it works."

Are Tim and I arguing? I don't like the way this feels in the pit of my stomach. "Okay, I'll give you that one. Why don't we think about this and talk about it later? The whole thing has caught me by surprise, so I might say something I don't mean."

"Yeah, and I suggest picking up one of the papers so you can see it for yourself."

After we end our call, I instruct the driver to make a stop at a grocery store. He waits as I run inside, grab a copy of *Famous People News*, and pay for it. Rather than risk his smirks, I drop the paper into my tote before I get back into the cab.

My cell phone rings again, so I pull it out and look at the name. Mother. No doubt someone has told her, or will tell her, about the article since I can't imagine her seeing it for herself. I decide to let the call go to voice mail and call Mother back later when I'm in the privacy of my townhouse . . . after I have a chance to read and dissect the article.

The image of Mother finding out I'm the subject of celebrity news makes me smile at the irony. She's above reading the gossip rags that I used to peruse while standing in line in the grocery store. I remember her swatting at my hand when I reached for one when I was in middle school. "That's just trash," she said. "And we're not trashy people."

Well, apparently that's changed with my success. And now that I think about it, whose place is it to call someone else trashy? I'm sure Mother hasn't thought this all the way through because she's a big believer in helping the downtrodden, even though she's way too caught up in her own intellectualism to get too close to anyone beneath her status. From a very early age she taught me how to use long words when shorter ones would have been perfectly suitable. Now I have to stop and think before speaking to keep from sounding like an intellectual snob. I also have to concentrate hard on not correcting people when they use bad grammar, which is quite a challenge when I'm with Tim. He tries harder than anyone I know, but his country talk is imbedded in his roots. Most of the time I find that quite charming, and I certainly don't want to change him, even though he seems to constantly struggle with trying to impress me.

"Here ya go, Ms. Slater," the cab driver says as he takes the fare I hand him. "Need change?" The fact that he used my name sends shivers down my spine. I pray he doesn't get greedy and sell my address to the tabloids.

"No thanks, but there is one thing I would like."

He grins. "What's that?"

I hand him an extra twenty. "Can you keep my identity and address—"

A horrified look washes over his face as he takes the money. "I'm a professional, Ms. Slater. I would never stoop so low as to divulge anything about one of my clients." He pulls out a business card. "You will call me next time you need a ride, won't you?"

That's the least I can do. "Yes, of course."

"Don't you worry about me saying anything to anyone." He runs his fingers over his closed lips.

"Thanks."

I pull my suitcase inside and take my time putting everything away. Then I fix a pot of coffee and sit down to read the article. It's really not that bad. They got a few facts wrong, but it doesn't make me look like a bad person, which was what I had feared.

Now I need to call Mother. I take a few deep breaths and press her number on speed dial. She answers with a lecture.

"How many times have I told you to stay away from those magazines, Priscilla? Doesn't anything I say get through to you? First you flunk out of college—"

"I didn't flunk out, Mother. I quit college, remember?"

"Okay, but what do you think you're doing, getting your name plastered all over the scandal rags?"

"My name isn't plastered all over them. It happened one time, and it was an innocent article. Have you even read it?" The mental image of Mother sitting down reading one of those magazines makes me smile.

"Of course I did. My daughter's in there. And I thought you and Tim were just good friends. When did that change, and why didn't you tell me about it?"

"You didn't actually believe what you read, did you?"

"The picture can't lie. I know what I saw. The way you two were looking at each other is pretty telling."

I spend the next fifteen minutes explaining what actually happened and defending myself. "I promise that if I ever fall in love, I'll tell you about it before I tell some reporter I don't even know."

"That would be nice."

"I better go now. I have to get up early."

"One more thing, Priscilla. I'm not saying I like seeing your picture in that . . . magazine, and I'm not trying to tell you how to run your life, but you and Tim . . . well, y'all do make a nice-looking couple."

I refuse to participate in this conversation any longer, now that she's taken it to a different place. "Bye, Mother. I love you."

"Okay, I can take a hint. Love you too."

"See you in a few weeks?"

"Don't forget, you need to give me an exact date as soon as you know."

"I'll call soon."

9
Laura

Did you hear about Priscilla?"

I'm standin' in the Piggly Wiggly with my second-to-youngest child, wishin' the woman in front of me didn't have so many coupons. I've tried couponing, but I can't seem to get everything organized, even in those little pouchy things, and cashiers get annoyed when half the coupons I hand 'em have expired.

Bonnie Sue is thumbin' through one of the magazines, poppin' her gum like she always does when she goes shoppin' with me. I woulda left her at home, but Renee's there with her boyfriend, and Bonnie Sue can't seem to keep her smart-aleck comments to herself, which gets Renee all hoppin' mad, and they wind up fightin' like a coupla yard dogs.

"What about Priscilla?"

"Look at this." She shoves the magazine in front of my nose, and I have to lean back to see what she's pointin' to.

"Is that . . . ?" I squint my eyes and read the caption beneath the picture. "Why that's Priscilla Slater and Tim."

"Can you buy me this magazine, Mama? Please?"

Rather than start an argument I know I'll never win, I make a quick decision. "Sure, and grab me a copy while you're at it."

Bonnie Sue's chin drops, exposing a wad of over-chewed gum and her slightly crooked teeth from not wearing her retainer like the orthodontist instructed. I start to comment but think better of it since she's recovered and is doing what I told her to, a rare thing these days.

Actually, Bonnie Sue has turned out to be a decent kid if you don't count her snot-face comments just because she's a cheerleader and popular with the boys. Renee is the one I'm most worried about now. For years she managed to fly under the radar as the second oldest of my young'uns and older of the two girls, but lately, ever since she started seein' this boy Wilson, she's different. Pete doesn't like the boy—says he's nothin' but trouble, but I remind him that people said the same thing about him when he was that age. My issue is with Renee, who used to be opinionated as all get out but now can't seem to make a decision before consulting Wilson. And that boy has some mighty strong opinions.

Bonnie Sue actually helps me put the groceries in the back of the minivan that I'm tryin' to talk Pete into lettin' me trade in for an SUV. After we get the bags situated, we get into the front seat at the same time. Bonnie Sue is still hangin' on to her copy of *Famous People News.*

I reach over and try to take it from her. "Here, let me see that."

She jerks it away from me, and I'm left holdin' onto a corner. "Now look what you went and done, Mama. You ripped my magazine."

"You can have mine. It's not ripped."

"Okay." She fidgets with her seatbelt, so I take advantage of her guard bein' down and yank the magazine out of her lap. "What're you doin', Mama? I was gonna read that."

"I just wanna see what they said about Priscilla."

Bonnie Sue sighs as I skim the article and see that there isn't much in there I don't already know, except maybe since I last saw Priscilla and Tim they might have gone and gotten romantic. But I suspect that's a misprint.

I toss the magazine back at her. "Here. I gotta drive home so the frozen food don't—I mean doesn't—thaw out."

Bonnie Sue thumbs through the magazine before closing it and dropping it to the floor. "I think it's so cool that we actually know someone famous. Do you think she might hire me when I'm done with beauty school?"

At the stop sign, I tip my head toward her and give her my "mom" look. "You do realize that becomin' a hairdresser isn't likely to make you famous, right?"

"That's what happened to Priscilla. It can happen to me."

"There's a lot more to Priscilla than that, Bonnie Sue. Did you know that she was voted 'Most Likely to Succeed'?"

"Yeah, and she *is* the most successful. So what's your point?"

"If we'd known she was gonna drop outta college and become a hairdresser, I don't think a one of us woulda voted for her."

Bonnie Sue gives me a look of utter confusion. "So you and all your friends voted for her just because y'all thought she was gonna get a college degree?"

"She was the smartest girl in the whole school. She even beat out Didi Holcomb by a smidge for valedictorian."

"I still don't get what your point is, Mama. You're talkin' in circles."

My daughter's right, but I'm not about to let her know I don't have a point, except that I want her to go to college. I mean, isn't that what all parents want for their young'uns? I pull into the driveway and turn to Bonnie Sue. "Give me a hand with the groceries, will ya?"

She carries two bags, and I carry the other five into the kitchen, slammin' the door behind me with my foot. I talk about how college will open more doors to her future and give her more opportunities than I'll ever have.

"Bubba didn't go to college, and Renee's not doin' so good no more." Bonnie Sue shakes her head. "She used to be the smart one in the family, but now . . . " She nods toward the living room where Renee and Wilson sit watchin' some hokey wrestlin' match on TV. " . . . not so much."

"Then it's up to you, Bonnie Sue. Someone in this family has to do something smart."

"Jack wants to be a rocket scientist." She rips into the bag of chips and stuffs one into her mouth. "That's smart."

As if he'll ever do that. My youngest child has gone from wanting to be a superhero to private investigator to astronaut and now rocket scientist. No tellin' what he'll wind up doin', but I'd be willin' to bet his bronzed baby shoes it won't be none of those things. Pete's tryin' to get him to learn a trade, but the boy hates workin' with his hands, unless it involves food or computers. I commented that he might wanna become a chef, but Pete says no boy of his is gonna have a job workin' in the kitchen. He considers that women's work. Obviously he hasn't seen much on the Food Network. My favorite chefs are the men, no offense to the Barefoot Contessa or Rachel. Give me a man holdin' a spatula in one hand and a potholder in the other, and I promise you he owns a piece of my heart.

Bonnie Sue hovers in the kitchen eatin' chips while I put everything away. Once there's nothin' left to be done, she brushes her hands together. "If you don't need me no more, I wanna go call Taylor."

"Go on ahead. I'll call you back down when supper's ready."

She stops in the doorway and turns to face me. "We're not havin' nothin' yucky, are we?"

"All depends on what you call yucky." I give her my evilest grin.

She plugs her nose. "I hate fish."

"We're not havin' fish, but I'm gonna try to fix somethin' healthy."

"One of your casseroles?" Her eyes light up.

"Prob'ly not. I used to think I was fixin' healthy food, 'til Mama's nutritionist told me all that fattenin' cheese was artery cloggin'."

She groans and walks out of the kitchen mumblin' something about her mama turnin' into a health-food nut. That's not such a bad idea, after seein' my mama suffer so bad after her heart attack. I never realized how miserable bein' in the hospital could be. I used to think all you had to do was lie in bed while nurses waited on you hand and foot. But no, they got Mama goin' to therapy and meetin' with all kinds of folks tellin' her she's gotta work at gettin' healthy if she doesn't wanna die young. I can't imagine her goin' for two-mile walks every single day, but she says she's gonna do it, and Randy's gonna go with her.

In the meantime, I'm havin' to learn a whole new way of cookin'. I burned a few meals last week, but I'm startin' to get the hang of sautéing with cookin' spray and olive oil. The hardest part is keepin' the family from addin' a plop of butter to everything once it's on their plates. I don't even put it on the table, but I can pretty much count on one of the boys to hop up and fetch it from the fridge for Pete. Little Jack will do just about anything to get an *attaboy* from his daddy.

Speakin' of the devil, I hear Pete stompin' his feet, tryin' to get the mud off before enterin' the house. He parks his truck so close to the edge of the driveway, he has to walk through the yard, and he's worn out the grass, so he gets mud in his boot tread.

"Hey, Miss Pudge." He comes up behind me, puts his arms around my waist, and gives me a kiss on the neck. I used to balk at his annoying term of endearment, but I know it's his way of sayin' he loves me.

"Hey, yourself." I tip my head toward the tater bin. "Would you mind grabbin' me a coupla big potatoes?"

"Sure." He leans over, inspects the contents, and pulls out a bunch of potatoes. "Is that enough?"

"More than enough." I rinse my hands, dry them, and take all but the two biggest potatoes and toss 'em back into the bin.

"Hey, what're you doin'? Are you just cookin' for me 'n you?"

"No, everyone will be here, but we're cuttin' back."

He groans. "I don't reckon you're gonna fry or mash 'em neither."

"You reckon right." I pick up one of the potatoes and inspect it. "I'm gonna slice 'em real thin and roast 'em."

Pete gives me a long, silent look and leaves the kitchen mumbling somethin' about gettin' sick of oven-baked potato chips. And I don't feel guilty because I'm doing it to get my family healthy.

An hour later the family and Wilson sit down at the table. I never ask Wilson to join us, but I reckon since he's so in love with Renee he figures he doesn't have to be asked.

Pete glares at him before turning to Bubba. "Wanna say the blessin', son?"

Bubba stares at the food on his plate and slowly shakes his head. "There's not much here to bless, is there?"

In spite of the fact that Pete most likely agrees with Bubba, he stabs his finger toward our oldest child. "You better be thankful you have anything to eat. There are homeless people in this world who'd give up their favorite corner on the street to have what you got." Bless his heart, I know he doesn't mean it, but at least he's still showin' his support in front of the kids.

After Bubba finishes his blessin', skimpy as it is, Bonnie Sue turns to Pete. "Did Mama tell you about Priscilla havin' her picture in the magazine?"

Pete looks at Bonnie Sue, his fork suspended between his plate and his mouth. "What magazine?"

"*Famous People News.*" Bonnie Sue grins at me. "Ain't that right, Mama? Wasn't Priscilla's picture in there?"

I nod, but before I have a chance to say a word, Wilson pipes up. "My mama says that's the best magazine they is. She goes to the grocery store on Tuesdays on account of that's when it comes out, and she can be the first to know everything."

Why am I not surprised? "Is that right, Wilson?"

His mouth is full of steamed vegetables as he speaks. "My mama, she likes to read. Papa says that's why she's so smart." He shovels another forkful of food into his still half-full pie hole. At least someone at the dinner table likes my cookin'.

Pete stares at Wilson with a disgusted look on his face and turns back to me. "So what's the latest with the reunion? Does it look like everyone will be there this year?"

10
Priscilla

Mandy has a mile-long list for me when I walk into the Jackson office. "These are all people who need to talk to you, and when you're done getting back to them, I have something I wanna discuss."

I'm used to Mandy's bossiness, but something about her is different this time. She doesn't look me directly in the eye. Instead, she gives me quick glances and looks away, almost as though she's afraid of something.

"Do you want to talk first?" I stand over her, looking down at the top of her head that's bent over her desk.

"No, that's okay. I can wait."

I walk back to the tiny room in the corner of our upstairs office suite. We talked about moving, but we couldn't find a new location that makes sense, so here we are in the same spot. After Mandy took over my old office—the big one with the power desk, picture window, and cool phone with all the buttons I still haven't figured out—I started working from home when I was in Jackson. But there have been some days when I need to be here, so we converted one of the supply closets to a small makeshift office for me, complete with a table barely big enough for my laptop, a much less sophisticated phone, and a chair. I leave the door open to keep from feeling claustrophobic and to get air.

As I work my way down the list, I spot a name I'm not familiar with, so I buzz Mandy. "Do you know who Beth Fay Swanson is?"

"No, but she said you would."

I put my phone back on the cradle and stare at the name, trying to figure out who she is. It's vaguely familiar, but nothing comes to me. Finally, I just pick up the phone and punch in her number. The instant she answers, I remember her voice from the restaurant. She's the fan who just had to take my picture.

"Oh, Ms. Slater, I'm so glad you called me back. The man at *Famous People News* said I'd probably never hear from you, and if I did, it would be one of your lawyers calling me back with threats."

"What are you talking about?"

"After you gave me the idea to go to the tabloids, I did just that. The man who gave me the money said you would come after me with the big guns."

"You're the one who sold my picture to the magazine?"

"Yes."

I'm stunned silent, but only for a moment. "I thought you just wanted our picture for personal use. I never would have—"

"I hope you understand I never would have taken money if my husband hadn't left me with a mortgage and a kid in college, and I had something that was worth some money, and I didn't exactly have a choice. It's hard being a single mom, ya know?" She pauses. "I hope you're not too upset, but I had to do it."

"So you said." I sigh. "What do you want from me now?"

"A job."

"A job?" This is turning into one of the strangest conversations I can ever remember having, and I have to hand it to her . . . she has guts.

"My friends all say you probably have people to look after you, since you're a celebrity, and I'm really good at a lot of different things. I don't have a formal education, but I can type, and I learn fast." She stops to take an audible breath. "If you need a gofer, I'm your girl 'cause now that my son is away at college, I can travel. Ms. Slater, I really need a job, and I'll do anything. I was in New York interviewing for a job that I didn't get, and I live in Raleigh, but I don't mind—"

"And you don't mind selling information to the magazines to make a buck. Ms. Swanson, I don't know what your game is, but you have some nerve calling me, let alone asking for a job."

There's a long pause over the phone line then a click. I hold the phone out and stare at it for a moment before dropping it back in the cradle. My mind races with all sorts of things, starting with the shock of that woman having the gall to want something from me after what she did.

I bury my face in my hands and try to make some sense of it. This is one of the weirdest situations I've ever been in, but as I think about what she'd told me about being a single mom and all, I can understand why she'd do what she did. Desperation sometimes causes people to do things they wouldn't ordinarily do.

Then the thought hits that I really do need someone else on my staff to help me with some of the minutiae of my life. But there's no way I'd even consider hiring that woman after what she did. Or maybe I would. Hmm.

The very idea of her request makes me laugh at the absurdity of the mere thought of hiring her. How would I ever be able to trust her? That old saying about keeping your friends close and your enemies closer pops into my head.

I work hard all afternoon at putting her out of my mind, but the more I think about all the things I have to do, the more I realize how much I need assistance. Getting to the network on time, with all the things I have to lug and contacts I have to make while I'm there, has been extremely stressful. Having someone with me would ease the burden, but it would have to be someone who isn't shy or reserved. Someone who is willing to speak to anyone at any level. Someone who doesn't worry about what other people think. I can't believe what I'm thinking: someone like Beth Fay Swanson. As bothersome as her actions were, I have a gut feeling about her—that she's not a bad person but someone who doesn't mind doing whatever she has to do to get the job done. At least she had the decency to call me and admit what she'd done. Besides, what she did isn't illegal, and I have to admit it's been good publicity for the Ms. Prissy Big Hair system, not to mention the fact that that one picture in the tabloid has significantly increased business for Tim. But I can't leave Mandy out of the equation, since she's been with me so long. She deserves the first crack at a new opportunity before I go making an offer to some stranger.

Instead of picking the phone back up to talk to Mandy, I get up and walk to her office. The door isn't all the way shut, so I knock before pushing it open. She looks annoyed until she realizes it's me.

"Need something?"

"Would you be interested in traveling?"

"You mean for the job?"

I nod. "Yes, I think it would be nice to have someone travel with me when I visit the salons and TVNS."

Her forehead crinkles, and she purses her lips. "I'm sorry, Priscilla, but I don't think I can do it. This guy I've been dating

. . . well, you know how that is . . . and I'm needed here . . . and . . ." She gives me a puppy-dog face and a shrug.

Before she has a chance to finish her thoughts, I nod. "You're right. But I still need someone."

Mandy narrows her eyes, folds her hands beneath her chin, and studies me for a few seconds. "I can tell you're up to somethin', Priscilla. Do you have someone in mind to hire?"

I close the door and pull a chair up to her desk. "You're going to think I'm nuts, but here's what I'm thinking." I tell her my thoughts about Beth Fay, and to my surprise she doesn't tell me I'm crazy.

"Yeah, she's got . . . a lot of nerve to do what she did, and that's exactly what you need. When I heard about her, I thought it sounded like something I might have done back when I was younger. How old is this woman, anyway?"

I smile. "Older than either of us."

"Oh." She chews her bottom lip then nods. "You could hire her on a temporary basis to see how she works out before you commit to her long-term."

I stand up and smile down at Mandy. "Brilliant idea. Thanks for helping me think through this."

"No problem. I've worked for you a long time, and I'm the first to admit you had your hands full with me. The fact that you saw something in me, made me want to work that much harder. Maybe that'll be the case with this Beth Fay person." She makes a face. "But considering what she did, you still need to be careful."

"Oh, trust me, I'll never turn my back on her or put myself in a dangerous position."

"Yeah, like don't let her stay in your hotel room with you." She smiles. "You know what you're doing, so if it seems right, then go for it."

"I sure hope it's the right thing." I pause. "You mentioned that you wanted to talk to me about something."

She grins back at me. "We can talk about it when I remember what it is."

After I leave Mandy's office, I give Tim a call and tell him what's transpired.

He gasps. "You're kiddin', right?"

"No, I'm totally serious." Then I explain my thoughts and tell him what Mandy said.

He laughs. "My granny used to say 'Keep your friends close but your enemies closer.' "

So that's where I heard it. "She's not exactly an enemy."

"Priscilla, this sounds crazy, but I know what Mandy's saying. You've had good instincts so far. So hire her."

"Seriously?"

"Yeah, you know you wanna do it."

"Wanting to do something isn't a valid enough reason." Why do I feel as though I'm arguing with myself?

"Maybe not, but it's not something you can't undo. Since you live your life in a fishbowl now, it might do you some good to have someone help you manage things. I agree with Mandy about bringing her on as a temp."

"Tim, you have such a logical mind, but this is different. So tell me what's going on with your uncle."

Once again, he laughs, snorting this time. "He just wants to go fishin', and I'm the most convenient person to bring up here, since I'm not tied down with a wife and kids." I detect a note of sadness in his voice. He clears his throat. "Back to this Beth Fay woman. When she came up to us in that restaurant, I didn't get that sick feelin' in my gut like I did when I met Maurice. I mean, I don't think she's out to hurt you. She's just tryin' to make it in this world, and she saw an opportunity."

"I hope she's not so opportunistic that she'd try to hurt me."

"I don't think she'd try to hurt you. Besides, you already know what she's capable of doing, so you can watch her like a hawk. You might even wanna offer her a bonus for some extra publicity. She's already told you she needs the extra money, and that'll be cheaper than hirin' a real publicist."

"Thanks, Tim. I'll call the woman back and see if she's agreeable to going through a temp agency."

"Tell her *Brad* said hey."

I place a call to my favorite temp agency to ask how to proceed. In the past, when Mandy and I have needed temp workers, we've called the agency, and they've found the candidates. This is the first time I've sent people to them.

After they explain all the steps, I take a deep breath and punch in Beth Fay's number. She seems shocked that I bothered to call back. "I'm so sorry, Ms. Slater. I don't know what I was thinking. That's really not like me, and if there's anything I can do to make it up to you—"

"Before you get too carried away apologizing, hear me out."

I explain that I want to hire her through a temp agency to see how things go. Every once in a while, she asks a question, like if there's a chance she'll be hired permanently or if there will be benefits because the ones through the temp agency aren't as good as the ones we have here. I tell her I can't make any promises.

"So you want me to just pick up and move without anything solid?"

I wonder if I've just made a huge mistake offering her this job. "You don't have to move, Beth Fay. I'll need you to travel, starting with a week here in my Jackson office. I'll cover all your expenses while you're here."

"In that case, I might consider it."

Odd comment coming from this woman. "I want you to spend some time learning about the company before we proceed, so it's pretty important. My assistant, Mandy, will work with you."

Beth Fay asks a few questions, and then there's silence. It's time to pop the question. "Well, are you interested in moving forward?"

Without a moment's hesitation, she blurts, "Yes. When can I start?"

I give her the step-by-step instructions from the temp agency. "After you get everything squared away with them, they'll call me, and we'll proceed from there."

About thirty seconds after we hang up, Mandy appears at my door grinning. "So you're hiring the stalker, huh?"

"Looks like I am. I hope I'm not taking on a problem."

"What's the worst that can happen? You're bringing a stalker onboard so you can keep an eye on her, and in the meantime, you'll get some work out of her."

"That's pretty much what Tim said. Did you remember what you wanted to discuss with me?"

"Yes, but this might not be a good time."

I fold my arms and lean against her desk. "Spit it out, Mandy."

"Well, you know how much you've been gone and all, leaving me with all this work. It's not that I don't like my job or anything, but—"

"Would you like a raise?" I look her in the eye.

Her lips twitch, and she nods. "Yes."

"Okay, you've got it."

A look of surprise flashes across her face, and she starts to jump up. I know she's coming in for a hug, but I'm really not in the mood, so I take a step back and smile. "I'll make sure it's in your next paycheck."

She sits back down in her chair, still smiling. "Thanks, Priscilla. You don't know how much—"

I hold up my hand. "Don't worry about it."

At the end of the day, I hear back from the temp agency letting me know they've got Beth Fay Swanson on their payroll, and they're assigning her to me. And she's starting the following Monday.

11
Tim

Priscilla not only looks hot but is also the sweetest woman I ever had the pleasure of bein' around. Who else do I know would hire someone who took her picture and sold it to some scandal rag? I understand why Beth Fay done what she did—desperation makes folks do all kinds of things—but most people in Priscilla's position woulda threatened a lawsuit, turned, and run. Priscilla don't just look at what a person does. She gets right to the heart of things.

It's early Monday mornin', and I'm flyin' back down to Mississippi to talk to my landlord about cuttin' my lease short. I doubt he'll do that, but it's worth a try. Uncle Hugh is so eager to get down to Vancleave so he can relax that he wants me trained to take over the company within a week or two after Priscilla's reunion. Uncle Hugh and Aunt Tammy said I could stay in their house that they aren't willin' to give up just yet. I never had a whole, big ol' honkin' house to myself before, so I'll prob'ly enjoy it for a while, 'til the newness wears off.

At least Uncle Hugh's not askin' me *not* to go to the reunion, 'cause that would be a deal-breaker. I'm not about to let my favorite girl down, even if she's not as smitten as I am. Or was.

I've been tryin' to move on and set my sights on someone else since Priscilla has made it very clear we're not meant to be together. She never led me on, but until her high school crush Maurice came up to her and got her head spinnin' with empty promises, I had hoped she might eventually see me as husband —or at least boyfriend—material. When I seen how fast she took off after him, I knew that was just false hope.

I'm not a bad-lookin' guy, and I'm real clean on account of I hafta be for my job in the beauty business. Last thing I do every mornin' before I head out the door is check to make sure my fingernails is clean. And I don't have a lack of women in my path 'cause that's mostly who I talk to when I try to sell 'em products from Uncle Hugh's company. Priscilla tells me I'm successful 'cause I have that little-boy charm so many girls think is attractive. I think it's the self-made dimple in my left cheek. That happened when I fell on Mama's rake. The doctor made stitches that he said would be nearly invisible, except when I smile. And I smile a lot 'cause it shows my dimple, and a salesman's gotta do whatever it takes to get results.

After my plane lands, I call Priscilla to let her know I'm back in town. I'd like to see how she and that Beth Fay woman are gettin' along. The very thought of the gall it took to hit Priscilla up for a job after what she done, sellin' that story to the tabloid, is so far beyond anything I ever seen; I know she's perfect to work for Priscilla. I just hope this don't give other folks ideas. I'll have to talk to Priscilla about that.

She don't answer her cell phone, so I call the office. Mandy's latest assistant answers the phone. "Is Priscilla in the office?"

"Hold please." She clicks the *Hold* button before I tell her who's calling. It's always easy to tell who's been trained and who's brand-new in that office 'cause once someone's been there a while, they learn how to make small talk. Priscilla insists on having a friendly atmosphere.

"Priscilla Slater. May I help you?"

I feel my dimple deepen as I grin. "You sound so professional. So how's the new girl workin' out?"

"Oh, hi, Tim. If you're talking about Beth Fay, she just started, and Mandy's training her. In fact, I think she answered the phone."

That explains a lot. "I just got back to Jackson. Mind if I stop by later?"

"Sure, how about lunch? I'm treating Mandy and Beth Fay, and I'd love to have you join us."

"Can't think of nothin' I'd like better than to have lunch with three beautiful women."

Priscilla lets loose with one of her belly laughs that still sends electricity throughout my body. And I'm talkin' set-the-house-on-fire electric sparks. "You're such a salesman, Tim."

"Want me to come by the office or meet y'all somewhere?"

"Hold on a sec." Priscilla puts me on hold and comes back in half a minute. "How about meeting us at the Natural Blossom?"

"That place don't serve meat." I've never been there before, but I drove by a coupla times, and between the pink awning and fancy writin' on the window, I can tell it's a girl-food place.

"Mandy's on one of her diets."

"In that case, sure, I'll meet you there, but don't get all bent outta shape if I don't eat nothin'. They do have sweet tea, don't they?"

"Um . . . I'm not sure."

What kinda place don't have meat or sweet tea? I wonder how they can even stay in business in Mississippi. I mean, this ain't New York or San Francisco, where folks suffer through cardboard meals and pretend they're satisfied.

I pile all my paperwork in the corner of my home office and plop a book down on top of it to keep it in place. You'd think with computers bein' in charge of business, folks wouldn't waste so much paper. But naw, that's not the case in the beauty business. I reckon they're so busy learnin' new ways to do hair a lot of 'em haven't gotten past learnin' how to send e-mail. I'm not talkin 'bout Priscilla, but she leaves all the orderin' up to her salon managers. Out of the hundred or so salons, only about a dozen of them send their orders online. Maybe one of these days I can change that, but right now I have to psych myself up for hangin' out with three women at a granola-girl restaurant. I shudder at the mere thought of all that healthy food sittin' lifelessly on that plate in front of me.

As soon as I swing my car into the parkin' lot, I spot that woman we seen in New York standin' by the door of Priscilla's car, lookin' like she don't know what hit her. She glances up, and I can tell the moment she recognizes me by the look of pure panic in her eyes.

Priscilla says somethin' to Mandy, looks at the stalker, and then turns to face me. She waves and motions for me to park alongside her car.

When I get out, I walk toward the stalker with my hand out, hopin' to make her relax. But she don't. She just backs away and looks over her shoulder at Priscilla, who nods.

"Mr. Puckett, I'm so sorry about what happened . . . what I did—"

"Well, you're a lucky girl," I say, interrupting her. "You got a job with the best boss in the South outta the deal."

Priscilla steps between me and the stalker. I remember her a little different, though. Looks like she cut her shoulder-length hair, and now it's in one of them bobs. "Tim, this is Beth Fay Swanson, and she'll be working with me over the next few months."

I reckon it's time to stop thinkin' of her as the stalker since I'll prob'ly have to deal with her. "Nice meetin' you, Beth Fay."

Mandy looks amused, and I'm sure she is. She's always enjoyed drama, and even though there's no screamin' or yellin' goin' on, there's plenty of silent drama to keep her entertained.

As soon as we walk into the restaurant, some woman with unnatural lookin' black hair, a fluffy almost-white top that looks like it's been dipped in tea, a long skirt that looks too big for her, and some ugly old brown sandals greets us. She's not wearin' a drop of makeup, but at least she seems happy if her grin is any indication.

"Follow me." She turns and walks toward the back of the restaurant, stops, and gestures toward a table. "Will this be okay?"

"Perfect." Priscilla winks at me as I hold her chair.

I try to get around to hold all the ladies' chairs, but the stal—um . . . Beth Fay and Mandy are already sittin' by the time I get to 'em. The black-haired woman remains standing by the table until we're all in our seats.

"We run a green restaurant, so we don't have menus. Instead, we have everything noted up there." She points to a wall with all sorts of things like whole-grain pizza with soy-based toppings and veggie shreds, vegan-rella sandwiches, and sprout salads. And the prices next to 'em? Boy howdy, you'd think they used the finest beef that ever walked based on how much stuff costs.

"Do you have anything good?" I ask.

She smiles down at me like she has practice humoring real meat-eatin' men before. "It's all delicious. If you like south-of-the-border flavors, I'd like to recommend our veggie tacos. That's what most . . . nonvegan people seem to enjoy."

I don't see that I have much choice, so I nod. "Sounds good. Bring it on."

Priscilla says she'll have the same, and Beth Fay nods her agreement as well. Mandy, who obviously knows the routine here, asks for somethin' in what sounds like a completely different language.

"And to drink?" Again, the woman's amused expression is focused on me.

"Sweet tea." I lean back, fold my arms, and silently dare her to tell me they don't carry the southern staple.

She nods and turns to the ladies who all give her their drink order. "I'll have your server bring your drinks right away."

After the black-haired lady leaves, Mandy starts talkin'. "I'm not only eating vegan these days. I'm into raw foods."

Mandy is always into somethin' different, so I don't even bother askin' questions, even though I have no idea what she's talkin' about. I figure the wind'll blow in even more change by next time I see her, and it'll all be for naught.

A younger woman with wavy red hair, blue jeans, and a faded blue T-shirt brings us our drinks. She sets a glass filled with pale greenish-yellow liquid down in front of me. I push it toward her. "I ordered sweet tea."

"This is sweet tea. It's the finest organic green tea we can find, and it's sweetened with agave nectar." Her smile is almost an exact replica of the black-haired woman's, and it unnerves me. Why did I agree to come to this crazy place?

I start to say somethin', but I see Priscilla starin' at me, so I face her. She winks, letting me know she understands.

Me and Priscilla both start to lift our glasses to take swigs of our drinks, when stalker-lady pipes up. "Ms. Slater, I thought you were a Christian."

Priscilla sets her glass down on the table and gives Beth Fay a curious look. "I am."

"Don't you say the blessing before you start your meals?"

Now don't that beat all—the stalker callin' out her boss on blessin' our meal. I'm not so sure what we got to bless at this place, but Priscilla tightens her lips and nods before closing her eyes. I don't believe I ever seen no one unnerve my favorite girl before.

12
Priscilla

After work I drive home still in a daze from the day spent with Beth Fay Swanson. She's not terrible, but she does create tension. Fortunately, she seems to amuse Mandy, so at least I don't have to worry about upsetting the rest of my staff. Mandy hovers over her like a vulture, making sure she says the right things on the phone and understands our system. I've asked Mandy to train her on some of the finer points so she'll know what to do when we travel together. The mere thought of that sends a shiver of regret down my spine.

I get to my townhouse and head straight to the kitchen, where I down a glass of water and grab a box of melt-in-your-mouth butter crackers. Lunch today was interesting but not very filling, so I've been starving all afternoon. No wonder Mandy's getting so skinny.

Before I have a chance to open my laptop, my cell phone rings. I look at caller ID and see that it's coming from the office. *Lord, please don't let there be another problem with Beth Fay.*

"Hey, Priscilla. That new girl's a trip, isn't she?"

I laugh. "I guess that's one way of putting it."

"She's actually okay, once you get past her nervousness. I can sorta see myself in her . . . but just a little bit. She's feeling the same way I did when I first started."

"But you didn't sell my story to the tabloids."

"I thought you might still be thinking about that. Priscilla, you really need to let go of that issue, or you'll never be able to work with Beth Fay. I think she feels really bad about calling that reporter, but look at it from her perspective."

"She needed money." I clear my throat and add, "And she wanted her ten minutes of fame?"

"Oh, trust me, she didn't even think of fame. Her mortgage was a month overdue, and she has to come up with the money to buy her son's books for college this fall. People do all kinds of things when they're desperate, and the opportunity was right there under her nose. I don't think she would've done that under normal conditions." She clears her throat. "She's also a committed Christian, which is ramping up her guilt and making her act a little odd at times."

Since when did Mandy start caring enough about other people to see all this? "You learned all this about her today?"

"Yes, I did, and you would've too if you'd spent more time with her."

Now I'm the one feeling the guilt. "I'll have to correct that tomorrow."

"Actually, tomorrow is what I'm calling about. Sheila just called and asked if you could go to the Piney Point salon to approve some construction details on the addition."

"I'll be there in a couple of weeks."

"That's a problem because the construction company you wanna go with is booked tight. They just had a cancellation, so they were able to work you in this week."

"Oh." Piney Point is a solid two-hour drive, and I already have enough to keep me busy before I go for the reunion. "Can't they fax or e-mail me the plans?"

"She wants you there to talk to the contractor."

I've always been able to count on Sheila to handle anything that comes up, so it must be important for me to be there. I let out a deep sigh. "Okay, I'll call her back."

"Have a good night, Priscilla."

"Mandy, have I told you lately how much I appreciate you?"

She laughs. "Yes, but it's always nice to hear."

"Well, I do appreciate you. A lot. And now I want you to put down the phone, get your things, and go home. It'll all be there tomorrow, and I don't want you to burn out."

"G'night, Priscilla. Have a safe trip to Piney Point."

Rather than leaving now and risk upsetting Mother who seems agitated every time my plans change, I decide to drive to Piney Point early in the morning and return as soon as my work is done there. I call the Piney Point salon with the hope of Sheila still being there. And she answers the phone, her voice sounding more strained than usual.

"I'm so sorry you're having to take time out of your oh-so-busy schedule, but the new owner of the tub and spa company refuses to talk to anyone but you."

"Sheila!"

"I'm sorry, Priscilla." She took a deep breath. "It's just that I'm exhausted and a tad frustrated. I shouldn't take it out on you."

"I understand." I pause. "Who is this person again?"

"It *was* Luke Manning from Hattiesburg, but he recently sold his company, and the new owner has a whole different set of rules. When their assistant called and told me you had to be here, I tried everything I could think of to get them to change their mind. I even said we might have to go shoppin' for another contractor."

"Shouldn't we do that anyway, now that Luke is out of the picture? The reason we chose his company was his expertise with tubs and spas."

"He's still in charge of managing the project since he's the one with the contractor's license, so I think it's best to stick with them." I can hear the frustration in her voice, so I don't press.

"What time will they be there?"

"Early in the mornin'. I'm so sorry, Priscilla. If you wanna come stay at my place, I can clear off the guest bed."

"I appreciate that, but I'll wait until morning to drive over."

"The offer stands for tomorrow night too."

Sheila has a heart of pure gold. Her husband is a plumber, and he's managed to do quite a bit of work for the salons in Piney Point and Hattiesburg, and he refuses to take payment for more than the cost of materials. The only way they let me show my appreciation is to pad Sheila's quarterly bonuses . . . and I do.

After I get off the phone with Sheila, it rings again. This time it's Tim.

"Mind if I come over? I got somethin' I need to give ya."

I explain what's going on with the salon, but he's still emphatic about wanting to see me. "Okay, but not for long. I have to get up early in the morning."

Less than five minutes later, Tim is standing at my door, thrusting a bouquet of flowers toward me. "Here. I figure you need these."

I laugh as I take the flowers. "Come on in, Tim. Want something to drink?"

He narrows his eyes with a dubious look. "Do you have *real* sweet tea?"

"Yes, I believe I do."

I pour two glasses of tea and put the bouquet into a vase with water before sitting down at the kitchen table with Tim. It feels cozy to be here with someone who has accepted me for who I am deep down rather than my public persona that seems to grow bigger and more unreal by the day.

"So what's on your mind?" I ask.

He sips his tea and shakes his head. "I don't know what's goin' on, Priscilla, but it seems like everything keeps changin' and gettin' weirder by the day."

"True."

"Stuff I never dreamed of happenin' is smackin' me in the face every time I turn around. I mean, look at me havin' to make a decision about movin' to New York and becomin' CEO of a big ol' beauty supply company. And havin' my picture in a magazine that millions of people read." He gives me a weary look. "And you. I don't know why we thought it would be a good idea for you to hire that stalker lady."

I smile. "According to Mandy, she's not so bad." I explain what Mandy said, and he listens with rapt attention.

"That's all well and good, but there had to be another way. What if she didn't see us that night? What would she have done?"

"Maybe it's all part of God's plan for us to be there and for her to do what she did."

Tim scrunches up his face. "Now that I done got myself all Christianed up, thanks to you"—he offers a goofy smile—"I see a lot of what you always talked about, but this is a stretch." He looks at me with a half grin. "You have to admit that, Priscilla."

"Maybe." I shrug. "But we're in this situation, and I plan to do whatever it takes to make the best of it. Don't forget, Mandy seems to like her."

"I reckon she must be okay then, since Mandy don't like many people."

Tim doesn't have to come out and say this, but I know he dated Mandy for a few months. Things were awkward around the office after they stopped seeing each other, but time passed, and they learned to deal with each other on a professional level again. Mandy informed me back then that all Tim ever talked about was me, so she brought up all her old boyfriends. Even though I haven't dated much, I know that's not a good move for any kind of relationship.

Since Tim obviously has something important to discuss with me, and it's getting late, I change the subject. "So what's on your mind, Tim? Why did you need to see me tonight?"

He leans forward enough to access his hip pocket and pulls out a folded but wrinkled sheet of paper. "When Mandy told me you was goin' . . . I mean *were* goin' to Piney Point, I thought I'd have you deliver somethin' to Laura."

I hadn't planned to visit Laura, but I can't turn Tim down on anything he asks me to do. After all, he continues to save the day at my class reunions.

"It's a list of things she needs to do before I get there this year." He holds my gaze. "It *is* still okay with you if I go this year, isn't it?"

"Yes . . . yes, of course it's okay. It's better than okay. I think you're one of the most important people at all my reunions."

He shakes his head, but I can tell he's pleased. "Naw, that's not true, but I do like to help out."

I hold up the paper as I stand. "I'll give this to Laura. I'm sure she appreciates everything you do."

Tim finishes his tea, and I walk him to the door. "Drive carefully, Priscilla, and remember that speed trap in Magee."

"I'll be careful." I stand on my tiptoes and give him a kiss on the cheek before I close the door behind him.

My eyes pop open a half hour before my alarm is set to go off, so I get out of bed and start getting ready for the day. I pack a small bag, just in case something goes wrong and I have to stay overnight, although I fully intend to come back to Jackson, even if I finish late.

Rather than let my mind take over, I listen to music all the way to Piney Point. The salon has just opened when I arrive, and Sheila is standing behind the reception desk.

She looks up. "Hoo boy, you didn't waste any time gettin' here this mornin', did you? You musta got up with the chickens."

"You said the contractor will be here early, and I don't want to keep anyone waiting. So what's the deal? I thought everything was settled with the spa expansion."

"Yeah, I thought so too, but I couldn't sway Luke when he called and said the new owner insisted on talkin' to you." She glances up at the wall clock. "They should be here in about a half hour."

That gives me just enough time to walk through the salon and say hi to everyone. I know about half the hairdressers, and they all give me a warm greeting and a hug. Some of the newer ones appear nervous that I'm in the building, so I just tell them I'm happy they're there and keep moving.

"Where's Chester?"

Sheila points to the back. "Ever since the facials got so popular, he spends most of his time in the back room."

Before going back there, I pull Sheila into the break room that's much nicer than the old one. The salon had become so popular we had to add hairdressers, and there wasn't much room in our previous location.

Once we're in the break room, Sheila pours both of us cups of coffee and sets them on one of the round tables. "Have a seat. Want a pastry?"

"I better not." After she sits down adjacent to me, I lean toward her. "So how are things around here?"

"Hunky-dory." She grins. "I mean it, Priscilla. All the hairdressers are happy to be workin' for you, and customers love the braggin' rights that come with your Ms. Prissy Big Hair fame."

"Did you see the tabloid—?"

A knock sounds at the door, and we both look up. One of the newer hairdressers is standing there, looking nervous.

"Whatcha need, Melanie?" Sheila asks.

"That construction guy is here, and he says he has an appointment with Pris . . . Ms. Slater."

"Please call me Priscilla." I give her the warmest smile I can manage. "Why don't you send him on back here?"

"Okay." She disappears quickly.

"Want me to leave, or should I stick around?" Sheila asks.

"Stay, please."

I hear men's voices as they get close to the break room. Sheila and I both glance up in time to see Luke Manning standing in the doorway. "Ladies," he says as he tips his head. "Priscilla, I'm sorry I had to interrupt whatever business you got goin' up in Jackson, but Maurice here . . . "

The sound of Maurice's name and the sight of his face as he steps from behind the door makes my ears ring and my blood boil. "What—?"

"Is that any way to welcome an old friend?" He walks into the break room like he owns the place and opens his arms for a hug.

I cringe and manage to squirm away from his embrace. As much as I'd like to cancel this addition, I've promised it to my employees and customers, so I have to go through with it. "Let's get on with this, Maurice. I don't have all day."

Luke looks back and forth between Maurice and me, and I see the transformation as he realizes there's something else going on. "Priscilla, you can count on me to make sure everything goes well." He shoots a brief glance at Maurice. "I'll do the final inspection when it's over."

I smile at Luke and nod. "Thank you."

13
Trudy

Did you get the package I sent?" Mama asks during our Sunday-night phone call.

"Yes, thank you. I have some exciting news to tell you."

"You met a man?"

"No, Mama. I just got a huge promotion at work. I'll be making more money and—"

"Have you had a chance to look at Priscilla Slater's picture in the *Famous People News*?" She's practically breathless with excitement as she adds, "There she is, right smack dab on the front page!"

"I saw that." I also noticed that Priscilla is wearing an outfit that is obviously expensive but wrong for her figure type because it emphasizes her sharp features. I shudder as I realize Mama ignored my good news. "Did you even hear what I said about the promotion?"

"Yes, of course, I heard you." Without skipping a beat, she adds, "It's hard to believe one of our own is in the Hollywood magazines, and she's not even *in* Hollywood."

"Mama, *Famous People News* is not exactly a—"

"I know, I know, it's a scandal rag, but most of the time there's at least a grain of truth to what they say."

"Well, if Priscilla Slater wants to date Tim, that's her business. I don't know why it has to be plastered all over the tabloids."

"Because, my sweet, beautiful daughter, anything Priscilla Slater does these days is news. Big news. She's making women all over the country look gorgeous with something we women in the South have known all along." She pauses barely long enough to catch a breath. "Which means you need to get on the stick and do somethin' about yourself, now that the market for available men is shrinkin', and more women are gettin' beautiful by the day. You'll never find a husband if you don't concentrate on what men want."

"I make women beautiful too." The instant I say those words, I realize how pitiful and desperate for her approval I sound.

"Oh, I'm sure you do a nice job of waitin' on your customers and helpin' them pick out clothes and all, but we both know it's the hair—"

"Okay, Mama."

"You better pay attention to me, Trudy. Last time you listened to me, you caught yourself a husband, and you lost him when you didn't heed my advice."

I want to gag. Mama's still on her kick about getting me married off, never mind the fact that it's my life, and I'm perfectly happy with it. Well, maybe not perfectly . . . but mostly. My job is one that almost any style-conscious single woman would die for, and it's getting better all the time.

Before I have a chance to change the subject, Mama continues her rant. "Trudy, you need to do somethin' about them hips of yours. No man likes to be with a woman who lets herself go."

Anger burns in my chest, and I have to take a deep breath to keep from exploding with what I really think. "Mama, I have not let myself go. Maybe I've spread out a tad, but I'm eatin' healthy and working out."

"Workin' out?" She makes one of her disapproving sounds—sort of a cross between a cluck and a grunt. "Don't go gettin' all muscular on me. Men don't like that either."

Quite frankly, I'm sick of worrying about what men want. I've come to the conclusion that I have to be satisfied with my life, and if I just happen to meet a man who likes me for who I am, he's the right guy for me. I mean, I married Michael and tried to live up to his expectations and look what happened.

"Did you try on the latest Spanx I sent? It's got extra reinforcement in the rear, which you need right now."

"No, I haven't tried on the new Spanx. Mama, you don't have to send me that stuff because I can get it at the store where I work with my executive discount."

Mama gasps. "Don't buy it where you work. You wouldn't want the folks you work with to know you're relyin' on Spanx to keep your figure."

"That's not a problem. Most people wear shapewear of some sort, so no one thinks anything about it." This conversation is wearing on my last nerve, but Mama has to have her say, or I'll wind up paying for it later . . . along with everything else she doesn't like about me.

"If that's what you think, you're not as smart as I thought you were." This is coming from a woman who was always embarrassed to buy her own feminine hygiene products, so she sent Daddy out to get them until us girls were tall enough to see over the counter.

I'll never forget Mama standing a couple aisles over, pretending she didn't know what we were up to, as if the store clerk wasn't aware we weren't even old enough to use the things.

Then there was the time Mama waited in the car after sending me inside the drugstore to buy feminine napkins. When I came out with the prettiest dinner napkins I could find, she about had a hissy fit.

"You still there, Trudy?" Mama jolts me out of my memories, but I'm still smiling. "You haven't been listenin' to a word I said, have you?"

"Of course, I'm listening, Mama. It's just that I have a bunch of stuff to do before I go to bed tonight."

"You always have somethin' to do when I talk about anything you find distasteful."

She's right, but really, what purpose does all this discussion about my large-and-still-expanding hips and thighs serve? If I do what she wants and focus my entire existence on finding a suitable man to make into a husband, I won't be able to enjoy my life. Now that I've had a good taste of life on my own without worrying about what everyone thinks of me—well most of the time, anyway—I'm actually having some fun. I have a job I love, some friends I can go out with once in a while, a church I attend when I'm in Atlanta, and an apartment of my own that I can escape to when the fun I'm having becomes too exhausting.

"Trudy!"

I sigh. "Yes, Mama?"

"There you go again, driftin' off when I'm tryin' to help you."

"Okay, I'll try on the Spanx and let you know if it fits."

"There's one more thing I wanna talk about before we go. What do you know about Tim Puckett?"

"Tim Puckett? You mean Priscilla's guy?"

"Yeah. That article mentioned that he comes from a highly successful beauty supply family."

"Yeah, I know he sells beauty products, but I'm not so sure of that part about the family."

Now it's Mama's turn to sigh. "You better check your facts. I know you don't put much credence in *Famous People News*, but I just happen to believe they might be right."

"And what do you want me to do with this information, Mama?"

"Don't get smart with me, young lady. You're still my daughter, and I deserve respect."

"Sorry."

"It's always good to know about people you come into contact with. No point in walkin' around with your head in a cloud."

What she's saying is that I need to do some background checking on anyone I get involved with to make sure they have the right financial means or social standing—or even better, both. "I'll be just fine. Now I really gotta go."

I hang up and glance at myself in the mirror. My forehead is all scrunched, and my mouth looks like I've been sucking lemons. Mama does that to me.

My work demands most of my time and even more of my thoughts over the next week, so I'm able to push my conversation with Mama to the back of my mind. When Sunday night rolls around, I'm half tempted not to answer Mama's call. But I can't bring myself to ignore her. After all, she's the one who brought me into this world, so that accounts for something.

"I got all the information on Tim Puckett," she says before I even have a chance to say *hello*. "He's a college graduate, and his uncle hired him as soon as he graduated. He managed to triple sales in his territory in the first two years he took over, and that's when his uncle saw that he had the perfect person to pass his business to when it came time to retire."

Dang, Mama's good. She should have been a private investigator. But I still don't know what she's getting at.

"Now before you go gettin' all huffy on me about pryin', I want you to know all I had to do was ask Sheila down at the Cut 'n Curl if she knew anything about Tim. And what she didn't tell me, Chester filled in. That man knows more gossip than the rest of the stylists combined."

"Did they tell you when Tim and Priscilla are planning to get married?"

"Are they—?" Mama clears her throat. "Was that sarcasm? 'Cause I don't think Priscilla's interested in Tim as a potential suitor. You, on the other hand—"

"Please stop doing this. I'm not getting together with Tim. First of all, when I see him, he's always with Priscilla. And secondly, I doubt he gives me a second thought when he leaves Piney Point."

"That's your fault, Trudy. You have to do somethin' to make yourself stand out, especially for a man like Tim."

She's obviously ignoring the first reason—that he comes to Piney Point to be with Priscilla. "So what are you suggesting I do, Mama?"

"You really wanna know?" She doesn't give me a chance to answer. "Here's how you get Tim Puckett's attention."

I sit there and listen to her talk about my hair, my conversation, and my *behind*. She has a plan for everything but what really matters.

"But Mama, what if I do all that, and he still isn't interested?"

"Oh, he will be, but don't worry about a thing. If you do what I tell you to, men'll be all lined up at the reunion wantin' to be with you."

There's not a single man who'll be at the reunion that *I* want to be with, but that's a whole 'nother subject. "I'll try on the Spanx you sent," I say to get her mind off Tim. "But now I gotta go. I have a bunch of stuff I have to get done so I can take off a couple days for the reunion."

"I'll see what else I can find out about Tim."

"Okay, Mama. Do what you feel like you gotta do. I love you."

I'm exhausted after I hang up. One of these days, I'm afraid I'll wind up telling her what I'm really thinking, and then I'll wind up with a mess I won't be able to clean up. As much as I love Mama, she needs to know when to let up.

14
Priscilla

I swanee, that woman's got somethin' up her sleeve." Sheila shakes her head and sighs. "Trudy's mama sets her mind to somethin', and she don't let up."

I can't help but laugh. Nothing has changed in Piney Point. "At least you didn't have to grow up with her being your mother."

"I reckon you're right. Amazin' how Trudy's managed to pull herself away long enough to actually *have* her own life. After Michael up and left her for Bimbo Number One, I was afraid she might fall apart."

Talking about clients and their daughters has never felt right, so I change the topic. "Are we heavily booked for the reunion yet?"

"If you're askin' if we got openings, we still have a few, but it looks like you'll have more folks at this one than the last one."

"I'll take as many appointments as we can cram into that week."

"Good 'cause it looks like you'll be in high demand." Sheila grins at me. "When you goin' back up to New York?"

"I have to fly up for a quick airing the week before the reunion."

"Don't forget to let me know when you find out the time. I like to make sure everyone gets to see you when you're on."

I give her a hug. "You're awesome, Sheila. I really appreciate all your support."

"Hey, how about me?" Chester joins us. "I'm supportive too."

Sheila rolls her eyes. "She never said you wasn't."

"Y'all are all wonderful." I glance at my watch and back toward the door. "I need to get going so I can stop off and see my mother and make it back to Jackson before Mandy leaves for the day."

All the way to my parents' house—correction, Mother's house—I fidget with buttons on the dashboard console. First it's too hot, then too cold. After I get the air conditioner set just right, I press the volume button on the radio. I know why I'm so uncomfortable, but that doesn't make it any better.

Ever since Dad moved out of the house he's shared with Mother most of their married life, the place doesn't seem like home. I'd always assumed that house would be a safe haven for me. Mother told me that the day after their divorce was final, she had a shopping spree in a furniture store, and the next day she spent the rest of her decorating budget shopping for linens. The place doesn't even hold a hint of Dad anymore.

As soon as I turn the corner toward Mother's house, I blink. It's been painted yellow. I feel a lurching sensation in my chest. Dad always said he could never live in a yellow house. This is like the final nail in the coffin of my stability.

Mother is waiting for me in the kitchen. I can tell she's eager for me to leave by the way she jumps up, offers me coffee, and sets it down, while she constantly glances at her handbag that's perched on the counter by the door.

"Have you seen Dad?" I ask.

She makes a face and shakes her head. "Now why would you ask such a question? You know we both still teach at the college."

"I tried calling him last week, but he never answers his house or cell phone."

Mother picks up a napkin and starts fidgeting with it. "I'm sure he's plenty busy, between teaching and his very active social life."

I can tell I've hit on a touchy topic, so I shift to her. "So how are the Classy Lassies?"

An expression of annoyance flickers across her face, but she quickly recovers. "They're talking about breaking away from the Red Hats and having their own organization."

"What would be the point of that?"

"You're asking a lot of questions, Priscilla. Is that why you're here . . . to grill me?"

"No, of course not. I just wanted to stop by and see you since I'm in town."

"Did you decide when you'll be here for the reunion?"

"Yes, in about a week." I take one more sip of coffee before carrying it to the sink and dumping the rest. I rinse the cup and stick it in the dishwasher. "I guess I need to go so I can talk to Mandy."

"How's Tim?"

"He's doing just fine, I guess."

"I can't believe you're still stringing him along. Most men wouldn't put up with that."

I open my mouth to argue but realize she's just spoiling for a fight, so I nod. "Okay, fine."

She purses her lips and shakes her head. "I'm serious, Priscilla."

"Don't worry about me. I'll be just fine. You need to concentrate on yourself now."

We have a short stare-down, but when my stomach begins to roil, I take a step back. "See you soon."

Mother stands at the door until I get in the car. As soon as I turn the ignition, I realize we never hugged. Intense sadness washes over me.

I plug my iPod into the stereo and crank up the volume to drown out my gloomy thoughts. No point in crying or even worrying about something I can't control. There's a crash on the interstate, so it takes me a tad longer to get to Jackson than usual, but I still make it before quitting time. Still, my nerves are on edge.

Mandy is hovering over her new assistant as I enter the reception area of our office building. She glances up and smiles. "Hey, Priscilla. I'd like you to meet Blair."

A softly pretty young woman with strawberry blonde hair and blue eyes looks up at me and offers a shy smile. "Hi, Ms. Slater."

I extend my hand. "Please call me Priscilla. We're rather informal around here."

She looks at my hand and turns to Mandy, who nods and whispers, "Shake her hand."

Blair wipes her hand on the side of her pants and places it in mine. I can tell she's inexperienced, but there's no doubt Mandy will give her a crash course in business etiquette. She's trained more assistants in five years than I'd like. I've had talks with her, but she's adamant about things running her way, and she reminds me that it took me several tries before I found her. My controlling nature wants to take over, but I hold back. Mandy is always in the office, and I'm not, and since I haven't had to worry about things going well in years, I've decided to let her do things her way.

I sidestep around Blair and look at Mandy. "Where's Beth Fay?"

"She has some business back in Raleigh, so I told her to go back home until you need her."

"Oh." I look down at Blair who is now fidgeting with small items on her desk. "So how do you like working here, Blair?"

"I like it so far."

"So are you from Jackson?"

"No, ma'am. I moved here from Alabama two years ago."

Mandy watches me with an odd expression as I chat with Blair, so I face her head-on. "Do you need something?" I ask.

"Um . . . yeah. Can I see you in my office?"

Blair's eyes pop open wide. "Did I say something wrong?"

"No, you're fine," Mandy says as she brushes past me and leads the way. "But I'm not so sure Priscilla is."

That's an odd comment. I follow her into her office, and she closes the door right behind me.

"What's up?" I ask.

Mandy plants her hands on her hips and gives me the same look Mother used to have when I did something she didn't like. "That's what I want to know. You're nervous as a cat in a roomful of rocking chairs."

"You wanted to talk to me about being nervous?"

"Yeah. I'm worried about you, Priscilla. Ever since you had your picture plastered all over the magazines, you've acted weird."

"It was only one magazine . . . and how would you know how I've been acting?"

"Every time we talk, I sense something different about you. You used to be so warm, and now you talk to me like I'm a stranger."

"I do?"

She nods. "I reckon it's normal for people to behave that way when they get famous, but don't lose who you are."

At this very moment, I'm not sure who I am or who I'm talking to. It feels surreal being lectured to by the assistant I wasn't even certain about keeping the first six months of her employment. But then a lot of things have been different lately, so maybe she's right.

"Sorry, Mandy. I suppose things have been a bit off-kilter for me since TVNS added more Big Hair shows. I'll try to be nicer."

"Oh, I'm not sayin' you're not nice. In fact, I think you might be nicer than usual. It's just that that warmth I used to see in you has cooled off, and it's like you have a shield around you."

Oh wow. Now I realize I'm actually leaning away from her, something I've never done before. Once I get to know someone, my personal space shrinks. I totally see what she's saying. So I do what I think will make up for my distant behavior and reach out for a hug. She smiles and hugs me back.

"That's much better." Mandy rocks back and leans against the edge of her desk. "So what do you think about Blair?"

"She seems really nice. Do you think she's the one?"

Mandy laughs. "You make this sound like a marriage."

"Well, it sort of is. Working in the same office with someone eight hours a day, five days a week makes you practically related."

"I get that. And yes, I think she just might be the one. She actually listens to me, and she does what I tell her to."

I tip my head toward her. "You do realize a good working relationship involves more than her taking orders from you."

"I *am* the boss . . . at least I am when you're not here."

"Yes, but that shouldn't make you a dictator." I've been itching to say those words to her for years, but every time I planned to have this talk with her, something else more critical happened, and the moments were lost.

Mandy frowns and chews on her bottom lip. I allow silence to fall between us as she ponders my comment. Finally, she smiles and nods. "Now that I think about it, I remember you asking my opinion and actually taking it sometimes."

"How did that make you feel?" I relax as I realize the tables have turned, and the conversation is about Mandy's behavior rather than mine.

"Like you trusted me and valued what I had to say."

"Do you like Blair?"

"Yes." She sighs. "Very much. We have a lot in common, and she wants to do a good job. I've never once caught her doing her nails or having long personal conversations on the phone."

I have to stifle a laugh. She just described what I caught her doing many times when she first started.

"Priscilla?"

I lift my eyebrows. "Yes?"

"Why did you put up with me? I was horrible in the beginning, but you never gave up. I remember wondering several times why you didn't give me the axe."

I don't tell Mandy that I sometimes wondered the same thing. "Don't forget to listen to Blair's ideas. The people you surround yourself with can make you look like a genius."

The message slowly sinks in, and she gives me one of her widest smiles. "Thanks, Priscilla. You're the best!"

"And so are you. Now let's go back out there so Blair doesn't think we're leaving her out of the fun."

Blair appears nervous as she glances up at us. I smile and tell her how happy I am that she's with the company, and she instantly relaxes. Mandy takes the cue and expounds on some of the things Blair has done well.

"She's super organized, and I never have to remind her to be polite to people when they call." Mandy looks at me before turning back to Blair. "As soon as you get more comfortable with the job, I'd like to have regular brainstorming sessions to get your input about some of the office procedures."

"Great idea," I say to back her up. "It's always good to keep improving. How are you with technology, Blair?"

She self-consciously shrugs. "I sort of know my way around the techie-world."

Mandy chuckles. "Don't get all shy about your knowledge, Blair. You got some mad techie skills." She looks up at me. "Did I tell you she has her certificate in computer application?"

"That'll come in handy around here." I move toward the door. "Since y'all have everything under control here, I feel really good about taking some time off for my twentieth reunion."

Mandy turns to Blair to explain. "She says she's taking time off, but this is when she goes back to her hometown and does hair. It's sort of a ritual."

"I don't know about that. All I know is that I enjoy doing the very thing that gave me my big break."

"It was nice meeting you, Ms. Sla—I mean Priscilla. I hope to get to know you better."

"Trust me, you will." Mandy glances back and forth between Blair and me and gives me a wink. "Priscilla still keeps a small office here, and she actually uses it once in a while, when she's not traveling."

Before I leave, Beth Fay calls and asks when I'll need her to travel again. "I'm pet sitting for my neighbor this week, but I can get someone else if you need me right away."

"Don't worry about it now. I'll call you on Saturday, and we can go over our itinerary."

On the way to my Jackson townhouse, I think about Mandy's last comment. She's right about the once-in-a-while thing. Ever since I got my coveted gig at TVNS, I travel more than I stay put, and it's starting to take its toll on me. I thought having condos in strategic locations between Mississippi and New York would give me a feeling of being home wherever I was, but that hasn't been the case.

15
Celeste

What's wrong, Celeste?" The look on Jimmy's face *almost* matches the way I feel. Almost.

I slowly sit up in bed and bury my face in my hands. "I wish I knew. I haven't felt good in a while. I was dizzy last week, and ever' mornin' this week, I been feelin' like I took a roller coaster ride that wouldn't stop."

"Maybe you got a bug." He throws the covers off and sits up on his side of the bed. "There's somethin' goin' around."

"The problem is I ain't been around."

"Want me to get you some coffee and bring it to you?"

I shudder. Normally I love coffee first thing in the mornin', but the very thought of havin' to smell it makes me want to wretch. "No."

"Okay, just askin'. I gotta go get me some so I can wake up. Holler if you need me."

As soon as Jimmy leaves the bedroom, I flop back down on my pillow. All sorts of things run through my head. If this had just started, I wouldn't think much about it, but for two weeks? What if I have some dreaded disease? What if I have cancer? I reflect on some of my former patients who had various kinds of cancer, and I remember some of them bein' sick—either from the chemo or the disease.

An overwhelmin' sadness washes over me. *Life has just started gettin' good for me and Jimmy, Lord. Why does this have to happen now?*

Jimmy reappears in the doorway lookin' at me like he don't know if he should get closer or keep his distance. "Maybe you should see the doctor."

"I hate goin' to the doctor. You know that."

"Yeah I do, and I'm the same way, but maybe she can help."

"If I don't feel better by tomorrow, I'll call her office and see when she can fit me in."

"I done called her office." He walks toward me, pulls his hand out from behind his back, and hands me a piece of paper with his scribblin' on it. "The receptionist was in early, and she said the doctor can see you this afternoon."

I groan. "I don't wanna go nowhere. I just wanna stay home and sleep."

Jimmy looks panicked as he ambles toward me. "Celeste honey, you can't ignore this and think it'll go away . . . not after this long. We need to find out what's wrong with you so the doctor can fix it."

"What if—?" My chin starts to quiverin' like it always does right before I cry. I don't wanna do that first thing in the mornin'—at least not on a day when Jimmy has a big meetin'. I take a deep breath and nod. "Okay, I'll go."

He sits down on the edge of the bed and takes my hand. "Promise?"

I nod and force myself to smile back at him. Jimmy has turned out to be ten thousand times better at this husband thing than I ever expected.

After Jimmy leaves for work, I set the clock and lie back down to catch some more sleep. Seems lately that's all I wanna do. If I didn't just get over my period a few days ago, I'd think I was pregnant. But I can't be. Can I?

The clock goes off, but I don't get up right away. I'm afraid to sit up too fast for fear I'll start havin' the dry heaves like I done yesterday. But I don't. In fact, I'm actually hungry, so I get up and head for the kitchen. What I want is some leftover chili, but I know better than to do that right off the bat. I pull out some crackers and nibble on them to see how my stomach takes to food. When I'm sure I can keep food down, I fix myself a small bowl of chili and heat it up in the microwave. It don't take me long to scarf it down on account of I haven't eaten since last night, and the day is half over.

It's temptin' to call the doctor's office and cancel my appointment, but a promise is a promise, and I don't wanna disappoint Jimmy. So I take a shower, fix my hair, and put on some makeup. My face is gettin' sorta puffy. When it's time to take off my robe and get dressed, I notice my face ain't the only swollen thing on me. I never had to worry about gainin' weight before, but it looks like I might need to think about it now.

I get to the doctor's office fifteen minutes early. The receptionist hands me a cup and tells me to "go" in it. A half hour later I'm sittin' in the examinin' room, wearin' a paper gown, lookin' at a grinnin' doctor.

"So how're you feeling, Mrs. Shackleford?"

"Right now just fine, but I think I need to go on a diet."

When she laughs, I think she has the strangest sense of humor.

"What's so funny?"

She shakes her head and sits down at her computer. "Tell me your symptoms."

"I been feelin' all pukey for a coupla weeks, and I'm so tired all the time. I ain't never been one to take naps, but now I find myself lying down once, sometimes twice a day. Oh, and I have to pee a lot. I can't even get through the night without havin' to get up at least once."

She nods. "How about tenderness? Are you hurting anywhere?"

"Just around my boobs. I seen this mornin' that they's all puffy."

Doctor Farrow is startin' to look like a bobblehead, she's noddin' so much. "That's normal."

"It is?"

"Yes." She scoots her chair around to face me as I sit at the edge of the examinin' table. "Your quick pregnancy test came out positive, and all your symptoms are typical of women in their first trimester."

Knock me down with a feather. "Pregnant? But I just got over my period."

"That happens sometimes. Was it heavy?"

"No," I say as I think back. "It was a little lighter than usual and only lasted two or three days."

"Let's do a full examination to make sure everything is okay. We'll need to schedule you an appointment with an OB-GYN." She finishes her exam, pokin' and proddin' me in all sorts of unmentionable places, and tells me to put my clothes on so we can talk.

I feel all weird and conflicted as I get dressed. My mind races, and my body tingles with the news. The nurse grins at me when she comes to take me to the doctor's office. "Congratulations, Mrs. Shackleford. I have three children, and they've been such blessings to my husband and me."

I smile back and thank her. Dr. Farrow comes in and sits down behind her desk. "Any questions?"

"I have so many I don't even know where to start."

"Tell you what . . . " She leans forward and hands me a slip of paper with an appointment written on it. "Jot down all your questions and ask the obstetrician. In the meantime, avoid cigarettes, alcohol, and any medication. Do you drink coffee?"

"Until I started gettin' sick, I drank almost a pot a day. But I don't smoke or drink no alcohol."

"You'll want to cut back on your caffeine." She tells me more things I need to avoid. "The receptionist will give you a list of precautions, and I'm sure the obstetrician will have more."

I head home with a list of things to do, what to eat, and what I need to stay away from. And I feel like I'm livin' in some sort of crazy dream. I pinch myself to make sure it's real.

Once I get to the house, I pick up the phone to call Jimmy, but I can't bring myself to give him this news without lookin' him in the eye. Me and him have talked about havin' young'uns, but we never actually decided if it was somethin' we wanted to do. He's good around other people's kids, but I've noticed he's always ready to hand 'em back to their parents after about five minutes. What if he don't want this baby in my belly?

I rub my abdomen and think about the miracle of the life growin' inside me. No matter how much I thought about it or talked about bein' a mama, the reality wasn't . . . well, real. And now it is.

The list the doctor gave me includes takin' a prenatal vitamin, eatin' lots of vegetables, bookin' appointments to see the new doctor she referred me to, tourin' the hospital maternity ward, birthin' classes, and . . . . I take a deep breath. I never knew there was so much to bein' pregnant. All I ever thought folks did was swell up like a blimp, eat whatever they craved, waddle like a duck, and holler at their husbands when it's time to go to the hospital to deliver the baby. But the list makes sense. After all, this child is dependin' on me for everything—from good nutrition to stayin' safe.

That's when it dawns on me that I'm gonna be responsible for another human bein' for the next . . . eighteen years? An image of Laura and Pete's young'uns flashes through my mind, and I shudder. What if this baby turns out like them brats? I have to sit down and take a few deep breaths before I fall over. Life is definitely about to change for me and Jimmy. Fear ripples through me, so I breathe even deeper. *Lord, don't let me fall apart. Give me the strength to do whatever I gotta do for this kid.*

About an hour later the phone rings, and I know it's Jimmy. I don't answer it 'cause I don't know what to say. He leaves a frantic message tellin' me he's worried sick and to call him right back. So I do.

"What did the doctor say?"

I inhale and slowly let out my breath. "I don't wanna tell you on the phone."

"Celeste, don't do this to me. I can't come home now . . . unless. . . . Is it serious?"

"Yes, it's serious, but the news can wait. Don't worry. I'm fine. We can talk about it durin' supper."

"Aw, Celeste, don't do this to me."

"I'm not doin' nothin' to you." The instant those words escape my lips I regret the snippiness of them. "Sorry. I'm just not myself."

"That does it. I'm coming home now."

Before I have a chance to tell him not to, he hangs up. I start to make a pot of coffee, but the doctor's list of what to avoid pops into my head. I pour myself a glass of water instead. And I add a wedge of lemon and some sugar to make it taste good. I've never understood how people could drink plain ol' water. It don't taste like nothin'.

Even though I'm expectin' Jimmy home, I'm surprised when I hear his car door slam ten minutes later. It normally takes him at least fifteen or twenty minutes to get home.

He walks in and stands there, starin' at me, almost like he's scared to say anything or get closer. My heart pounds at the thought that he might not be happy about me bein' pregnant.

"Are you . . . is everything . . . I mean . . . " He swallows hard and takes a tentative step forward.

I point to his chair at the kitchen table. "Come sit down, Jimmy."

"Why can't I stand?"

"Oh, trust me on this. You'll need to be sittin' down for this news."

His face is all crinkly with worry as he sits down and folds his hands on the table. "Okay, give it to me straight, Celeste. I wanna hear the news." He blinks, looks at me, and reaches for my hand, almost as if he's afraid to touch me. "I want you to know I'm here for you no matter what it is."

I open my mouth to tell him we're gonna have a baby, but my voice catches. I clear my throat and grip his hand real tight so he can't let go. "I'm pregnant."

The message don't register right away, but I can tell when it does about ten seconds later. His eyebrows shoot near 'bout up to the ceiling. And he smiles.

"I know we didn't plan this, and I didn't mean to do it without discussin' it first, but . . . " I lift my shoulders and let them drop as I shake my head. "It just happened."

Jimmy takes a deep breath as he stands and stretches his arms straight up. When he brings them back down, he scoops me up into his arms and gives me the biggest hug ever. "You just made me the happiest man on the Miss'ippi Gulf Coast."

"You're happy about it?"

"Boy howdy, am I ever!" He lowers me back to the chair. "Only thing is I'm worried about you. Will you be able to get through nine months of bein' sick?"

"I don't think it'll last all nine months." Then I tell him what all the doctor said and about making an appointment with the obstetrician.

"This is great! I can't wait to tell everyone at the reunion."

The very thought of going to the reunion feelin' as awful as I have been lately sends my stomach churnin' again. I have puffy cheeks, and my hair has taken on a life of its own—but fortunately not as bad as it was before the makeover Priscilla gave me ten years ago.

"I'm not so sure I wanna go to that."

His smile fades. "What are you talkin' about, Celeste? We hafta go now. Don't you see how important this is? Me and you will be like the stars of the party, with you pregnant and all. Folks will see us as one of them now."

Maybe he's right. Jimmy and I was both outcasts during our high school days, and no one gave us the time of day until they needed our help for the reunions. I don't know why, but I get what he's sayin' about fittin' in, now that we're in a family way.

"I gotta get back to work, but I'm takin' you out for supper to celebrate. Anywhere you wanna go." He leans over and gives me a kiss on the cheek. "Start thinkin' about what you wanna eat."

After he leaves, I call Laura and tell her we'll be at the reunion. "We have some excitin' news to share."

"Are you finally pregnant?" she asks.

I want to smack her. "Yes, but don't tell anyone. We want to let everyone know."

"Don't worry about me. I got too much to do to worry about spreadin' someone else's news."

As soon as we hang up, I have no doubt everyone will know by the time me and Jimmy roll into town. Oh well. At least me and him's in this together. And I'm startin' to crave watermelon.

16
Priscilla

The camera lights are hot as I take my position on the blue dot beside Felicity Rhodes, the show host I work with most of the time. She's been my favorite since before I ever got on TVNS, and that hasn't changed. There's something warm and natural about her style that puts everyone at ease—from the vendors to the customers who can't wait to see the next product she's excited about. And from what I can tell, she's truly excited about every single thing TVNS sells. Like everyone else there, she's tense right before showtime, but it's understood because everyone else is too.

"You look fabulous today, Priscilla," she whispers as the camera crew does their thing. We still have a few minutes before we're on air. "Is there any truth to what I read in *Famous People News*?"

"Not even a grain of truth. Tim and I have been friends for years." The makeup person approaches and brushes something across my chin, which I tilt toward her.

"He sure is cute." Felicity holds still while the hair stylist sprays a stray strand. "Friendship is a good place to start. In fact, my husband and I were both dating other people when we met. We enjoyed so many things in common, after we broke up with the other people, it was only natural for us to continue hanging out."

"That's really nice." I understand exactly what she's saying, but how do I explain the part about the chemistry—that special spark and music in my ears—not being there. That might have changed a little bit lately, but I've attributed that feeling to exhaustion-based vulnerability.

I'm thankful when the producer lets us know we only have a few seconds before we air. And then I'm on. Being in front of the camera is fun for me. I feel as though I'm playing a part, and since I know what I'm talking about when it comes to hair, I know I sound natural.

As the hour goes on, I find myself laughing and joking with Felicity and the people who call in to share their testimonials with us. One woman claims the Ms. Prissy Big Hair system has added a spark to her marriage. She actually giggles when she says, "He says I'm hotter than I was when we first got married."

Felicity has a cute comeback, and the woman goes on to say she'd never be without my products, and she's excited to try my new and improved line. The next woman comes on air to say she bought the kit after seeing how pretty it made someone else's hair. I'm feeling really good about things until someone stuns me with the question, "Why are you denying your relationship with that man I saw you with in the magazine? It's obvious the two of you are meant for each other."

When Felicity sees that I'm speechless, she takes over, and the camera pans away from me and zooms in on her. I sure hope Tim isn't watching, but I suspect he is, since he always has in the past.

Each time I've been on air at TVNS, we sell out before the show is over, and this is no exception, even though I upped my order by fifty percent. "That's all we've got, folks." Felicity's voice practically purrs as she lets the audience know that I'll be back soon with even more products that are formulated to give women full, lustrous hair that will turn heads whenever they enter a room. "Here's Lawrence Holt with the latest in home design." We both hold our smiles until we get the signal we're off the air.

"Now that's what I'd call a successful show." Felicity unclips her own microphone, and I follow suit. "Ms. Prissy Big Hair has turned out to be one of our most profitable products." She places her hand on my shoulder. "I bet you're feeling really good about that."

"Yes, it does feel good." I try my best to act more enthusiastic than I actually am, but I think she can see through me, even though she doesn't say anything about it. Instead, she asks me to join her for coffee at the TVNS cafeteria, where all the employees, show hosts, and vendors congregate and enjoy one another's company. I accept.

It's mid-afternoon, so most of the lunch crowd has gone back to work. What we see now are camera crewmembers and a few corporate executives who are stealing a quick break between meetings. A few people lift their hands in acknowledgment of either Felicity or me, but no one is fazed by either of our notoriety. It's nice to go somewhere and not have people staring.

As soon as we're seated with our coffee, Felicity leans forward, until her face is inches from mine. "So tell me more about this Tim guy." I don't respond right away, so she continues. "I know you say you're just friends, but I'd like to hear all about him."

I lean back and laugh. "Are you saying you don't believe me?"

"I never said that, but just in case something does come of your relationship, I'd like to be in on at least some of it." She tilts her head. "I mean, we are friends now, right?"

The look on her face is so filled with curiosity it's comical. "Okay, so what do you want to know about him?"

"Where's he from, how did you meet, what do the two of you do when you're together, and . . . well, you know, all the normal stuff."

"He's from Mississippi; we met in the first salon I ever bought when he called on me for his uncle's beauty supply company; we mostly talk about business or whatever class reunion I have coming up, and that's about it."

Felicity shakes her head. "That can't possibly be all. What do you see in him . . . I mean as a friend?"

I think for a moment before I answer. "He's very sweet, he's polite, and he seems to want to make me happy. I also like the fact that he respects me and sincerely wants me to be successful."

"Sounds like a great catch to me. So what's holding you back?"

"Nothing but the fact that he and I will always be friends."

Felicity plays with her spoon for a moment before putting it down and looking back at me. "I know you're not asking for advice, but I think we know each other well enough to speak our minds." She looks at me expectantly and smiles when I nod. "It isn't every day you find a man as cute and sweet as Tim yet who respects you as you say he does."

Her words are very true, I think as I reflect on my crush-gone-bad on Maurice. All he cared about was what I could do for him, while Tim waits on the sidelines, at the ready to help me accomplish whatever I want to do.

I decide it's time to turn the tables, so I ask her some questions about her husband. Her expression softens to the point of dreaminess as she shares stories about how she discovered he was the one. I'm amazed by the similarities between her and her husband, Reggie, and Tim and me.

"Reggie really liked my friend Stacy, but she never saw the value in his decency. All she wanted was someone who could make a lot of money and let her buy whatever she wanted. Reggie wanted to go into the military after college, and that wasn't good enough for her."

"Did he follow his dream?"

Felicity nods and blushes. "Yes, but he and I had become such good friends, it was tough to see him go. I think I sort of knew he was the one because I missed him so much after he left."

"That must have been tough."

"It was, especially since I figured we'd always just be good friends. I was thrilled when he decided to give up his commission and stay here in New York. Of course, at the time, I didn't realize he was planning to take our relationship to a more romantic level." She sighs. "I'll never forget his proposal."

"Tell me about it."

Felicity shares how Reggie had asked her to go on a picnic on Staten Island. "It started out such a pretty day—not a cloud in the sky—but the air was a bit nippy since it was October. I forgot to bring a sweater, so he pulled a blanket out of his trunk and wrapped it around both of us." She rubs her arms. "It gives me goose bumps just thinking about how I felt, being so close to him."

"Did he propose then?"

"No, not yet. I could tell he was nervous, but he insisted we go to a certain spot at the park, even though there were other really pretty places. I went along with him, but I was beginning to wonder if something was wrong with him." She giggles. "He says he was bitten by the love bug, and that's why half of what he did made no sense."

"So did he propose during your picnic?"

She shakes her head. "No, we ate mostly in silence. I kept asking him if he was upset because he didn't eat much, and he kept looking around me for something. Finally, I'd had enough. I stood up and told him that I was disappointed in how little attention he was giving me, and if he wanted to be elsewhere, then go right ahead. He stood and told me there was nowhere else he'd rather be, and he started to lean down to kiss me. We'd kissed before, but this one was different. It was so . . . " Her eyes practically roll back in her head, and she makes a swooning sound. "So heavenly." She straightens up and squares her shoulders. "Then suddenly, he was distracted again. Right when I was about to let him have it, he pointed to something behind me. I turned around, and there was a beautiful horse and carriage. Come to find out, that's what he'd been watching for. We tossed all our picnic stuff into his trunk so we could go for a ride in the carriage. We'd barely rounded the first corner when he told me he couldn't wait any longer. I was never so surprised as I was when he pulled that little box out of his pocket and asked me to marry him."

"That's very sweet." I wonder if anything even close to that romantic will ever happen to me.

"I know. And remember, we didn't start out with all the bells ringing between us. Our relationship was more like a pair of comfortable sneakers, until we both decided we were perfect for each other."

"Okay, that's fine for y'all, but Tim's and my relationship is nothing like that."

"Whoever said it was? All relationships are different. You can't compare yours to mine, but don't try to compare it to something in a fairy tale either."

17
Tim

I'm sittin' here watchin' Priscilla on TV, when that woman calls in and asks about the magazine article. Priscilla looks like she done seen a ghost. Her reaction sorta hurts my feelings, but I do understand. Me and her's got somethin' special, and TVNS isn't the place to talk about it.

Uncle Hugh calls, and we talk about business for a few minutes, even though I know he'll bring up Priscilla since he don't miss a single time she's on. "Tim, you need to quit messin' around and make that woman yours. Even her audience agrees."

"It's not that simple, Uncle Hugh. Priscilla has a mind of her own."

"So you do love her."

"Yeah, I reckon I do. But that don't mean she loves me back."

"Then give her a reason to."

I been givin' her plenty of reasons to love me back. I listen to her when she needs to talk—somethin' Mama always says is the best thing a man can do. I help her when she needs me, like for her class reunions. When Uncle Hugh's company has specials on products, she's always the first to know.

"Timmy, you still there?"

"Uh . . . yeah, I'm here."

"Priscilla needs to see your value as a man she can fall in love with."

"But I—"

"I'm not talkin' about stuff you do for her. She needs to understand there's more to you than meets the eye."

"That sounds like girl talk."

He laughs. "It is, and it's obviously not something that comes natural to any of us guys. I learned it from Tammy. She once told me she always thought of me as a nice guy, but it's my mysterious side that grabbed her heart."

"You have a mysterious side?"

"Obviously I do." He chuckles and clears his throat. "So you need one of those intangible qualities that will make her heart go pitty-pat."

"Um . . . how do you spell that?" I pull a pen from my pocket and hold it over some scratch paper.

"How do I spell what?"

"That word . . . that quality you said I need."

"Oh, intangible?"

"Yeah, that's the word. I've heard it before, but I don't know exactly what it means."

He tries to spell it but can't, so he tells me the definition. After we hang up, I think about what he says the word means. *Something you can't touch, feel, smell, or see, even though it's real. Like life insurance.*

So I need to make her see my value without coming right out and showing it to her. I'm not sure how I'm gonna do that, but it makes sense in some sort of, well, *intangible* way.

All this talkin' about what it'll take to make Priscilla love me leads me to believe I've been too easy. She obviously don't mind workin' hard for what she wants. Maybe if I don't hang around her so much, she'll have to work to get near me. It might backfire, but I figure I don't have nothin' to lose since it's been more than a decade of me wantin' her and her seein' me as just a good friend. I don't think that'll change, but it's worth a shot.

Now I have to find some way to be nearby but not too available. That's my challenge, and I can only hope I'm up to it. It's just gonna be hard not to run to her rescue if she gives even a hint of bein' in distress.

I'm on my way to the office early the next morning when my cell phone rings. I see that it's Priscilla, and I'm half tempted to not answer. But that don't seem right, so I click the answer button.

"Did you see the show yesterday?" Her tone is a tad strange, almost like she's hopin' I didn't see her.

"Yes, I saw it."

"What did you think?"

"You done good, Priscilla . . . I mean you did a nice job."

She don't speak right away, but I hear her breathin'. It takes every single solitary ounce of self-restraint to not say more, but I hold back. "We sold out early."

"Yes, I know."

"Tim, are you okay?"

"I'm just fine, Priscilla. Why?"

"Because you're acting rather strange. You don't sound like yourself."

I'm not sure if that's a good thing or not, but once again, I resist my urge to explain the real reason. "I'm on my way to work."

"Oh, that's probably why. So how do you like running the company?"

Sounds like she's in the mood to chat. "It's okay." What I would have said before was that I would much rather be back on my route so I could see her more often, but I don't. "I still have quite a bit to learn, but Uncle Hugh seems to think I'm doin' a fine job."

"No doubt you are." Do I hear a hint of disappointment in her voice? My heart aches for her, but I have to stand firm on this intangible quality thing. It's time for her to see somethin' she can't really *see* rather than have me at her beck and call. "Sounds like you're busy."

Oh man, I'm dyin' to see if she has time to hang out after I get off work, and I'm about to say somethin' along those lines, but I bite my bottom lip 'til the urge goes away. "I reckon I better run now. I'm at the office buildin', and I have a ton of work to do."

"Call me soon, okay?"

"You bet." I click the *Off* button and drop the phone into my pocket. This is gonna be much harder than I ever imagined. I need to come up with that intangible thing soon, or I just might lose my mind.

Good thing there's a phone call waitin' for me when I get to the office 'cause it instantly gets my mind off my feelings for Priscilla. After that, I have a meetin' with a new product manufacturer, and then it's lunchtime, which turns out to be a workin' lunch on account of there's so much to do. Seein' how much goes into runnin' a company my respect flies sky high for Uncle Hugh. No wonder he was ready to take off and move to his fish camp in Vancleave. He still calls me every single day. I tell him he don't need to do that—if I need him I'll call him. And he says he'll quit, but he don't.

I tackle paperwork all afternoon, with one interruption after another from our sales managers wantin' this or needin' that. Makes me feel awful for all those times I didn't think twice about callin' up Uncle Hugh for stupid stuff. Maybe if he made me sit in his office for a whole workday to see how hard he worked, I woulda not bugged him so much. I look back and remember how he always seemed to have time for me, no matter what time of day it was. How he managed to keep his wits about him is beyond me. As it is, I wanna open the window and holler as loud as I can, just to let off some steam. Now I see why all the bars is full after quittin' time. Them people just need to unwind.

If I hadn't seen such carryin' on from Pete Moss when he got all liquored up, I mighta joined the fellows down at the After Hours Pub. But I don't have enough confidence in how I'll behave to risk doin' that. I'm afraid once I start drinkin', I might like it so much I won't be able to quit.

18
Priscilla

Something is happening between Tim and me, and I'm not so sure I like it. He's acting distant—something I've never seen him do before. Maybe it's his new position with Hugh Puckett's company, or maybe he's just lost interest in me. If that's the case, it's probably for the best.

My flight back to Jackson is uneventful, with the exception of a crying baby. But even that doesn't bother me as much as it used to. In fact, I have a powerful urge to lean over and see the child, and when I do, my heart does a flip-flop when I take in her chubby little cheeks and pouty lips. *Lord, what is happening to me?*

As my business grows, so does the amount of luggage I have to check. The folks at TVNS have asked me to have a change of clothes for each segment of airtime. They've offered to let me wear some of the clothes they sell, but until I get there, I never know what they'll have, so I bring my own wardrobe. Beth Fay wasn't able to travel with me this time, so all the work falls on my shoulders.

It takes me an hour to get my bags, pile them into my car, and drive home. As soon as I open the door, a feeling of comfort surrounds me. No matter how many condos I have up and down the East Coast, this place feels the most like home.

I mentally swat away my feelings of needing stability that have haunted me more frequently over the past several months as I toss the biggest suitcase onto my bed to empty it. After a trip like this, I used to come home exhausted, but now I'm restless. Something isn't right with me, and I have no idea what it is. I don't want to go anywhere, but I have the urge to do something familiar.

After all my things are put away, I change into sweats and pad barefooted into the kitchen, where I pour myself a bowl of sugary cereal. I take that to my favorite chair in front of the TV, pick up the remote, and channel surf until I find a rerun of an old sitcom. Nostalgia washes over me and swirls around, bringing comfort to my soul. And then during the first commercial break, it hits me. I know exactly what's wrong. I've accomplished all my goals, and now I don't know what to do without something to strive for. Now I'm on that hamster wheel that I've been avoiding all my adult life. Ugh.

I force myself to finish watching the show that I remember seeing at least fifteen years ago. As soon as it's over, I lift the remote and turn off the TV before going back into the kitchen and pouring another bowl of cereal that I place on the small bistro-style kitchen table, where I do my best brainstorming. I have to come up with another goal, or I'll never be happy again. That saying about enjoying the journey pops into my mind, so I jot that down on the notepad I keep on the table. Whatever I choose to embark on next must have a journey worth traveling, or I'll lose interest and be right back to where I am now.

This isn't as easy as it once was, now that I've forged a path in the beauty business. Whatever I choose to do has to make sense to where I am today.

I write *beauty*, *fashion*, and *passion* across the top of the page before listing my ideas beneath them. Whatever comes to mind is what I write, without editing or deleting anything. As the ideas flow, my lists grow longer, and it doesn't take long before I see a plan emerge. My passion is still beauty related, and I like the idea of being on TVNS. However, I don't enjoy the travel as much as I thought I would, so I need to find another way to have my product line on air without physically being the one to go to New York every time. Now that I'm fairly certain that Beth Fay is harmless, I think she just might be the person who can help me out with this. She's expressed her desire to become famous, so I'm thinking I might be able to train her to be the TV spokesperson. I'm sure she'll be much happier doing that than sitting on the sidelines, behind the cameras, watching me and waiting for whatever comes next. She'll be the person in the limelight, and if I can keep her from becoming a diva, I think she'll be perfect. As it is, she's using most of my products and looking absolutely stunning because of it. I glance up at the clock and see that it's too late to call her, but that's okay. At least I'll be able to go to sleep, knowing I have a plan . . . or at least part of a plan that I'll be able to finish once I have her trained.

I wake up early the next morning and resist the urge to call Beth Fay. This is something I'd like to discuss with Mandy first, which shows me how much I've come to trust and depend on my assistant.

Her car is in the parking lot when I arrive a half-hour before she's supposed to be there. As soon as I walk in, she comes to the door of her office. "What are you doing here so early? I figured you'd be in late since you just got back from New York."

"I couldn't wait to talk to you about a new idea." I gesture toward her office. "Let's sit down and get started."

"Want some coffee first?"

"Sure." I start to follow her, but she tells me to go sit down, and she'll get it.

Once we have our coffee, we settle into position in her office for what I suspect will be a long meeting. The instant I tell her my thoughts, her eyes light up. "Perfect! That might be the very thing that'll light the fire under that woman and at the same time give you a chance to regroup."

"So you like it, huh? I wasn't sure you'd go along with it."

"I love the idea, and I think Beth Fay will too. Just don't expect this to hold her interest more than a couple years, if that."

"You don't think it will?"

Mandy shakes her head. "Not being the drama queen she is. She's nice and all, but she likes to keep excitement stirring in her life. Your plan will give her that for a while, but we'll need to keep a careful watch on her to prevent some sort of disaster once she gets bored."

"I think you're right."

"Oh, trust me, I know I am. I've hired enough drama queens to know them when I see them." When I don't respond, Mandy continues. "And based on the nature of being on air and people fawning over her, this plan might hold her interest longer than anything else." She smiles. "I wondered how long she'd be satisfied with being your shadow."

"You know that's never how I saw her."

"Of course I know that, but she's different." Mandy drums her fingers on her desk, and I lean back to think about what to do next.

"I guess I'll need to do some rehearsing with her," I say.

Mandy nods. "Maybe even have someone videotape her so she can see how she comes across."

"That's what the production people at TVNS did with me. Oh, that reminds me. Before I go through with this plan, I'll need to talk with the representative there to make sure it's okay."

"Even before you do that, why don't we feature Beth Fay in a print ad to give her some visibility and some celebrity status?"

"Great idea, Mandy. You're brilliant."

"That's why you hired me, right?"

"Yes, of course." She and I both know that's not exactly how things started out with us. I hired her because I was desperate for a warm body to sit in the reception area of my corporate office, and she just happened to be in the right place at the right time, but we never discuss that because it's pointless to bring up the past with everything being just fine between us now.

I call Beth Fay to find out when she'll be free again. She says she's not sure, but when I tell her we'd like to feature her in an ad, she's suddenly available next week. I'll be in Piney Point for the reunion, but I trust Mandy to take care of the details.

Mandy and I plan what needs to be done while I'm away. Blair has turned out to be efficient and seems satisfied with her job, which is refreshing since by this time, most of the receptionists Mandy has hired have one foot out the door.

"I have a feeling Blair sees this as a career position." Mandy slowly shakes her head. "I don't get it, but it's nice to have someone who isn't always on the phone, trying to sneak interviews with other companies. There's something different about her. She seems content all the time."

That sounds good to me. "Maybe she'll stick around long enough for me to get to know her. What do you think about the three of us going out for dinner after work?"

"Great idea. Want me to ask her, or would you rather do it yourself?"

I stand up and back toward the door. "Let me talk to her."

Blair is on the phone, taking notes when I walk out to the reception area. She glances up at me, smiles, and resumes jotting something down. When she's finished with the call, she hands me the note. "A new product line from California. Here's the man's name and number."

I stuff the paper into my briefcase and sit in the chair beside her desk. "How would you like to go to dinner with Mandy and me after work?"

Instead of answering immediately, she scrunches up her forehead and rubs her chin. "How long will it take?"

"Oh, do you have to be someplace? We can make it another time if tonight's not convenient."

"My little sister is in the hospital, and I promised my mother I'd go sit with her so she can go help out at the church."

"Your little sister is in the hospital?" Why don't I know this? I wish Mandy had filled me in a little more.

"Yes." She glances at Mandy who has appeared at the door with a questioning look. "Sorry I didn't tell you, but I didn't want to burden you with my problems."

Okay, so Mandy didn't know either. "Don't worry about that being a burden." I feel a lump form in my throat. "Is there anything I can do to help?"

Blair slowly shakes her head and lowers her gaze to her desk before I see the first tear splat on the blotter. "She's having some complications from chemotherapy, so they're keeping her in the hospital for observation."

"Oh, Blair, why didn't you say something?" Mandy doesn't hesitate to close the gap and put her arm around her assistant.

"On my last job, I was told to keep my personal life out of the business." She glances up with misty eyes, and her chin quivers.

"That's totally not us." Mandy looks to me for reassurance.

"Mandy's right. We care about the people who work for the Cut 'n Curl, and we want to help wherever and whenever we can."

That's all it takes for the dam to break. Blair starts boo-hooing, and Mandy excuses herself to get tissues.

"Look, Blair, if you need to take care of your sister, we understand. Just please don't bottle up your worries, because we might be able to do something."

Blair looks me in the eye. "What can y'all do?"

I take a deep breath and decide to share my faith. "We can pray. I'm very good at that."

A slight grin forms on her lips. "That's another thing I wasn't sure I could talk about. My family has always gone to church, but my last boss . . . " She sniffles as she takes the tissue Mandy hands her. "Well, he told me to leave my religion at home and concentrate on the job when I'm at work."

"You didn't get fired for your faith, did you?" I narrow my eyes.

"Oh, no, I didn't get fired. I walked out when he told me I had to work overtime on a night when he knew I was supposed to sing in church."

Mandy and I exchange a look before I lean toward Blair and whisper, "If you have to leave early for church, we understand. This business is for people and about people, and most of us here are believers. And we don't always have to agree about everything, so if you have a difference of opinion, don't be afraid to state it. Just remember, though, that you might wind up with a spirited discussion as a result."

"You can say that again," Mandy added.

"So is there anything we can do besides pray?" I ask.

"Well . . . " Blair looks at Mandy then at me. "My mama is a big fan of yours, and she'd really enjoy meeting you. Can she come here sometime . . . I mean . . . I'll tell her she can't stay long."

"That's fine, but I have an even better idea. Why don't we go pick up some food and bring dinner to your mother and sister in the hospital?"

Mandy makes a face. "I'm not so sure I want to be around sick people."

I level her with one of my mock-stern looks. "Afraid you might learn something?"

Blair laughs. "The kids in the section where my sister is would love to see some new faces."

"That settles it." I point to the phone. "Call your sister's favorite restaurant and place an order. I like just about anything, so I'll have whatever she wants."

Mandy sighs. "Okay, I guess I'll go too."

It takes Blair about ten minutes to find out what her mother and sister want and to call the order in to the Thai restaurant near the hospital. I tell them to go on ahead, and I'll pick up the food.

Joy fills my heart. Maybe taking the focus off my career goals for a change is just what I need.

I arrive in the hospital parking lot with two bags filled with containers of food. Blair and Mandy meet me by the entrance and offer to help.

"I need to warn you that most of the kids in Haley's unit are bald from the chemo treatments."

An idea flickers in my mind, but I don't say anything just yet. We walk inside and go up in the elevator to the children's unit. The second we step out, we're greeted by a sweet-looking woman about my mother's age and the cutest little bald-headed girl I think I've ever seen.

Blair's mother gives her daughter a hug and turns to me. "So this is your boss lady?"

"Mama, I'd like you to meet Priscilla and Mandy, who manages the Cut 'n Curl office."

I see stars in Blair's mother's eyes as she shakes my hand. "Please call me Irma. It's so nice to meet you, Priscilla." She turns to Mandy and pats her arm. "You too, Mandy."

"Mandy is Blair's immediate supervisor since I travel so much. In fact, she's the one who hired her."

"Thank you so much for giving my girl a chance. She hasn't had it easy, with all we have to deal with."

Blair's little sister stares up at me, her smile warming me all over. I lean over and grin right back at her.

"You are so cute!"

She pulls her bottom lip between her teeth and looks down at the floor. Her mother puts her hands on Haley's shoulders. "My baby's always been shy around people she doesn't know."

I nod. "Haley, I hear you like Thai food." When she nods, I wink. "So do I, so I brought some for supper. Do you think we should share?"

She giggles and nods. Irma's chin quivers as she sees us interacting.

As we eat, I'm pleased that Haley grows more comfortable, and she actually asks questions. "Do you like being on TV?"

"Sometimes," I admit. "But sometimes I like not being on TV too."

Haley turns to Mandy. "Are you famous like Miss Priscilla?"

Mandy shakes her head. "No, I'm not the least bit famous, and I don't wanna be either."

"How about you, Haley?" I ask. "Would you like to be famous?"

She adamantly nods. "When my hair grows back, I wanna be famous and be on TV, just like you."

Her innocence touches my heart in a way I've never experienced before. After we finish eating, I pull Irma to the side.

"How would you feel about Haley getting a wig from one of my customers?" I explain how every now and then, one of the Cut 'n Curl customers wants to donate hair to the Locks of Love organization.

Irma's eyes light up. "She would absolutely love that!"

My heart practically explodes with gladness as I realize I've found something that I don't think I'll ever get tired of. I want to help these children feel better about themselves, and my business is in the ideal position to help.

19
Laura

"You know I don't much like that boy Renee's hangin' all over." Pete gently brushes past me to get a glass from the cupboard. He turns on the faucet, fills the glass, downs the water, and fills it up again. Ever since he gave up alcohol, he started drinkin' enough water to drown a fish. "Can't you make him go away?"

I level him with one of my looks. "I've talked to her about their . . . affection, and she says they're not into hidin' their love."

"That's ridiculous." Pete sips his second glass of water and scowls. "Kids have been hidin' their affection since the beginnin' of time, and that's the way it should stay. Parents shouldn't hafta see their young'uns gettin' groped."

"Why don't you talk to her?"

He shrugs, still frowning. "What's the point? Anything I tell these kids goes in one ear and out the other."

"If I tell her, it won't even make it to her ears. I think there's some sort of mama-censor monster that protects our young'uns from hearin' our advice." I sigh. "I'd like to tell that boy to get lost, but I'm afraid the one we'd lose is Renee." I look at my husband. "I wish someone woulda told us this might happen."

Pete actually cracks a smile as he sets down his water glass. "C'mere, Miss Pudge."

"Don't call me that. I want credit for those twenty pounds I lost."

"Okay, Skinny Lady, I wanna hold you."

I take a step toward the only man I've ever loved—the one I've been through thick and thin with, and I'm talkin' so thin I wasn't even sure it was there sometimes. As I snuggle into his arms, I feel our heartbeats hammerin' away in a familiar rhythm that lets me know we're meant to be together forever. Pete tips my face up toward his and leans down to kiss me.

"Ew, gross." I yank my head around to see our third kid, Bonnie Sue, standin' at the kitchen door. "Do y'all hafta do that in front of everybody?"

Pete chuckles as he keeps his hold on me. "Last I checked me and your mama was the only ones in the room."

"Mamas and daddies should never act that way." She lifts an arm to shield her eyes from the sight of us.

"How do you think you got here, young lady?" Pete glances down at me and winks.

Bonnie Sue grunts. "That's disgusting."

"Maybe so," Pete says, "but have you ever thought about it?"

Our daughter makes the worst face I've ever seen as she holds up her hand. "I am so outta here." She makes a gagging sound as she leaves the kitchen.

Pete turns around to face me, grinnin' real big. "That's one way to have our alone time. All we have to do is act romantic, and our young'uns run away so fast you'd think they had a skunk chasin' 'em."

We hear Bonnie Sue shoutin' in the living room about how disgustin' her sister is bein' with Wilson. I couldn't agree with her more.

Pete snorts. "No wonder that Bonnie Sue ain't been able to hold onto a boyfriend. At least we prob'ly won't have to worry about her havin' to get married."

"That's no guarantee."

He lets go of me, picks up his glass of water, and chugs all but the last few sips. "I know that, but that don't mean I can't have wishful thinkin'. It's goin' all through me to see that boy's hands on Renee."

"Me too. But at least we know where they are."

Pete nods. "Yeah, at least for now we do. I don't know how long that'll be the case, though."

Nothing much has changed from one generation to the next. Little kids look up to their mamas and daddies, then they become preteen monsters. As they pass through their teenage years, hormones rule and misplace their brain cells. I've heard that in a few years, they'll find 'em, and that's when Pete and I'll be able to reminisce the good ol' days that never were.

"So how many folks do you reckon will be at the reunion this year?" Pete dumps the water and pours himself a fresh glass. Ever since he quit drinkin' he has a thing about his water bein' fresh.

"More than we had in our class. We're gettin' calls from people a year ahead and a year behind us. Seems we throw the best parties, and they wanna be part of the fun."

Pete looks at me with a half-grin and shakes his head. "It's not that we have the best parties. They just don't wanna miss out on bein' in on the earliest gossip."

"Yeah, you're prob'ly right. Some earth-shatterin' drama always happens at our reunions."

"One thing you can count on this year, Skinny Lady, is I won't cause none of that drama. I'm sober, and I plan to stay that way."

I'm so proud of my husband I could spit, I think as I pick up my dishrag and start wipin' the countertops. Once upon a time, I had a little fear that if Pete ever stayed on the straight-and-narrow, he'd lose interest in me. When I realized that wouldn't happen, I've been able to enjoy a husband who loves me without the fog.

The phone rings, and since Pete doesn't appear eager to answer it, I put down my rag and lift the receiver. It's Didi Holcomb, and she sounds like she has a cold . . . or she's been cryin'.

"I-I'm calling to cancel my place at the reunion." She sniffles.

"What's the matter, Didi? You sick or somethin'?"

"Uh . . . yes, I'm very sick."

I want to ask more questions, but Didi has one of those personalities that puts people in their places, even when she doesn't say anything. "Okay, I'll try and see if I can get you your money back, but I can't guarantee—"

"Don't worry about it. I never expect to see any of my money again."

Whoa. Somethin' is buggin' her real bad. I swallow hard before blurting, "Do you need to talk, Didi? You can come over if you want to."

The sudden silence makes me wish I hadn't invited her over, but to my surprise, she speaks up. "Yes, I'd love to talk. May I come now?"

"Sure. Come on over."

As soon as I hang up, I scurry around the kitchen puttin' things away that we normally leave out. I run out to the livin' room and tell Renee she needs to pull herself away from Wilson long enough to help me straighten up a bit. She groans and starts to complain, but I give her one of them looks that lets her know I mean business. That doesn't stop the grumblin', but she does go into action.

I holler up the stairs to Pete to let him know we're about to have company, and he's not to come down unless he's fully clothed. He hollers back, "Who'd come over here at this hour?"

"It's just seven-thirty, Pete."

"My show'll be on in half an hour."

I don't even bother commenting on that. Instead I toss a few stray shoes into the coat closet. I'm about to head back into the kitchen when the doorbell rings. That girl didn't waste a second gettin' over here.

When I fling the door open, I'm shocked to see a mess of a woman with ratty hair, no makeup, and a wrinkled T-shirt that came from some bank's grand opening. I do my best not to let on as I take a step back. "C'mon in, Didi. Do you wanna sit in the livin' room or in the kitchen?"

She steps inside and looks around. "Let's go to the kitchen."

Once we're there, I'm not sure what to do next, so I point to the table. "Have a seat, and I'll put on some coffee."

"It's too late for coffee."

"How about tea or water?"

She shakes her head. "I don't want anything but a few questions answered."

The way she says that sounds like she's about to accuse me of something, and I get nervous. I don't think I've done anything to her, but I can be clueless at times. I pour myself a glass of tea and join her at the table. "So what's on your mind, Didi?"

"You and Priscilla are pretty good friends, aren't you?"

Didi obviously doesn't know either Priscilla or me very well if she's wonderin' that, and I don't know what she's gettin' at, so I bob my head. "Why do you ask?"

She props her elbow on the table and leans toward me. "What does she have that I don't?"

"I don't know what you're talkin' about, Didi."

"Seems like Priscilla gets everything she wants. She beat me out of valedictorian, she's a successful businesswoman, and now she's famous."

I tilt my head and look at Didi in a way I've never seen her. The woman is downright jealous. "It's not like you're not accomplished, Didi. Look at you." I hold my hands out toward her. "You're a doctor."

She snorts. "Yeah, a pitiful doctor who doesn't have the sense to know when she's being used."

Now we're gettin' to the good stuff. "So is this really about Maurice?"

"It's about how I always get whatever Priscilla doesn't want, and I'm getting sick and tired of never being first choice."

"Are you saying Maurice wants Priscilla?"

Didi closes her eyes and swallows before giving me the most pained look I've ever seen. "I have no idea what Maurice wants, and I'm not sure he knows either. But what I do know is that every time things start to look good for us, Priscilla finds a way to jump between us."

This is makin' no sense. I just happen to know Priscilla can't stand Maurice—ever since somethin' he did after the last reunion. Besides, Priscilla hasn't even been to town much lately, and I've seen him enough to know he's been here, so how can Priscilla come between Didi and Maurice?

"Are you sure it's Priscilla and not someone . . . or somethin' else?"

"Oh, it's Priscilla, all right. Did you see that magazine article about her and that guy she keeps bringing around?" She reaches for the saltshaker and starts fiddlin' with it. "It's like she can't stand seeing me happy."

"I could be wrong, Didi, but I don't think that magazine article has anything to do with tryin' to keep you from bein' happy. In fact, from what I've heard, she wasn't even the first to know about it."

"See? I knew you'd stick up for her. Everyone wants to take her side." Didi stands up and lifts her hands in the air like she's givin' up. "What's with everyone? Are you all a bunch of puppets that Priscilla Slater can manipulate?" She snorts. "Obviously you are."

That does it. I'm sick and tired of this woman's whiny-butt nonsense. I stand up and jab my finger toward her chair. "Sit back down, Didi Holcomb, and listen to me." The sternness of my own voice surprises even me, and it gives me the energy to keep goin'.

Didi's eyes widen, and she does as I say. Her mouth opens a fraction of an inch, but she doesn't say a word. Instead, she continues watching me as if she thinks I might do somethin' crazy. Good. That's where she needs to stay 'til I'm done.

"You gotta get over yourself, Didi. No one has set out to hurt you but you, yourself."

"What?"

"I think you heard me. The only person who can determine what happens in your life is you. If you keep harpin' on this Priscilla thang, thinkin' you have to compete with her for everything, you'll never be happy. I can guarantee you she's not givin' you a second thought, unless it's pity when she sees you all lovey-dovey with that loser you been engaged to."

I can't believe I just said that, and from the look on Didi's face, she can't either. I know I done said too much already, and for some reason I can't stop.

"Priscilla has always wanted to be a hairdresser, ever since I can remember. And she did it, even though her mama and daddy thought she was too good for that kind of work. She's a smart girl—too smart to let her snobby parents bully her into stayin' in college."

"You would say that, being one of her closest friends," Didi says with a smirk.

"That's another thing you got wrong, Didi. I don't like Priscilla any more than you do, but that doesn't mean I don't respect what she's done with her life." The instant those words leave my mouth, I wanna crawl into a hole. I never ever told anyone I didn't like Priscilla, and I'm not even sure that's true. In fact, now that I think about it, I might be just as jealous of the woman as Didi always has been.

"So, the truth comes out." A smile forms on Didi's lips, and I want to rip it right off. "How would you like to help me bring her down a notch at the reunion?"

Ten years ago, I might have wanted to participate in somethin' underhanded to hurt Priscilla, but now that I finally have my life together, I see how pitiful that type of thinkin' is. "No, Didi. I'm not about to lower myself to be mean to someone just 'cause I'm not happy with my own life. And you need to rethink it too, or you might make yourself even more miserable than you already are . . . if that's possible."

Her chin quivers, and she starts to stand up. But then the sobs hit her, and she falls back down into her chair and slowly curls up with her face in her hands and her elbows in her lap. I stand there lookin' down at her, knowin' there's nothin' I can do to help.

20
Priscilla

Life is much sweeter, now that I've got something to look forward to. After meeting Blair's little sister who is twelve years younger than she is, I know that I have to do whatever I can to make her life better.

"Wow." Mandy looks at me with a smile of amazement. "You really are a new person today. I can't get over how one visit to the children's cancer unit has gotten you all excited again."

"Those kids really grabbed my heart." I pause and study Mandy. "Didn't that affect you?"

"Well, sort of. I feel sorry for them, but I don't plan to keep going back."

I want to shake Mandy, but that's only because I'm so fired up over plans to help the children I expect everyone to feel the same way. This isn't new for me. Back in high school, I got upset that people turned me down when I collected coats and blankets for homeless people. Now I understand that other people might not feel my passion.

"So when are you visiting them again?" Mandy asks.

"I'm having all my salons collect hair for Locks of Love."

"That's really nice." She picks up a piece of paper and hands it to me. "Take a look at this."

As I read it, I'm impressed by how quickly she acted. "You wrote a press release about it. Thank you so much, Mandy."

"It's the least I could do since it's so important to you . . . and Blair."

"You really like her, don't you?"

Mandy nods. "Yes, she's been the best of all the people I've ever hired. She's never given me attitude about anything."

"Good. We need to do whatever we can to keep her happy working here."

"Oh, I almost forgot something. You have an appointment with some equipment rep who says he can save us a bunch of money on electricity with his line of dryers and tools."

"Do I have time to grab some breakfast?"

"Not unless you can eat it in the next fifteen minutes. He wanted to come next week, but since you'll be in Piney Point, I worked him in this morning."

As if on cue, Mandy's phone lights up. She grabs the phone, answers it, and says, "She'll be right out." Mandy hangs up the phone and nods toward the door. "Looks like he's here early."

I open Mandy's office door expecting your run-of-the-mill beauty supply salesman but find myself speechless when I come face-to-face with the best-looking man I've ever laid eyes on. Fortunately, I've worked hard at maintaining my composure in all circumstances, and being on air has given me the acting experience, so I recover quickly and smile. "You must be the equipment salesman who couldn't wait until I got back from my trip."

He grins as he takes my extended hand in both of his. "And you must be the most gorgeous beauty salon chain owner I've ever seen in my entire life. I'm thrilled to finally meet you." Oh, he's slick. He pulls a card from his pocket and hands it to me.

"My name is Rick Crenshaw, and I have a line of products that every salon needs."

"And why do you say that, Rick?" I gesture toward the hall leading to my office.

He nods. "I'll follow you."

I lead him to my tiny office and go around behind my desk to put some space between us . . . and to keep some authority in the situation. The last thing I need is for him to think he has any sort of power over me. I wipe my hands on the sides of my pants as discreetly as possible.

We start out discussing the equipment currently in our salons, and he shows me some examples of the line that he created. The more he talks about how efficient his line is, the more impressed I am. He clearly understands both the aesthetic and the business sides of the industry.

"So why did you choose to target the beauty industry with your product line?" I fold my hands on my desk and hold his gaze . . . and my breath.

"Excellent question, and you're not the first to ask. My mother and aunt both own salons, and they constantly complained about the cost of power continuing to rise and eating into their profits. I'd been working as an electrical engineer, and I hated my job, so I decided to come up with something that would help them and the thousands of other salon owners in the country." He flashes a smile full of not-quite-straight-but-very-white teeth, making me internally swoon. It's been a long time since I've had this kind of reaction over a man.

The more he talks the more I want to hear. I ask as many questions as I think I can get away with and not be too obvious . . . or desperate. Although I've seen a similar product line, his presentation is fresh and intriguing.

Mandy buzzes my phone to let me know my next appointment has arrived. I hate that I have to end this meeting, but it's probably for the best anyway, since I'm not sure if I have enough self-restraint to hold back making a fool of myself.

He packs up his products and takes a step toward the door, then stops. I almost bump into him, and we both laugh.

"I hate to be presumptuous, but would you care to have dinner with me sometime soon?"

My face flames with excitement, so I avert my gaze to something behind him. He turns to see what I'm looking at, and I clear my throat. "I would love to."

"Since you have another appointment, I'll call you later this afternoon to make plans."

I nod. "Okay. I'll be in afternoon meetings until around four."

"Will you be free after that?" I'm afraid if he keeps gazing at me like this, he might melt my toenail polish.

"Unless something comes up, I should be."

"Why don't we plan on dinner tonight? I can pick you up here or meet you wherever you'd like to go."

"Tonight?" My voice comes out in a squeak, so I clear my throat again.

"I hope you're not coming down with something. You're such a busy woman."

"I'm fine. Why don't we meet at Lorenzo's?" When he gives me a blank look, I add, "It's a steak and seafood restaurant about three blocks from here."

"Oh, I think I passed it. How's seven?"

"Perfect. We'll need a reservation. Would you like me to call and make one?"

"Yes, if you don't mind. See you there at seven unless I hear otherwise."

Once he's gone, Mandy runs back to my office and closes the door behind herself. "That man is so hot."

My lips are dry, so I lick them and look down at my desk as I sit. "Yes, he is rather attractive."

"Priscilla, I know you like him. Otherwise, why would you accept a dinner date?" She narrows her gaze. "And don't tell me it's only about business."

"What else would it be?" I challenge her with lifted eyebrows and a half-grin.

She giggles as she walks out of my office. "I'll send your next appointment on back . . . and I'll call Lorenzo's to book your reservation."

The day drags on, and it seems like forever before time to meet Rick at Lorenzo's. A few times during the afternoon I've been tempted to call and cancel. I don't know this guy, so my reaction scares me. Mandy keeps looking at me and cracking up laughing.

I arrive at Lorenzo's, super excited but half hoping Rick doesn't show up so I can slink back to my comfort zone. The doorman opens the heavy wooden door, and there stands Rick, an expectant expression on his face, looking even better than I remembered from this morning.

We both start talking at the same time, until the maître d' makes a sound to get our attention. Rick places his hand on the small of my back, and we follow the man to our table.

Throughout dinner, I find myself falling faster and faster into that hole of infatuation—deeper than the one I was in for Maurice. Rick sure does know how to hold my attention.

"So what are your passions?" He props his elbows on the table, folds his hands, and waits for me to answer, never once taking his gaze off mine.

"Until recently, my biggest passion was building my business and getting established on TVNS. Now that I've managed to do that, I'm starting to look outside myself."

"That's always a good thing to do." He leans back. "Especially since everything you've concentrated on in the past is business related."

"I know, and now that I look back, I realize how impersonal my goals were." I make an apologetic face. "Then I met Blair's little sister, and she totally won my heart." I tell him the story about going to the children's cancer unit at the hospital and how I plan to do whatever I can to help them. "How about you? What are your passions?"

"Well, I'm a southern boy, so college football is one of them. I'm not much for hunting, but I've been known to drown a few worms at my dad's favorite fishing hole."

"You sound like a man's man."

He tips his head to one side and takes my hand. "Maybe I am, but I sure do appreciate a beautiful, fun, smart, witty woman."

I force myself to look down and try not to let him see me sigh.

21
Trudy

Hey, Trudy."

I glance up and see Darryl Conrad, the man who's been living at the other end of my building for the past year and a half while his house is being built. He once told me he's waited long enough to find the woman of his dreams, and since the Lord hasn't seen fit to bring her to him yet, he's moving on with his life. I totally get that.

"Hey, Darryl." I slam my car door shut and start walking toward the apartment building

"Haven't seen you around much lately. Been workin' hard?"

"Always." I stop, shield my eyes from the late afternoon sun, and smile at him. Darryl's not a bad-looking man, but I wouldn't call him handsome either. He's definitely not someone I'd notice in a crowded room.

"Be careful about that, or you'll look back and wonder where your life went."

His smile is warm and genuine. I suspect he was one of those guys in high school who made good grades, joined a club or two, and otherwise flew under the radar. Girls like I was back then wouldn't have given him the time of day. Such a pity. I get an idea.

"Hey, Darryl, whatcha doin' for supper?"

"I haven't thought that far into the future yet." He laughs. "Why? What are you doing?"

"Thinkin' about going out for Mexican food."

He takes a step toward me. "Care to have company?"

"I thought you'd never ask."

"Have you tried that new place, Casa Enchilada's?"

I giggle. "I was there the night they opened. It's good."

"Wanna go there?"

"Of course. Let's go early, and maybe we'll have time to walk off some of the calories afterward."

"Great idea!" He points to his apartment. "I'm going to change into some jeans first."

"See ya back here in about fifteen minutes?"

"It's a date." His stride quickens, and in a matter of seconds, he's disappeared inside the building.

As I get ready, I realize this actually is a date—something I haven't had in months. Last time I went out with a man, he bored me to tears with his techie talk, and I swore off men—at least for a while. Seems like the good-looking guys think about themselves too much, but the geeky ones speak a language that might as well be Martian as far as I'm concerned. The only tech stuff I want to know about is what I have to use on the job. I can text message on my phone, but I don't wanna know how it works. All I care about is whether or not the person received it.

Darryl's waiting for me when I go back outside. "I'll drive," he says. He looks me up and down. "Lookin' good, Trudy." He laughs softly as though he just thought of a private joke. "But then you always do."

"Thank you." He jumps in front of me and opens the passenger door, something not many guys seem to be doing these days. I like it.

As he drives to Casa Enchilada, we chatter nonstop about everything under the sun. I'm comfortable around Darryl, and it appears he feels the same way about me, which is rather unusual, if I must say so myself. I mean, being a former beauty queen has its drawbacks, and one of them is that men seem to be intimidated by the way I look, even now with these thunder thighs.

I study his profile and wonder why I've never noticed his great cheekbones and his strong chin. "So how's the house coming along?"

"We had a slight weather delay, but we're back on track. Wanna see it sometime?"

"I'd love to!"

Once inside the restaurant, the server brings us some chips and salsa. "Our special tonight is a spinach enchilada platter with rice and beans."

Darryl nods toward me. "Ladies first."

"The spinach enchilada sounds good. I'll have that."

"Ditto." Darryl folds his hands on the table. "That was easy enough."

"I know." Everything is easy with Darryl—conversation, laughter, and just bein' with him.

Throughout the meal, he never once looks at me like I've lost my mind—even when I polish off the last bit of rice and scrape the sauce from the enchilada with one of the chips. These days, I have no self-control when I eat certain types of foods, and Mexican is one of them.

Darryl gently pushes my hand away when I reach for the bill. "My treat."

"But I asked you."

"Yes, I know, but that's only because I hadn't gotten around to asking you first."

He's such a sweetheart. "Okay, but next time is my treat."

Our gazes lock, and I feel a tiny flicker in my chest. That's when it hits me. I'm really attracted to Darryl, and I want to spend more time with him.

"So where would you like to go for our walk?" He turns the key in the ignition.

"What are my choices?"

"We could go back to the apartment complex and walk around there, or we could go to the mall."

I smile at him. "I work at the mall, so nix that idea."

He shrugs. "Apartment complex it is then . . . unless you have a better idea."

At this moment it doesn't matter a hill of beans where we are, as long as I'm with Darryl. I haven't felt like this since me and Michael were an item.

I put my purse in my apartment, stuff the key into my pocket, and join Darryl back outside. "Couldn't be a better night for walking."

We walk and talk about whatever pops into our minds. And we laugh at things I ordinarily wouldn't think are funny. I want this evening to last forever, and if my intuition is as good as it always has been, Darryl feels the same way.

After we round the tennis courts and start back, he stops, takes me by the hand, and turns me around to face him. "Are you dating anyone, Trudy?"

"No." My heart hammers as he takes my other hand and looks down at me with gentle eyes. "Are you?"

"Not until now." We continue lookin' at each other, until he pulls me close. "I like you, Trudy. You're fun and very sweet and super smart. Most pretty girls lack one of those."

I laugh. It sure does feel nice to hear those words. "I hope I don't disappoint you."

"I don't think you will." He lets go of my hands, cups my face, and drops a brief kiss on my lips. "We need to start talking about what to do on our next date."

I suggest a movie, but he says that's not a good idea so early in our relationship since we can't talk and get to know each other better. "How about skating?" I'm half kidding, thinkin' there's no way he'll wanna do that.

He surprises me. "Sounds like fun. I haven't skated since I was a kid."

"Same here. That should be hilarious."

"I'll bring my good camera to capture those funny moments. My parents gave me an expensive camera for my birthday, and until now I haven't had a chance to put it to good use."

"I don't know about pictures." I used to be a camera hog, but not so much now.

He makes a silly face. "Aw, c'mon, Trudy. No one will believe me when I tell them I'm hanging out with such a pretty girl, unless I show proof."

Flattery like this used to go straight to my head, but now it's grabbing my heart. "Okay, but you have to promise to give me final approval on what you keep and what you delete."

He makes a cross over his heart. "I promise."

As I lie in bed later, I reflect on my time with Darryl. He's much better looking than I ever realized before now, and I appreciate the fact that I can take everything he says at face value without having to analyze it later.

22
Priscilla

I'm sitting in my office finishing up a report when I notice movement in the doorway. My heart hammers when I realize it's Rick.

"No one was at the front desk, so I figured it was okay to come on back."

"Blair's having her weekly meeting with Mandy in her office."

He walks on in without waiting for an invitation, which is just fine with me. "Good to know she's not sleeping on the job."

"Have a seat?"

He pulls a chair around to the side of my desk and makes himself comfortable. "So what's new with you?"

I tell him about my busy day. He reaches for my hand and gently massages it, all the while looking at me with eyes at half-mast. I'm not even sure he's listening to me, but his touch makes my words seem less significant.

After I finish talking about my work, he mentions how many people are jumping on his product line. "I'm gonna be a rich man once all these orders are shipped and paid for."

"Congratulations."

"Don't say that yet. I don't want to be jinxed."

"Are you superstitious?"

He shrugs. "Not really, but there's no point in tempting fate."

As intelligent as he is, he can't possibly mean that. I'm sure it's just an expression—at least that's what I hope. I laugh.

With a lifted eyebrow, he grins. "I like you, Priscilla."

Now that he's said that, I feel comfortable letting him know how I feel. "I like you too."

"Good. Now that we've got that out of the way, I guess we can officially say we're an item. Is that okay with you?"

Since we're now . . . an item, I wonder if I need to explain that I'm going to the reunion with Tim. Before I have a chance to bring it up, he glances at his watch and stands. "I better get going. I have a lunch appointment in a half hour."

I'm not sure what to do, now that our relationship has been defined. Should I give him a hug, a handshake, or just a parting comment? I assume the discomfort in the pit of my stomach is due to my lack of experience in the romance department. He backs toward the door and waves. "See ya soon, Priscilla. Don't work too hard."

Seconds after I hear the main door to the outside close behind Rick, Blair appears at my office door. "I hate to bother you, Priscilla, but my sister asked if you can come to her party at the hospital tonight."

"Her party?"

Blair nods. "It's her birthday."

How could I possibly turn down any child who has to celebrate her birthday in the cancer unit at the hospital? "I would love to."

Relief washes over Blair's face. "I was afraid . . . well, I thought you might be too busy. When I asked her what she wanted for her birthday, she said all she wanted was for you to come to her party."

My eyes sting, but I fight the tears to keep them from falling. "Blair, your sister is absolutely precious, and I'm honored she'd want me there."

"Good. She'll be happy when I tell her you're coming. The party starts right after dinner—like around six-thirty."

Blair heads back to the reception area, and I busy myself with the project I'm working on. Since I'll be out of the office all next week, I ask Mandy to bring me some lunch from the deli.

An hour later, Tim shows up at the office, a white bag in his hand, a silly grin on his lips. "Hungry?"

"Yes, Mandy—"

"She told me to bring this on back to you." He drops the bag on my desk and tips his head toward the side chair. "Mind if I sit?"

I push my work to the side, pull the bag closer, and nod. "Sure, have a seat. What are you doing in Jackson?"

"Visiting you."

I hold up half the sandwich. "I can't eat all this. Want half?"

"No thanks. I had lunch with Mandy and Blair."

"What do you think about Blair?"

"She seems like a good fit for your office." He crosses his leg and leans back in the chair. "Has she told you about her little sister?"

"Yes, in fact I've visited her, and it's heartbreaking." I nibble the edge of my sandwich and chew slowly.

"I know." Tim rubs his chin. "I'm trying to think of something to do at her party."

"You're going to her party?"

He grins. "I sort of have to. I volunteered to be the entertainment."

"That is so sweet, Tim."

"It'll be sweet if I can come up with some ideas. Got any suggestions?"

I think for a few seconds before I remember. "How about karaoke? You did that at the last reunion, remember?"

Tim groans. "I don't wanna scare the poor kids."

"How about some jokes? You've always been funny."

"Nah, I'm not sure the younger crowd will get me. I was thinkin' along the lines of magic tricks."

"If you can pull off enough magic tricks to hold their interest, it sounds like an excellent idea."

Tim leans forward. "I been doin' a little research on the Internet, and I saw some stuff that other people have done. I haven't met Haley yet, but I get along pretty well with most kids."

"That's because you're practically a kid yourself, Tim."

He laughs as he stands and straightens the front of his trousers. "Yeah, and I'll prob'ly always be that way. I reckon I better head on over to the party store and see what kinda props they have."

I finish half the sandwich and put the other half in the break-room refrigerator. After I complete my project, I make a few calls and start straightening up to leave. Blair buzzes me. "It's Rick Crenshaw on line one."

"Thanks, Blair." I clear my voice and punch the button. "Hey, Rick. How was your afternoon?"

"Perfect! And I plan to take you out to the best restaurant in town to celebrate."

Could life be any better? "When?"

"How about tonight?"

"Sorry, but I've already promised my assistant I'd visit her sister in the hospital."

"Tell her you'll go another time. This is big, and I want to share it with my best girl."

"I can't." Guilt replaces my joy as I realize I would rather be with Rick than go to the hospital. "It's her birthday."

"Oh." He actually sounds disappointed.

An idea pops into my mind. "Why don't you go with me, and we can go celebrate your news afterward?"

"I don't know, Priscilla. I'm not big on hospitals."

"We'll just be there a little while, and I don't think anyone on her floor is contagious or anything."

"If we keep it short, I suppose we can do that. Want me to pick you up at the office or your townhouse?"

"I'll go on home and change. You can pick me up there."

"See you in about an hour then."

This is turning out to be a banner day, but I still have an odd feeling about Rick. Mandy and Blair have already left, so I have to lock up as I leave. I get home, take a quick shower, and freshen my makeup before I pull on my favorite knit dress. I'm ready and waiting when the doorbell rings.

Rick greets me with a kiss on the cheek and leads me to his car. "So what's this we're celebrating?" I ask.

"I'm not telling you now. You'll have to wait until later."

I make a mocking groan as he walks straight to the driver's side of the car. I haven't dated much lately, but last time I went somewhere with Tim, he opened my door for me. Oh well, it's not really that important. I'm perfectly capable of getting into and out of a car without help from a man.

Rick pulls out of the driveway and heads south. I point my thumb over my shoulder. "Oh, the hospital is back that-a-way."

He lets out a breath of exasperation. "I was hoping you changed your mind."

"If you don't want to go—"

"I don't, but I'll do it for you." He stops at the end of the street, smiles, pulls my hand to his lips, and kisses the back of it. I expect a tingly sensation, but it doesn't happen.

"Thanks."

I give him directions to the hospital, and we're there in about fifteen minutes. As I put my hand on the door to open it, he touches my arm. "Will you be long? I mean, if this is a quick in-and-out thing, I can wait here for you."

"It might be a while. It takes a few minutes to get to her floor, and I'm sure there'll be cake and ice cream. A friend is providing entertainment, so I'd like to stick around for at least some of that."

Rick's face turns red, and I see his temples pulsing as he clenches his jaw. But he doesn't say anything as he gets out of the car and follows me.

When we get off the elevator on Haley's floor, Blair is right there waiting. She glances back and forth between Rick and me and gives me a questioning look.

I lean and glance around her. "Is Tim here yet?"

"He's in the men's room changing into his costume."

"Costume?" I smile. Tim really gets into whatever he commits to. "This should be interesting."

"Who's Tim?" Rick asks.

Mandy comes up from behind. "Tim Puckett is one of the sweetest men who ever lived. He likes to help out wherever he can."

I glance over my shoulder and see the disapproval on her face. Rick closes his eyes and shakes his head.

"Blair!" The sound of Haley's voice touches my heart. She's been through another round of chemo, and she's hoarse and weak, but she still has that sweet little smile on her face.

"Oh, for heaven's sake," Rick says. "That little girl is bald." When I try to ignore him and reach out to hug her, he grabs my arm and yanks me back. "Don't touch her!"

Blair looks like someone has thrown acid on her. Mandy takes Rick by the arm, pulls him away, and nods for me to go ahead. My heart melts at the sight of Haley's face as her eyes well with tears.

23
Tim

Nothin' I'd like better right now than to deck that guy Priscilla brung to the hospital. What was she thinkin'? He obviously don't like kids, and I'm pretty sure he thinks he's too good for any of us. Even when I say hey to him and try to shake his hand, he looks at me like he don't wanna be bothered. And he don't even shake my hand. If Priscilla is attracted to guys like him, I don't stand an ice cube's chance.

"I love the outfit, Tim." Mandy walks up and motions for Blair to join us. "You really do throw yourself into everything you do, don't you?"

"When I do somethin', I like to do it right. Nothin' half-baked for me." I used to say that different 'til Priscilla came along. It took me a while to clean up my language, but now it comes natural, and I don't hafta watch my mouth, no matter where I am.

"When you said you'd do some magic tricks, I expected a tux and top hat." Mandy leans back. "But I think the clown suit is much more fitting."

"I'll take that as a compliment. I figured if I mess up on the magic, I can do somethin' funny and the kids won't care that I don't know what I'm doin'." I turn to Blair. "When do you want me to get started?"

"The sooner the better," Priscilla's fella says. "We have dinner reservations in an hour."

I'm tempted to drag out the time to make them late, but that wouldn't be fair to my favorite girl, even though she's showin' some terrible judgment when it comes to men. I hope she sees the light before this sorry, no-good excuse for a man sweeps her completely off her feet, if he hasn't already.

One of the nurses gets everyone's attention and tells the kids to get their cake and take it to recreation room. I'm glad I'm wearin' gloves 'cause my palms is startin' to sweat. I never done magic before, and the only practice I had time for was this mornin', and it didn't go so good.

Priscilla keeps on lookin' at me like she's waitin' for approval or somethin'. Well, I got news for her—I'm not givin' it. I'm done pretendin', and even if I wasn't, I don't think I'm a good enough actor to make her think I like her date. Every time I see him put his hand on her shoulder I wanna puke.

Some of the kids come up to me and ask questions about my clown suit. I try to answer without talkin' 'cause the lady at the party store said most clowns don't talk. But that's too hard, so I stop pretendin' to be somethin' I'm not, and I do a little speakin'. I see a few shy kids hoverin' near the wall, clearly afraid of me. That's one thing the store lady was right about—a lot of folks is afraid of clowns.

One little boy points down at my oversize shoes. "Be careful you don't trip. I had some shoes that were too big for me, and I kept on falling 'til I grew into them."

I take a step and pretend to trip. When I catch myself, I hold up a finger and twirl it in a circle around my ear. He cracks up.

A little girl watches me with widened eyes, lookin' like she done seen a ghost. I take a chance and do a little jig right in front of her, hopin' to break the ice. When she smiles and claps, my heart near 'bout jumps outta my mouth. I could get used to this clown thing.

The head nurse lifts her hands over her head and claps. I imitate her, and it ain't long before everyone is clappin' their hands way up in the air. The nurse looks at me with a pretend frown and shakes her head. I can tell she's not mad on account of the twitchy thing her lips is doin'.

I point both hands to the kids and then to the cake table. The head nurse winks at me and mimics my gestures.

It takes the nurses and family members about fifteen minutes to get all the kids through the cake line and in the room where I'll be performin'. I stand by the door, waitin' for my cue. Priscilla and that man hang out at the back of the room, and I'm pretty sure she'd rather be up here with me than where she is. She keeps lookin' over at me and smilin'. My makeup is smilin' back at her.

Haley has a front row seat with her family. Blair mouths, "Do you need help?" I shake my head no. She puts her arm around her little sister, points to me, and whispers somethin' that makes the little girl laugh.

"Okay, Mr. Happy, you're on." Mandy makes a sweeping gesture toward the roomful of wigglin' kids. "Go break a leg."

With my stomach feelin' like it's done been turned inside out and my wringin'-wet gloves, I take my place at the front of the room. The second everyone sees me, they stop talkin', and a few of 'em even laugh. That gives me just enough confidence to start performin'.

Once I begin, I can tell that the kids like what I'm doin'. Now I'm on a roll. I mess up on near 'bout every single magic trick, but I do somethin' silly, and they laugh. By the time I'm done, the birthday girl has happy tears streamin' down her smilin' face. Everyone stands up and claps, makin' me feel all gooey inside . . . until I notice Priscilla and that man slip out the back of the room.

We already sang "Happy Birthday" to Haley, but I don't know what else to do but sing it again. No one seems to mind, and I'm pretty sure they don't know it's my ploy to get the attention off me.

A nurse comes up and tells the kids it's time to get ready for bed. Once all of 'em are out of the room, Mandy, Blair, and Blair's mama come up and heap me with praise. I thank them and try to act grateful, but my mind is still on Priscilla and what she thinks. It's hard watchin' the love of my life leavin' the party with another man.

24
Priscilla

Glad that's over." Rick puts the car into gear and pulls out of the hospital parking lot. "I'm just glad we got out of there in time to make our reservation."

"I thought it was really nice. Those kids need something to make them smile."

Rick snickers. "Oh, trust me, those kids have plenty to smile about. I'm sure they have all kinds of folks visiting and giving them things. That's what bleeding hearts do."

I look at him with a wary eye. "So you're saying you don't care about them?"

"Of course I'm not saying that. It's not that I don't care about them. It's more like I don't give them a second thought." He reaches for my hand and squeezes it. "Now let's stop talking about depressing things and concentrate on what really matters."

"What really matters to you, Rick?"

He stops at a light and gives me a secretive grin. "I'll tell you all about it over dinner. For now, I'll just say that I had a very good day."

I wonder how Blair's little sister's day was. For that matter, how was Blair's day, worrying about Haley, wondering if there's any way she can bring some sort of joy and happiness to the little girl on her birthday.

"Tim was sweet to go to so much trouble for those children."

Rick snorts. "He obviously doesn't have a life of his own. How do you know that loser anyway?"

Anger bursts through, and I can't control myself. "Are you always this boorish?"

"Boorish?" He grimaces. "Isn't that a rather harsh word?"

"Not as harsh as the way you're acting. Do you realize what is going on back at that hospital? We're talking life and death here—not some business conquest that'll pad your bank account." The shrillness of my own voice surprises me, but I don't stop. "Those medical people dedicate their entire lives to helping those children get well. Blair and her family center their lives on Haley because they don't want to let her down when she needs them. Tim has the decency to do something I just happen to know makes him very uncomfortable because he cares about others, which is more than I can say for you."

He flinches. "Ouch."

The chemistry I felt for Rick when we first met has turned into disdain, and I don't think there's anything I can do to change it. "Please take me home."

"You're kidding, right?"

"Nope." I fold my arms and dig my heels into the floorboard. Not only has the chemistry fizzled, anger is making me want to say something that would've gotten my mouth washed out with soap when I was a kid.

"Don't you want to hear about my fabulous day?" He puts his hand on my knee.

"Please remove your hand, Rick. You're in my space."

He lifts his hand as though he'd touched a lit match. "Okay, okay. I'll take you home. But don't expect me to come around anymore." He clears his throat. "It's your loss."

"Then I'll just have to suffer." How could I have been so easily fooled? You'd think I would've learned after Maurice.

He pulls up in front of my townhouse and sits there drumming his fingertips on the steering wheel. "We're here. Now get out."

No one has ever spoken to me like this—not even Maurice, who until now I've considered the rudest, most inconsiderate man on earth. "Oh, by the way, your equipment line is nothing but a bunch of recycled junk. I looked at something similar a couple years ago when Tim asked me what I thought about it."

He doesn't even bother looking me in the eye as I get out and slam the door. Before I even hit the front step, I hear tires squeal as he takes off. As I walk inside my townhouse, I feel like the stupidest woman on earth. How could I have missed all the signs of an arrogant, egotistical cad? It's not like he ever bothered acting humble. Then I think about the last words I said to him, and I cringe. Losing control is something I've never allowed myself to do.

For the next hour or so, I firmly lecture myself about caring for the wrong men and letting them get to me. Just like Maurice, Rick isn't worth an ounce of my energy. The very thought of his attitude toward the children who are in the hospital fighting for their lives gets my blood boiling, even though I keep telling myself to stop thinking about him.

I kick off my high heels and yank off the dress I'd carefully chosen for my celebratory date with Rick. As I pull on my comfy pajama bottoms and T-shirt, I think about the differences between Rick and Tim. What a sweet, gentle soul Tim is. I can't even compare him to Rick or Maurice, the guy I wasted my high-school crush on until I found out all he wanted was for me to finance his failing family business.

Too bad my business sense doesn't cross over to my personal life. All my life, I've heard about the tingly feeling girls get when Mr. Right comes along, and that's what I want. The problem with that is my tingly feeling so far has signified that I'm crushing on Mr. Wrong.

Fortunately, I'll be away from the office for a week, busy getting ready for my twentieth high school reunion. Based on past experience, I know I'll be busy doing hair and won't have a spare moment to think about personal matters, which is a good thing for me at the moment. However, there's still the matter of facing Mandy and Blair tomorrow at the office. The combination of Rick's behavior and the fact that they know he and I were supposed to go out for dinner after Haley's birthday party make me want to go into hiding and not face the questions I'm sure they'll have. But I can't do that. This is something I need to deal with immediately or risk losing respect from the very people I depend on.

I'm so restless I can't sleep. At the first hint of daybreak, I crawl out of bed, get ready for work, and grab a cup of coffee to go. For the first time in years, no one is at the office when I arrive.

Mandy comes in an hour later, flipping on lights, making all kinds of noise. "Priscilla? Are you in your office?" Her voice echoes down the hall.

"Yes, come on back."

The hallway is carpeted, but I can hear the whooshing sound as she approaches my doorway. "So how was your date?"

"It wasn't."

She widens her eyes and lifts a finger. "Hold that thought. I'll go get some coffee and be right back."

I formulate a short speech about how Rick and I are too different to make a relationship work. Maybe if I keep it brief, I'll be able to transition to a more comfortable topic, like work.

She arrives ten minutes later, cup of coffee in one hand and a picture in the other. "I brought you something." She drops the picture on my desk. "We took a picture of Tim and some of the kids, and I printed it out on my computer before I left this morning."

As I study the picture, I see joy on the faces of the children and Tim—even behind the makeup. It may be easy to fool adults, but from my experience, children are able to see through our facades. He sincerely cares about other people, and those kids know he was there for the right reasons.

"I sent you more pictures in an e-mail, but I thought this one would be good to frame for the office." Mandy sighs. "Too bad you don't have feelings for him because he sure does love you. When he talked about you on our dates, I knew I didn't stand a chance."

"I'm sorry." And I am in many ways.

"Don't be sorry. I have a great guy in my life now." Mandy takes a sip of her coffee while watching me look at the picture. "Okay, so tell me about your date-that-wasn't with Rick."

I lick my lips as I think about how trite my rehearsed response is. This isn't the time to rely on a rehearsed speech. "It ended right after we left the hospital."

"That bad, huh?"

I nod. "Afraid so."

"I was worried something like that might happen after I watched his reaction to the kids. He doesn't seem to have much compassion."

"Rick and I are so different—"

"Yeah, yeah, yeah. I get that you don't wanna say anything bad about him. You're that kind of person. But one thing you might wanna think about is finding someone to vent to. Bottling up all that emotion and anger can't be good for you."

"Anger? I'm not angry."

She stands and smiles at me over her coffee mug. "Sure you're not. So are you gonna buy that energy-saving product line Rick was trying to sell ya?"

I shake my head. "No, I think what we have is working out just fine."

Still smiling, she takes a step toward the door. "Whatcha got on your agenda for today?"

"As soon as I finish up here, I'm heading out. I figured it might be good to drive on over to Piney Point and get situated at Mother's house before I go to the Cut 'n Curl and Spa."

"Oh, that reminds me. I got some bids on your proposed day spa in Savannah. Looks like a lot of construction people need the work, so you should be able to get a decent deal."

"Why don't you go through them and select the top three for me to look at after I get back?"

She gives me a mock salute. "Yes, ma'am."

Mandy has come a long way since she's been here, and I can't imagine not having her in the office. I make a note on my cell phone to have something sent to show my appreciation. And while I'm at it, I'll get something for Blair and her sister.

It takes me a couple of hours to finish my work. I hug both Mandy and Blair on my way out the door. "Don't forget to have fun," Mandy whispers. She knows me too well.

Since I travel so much, I have a second set of toiletries already in my suitcase. All I have to do is pack enough clothes for the week. At least while I'm at Mother's I can do laundry.

I start out listening to the news on the radio, but when the newscasters start repeating what I already know, I plug in my iPod. The trip is always quicker when I don't get lost in my own thoughts.

Mother doesn't expect me until tomorrow, but I don't think she'll mind my coming early. In fact, she might even be happy to see me, now that she lives alone. Last time we chatted on the phone, I sensed a hint of loneliness.

When I pull onto the street where I grew up, I see a strange car parked in Mother's driveway. It probably belongs to one of her Classy Lassie Red Hat friends.

Using the key I've never removed from my key ring, I let myself into the house that's mostly dark, with the exception of the light from the kitchen that shines into the hallway and the flickering TV in the family room. Naturally, I assume Mother forgot to turn off the TV and is sitting in the kitchen chatting with whomever the car belongs to, so I reach over and flip the switch to the overhead light. And that's when I get the surprise of my life.

No. It can't be. The instant I see Mother all snuggled up on the sofa with a man . . . it gets even worse . . . . It's Mr. Barrymore, the retired principal from Piney Point High School. I just want to crawl into a hole and . . .

"What are you doing here tonight?" Mother stands up and straightens her blouse. "I didn't expect you until tomorrow."

25
Laura

You better tell Mama, or I will!" The sound of Bonnie Sue's screeching voice sends me flyin' up the stairs to see what's goin' on.

"If you do," Renee shouts back, "I'll tell her about the time you and all your little cheerleader friends skipped school and hung out with those frat boys in Hattiesburg."

Pete and I have had the toughest time keepin' Bonnie Sue from growin' up too fast, and there's no tellin' what kinda lies them college boys will tell to get what they want. I reach the top of the stairs, ready to light into Bonnie Sue, but I see Renee comin' outta the bathroom, her face streaked with tears. And they don't look like fresh tears either.

"What is goin' on up here?" I've managed to soften my voice, but I still plan to let Bonnie Sue know she's grounded for the summer.

Bonnie Sue pops her head out of her bedroom and smirks at her sister. "You gonna tell her, or do I have to?"

"You—"

Renee starts to call her sister a name, but I stop her. "There'll be no name-callin' here, young lady. One of y'all needs to start talkin', and I'm not waitin' all day." I prop my fist on my hip for extra emphasis.

Bonnie Sue snickers. "If you don't say it, I will."

"Okay, okay." Renee turns to me, chin quiverin', and blurts, "Mama, I'm pregnant."

My life has just gone from bein' slightly messy—okay, a total mess—to bein' a disaster. "What? How?"

Bonnie Sue laughs. "You should know, Mama. You had four young'uns."

I point my finger toward her room. "Get back in your room right now, Missy. I'll deal with you later." Skipping school doesn't sound quite as bad at the moment, but I can't tell her that. "And be prepared for a summer of hard work . . . around the house."

Bonnie Sue narrows her eyes at her sister and mouths something I can't quite decipher, but I suspect it involves pain later. When I glare at her, she bobs her head, pops back into her room, and slams the door behind her, leaving Renee and me facing each other.

"Mama, I didn't mean for it to happen." She lifts her hands to her face, and her whole entire body starts shakin'.

It breaks my heart to see my second-born in such sad shape, so I close the distance between us and wrap my arms around her. "I know you didn't mean for it to happen, but you did somethin' you knew you weren't s'posed to do, and that's what happens."

"Am I grounded too?" She separates two of her fingers and looks at me with one eye.

I slowly shake my head. "I could ground you, but I think you'll be payin' for this much longer than anything I can do to punish you. Have you been to the doctor?"

"No."

"How do you know you're . . . pregnant?" The word sticks in my throat, but I try not to let my child know how afraid I am.

"Home pregnancy test." She points to the package in the bathroom trashcan. "I was gonna wrap it in toilet paper, but Bonnie Sue walked in before I had a chance to."

"So when were you plannin' on tellin' us?"

Her chin quivers. "I don't know."

There are a lot of things I don't know, but one thing I do is that we can't pretend this isn't happenin'. "Do you wanna tell your daddy, or do you want me to?"

"Do we hafta tell him?"

Renee sure is actin' stupid for a girl who used to be so smart. "Do you think he won't notice when your belly starts growin'?"

"I don't know. He don't notice a lot of things."

She has a point, but I'm not gonna make this easy for her. "I think you should tell him, Renee."

Bonnie Sue opens her door a crack. "I'll tell him if you can't."

"Get back in your room, Bonnie Sue." After she closes her door, I turn back to Renee. "You better tell him before he finds out from someone else. Does Wilson know?"

"He's the one who got the home pregnancy test for me."

"Have you talked to him since you got the results?"

"Not yet." She sniffles and leans toward me, putting her arms around my neck. "Mama, I'm so scared."

"I know you are, honey, and you have every reason to be. Your daddy is gonna be furious."

"That's not what I'm scared of. What am I gonna do with a baby? I don't even like to babysit."

"It's different when the baby is your own." I can't believe I'm sayin' this, but I continue. "When that precious little package makes its appearance, you'll feel more love in your heart than you ever imagined possible."

"Mama!" Bonnie Sue's voice rings out from behind her closed door. "Can I come out now?"

I let out a deep sigh. "Okay, but you better behave. I'll deal with you later."

She comes waltzing outta her room lookin' like a diva. "Hey, Mama, you're gonna be a granny."

Now I'm ready to toss my cookies, but I swallow the lump that's still growin' in my throat and shake my head. "Bonnie Sue, if you keep this up, you'll stay grounded 'til you're outta high school, and that means no junior-senior prom for you."

Bonnie Sue scowls at Renee. "Looky what you gone and done. You're ruinin' everything for me."

"I wasn't even thinkin' about you, Bonnie Sue."

That's an understatement. "Girls, why don't the two of you talk quietly while I go figure out what to do next?"

I'm halfway down the stairs, when Renee hollers, "Mama, you're not gonna tell Daddy today, are you?"

"No, honey. Remember, I said you are."

"Can't we wait?" Her voice is much closer, so I stop and turn around to see her standin' at the top of the stairs, lookin' like the little girl I remember from back when she was still innocent.

Before I have a chance to answer, I hear Bonnie Sue snorting. "It's gonna be real obvious soon, you moron."

"There'll be no name-calling. I'll send your daddy up here when he gets home." They disappear, and I continue on downstairs.

When I get to the kitchen, Little Jack is sittin' at the table with a heapin' bowl of ice cream in front of him. "Don't eat too much, or you'll ruin your supper." That's not exactly true anymore, what with him growin' like a weed these days, but I been sayin' that since he was a toddler, and I'm not about to stop now.

"When can I get my permit?" He stabs the ice cream with his spoon and lifts a blob about twice the size of his mouth. "I can't wait to start drivin'."

I give him what I hope passes as a mama-worthy glance. "You're gonna have to wait. You're still not old enough."

"Daddy says I hafta know this book inside and out to take the test." He taps the drivers' test book in front of him. "Even if I start now, I'll never learn all this."

Sometimes I wonder how Jack made it this far in life. "You do realize there's a test involved, right?"

"Yeah, but it's just stupid stuff like 'What do you do at a stop sign?' I already know what to do."

"Jack, you know there's more to it than that."

He looks at me with wide eyes as he shoves a humongous bite of ice cream into his mouth and swallows, followed by a grimace. "Brain freeze."

My family may be dysfunctional, but I love every single person—even when I wonder if aliens might have taken over their brains. "Slow down."

"I really wanna drive." He keeps shoveling ice cream into his face until he gets another brain freeze. You'd think he might slow down to keep the same thing from happenin' again and again, which is the very reason both Pete and I are worried about him drivin' a car. No matter what he's doin', Jack doesn't seem to learn from mistakes. Our other young'uns learned early on that if somethin' hurt they needed to quit doin' whatever it was that caused the pain. I know we're not supposed to compare the kids to each other, but I can't help it.

Jack opens the book, takes a brief glance at it, and makes a face worse than when he had brain freeze. "This is stupid stuff. I'll never need to know all that."

"Maybe not, but it's better to learn it and not need it than to need it and not know it." Oh man, I'm startin' to sound like my mama.

Jack's chin falls slack. "Huh?"

"Never mind, sweetie." I figure when he's old enough to get his permit he'll do whatever it takes. He always does, and I have to admit I'm often surprised by the results.

"When's Daddy gettin' home?"

My husband walks in the door every evenin' around five o'clock, just like clockwork. "Same time as always."

"I'm starvin'."

I glance at Jack's empty ice cream bowl and shake my head. "I better put somethin' in the oven then, so we can eat when your daddy gets home."

Jack gets up, grabs the drivers' test study book, and leaves me alone in the kitchen. His bowl still sits on the table. I mumble as I carry it over to the sink and run some water in it. No matter how many times I remind him to clean up after himself, he still acts like he's got a maid. Pete says it's my fault for pickin' up after him, but I keep tellin' him that if I don't, our house will be condemned by the health department. That always gets a laugh from Pete, and then I wanna throw somethin' at him, but I don't 'cause I'd have to pick up the broken pieces, and I already have too much to do as it is.

I work hard on preparing a healthy meal that the family will eat, but it's challenging to cook without so much cheese. Especially the vegetables. My young'uns grew up eatin' all their veggies smothered in cheese, and now they act like I'm tryin' to poison them or somethin'.

Pete comes up and puts his arms around me as soon as he gets home. "What's for supper?" he whispers in my ear before he kisses my cheek.

"Baked chicken, seasoned brown rice, and a vegetable medley."

He leans back, crinkles his nose, and shakes his head. "I miss the old food. Can't you cook somethin' good once in a while?"

I don't see a problem with an occasional cheesy casserole, so I nod. "Maybe tomorrow night." Should I have him talk to Renee now or wait 'til after supper? Bonnie Sue interrupts my thoughts as she practically bounces into the kitchen.

"Hey, Daddy, you need to go upstairs and talk to Renee. Now."

When I see the look of exhaustion on Pete's face, I shake my head. "He just got home, Bonnie Sue. Give him some time to unwind."

She makes a smart-aleck face. "He might wanna start drinkin' again."

"Wha—?" Pete casts a puzzled glance in my direction.

Now that Bonnie Sue has already said too much, I nod toward the door. "Pete, why don't you go have a chat with your daughter? It'll be a few minutes before I have supper on the table."

Pete looks back and forth between Bonnie Sue and me before he leaves the kitchen. I wanna strangle Bonnie Sue.

"I bet Daddy hits the roof when he finds out."

I lift the lid on the pot of brown rice and put it back. I'm gettin' better with the healthy seasonings, and I've noticed the family is leavin' less on their plates.

"Are you givin' me the silent treatment?" Bonnie Sue asks.

I turn around, fold my arms, and try to bob my head like she does, but I still haven't mastered it. "Now why would I go and do that?"

Pete's been upstairs for near 'bout five minutes, and I still haven't heard a peep from him or Renee. That worries me.

Bonnie Sue's sittin' at the kitchen table, flippin' the pages of a fashion magazine she talked Pete into subscribing to for her.

I wipe my hands on the dishrag. "Keep an eye on supper, Bonnie Sue. I'll be right back." When she doesn't even bother to look up, I tap on the table until I get her attention. "If you smell somethin' burnin', turn off the stove."

I'm about halfway up the stairs when I hear whimperin'. "Daddy, I didn't mean for this to happen."

"I know you didn't, sweetie, but the good Lord sometimes makes things happen, even when we don't want them to. Where is Wilson?"

That's exactly what I want to know. I get to the closed door of Renee's bedroom and stop, plasterin' my ear to the door, but I still can't make out what she's sayin'.

26
Priscilla

I've been at Mother's for two days, and she's still annoyed that I interrupted her date with Mr. Barrymore. He didn't stay long after I arrived, but he's been back for a visit. Seeing him touching Mother gives me the creeps. I know it's not deemed inappropriate now, but it still seems so wrong to me.

Apparently Mother hasn't been comfortable letting people know about her new boyfriend because when I mention it at work, Sheila looks surprised. "I had no idea." If anyone in town knows something, Sheila does. "You can't really blame her, though. Mr. Barrymore is an attractive . . . older man."

I shudder. Who would ever look at a high school principal and think *attractive*? Certainly not me. The way he tries so hard to gain my approval only makes things worse. I don't need flowers from a man I don't want my mother dating. And to think I used to see him as a man of authority who deserves respect.

Fortunately, I don't have any appointments until tomorrow, so I can check on Laura and see if she needs anything. Tim says he'll be in Piney Point as soon as he can get away from the office. Apparently, his uncle plans to take a break from fishing to mind the office while Tim's gone.

A split second after I step up on the Moss's front porch, the door flies open, and their youngest child, Jack, runs out. Pete is right on his heels.

"Hey, Pete. Is Laura home?"

"Yeah, go ahead and let yourself in. Me and Jack's goin' for a drive, and I hafta get back to work before lunch, so I gotta run."

"Okay." I stand there and watch Pete back out of the driveway in Laura's car. Instead of letting myself in unannounced, I knock on the door, open it a few inches, and call out. "Anyone home?"

"Yeah, I'm in the kitchen. Come on back."

When I walk in, something seems strange about the place. It's a little too orderly and quiet to be the Moss's house—especially for a summer day.

Laura is sitting at the kitchen table, staring at a page in a fashion magazine. Something is definitely not right here.

"Hey, Priscilla. How ya been?"

"Um . . . " I glance around at the sparkling countertops. "Just fine. How about you?"

"Couldn't be better." She fakes a smile. Ah, now I can relax. It's all a show.

"So tell me what I can do to help with the reunion."

She tilts her head to one side. "Aren't you s'posed to be doin' people's hair this week? Last I heard, folks was gettin' on a waitin' list, hopin' you'd have some cancellations."

"Not today. I start tomorrow. I told Sheila I was working on reunion stuff."

"There's nothin' to do. We got all the place cards made, and we're havin' it catered." She closes the magazine and leans back. "Want some coffee?"

"That would be good."

She points to the coffeepot on the counter. "Then help yourself. The mugs are in the cupboard above the coffeepot."

I pour myself some coffee and carry it over to the table. "Mind if I sit here?"

"Of course, I don't mind."

Once I sit down, I look at her, and she smiles but doesn't say anything. "So how are the kids?"

She scrunches up her forehead. "Why? Have you heard somethin'?"

Ooh, touchy subject. "No. I just wondered how they're doing. Didn't your oldest son go into the military?"

"Yeah, Bubba's in the Army. He just left for boot camp."

"So how does he like it?"

Laura shrugs. "We haven't heard from him yet."

"How about your girls?"

Her expression tenses up even more, so I know I've hit on a sensitive topic. "Bonnie Sue is . . . well, she's Bonnie Sue. She hasn't changed much."

"Does she still want to be a hairdresser?"

"Are y'all talkin' about me?"

I look up and see Bonnie Sue coming toward us, so I stand and reach for a hug. She practically throws herself into my arms. "It's good to see you, Bonnie Sue."

"I can't believe you're actually here in my kitchen." The look of adoration on her face embarrasses me. "I'm callin' my friends."

Laura points to an empty chair. "Sit down, Bonnie Sue. She's here to help with the reunion."

"Have you told her about Renee?"

"What's going on with Renee?" I ask.

You'd think I hurt one of Laura's kids by the way she turns on me. "What's going on with Renee is none of your business, Priscilla."

I'm about to apologize when Bonnie Sue laughs. "Mama, it's not a secret no more. Wilson's been braggin' all over town that he knocked her up."

"You done said too much, Bonnie Sue. Go to your room."

Bonnie Sue gets up and grumbles all the way to the door. "It's not like the whole world doesn't already know."

Once we're alone, I turn to face Laura who won't look me in the eye. I'd give her a hug if I thought she'd let me. "Laura, I'm sorry if I came at a bad time. Would you like me to leave?"

She turns and faces me head-on, and I see her eyes mist over before a tear trickles down her cheek. "No, you might as well stick around, now that the cat's outta the bag. And you might as well know my life hasn't exactly been a picnic lately."

Laura's life has never been a picnic, but she's managed extremely well . . . at least, much better than I would under the circumstances. "There are worse things than your daughter being pregnant," I say, instantly wishing I'd kept my mouth shut. "I'm sorry. That was insensitive of me."

"No, you're right."

"How's Pete taking it?"

Laura shrugs. "Much better than I am. I think he's happy that Wilson doesn't want anything to do with Renee." She lifts her arms and lets them fall back to the table in obvious frustration. "'Cept to brag about what he did to my daughter."

"If you want to talk about anything, I'm a good listener." That's something that I had to learn as a hairdresser.

"How 'bout you talk to Renee?" A flash of hope flickers in Laura's eyes. "Maybe you can work some magic, like you did with Bonnie Sue."

I wouldn't exactly call what I did with Bonnie Sue magic. After she shoplifted a skirt, I brought her back to the store to talk to the manager. Chatting with a pregnant teenager is different. But I can't turn Laura down at a time like this.

"I'll be happy to. Just let me know when." Maybe she'll forget.

"How about now? She's up in her room. We can't get her to come out . . . not even to eat."

I swallow hard. "Okay. Which room is hers?"

"The one with the sign on the door that says *Keep Out*." She gestures toward the door. "Why don't you go on up?"

I pause for a moment, take a breath, nod, and forge ahead. One of the few things in life that intimidates me is a child—even teenagers—unless they're sitting in my salon chair, and even then I'm somewhat nervous. It's so hard to know what they're really thinking or if something I say might mess them up for life.

When I get to the top of the stairs, I clear my throat loud enough for anyone on the second floor to hear me. It takes me the better part of three seconds to find Renee's door. I knock on the door.

"Go away."

"Renee, it's me, Priscilla Slater. Can we please talk?"

"What are you doin' here?"

Um . . . I have no idea what I'm doing, but I don't want to tell her that. "I just want to chat with you for a few minutes."

Silence in situations like this makes me nervous, but fortunately, I don't have to wait long before she opens the door. "Did my mama tell you to come talk to me?"

"Yes." I'm not about to lie to a teenager who, as I remember from personal experience, will be able to see right through me at the first hint of an untruth. "I promise I won't stay long, unless you ask me to."

She flings the door open but wastes no time in running across her room and flinging herself over her twin bed. I stand in the doorway, not knowing what to do at first. When she doesn't bother to look up at me, I close the door and walk toward her bed.

After another few seconds of silence, she props her head on her hand and starts talking. "He told me he loved me, and I believed him. Now look at what a mess I'm in. My life is ruined."

"I don't think your life is ruined, Renee. You have a family that loves you. They'll be here for you no matter what."

"But I can't hang around here forever. I'm gonna be a mama. I hafta go find a job and an apartment, and . . . " She sniffles and casts a quick glance in my direction before flopping over on her back to stare up at the ceiling. "There's so much I hafta do, I don't know where to start."

"Why don't you make a list? You might find that it makes things less daunting." I watch her for a while before adding, "That's not all you're worried about is it?"

She shakes her head. "I don't know how to have a baby. It scares me half to death."

I totally understand what she's saying. I'd be afraid too, as I'm sure most women are. "You're not alone, Renee."

"Do you think Wilson will ever love me again?"

"I suspect Wilson never stopped loving you. He's probably just as scared as you are."

"Then why did he take off as soon as I told him I was pregnant?"

"Because he can." I lower myself to a sitting position on the edge of her bed. "But for obvious reasons, you can't. If he chooses not to come back, it's his loss." I know this deep down, but I'm not sure Renee believes me.

She sits up and looks at me with more hope in her eyes than I feel. "Do you really think he might?"

"There's no way for me to know since I've never met Wilson, but one thing I do know is that you have your whole life ahead of you. It's up to you to come to terms with your situation and make the most of what God has given you."

"You sound like Daddy."

"I do?" I can't imagine Pete saying those words. He must have changed more than I realized.

"I thought he'd kill me and then go after Wilson, but he took it better than Mama did. She says I'm too immature to have a baby."

"The best thing you can do right now, Renee, is to prove her wrong. Show her how grown up you've become."

Renee lifts the corner of her sheet and dries her tears. "I'll try."

I open my arms toward her. "Hug?"

She flings herself into my arms, nearly knocking me over. Once I'm past the shock, I discover I actually like being hugged by this woman-child. "If you ever feel like talking, give me a call." I reach into my handbag, pull out a card, and jot down my personal cell-phone number. "I almost always have my phone with me, except when I'm on air."

She smiles as she studies the card. "This is so cool. I have my very own personal TV star to talk to."

The Moss girls are way too easily impressed by fame. "Just remember you have to work hard for whatever you really want, and if that's what the Lord wants for you, you can have it."

After I leave, I go to Mother's house. It's the middle of the day, so I'm surprised to see her sitting in the kitchen.

"I thought you were teaching this summer."

"My first class isn't for another two hours."

I open the fridge and pull out some ham and cheese. "Want me to make you a sandwich?"

"No, I just had breakfast."

The conversation between us has always been somewhat stilted, but it's worse than ever now. I finish making my sandwich, cut it in half, and carry it over to the table. Before I have a chance to say a word, she starts in on me.

"If you don't like my choices, why don't you just go stay with your father?" Mother's chin juts in a defiant expression.

Mother is well aware that Dad has a one-bedroom apartment, so my staying there is not an option. Besides, ever since their divorce, I've seen things differently. I once blamed the tension on Mother, but now I realize how unsupportive Dad was and know he was at least half of the problem. "I don't want to cramp your style, so I'll probably not be around much." I hear how childish I sound, but when it comes to my mother's love life, I can't help it. She's always brought out the worst in me, and that's obviously not going to change any time soon.

27
Celeste

You wanna ride in the backseat, sweetie? It'll be a lot easier if you wanna lie down." Jimmy looks at me with concern. Ever since I told him I'm pregnant, you'd think I was fragile.

"Honey, you know I get carsick in the backseat."

"I got you some gingersnaps and ginger ale like that lady at the doctor's office told me to do. Maybe that'll make you feel better."

"I feel just fine . . . right now. Let's just get goin', and maybe I won't get sick."

Jimmy points to a small trashcan lined with a grocery store bag. "We'll bring that just in case." My husband would make someone a fine mama.

All the way to Piney Point, Jimmy hounds me with questions. "How you feelin'?" "There's a convenience store. Want me to stop?" "Need help putting your seat back so you can close your eyes?"

I appreciate all his concern, but what I really want is a normal conversation about anything but my pregnancy. It used to bug me that all we used to talk about was his company, but right now I'd give anything to hear how one of his clients had to increase surveillance on one of their employees.

"Have you been thinkin' about names?" Jimmy casts a brief glance in my direction before turning his attention back to the road.

"It's too early." I sigh. "We'll need to wait 'til they can tell if it's a girl or boy."

"We can make two lists—one with girl names and one with boy names. That way we're prepared."

"Why don't you do that?" He obviously won't let up on this subject, so I figure why bother fighting it. At least this is somethin' that'll keep him busy.

He nods. "Okay, and I'll start now. I been thinkin' we might wanna use family names. My great-uncle Harvey sure would be happy to have a young'un named after him."

"Harvey?" I shudder, and then I remember he has another uncle named Gaylord. "Maybe."

"You don't like the name Harvey?"

"It's a great name for your uncle, but I'm not so sure about namin' our baby that."

"We could name him Jimmy Junior and call him J. J." He turns to me and winks. "Or Bubba."

"That's Laura and Pete's oldest boy's name."

"You can have more than one Bubba."

"Yeah . . . um . . . I don't think so."

He gets a thoughtful look on his face. "Okay, I'll work some more on the boy name list. Now for the girls. Do you like Juanita? That was my grandma's name."

"It's okay."

"I like it 'cept it's hard to come up with a middle name to go with it."

I change position and settle in for a long ride filled with names flying at me, one after another. And I'm not disappointed. One thing I'm just now realizin' about my husband is how creative he can be.

"We can blend our names and call the kid Jimmeste or Celjim."

I give him one of the wifely looks I've mastered and shake my head. "I don't think so."

He laughs. "At least I'm tryin' to come up with somethin' good." Silence falls between us for all of thirty seconds before his face lights up. "Hey, I know. How about Apple or Cocoa?"

"Nah, them kinda names only work in Hollywood."

"I reckon you're right."

Time to change the subject. "Who all do you think will come to the reunion?"

"Pete said near 'bout everyone will be there. I'm glad 'cause last time we didn't have all that great a turnout."

"I'm curious about how everyone looks. The only one I seen lately is Priscilla, and that's just 'cause she's on TV all the time." I have mixed feelings about Priscilla. I hate the fact that she hasn't changed much, but I will always have a special place in my heart for the woman who showed me how to look beautiful.

"Do you think she'll bring that boy with her? What's his name?"

"Tim." Laura didn't mention him when I last spoke to her. "I don't know, but I hope so. He's a worker, that one."

"Too bad Priscilla can't find it in her heart to love him 'cause he sure is crazy about her . . . at least he was."

"I don't know if Priscilla can find it in her heart to love anyone but herself."

"Celeste! That ain't a very nice thing for you to say."

"I know." And I do know it's bad to say such stuff, but I can't help how I feel. "It's just that when all a woman thinks about is makin' a name for herself at the expense of everything else in life, it seems selfish."

"Or maybe she's not ready to settle down."

"Let's talk about somethin' else, Jimmy." Blabberin' about Priscilla annoys me so bad I wanna spit.

"She did do you a favor by showin' you how beautiful you can be."

I tilt my head toward him, lower my sunglasses so he catches the full effect, and give him one of them looks only a wife can do. "Did you hear me?"

He pulls his chin back. "Loud and clear."

"What do you think about the name Marybeth?"

"I dunno. It's okay I guess." He laughs.

Who knew pickin' a name would be so hard? Maybe a boy's name will be easier. "I like Matthew for a boy."

Jimmy shakes his head. "There's already too many of them."

"That's because it's a nice name."

"I still think we should consider namin' him after me. We can name him Jimmy and call him Bubba." He cuts a glance my way and grins. "Or Bubba-Jim."

I groan. "Let's both think on this and talk about it later."

"You were the one who brung it up," Jimmy reminds me.

"No, I don't think it was me. Regardless, I don't wanna keep spoutin' out stupid names just 'cause we ain't had time to think about it yet."

"Okay, okay. I wonder if Laura will want us to do somethin' at the reunion. You reckon she'll have a list of chores for us?"

"She never bothered to ask this time, so I won't do nothin', even if she asks me to." Laura can be mighty bossy, which is why I plan to steer clear of her until the actual party.

"That ain't right, Celeste. Laura's got her hands full with Pete and the young'uns." A frown covers Jimmy's face. "Now that Pete's sober, I won't have no one to drink with."

"You ain't had a drink in months, so why do you care?"

"Celeste," he says real slow, "that's part of the fun of reunions. Besides, it helps me loosen up to knock back a few."

"Maybe you don't need to loosen up so much."

"It wouldn't hurt for you to loosen up too. Maybe me and you can—"

"I'm pregnant, remember? Pregnant mamas ain't s'posed to drink alcohol 'cause it might hurt our baby."

"Oh." He chews on his bottom lip. "I have a picture of my mama drinkin' beer when she was pregnant with me."

"I'm not your mama."

"You can say that again." He reaches over, takes my hand, and lifts it to his lips for a kiss. "And I'm happy you're my wife. Have I told you lately how much I love you?"

I force myself to smile at Jimmy. When me and him first got together, it was more for companionship, and neither of us had people waitin' in line for dates. After a while, we got comfortable around each other, and at some point along the way it grew into love—but for the life of me, I can't pinpoint when that happened. All I know is that we might not have all the sizzle and pop some folks do, but we have a good marriage. Jimmy don't have to worry about me lookin' at some other man, and I don't think he's stupid enough to chase another woman 'cause I can be meaner'n a junkyard dog when I get all riled up.

"It'll be nice to see folks we haven't seen in years." I pull down the visor mirror and smooth my hair back. I've managed to keep up the beauty program Priscilla put me on, and my skin don't look like I've aged much since the last reunion. "I wonder if everyone will look old."

"Prob'ly." Jimmy laughs. "I seen Harold Fitzpatrick when he came down to the coast a few months ago. His hair is fallin' out."

I glance at my husband's head, but I don't mention that circular bald spot toward the back. When I told him about it last year, he said I was seein' things and that his hair is thick as ever. Whatever Jimmy can't see ain't there.

We arrive at the Olson Family Hotel on Main Street in Piney Point. It's a lot older than some of the places closer to Hattiesburg, but we done decided it'll be easier to participate in activities if we're right there in the heart of things.

"Wanna stay here while I run inside and get us a room?"

"Yeah. It shouldn't take long to get the room, since we have a reservation." Then it dawns on me. When I asked Jimmy to reserve the room, he didn't say nothin'. "You did make a reservation, right?"

"I . . . uh . . . no, I forgot."

Since I done been married five years, I know it won't do me a single solitary bit of good to fuss at Jimmy. It's too late to change things anyway. "Then I best go inside with you, since I know the Olsons better than you do."

"Tell ya what, Celeste. I'll stay in the car while you go inside."

Again, I figure it's best not to argue. I just grab my purse, get out of the car, and slam the door without botherin' to comment or even look at my husband. It might be pointless to say somethin', but I have this pent-up anger that's gotta get out.

I walk right up to the front desk and see Clyde Olson standin' there watchin' the TV on the counter. He laughs at somethin' he hears before turnin' to me. "Hey, there, Celeste. Haven't seen you in a while. What can I do for ya?"

"Hey, Clyde. Me and Jimmy need a room."

He shakes his head. "I don't know if we have anything available, with the reunion and all."

I used to babysit Clyde's brats—I mean young'uns—when him and his wife used to go out clubbin' back in the day, and

I remember them tellin' me there was always a room available for family when they came to town. "How 'bout that room on the third floor—the one at the end of the hall?"

He scrunches up his forehead and rubs his chin. "What are you talkin' about, Celeste?"

"You don't wanna mess with me right now, Clyde. I'm pregnant, Jimmy's out in the car, and I'm tired. Just give me the keys to that room, and everything will be okay."

"Hold on just a minute. Let me call my wife."

As he calls his wife, I stand there starin' at him and drummin' my fingers on the counter to make sure he don't forget how annoyed I can get. Last time—when he and his wife came home three hours after they was s'posed to—I read them the riot act and threatened to never babysit for them again. Since I was the only person who would even consider sittin' with his bratty kids, that scared them into promisin' never to do that again. And they didn't.

"Okay, Celeste. Rose said since no one else is usin' it, and you're practically family, we can let you have that room."

I smile and pull out my credit card. "I want your best rate too."

He holds up his hands. "We don't have a rate for the family room. It's on the house."

At least one thing is goin' right. "Why, thank you, Clyde. Me and Jimmy appreciate it. If you ever come down to Biloxi" —I don't know what's gotten into me. The very thought of entertainin' Clyde and Rose Olson and their brats sounds like a total nightmare—"maybe you can give us a call, and we can meet you for dinner."

"That would be real nice . . . that is, if we can ever get away."

He hands me a coupla keys, and I take off as fast as my swollen feet can carry me. Jimmy looks a little worried, until

I get in the car. "Okay, we got a room. Let's get our suitcases and get settled."

I decide not to mention the fact that our room is free. Jimmy don't need to think he done somethin' right by forgettin' to make the reservation.

28
Priscilla

On my way to the Piney Point salon, my mind swirls with activity, and right there in the center of my thoughts is Tim. I've been thinking about Tim quite a bit lately, but it makes sense with the class reunion coming up. If it weren't for him, I have a feeling the ten-year reunion would have been a total flop. But even though he made sure everything happened that was supposed to, we still had some issues . . . like Pete Moss getting drunk and crashing his truck.

The idea of thinking about Tim makes sense, but the precise thoughts are a bit disconcerting. After seeing him dressed as a clown and obviously enjoying the kids at Haley's birthday party, I can't help but compare him to other men I've felt that heart-fluttering, head-in-the-clouds chemistry with. My feelings for Tim have been positive, but I've never had that fiery-hot passion I expect in a romantic relationship. Being with him is comfortable, relaxed, and . . . well, easy. I can always be myself with him and not worry that he's looking over my shoulder for something . . . or someone better.

I arrive at Prissy's Cut 'n Curl and Ice Factory Day Spa and see a spot near the door. As I get closer, I notice that my name has been painted on the curb in front of the spot. "Reserved for Priscilla," and I smile.

There's a group of folks standing in the reception area, and they all turn to face me when I walk in. Chester is the first one to come forward with open arms. "Hey, girl. We wondered when you'd get here. How do you like what we've done?" He waves his arms around in a sweeping gesture.

The wall in front of me is covered with framed candid photos of the hairdressers and spa workers. I take a step back and look around for the full effect. Small white lights have been strategically placed to accent certain aspects of the room and décor, such as the ceiling-high wooden beam that's a replica of what used to support the ceiling and the old-fashioned elevator that took forever to get right. Knowing they went to all this trouble brings joy to my heart and a lump of pride to my throat.

"It's perfect." I sigh. "I couldn't have done better."

Chester glances over at Sheila and winks. "We kept remembering what you said about not wanting to compromise the integrity of the old ice factory."

"Y'all did a wonderful job."

Someone walks in behind me, and the crowd of employees disperses as the client steps up to the appointment desk and announces she's here for a facial. Chester enters something into the computer and leads her to the back.

"Wanna see your appointment calendar?" Sheila asks. "We tried to give you occasional breaks between clients, but it sure was difficult. It never was easy, but now that you're a TV star, everyone wants your hands on their hair."

I laugh. "I wouldn't exactly call myself a TV star."

"You do realize that near 'bout everyone in town watches every single show you're on, right?" Sheila plants a fist on her hip and chuckles as she shakes her head. "We even have a call chain to let folks know."

"Call chain?"

"Yeah, I call three people, and they call three people, and before ya know it, every household in Piney Point is made aware."

"Sort of like the church prayer chain."

Sheila nods. "Yeah, and we do that too. Most of us pray for you before you go on."

"I certainly appreciate that. Don't forget to add prayers for the production people. It gets rather crazy around the studios sometimes."

"Okay, I'll keep that in mind." She punches a few keys on the computer and motions for me to take a peek. "Looky here. You got appointments startin' in about fifteen minutes. I tried to give you a full hour lunch break, but with all the folks linin' up, I could only manage a half hour."

"That's okay." I'm actually glad I only have a half hour because I won't have as much time to think about my parents, Tim, and some of the other things that have been taking over my mind lately.

"We have a station set up for you, but if you want to swap with me, I understand."

Sheila has claimed the best position in the salon, since she's the manager. "No, I don't care where I am."

"If you change your mind, just holler. It's not a lot of trouble."

We exchange a glance, and practically a lifetime of respect flows between us. Sheila is a seasoned professional who doesn't mind working hard and learning whatever it takes to make her one of the best hairdressers in Piney Point. And I know she respects me for all I've managed to accomplish. One area where she's ahead of me is the relationship department. She's been married to the same man for decades, and I know they work hard at maintaining the spark in their relationship, which hasn't been easy, considering all they've been through. Between her long hours at the salon and his problems with lack of job security, even the best marriage would be tested.

My morning appointments are filled with as many questions about being on TV as information about hair. Every now and then, Sheila or Chester walks by and joins in the discussion. I enjoy the camaraderie that I don't normally have with my crazy-busy schedule.

It's almost lunchtime, and I'm about to finish with my last morning client's hair, when Sheila pops over to my station. "Tim's here. He wants to take you to lunch."

"Send him on back."

After Sheila goes to get Tim, my client's eyes light up. "Tim's that fella you were with in that magazine, isn't he?"

I nod. "Yes, Tim and I have been very good friends for quite a while."

"You know what they say about a man and woman being good friends, right?"

I'm tempted to ask who "they" are, but I don't want to anger her. Mother used to go ballistic when I said the vague "they."

Tim shows up with a smile. My client's chin drops. "You're even better looking in person than in your pictures."

"Pictures?" I say. "As in more than one?"

"Yes, one was in *Famous People News*, and then I saw another picture on *Entertainment Tonight*.

From behind me, I hear Sheila's voice. "Don't forget the series in the *Piney Point Herald*."

Tim and I look at each other in the mirror, and he starts laughing. "Some people go lookin' for fame and fortune, while others have it lookin' for them." He winks at me. "Looks like you fall in the second group, Priscilla."

I level him with a look filled with attitude. "Don't forget, Tim, I'm not the only person in those photos."

"Yeah, but I have to admit I'm mighty proud to be seen with you."

The look he gives me now is filled with question . . . and a hint of doubt. I swallow hard as my chest constricts. Something between us is changing, and I don't know how to act.

"Ready for lunch?" He lifts a sandwich bag. "I wasn't sure if you had something here or if you had time to get away, so I stopped off and picked up something for both of us."

"Whatcha got?" I nod toward the bag.

"Turkey sub with everything—all the veggies . . . and a bag of baked chips 'cause I know they're healthier."

"I'll have what you brought. My other lunch will still be good tomorrow."

As Tim follows me back to the break room, I sense that we're being watched. A glance over my shoulder confirms my hunch.

Without either of us having to say a word, Tim and I prepare our food. He unwraps the sandwiches and places them on paper towels, while I get drinks from the fridge—a cream soda for him and bottled water for me. I place the drinks on the table as he pours some of the baked chips beside the sandwiches. I find comfort in the familiar, and a peaceful wave flows through me.

"I been gettin' some serious attention around town this time." Tim lifts his sandwich and pauses. "That picture in the magazine sure did make the rounds."

"Does that upset you?"

He purses his lips and slowly shakes his head as he holds my gaze. "Nah, in fact, I sorta like it."

I laugh. "Not every guy would be that honest."

He wiggles his eyebrows. "Don't forget, Priscilla, I'm not every guy."

"You can say that again."

"Don't forget, Priscilla—"

I swat at him with a napkin.

He playfully holds up his arms as a shield. "Whoa there, girl. You don't have to go gettin' all violent on me. I was just doin' what you told me to."

"So far today, all my clients have seen at least one of the pictures, and they all say the same thing . . . " I grin and take a bite of my sandwich.

"What? That I'm the hottest guy in town, and they think we look like a royal couple?" I detect a hint of wishful thinking in his tone.

I swallow my food and smile. "Something like that."

Redness creeps up his neck and tinges his cheeks. He coughs. "I went by Pete and Laura's place, but no one answered the door. I think one of the kids was home 'cause I seen the blinds . . . er, I saw the blinds move."

"Don't take that personally."

"I won't. I know how they are. I just wanted to find out if Laura has my to-do list made yet."

"Did she say she was putting you to work?"

He shrugs. "She always does, and earlier she said she would, and I don't have any reason to believe anything will be different this time."

"You don't have to—"

He lifts a finger and raises his eyebrows. "I don't have to do anything, but I want to do everything I can to make the reunion a success."

"You're very sweet, Tim. I think everyone appreciates all your hard work."

"That's nice and all, but I'm doing this for one pers—"

Sheila shows up at the door, interrupting Tim. "Your first afternoon appointment is here early. I don't want to rush you. I just thought I'd let you know."

"Thanks, Sheila." I'm actually thankful she interrupted Tim because it sounded like he was about to get mushy, and I'm surprised by the way it makes me feel.

The rest of our lunchtime conversation switches to talk about less-personal topics. I'm relieved, and I think Tim might be too. Neither of us can finish our sandwiches.

"Why don't you go on out there and take care of your client?" he asks. "I'll clean up." When I look at him, he makes a shooing gesture. "Go on. You don't wanna keep folks waitin'."

"Thank you, Tim." I have to fight the tears that form at the backs of my eyes. Whatever is happening to me is foreign, and I'm so discombobulated I don't know what else to say, so I scurry out of the break room.

29
Tim

Me and Priscilla make quite a pair . . . although I'm not sure what we're a pair of. Some folks might say we act like a married couple, but others might think we need to move on. I'm somewhere in the middle . . . somewhere along the lines of confused about where we stand and wantin' to stand a whole lot closer. And from how I see Priscilla actin' lately, I'd be willin' to bet my fine leather briefcase Uncle Hugh gave me for my college graduation that she's just as confused as I am.

I head out of the salon and spa, straight for the Moss's house. If I don't catch someone home this time, I'll go back to my hotel room in Hattiesburg. I forgot to book a room in advance, so all the hotels in Piney Point were full up. But that's okay. I like Hattiesburg. It's more sophisticated and youthful, with all the college kids swarmin' around. I went to a smaller college, and that was okay at the time, but if I had it to do over again, I'd probably try to get into Southern Miss.

I pull up in front of the Moss house, park my car, get out, and head up the sidewalk. Before I get to the porch, the front door opens, and there stands Laura.

She's smilin'. That's rather shocking. "Hey, there, Tim. How's the poster boy?"

"Poster boy?"

"C'mon in, and I'll get you somethin' to drink." As we walk toward her kitchen, she keeps talkin'. "I hear girls all over the country have cut out your picture and hung it on their wall. You're gettin' to be a regular heartthrob."

"I never heard that."

"Oh, but it's true. In fact, Bonnie Sue—that's my second-youngest child—she says all her friends wanna meet you."

"I'm near 'bout old enough to be their"—I practically choke on the last word—"father."

Laura cracks up with laughter. "It happens. Even the best of us get older. Coffee, sweet tea, or Mountain Dew?"

"Tea would be good. I done had a sody pop over at the salon."

She pauses for a split-second. "I got me an appointment with Priscilla on Friday. I wanted one on Saturday, but Sheila says she's all booked solid."

"Want me to see if I can get her to switch things around for you?"

Her jaw tightens, and she shakes her head. "I'll be fine with Friday. She doesn't owe me a thing."

"But I think—"

She narrows her eyes and sticks out her chin. "I said no."

Now that's the Laura I remember. I lift my hands in surrender. "Okay, but if you change your mind, just give me the word."

"We have a bonfire planned, but I'm not so sure folks will wanna come since there won't be any alcohol."

I shrug. "I don't think that'll make much difference."

"You've obviously not been payin' much attention to where folks line up."

She has a point. "Maybe they've matured since then."

Laura leans back in her chair and lets out a deep laugh. "You're prob'ly the most mature person at any of our reunions, Tim."

"Maybe you think that 'cause you don't know me as well."

Laura's face crinkles into a genuine smile. "Sheila told me you took over your uncle's company. How's it goin' up in the Big Apple?"

"It's okay." I look Laura in the eye. "But I have to admit I miss bein' down here in the South."

"Yeah, I can imagine."

"Don't get me wrong. I'm livin' in a real nice house . . . Uncle Hugh and Aunt Tammy's lettin' me stay there rent-free and all, but . . . " I take a deep breath before I admit what's really wrong. "It's sorta lonely up there all by myself."

"You lived alone in Jackson, didn't you?"

"Yeah, but I always had folks around to do stuff with, ya know?"

Laura nods. "Yes, I know."

"But I didn't come here to talk about me. I want to pick up my to-do list. If you don't have one for me, we can make one now."

"You can start by vacuuming the living room, and after you're done there, you can mow the lawn. I'm sure Pete will appreciate that. The job went back to bein' his after Bubba left for boot camp." She chuckles. "But seriously, Tim, there's not much left to do. Now that Pete's sober, he's been a real big help with the reunion."

I know that should make me happy, and I sorta am . . . for Laura. But it also makes me wonder what I'm doin' here so early. I squirm around in my chair and try to come up with somethin' she might want me to do.

"Did you get the permit for the bonfire yet?"

Laura nods. "Pete got that a few days ago."

"Oh." I drum my fingers on the table and rack my brain for more ideas. "How about equipment? Do you have everything you need for the big party on Saturday?"

"The community center has everything, but we can prob'ly use you to help set up the tables and chairs."

I push my chair back from the table and stand up to leave. "In that case, I reckon I'll just head on over to Hattiesburg. There's a coupla new salons we're sellin' to, so maybe I can go introduce myself."

"That sounds like a good idea. I'm sure they'll enjoy meetin' you, since you're famous now." She glances at me, and I see that twinkle in her eye that lets me know she's teasin'.

I run my fingers through the top of my hair. "Maybe I should see if I can get Priscilla to freshen up my hair before I go meet these strangers . . . now that I'm so *famous*."

"Don't forget she's famous, too, and she's got all the business she can handle today." She stands up and turns to face me. "Tim, I know how annoyin' it can be for folks to give you unsolicited advice, but I got some for you."

"What's that?"

"Don't let time get away from you. If you want somethin', go after it with everything you've got. Even if you can't have it, at least you'll know you've tried your best." She smiles. "And then you can move on."

"True." I hold out my hand to let her know she can go first.

She places her hand on my arm. "Tim, if you still want to be with Priscilla, have a talk with her. I'm sorta surprised you're still single and hangin' around waitin' for her."

"I'm not exactly waitin' around and doin' nothin'."

"Are you datin' anyone?" She challenges me with one of the looks she gives her kids when she don't believe them.

"I might not be datin' anyone right now, but I have in the past. It's just that . . . well . . . "

"No one matches up to Priscilla, right?"

I nod. "Yeah, I reckon you could say that."

She opens her mouth to say somethin' when an ear-splittin' scream makes both of us near 'bout jump outta our skin. "Mama, come here! Quick! I'm bleedin' to death!"

30
Priscilla

Priscilla, Tim's on the phone, and he says it's urgent." Avery, one of the fresh-out-of-beauty-school new hires hands me the phone.

"Hey, Tim. What can I do for you?"

His voice sounds like he's been sucking helium it's so tight. And he's talking ninety miles an hour. "Slow down, Tim. I can't understand a thing you're saying."

I hear the muffled fumbling with his phone as he clears his throat and takes a very loud, deep breath. "Something terrible has happened here at the Mosses' house. Can you get away?"

As long as I've known him, Tim has never had this much of a sense of urgency, and I'm not about to let him down if he really needs me. The first image in my mind is Pete's truck wrapped around another tree. "Let me go wash the chemicals out of my client's hair, and I'll get one of the new hairdressers to finish up."

"Tim, are you on the phone with Priscilla?" Laura's voice rings in the background.

"Yeah. She's comin'."

"Tell her that's not necessary. Pete's comin' home, and we're takin' her to the emergency room."

"I called an ambulance."

Laura makes one of her growling sounds. "I told you not to do that."

"Tim," I say as crisply as I can. "What happened, and to whom?"

"Renee's bleedin' like a stuck pig. I mean there's a mess of blood all over the place." He clears his throat. "I think she might die if we don't get her to the hospital right away. Hold on . . . If you don't wanna go in an ambulance, I'll take her." I can tell he's talking to someone there.

Not knowing whether to go straight to the Moss's house or the hospital, I make a quick decision. "Why don't we hang up so you can help? Call me when you get to the hospital." I hear a siren in the background, followed by Laura yelling and her daughter screaming.

"Okay, sounds like the paramedics are here, and Laura's a basket case. She keeps talkin' about a baby. I think that woman mighta lost her mind."

"Renee's pregnant." Someone has to tell him, and obviously that little detail has slipped Laura's mind.

"She don't look—" He groans. "I gotta go. I'll call you back." He clicks off the phone before I have a chance to say another word.

By now I have a crowd gathered around me. Since I'm not sure what's happening, I don't have any information to give them. "I don't know anything yet. Avery, don't hesitate to interrupt me if Tim calls back."

She nods and takes the phone, and the crowd disperses. The only person still standing in my station is Sheila, who has her hand on her hip as she stares at the counter shaking her head. "Seems there's always somethin' happenin' with Laura and her brood."

I nod. "It does seem that way."

"Any idea what's goin' on this time?"

"Tim said something about Renee bleeding all over the place."

Sheila's eyes instantly widen. "She's the one's pregnant, right?"

I nod.

"I bet that girl's havin' a miscarriage. Poor baby. Any idea how far along she is?"

"I'm not sure, but I think it's still early in the pregnancy."

Sheila turns to leave but stops and looks at me with sadness. "Seems to me like Laura's not catchin' a break from anyone." She makes one of her clucking sounds with her tongue as she heads on back to her station, leaving me standing there, thinking about what she just said.

Sheila's right. Laura has always been a disaster magnet—mostly caused by her own actions, but that doesn't make it any less difficult. I want to do something to help her, but in this instance, I have no idea what will make her feel better and what might infuriate her. Laura Moss is difficult to gauge sometimes, and she tends to fly off the handle if she perceives my actions being anything close to dishonorable, even if I have the best of intentions.

When the timer dings, I quickly rinse the chemicals out of my client's hair and start working on the style. I'm barely finished when Avery appears at my station holding out the phone. "It's Tim."

"Thanks, Avery." I thank my client and let her know Avery will process her credit card and schedule her next appointment with another hairdresser. As soon as they leave, I lift the phone to my ear. "Hey, Tim. So what's the news?"

"Looks like Renee lost the baby. Laura's so upset no one can console her." He pauses. "Even Renee is tryin' to make her mama feel better."

"Do you think it would help for me to be there?"

Tim lets out a breath of exasperation. "No. I mean, I'd like you here, but Laura don't . . . well, she don't want no one with her but Pete."

"I understand." And I really do. If I had a tragedy, the last thing I'd want is a bunch of curious people standing around. "So what are you going to do now?"

"I don't know. I was over at the Moss's house tryin' to get my orders from Laura when this whole thing happened. Now I feel like I'm in the way."

"Tell you what, Tim. I can use your help here."

"You can?" I hear the hope lift his voice.

"Yes. Make sure Laura and Pete are okay, then come on over to the salon and spa." After we hang up, I run over to Sheila's station and pull her away.

"So how's the little Moss girl?"

"You were right. She had a miscarriage. And now we have to come up with something for Tim to do so he can feel useful."

Sheila grins and gives me a thumbs-up. "I know just the thing."

By the time Tim arrives, his face pale with fear, we have a list of things to keep Tim busy all afternoon. And it's useful stuff, like picking up lunch for all the hairdressers, taking Bonnie Sue and Jack Moss out for something to eat since their parents aren't home, and running a few errands for the salon and spa.

"After I finish up here, maybe you'll be done with the list." As I place my hand on his arm, he looks down at me with a tenderness I've never seen from any other man. My heart does a little flip, a totally new experience for me. I instantly pull my hand back, and the bond is broken. "Maybe we can go back over to the Moss's house and see how they're doing."

Tim continues looking at me as he nods and licks his lips. "I'll be back with lunch."

He's barely gone when Sheila pops up again. "That boy is still so in love with you he don't know what to do with himself."

Once again, I feel an unfamiliar tug in my chest. "Tim is truly one of the nicest people on earth."

"Yeah, he don't have a selfish bone in his body. What a great catch for the right woman." She narrows her eyes and gives me a long glance. "And I think that woman prob'ly knows it too, but she's got so many irons in the fire she wouldn't know love if it bit her in the . . . well, you know." She tilts her head to the side and gives me a goofy grin. "Get the drift?"

"Loud and clear."

That conversation plays in my head for the rest of the day. As I finish up with my final appointment, Tim appears. "I thought we'd go check on the Moss kids together. When I stopped by the hospital, Pete and Laura said they wanted to stick around with Renee until she can go back home, which'll prob'ly be mornin'. They wanna keep her overnight for observation since she bled so bad."

"Sounds good." I say good-bye to the people in the lobby and take off with Tim.

We're barely out the door when I hear Chester talking to one of the new hairdressers. "She might be famous now, but she's still one of us." That makes me smile. I glance over at Tim who winks but doesn't say a word.

Tim holds the door as I get into my car. "Why don't I follow you to your parents' . . . er, your mother's house, and we can go in my car?"

"Sounds good. Want me to call the Mosses, or do you want to just show up?"

"Why don't we just show up? Them young'uns need to stay on their toes. We don't need to warn 'em."

"Good thinking."

Mother is weeding her front flower garden as I pull into the driveway. She stops, turns and glances at me, and without even acknowledging my presence, turns back to what she's doing. I get out and walk over to her.

"Tim and I are taking two of Laura and Pete's children out to dinner. Would you like to join us?"

She gives me a look as though she thinks I've lost my mind. "Whatever would I do that for?" She plucks another weed before stopping and casting a curious glance at Tim who has just pulled into the driveway behind my car. "The Mosses have four children. Why would you only take two of them out for dinner?"

"One has moved out, and the other is in the hospital."

"Oh." She stands. "What happened?"

As I explain, she shakes her head. "That's what happens when people marry the wrong person or marry too young. Laura made both of those mistakes."

I don't mention the fact that both she and my dad have made one of the mistakes—marrying the wrong person. So we glare at each other.

Tim saves the moment by joining us. "Hey, there, Ms. Slater. Your flowers are lookin' good."

Mother's face lights up, causing a jealous twinge through my heart. "Thank you, Tim. It's nice to know someone appreciates natural beauty." Her words are meant to hurt me, I'm sure, but I've dealt with her anger toward my profession so long it doesn't even bother me. I'm way past that, but it would still be nice to hear something positive from her once in a while. I don't know what more I could do to impress her.

Tim glances back and forth between Mother and me. "Ready, Priscilla?"

"I sure am."

We're halfway across the yard when Tim stops. "Would you like us to bring you somethin', Ms. Slater?"

"No thanks, Tim, but it's sweet of you to ask." She watches us as we get into the car before resuming her weeding.

"Mother probably wonders why you even want to be friends with me."

Tim gives me a reassuring smile and places his hand on mine. "That's not true, and you know it. Your mother loves you."

I'm sure he's right, but it still hurts to know she doesn't approve of anything in my life. "She has an odd way of showing it."

"Some folks don't know how to show love, and it comes out lookin' like somethin' else."

I wonder if there's a hidden meaning behind that statement, and then I remember this is Tim we're talking about. One of the most endearing qualities in him is his transparency.

When we pull up in front of the Mosses' house, I notice the blinds moving in one of the windows. "They know we're here."

Tim nods. "Yeah, I saw that. What do you reckon they'll wanna eat?"

"I don't know. McDonald's Happy Meals maybe?"

"I think they're a little old for Happy Meals." He chuckles. "But so am I, and I like 'em."

By the time we get to the front door, Bonnie Sue has it open, and she's standing there smiling at us. "This is so awesome." She pulls her cell phone out from behind her back and aims it at us. "Hold still for a sec so I can take a picture. My friends will be so jealous."

"Let's make it real good," Tim whispers. "I don't wanna disappoint her friends."

When I nod, he grabs my hand and gives me a look that practically melts my insides, all the way to my toes. I don't want this moment to end, but as soon as Bonnie Sue clears her throat, Tim drops my hand and gestures for me to go ahead of him. Bonnie Sue takes it all in, making me wonder what she's thinking.

"Me and Priscilla are here to take you and your little brother to dinner."

"Cool." She walks over to the bottom of the stairs. "Jack, get your hiney down here right now. We're goin' out to dinner with famous people."

"I'm not hungry." Jack's voice is very high-pitched.

A look of concern crosses Tim's face. "Want me to go up there and see about him?"

Bonnie Sue rolls her eyes. "He's just bein' a big baby 'cause he's not gettin' much attention from Mama and Daddy, now that Renee's pregnant. When that baby comes, Jack won't be the youngest no more, and then he'll know what it's like to be a middle child."

Tim gives me a look, and I shrug. Bonnie Sue obviously isn't aware that there won't be a baby—at least not this time.

He looks back at Bonnie Sue. "Go get yourself ready to go."

She holds her hands out. "I'm always ready."

31
Laura

My heart aches for my second-born who has just experienced the loss of her own child. I wanna smack one of the doctors who came in and acted all cheerful, sayin' things like, "Looks like you're off the hook this time," and, "You better think twice before you get yourself in this situation again." He musta skipped out on the compassion class in medical school.

"Mama, can you call Wilson and tell him about the baby?"

The look on Pete's face reminds me of a charging bull. "That boy don't need to know nothin'," Pete says. "He wasn't even decent enough to stand by you when you was carryin' his baby, so why would you wanna have anything to do with him now?"

I tug on Pete's shirt and shake my head when he looks at me. "Not now," I mouth. I let go of him and step closer to the head of Renee's bed. "Your daddy will stay here while I go call Wilson."

"Laura." Pete's tone is low and commanding, and that makes me pause. But I'm still not gonna let him hold me back from doin' what our daughter wants.

"I'll be back in a few minutes." I dart out of the room before he has a chance to say another word. I'm not in the mood for arguin'.

Back before they got too lovey-dovey, I put Wilson's number in my cell phone, just in case I ever needed it. I'm glad I didn't follow through on deleting it.

He don't answer, so I leave a message that he needs to call me back. Before I click the *Off* button, I add, "It's urgent."

A few seconds later, my phone vibrates, and I see that it's Wilson. "I'm sorry, Mrs. Moss, but I'm out of town right now, and I can't—"

"Stop right now, Wilson. I'm not askin' you to come over or do anything else for that matter. I'm callin' 'cause Renee asked me to let you know she lost the baby."

"She did?" His voice sounds way too joyful for the moment. "Can I come see her now?"

"I thought you were out of town." Anger returns and simmers throughout my body. I can only imagine what Pete will do to the boy if he shows up.

"Well, I sorta—"

"No. If you so much as come within ten feet of my daughter, I'll—" I stop myself before I say somethin' he can use in a court of law. "Just stay away, Wilson, and everyone will be fine."

"You can't stop me—"

I click my phone off and drop it into my purse. What Renee ever saw in that boy is beyond anything I can imagine. Her daddy may have been a drunk when I married him, but he has always had more heart in his little toe than Wilson has in his entire body. And no matter how much Pete had to drink, I never worried about him leavin' me.

Pete and Renee are deep in a conversation when I enter the room, and as I get closer, I can see that Renee is close to tears. "But, Daddy, I love him."

"You just think you do." Pete sounds frustrated, but he's hangin' in there. "Love is a whole lot more than how you feel when you're kissin' or . . . touchin' each other."

Renee turns to me. "Mama, Daddy says Wilson don't love me."

I give Pete a look and hope he gets the silent hint that I wanna talk to our daughter alone. But he doesn't.

"Tell your daughter there's more to love than—" He cuts himself off as he casts a helpless look my way.

Renee sniffles as I get closer. I grab a tissue from the table and hand it to her. "Your daddy's right. One of the most important things about love is knowin' the other person will be there for you no matter what. Wilson hasn't exactly been there for you."

"I'm not stupid," she says. "Daddy hasn't always been around when you needed him."

Pete's chin quivers, and that sends daggers shooting through my heart. I touch his shoulder and nod toward the door. "Let me talk to her, okay? Why don't you go call the house and see how Bonnie Sue and Jack are doin'?"

As soon as Pete is gone, the corners of Renee's lips turn downward. "Daddy used to get drunk and go to jail, and you never once told him he couldn't come back."

I suck in a deep breath to keep from blastin' her with a piece of my mind. I need to keep my head so she don't think I'm just havin' a tantrum. "Your father has never once willingly left us, no matter what. Even when he was drunk, he was there for all of us. He never . . . well, he hardly ever took off from work 'cause he knew he had to support his family." I swallow hard. "He had a sickness, and that's different."

Renee turns her head away, but I still manage to see a tear escape and roll down her face. I wanna hold her and tell her that everything will be all right, but based on my own life, I'm not sure that'll always be the case. The last thing my daughter needs right now is a lie, even if it is to make her feel better.

"If you wanna see Wilson, that's up to you. Just don't forget what he did when you really needed him."

"I'm not stupid." Renee turns back and looks me in the eye. "But don't you think he can change?" She sniffles and swallows hard. "I mean, if I love him enough . . . " Her voice trails off as she turns away.

Some of my Bible lessons about repentance and forgiveness come to mind, but I know how much Renee hates being preached at. I can still use what I know, but I have to be subtle, or she'll tune me right out.

"I know you're not stupid, Renee. In fact, you're very smart. As for Wilson changin', he has to want to change and do it for the right reasons."

"How do you know he don't wanna change?"

"I never said I thought he didn't wanna change." I dig deep and try not to let my opinion of Wilson color what I'm tryin' to tell her. "If he is sincerely sorry for abandoning you, then I reckon you should forgive him. But that doesn't mean you have to let him back into your life, only to do it again."

"If he's really sorry, he won't do it again." Before I have a chance to say another word, she mentions exactly what's on my mind. "But then I'll have to figure out if he's really sorry or just sayin' he is to get me to . . . " She gives me a pained look. "You know."

I nod. "Yes, sweetie, I do know. That feelin' you get when you're crazy about a boy can make even a smart girl lose her head."

"Mama, I love Wilson." Her chin quivers. "I can't help it."

"Maybe you just think you love him, honey."

Renee opens her mouth, but she's interrupted as Pete comes stormin' into the room. "No one's answerin' the phone. Them young'uns know they're not s'posed to go nowhere without askin'."

I slap my forehead. "I forgot to tell you. Tim said he'd stop by and take them out to eat so we don't have to worry about feedin' 'em."

Pete looks up at the ceiling, puffs his cheeks, and lets out a breath. "I near 'bout lost my mind with worry."

I look down at Renee and smile. "See what I'm talkin' about? That's a man who loves his family so much he just about loses his mind with worry when he doesn't know where they are."

Renee closes her eyes and shakes her head. "Mama."

"It's true. If your daddy didn't worry about y'all, I'd be mad at him."

"You shoulda told me." Pete purses his lips. "What if I had a mind to call the police before comin' in here."

"Why would you call the cops? It ain't like y'all have babies in the house." Renee focuses on Pete. "You need to stop treatin' us like we don't know nothin'. Trust us."

Pete and I exchange a glance. I'm sure he's thinkin' the same thing I am—that if we kept better track of 'em, Renee wouldn't even be lyin' here in a hospital bed.

"Or maybe you can't." Renee turns away. "At least not me anyway."

"Honey, it has nothin' to do with trust. It's all about makin' decisions that are right for you. Your daddy and I don't think Wilson's right for you."

"Did your mama think Daddy was right for you?" Her face holds even more challenge than her question.

I glance over at Pete who is waiting for my answer. "She does now."

"Well, I just happen to know she was furious when you told her you were marryin' Daddy, and she even threatened to disown you."

Pete steps up between Renee and me. "This has nothin' to do with us, young lady. This is all about you. After we get you outta here, we need to have a serious little chat about your future . . . and one that don't include that sorry, good-for-nothin' loser you think you might be in love with. He is not welcome in our house, ever again."

"But Daddy . . . " Renee looks at me and blinks as her chin quivers. "If I can't bring him to the house, I'll just go somewhere else and see him."

"You will not—"

I grab Pete's belt and pull him away. "This isn't a good time for that, Pete."

"Okay." He holds up his hands and walks over to the chair in the corner of the room. "It's never a good time, but one of these days it'll be too late, and you'll wish you made it a good time."

The doctor comes in with one of the nurses and gently nudges me and Pete out of the room. I hear voices in the room, but I can't make out what they're sayin'. Pete is still so upset he can't say much without it soundin' like he's arguin', so I don't even bother strikin' up a conversation with him.

After the doctor finishes examinin' Renee, he comes out and says she needs to get some rest and that she can go home in the mornin'. "I gave her a sedative, so she should sleep pretty well tonight. Why don't the two of you go on home and come back refreshed?"

"I wanna stay here." Pete folds his arms and plants his feet about two feet apart. My heart hammers at the sight of my knight in denim.

"Suit yourself." The doctor lifts his hand in a wave. "I need to finish my rounds before I leave. Have a good evening, folks."

Once he's gone, I let Pete know I'm tired and I'd like to sleep in my own bed. "You heard what the doctor said." I take his hand in mine and tug him toward the elevator. "Please drive me home, Pete. I don't wanna have to call someone."

His shoulders rise and fall as he finally gives in. "Oh all right. But you better be ready to come back here at the crack of dawn, or I'm comin' without ya."

"Of course."

The house is quiet when we walk in. "Tim and Priscilla must have taken 'em someplace real good," Pete says.

"That reminds me. We haven't eaten yet. Did you want me to fix us somethin', or do you wanna do carryout?"

"Can you cook one of them fancy casseroles like you used to make?"

"I'll be happy to. Why don't you go have a seat in your recliner, and I'll call you when it's ready?"

He heads off for the family room without an argument. My husband is exhausted from all the emotional trauma we've been through ever since we found out Renee was pregnant with Wilson's baby.

I dump all the cheese I have over the frozen vegetables in the casserole dish, which isn't much since we've cut back. The cream soup in the pantry should give it the richness and flavor Pete likes. I finish mixin' everything and shove it into the oven when I hear the front door slam and my young'uns laughin' like they're at a party.

"Mama, you shoulda seen Tim." Jack snickers as he enters the kitchen. "He does the best impressions."

Tim walks in behind Jack, his face red. "They're not that good."

"Yeah, they are. Show her how you do that guy on the music show."

Bonnie Sue and Priscilla haven't come back to the kitchen, so I wipe my hands to go see where they are. "Just a minute." I walk through the family room and see that Pete's snorin' in his chair, and he's alone. "Bonnie Sue," I holler as I walk through the house, half hopin' I'll wake my husband so supper doesn't go to waste.

"We're upstairs, Mama. Priscilla said she'd show me how to mix and match my old clothes to make it look like I have new outfits."

"Okay. I was just checkin' to make sure you're okay."

I start back to the kitchen when I hear Bonnie Sue talkin' to Priscilla. "Mama worries too much. She thinks I'm gonna mess up like Renee did."

Before I have a chance to holler that I heard her, Priscilla speaks. "Your mother protects you because she loves you."

At least Priscilla is stickin' up for me. I'm not so sure I woulda done the same for her.

I get back to the kitchen in time to see Tim actin' all goofy, makin' Jack howl with laughter. "Some boys never grow up." I smile as I say that to make sure Tim knows I'm just funnin' him.

"That's not the whole truth." Tim makes another funny face. "Deep down, *none* of us ever grow up, but we hafta act like men to keep you ladies happy."

"True. So where did y'all eat?"

"Olson's Diner." Jack rubs his belly. "I had the meatloaf and smashed taters, and they was real good."

At least I have some comfort knowin' my young'uns had a square meal. I look at Tim. "Thanks for takin' Jack and Bonnie Sue out to eat."

"It was our pleasure." He slips into his regular self and sits down at the table. "So how's Renee feelin'?"

"Better, but I'm worried she'll get back with that loser Wilson."

Tim frowns and shakes his head. "Maybe not. She's a smart girl."

"Now that she's not pregnant anymore, he wants to see her again." I open the oven door to make sure the cheese isn't burning before closing it and turning around to face Tim. "Pete's furious."

"I understand Pete's feelings," Tim says slowly, "but I do think it's best if Renee's the one makin' the decision. Otherwise, you'll wind up with a battle on your hands."

"Oh, I know it."

"From what I've seen, teenagers and young adults think they know more than their mamas and daddies."

I tilt my head and give him a long look. "Are you sure you're not a parent, Tim? You sure do know a lot about young'uns."

"That's 'cause I still sorta think like they do." He makes a face at Jack. "Mama says it's a wonder I can make it on my own since I never grew up."

Bonnie Sue comes waltzin' into the kitchen wearin' an outfit I never saw before. "Did you just buy that?"

"No." She smiles and points her thumb at Priscilla who is right behind her. "Priscilla took pieces of other outfits and put them together for me. Ain't it cute?"

"*Isn't* it cute?" You'd think she'd talk right by now.

"That's what I'm sayin'. I love havin' her here, Mama . . . "

She has that look on her face like she wants to add, *Can we keep her?* But that's just my memory playin' tricks on me. Back when she was a little girl, she used to bring home stray animals and beg us to let her keep 'em.

Priscilla smiles back at Bonnie Sue, sorta like they're in on a secret or somethin'. "I used to have to get creative when I was your age because my mother didn't understand why anyone would be interested in the latest fashion."

"Oh, I understand wantin' to be stylish and all, but . . . " I look at my daughter who isn't payin' an ounce of attention to me 'cause she's lookin' at Priscilla with adoring eyes.

"You look cute, Bonnie Sue. And Priscilla, I appreciate you helpin' her out. We can't afford all that many new clothes for the young'uns these days."

Priscilla smiles at me. "Did you know that most of the clothes I wore in high school came from thrift shops and discount stores?"

"No, I didn't know that." I look away as fast as I can. "I best be gettin' supper on the table before it's too late. Pete was starvin' when we left the hospital."

Tim glances over at Priscilla. "I reckon we best be gettin' along so y'all can have some family time."

Priscilla nods at him and takes a step toward me. "Laura, if you want to change your appointment to Saturday morning, I'll work it out."

"You don't hafta do that." I know she's bein' extra nice to me on account of all we've been through, and I appreciate it, but I'm not used to folks makin' an extra effort for me.

"But I want to. I'll call you in the morning with the new time. Do you mind if it's early morning?"

"That's probably best for me," I admit. "Thanks. Bonnie Sue, go wake your daddy up and tell him his supper's ready."

32
Priscilla

I don't know why it's so difficult for Laura to accept favors." I look at Tim as he drives me back to my mother's house. "All I have to do is go in a little bit early and move my next client back by half an hour."

"It's pride." Tim pulls up to a stop sign and looks at me for a moment before turning his attention back to the road. "And I'm not sure she feels worthy."

"That's just silly."

"Maybe to you." He purses his lips, so I know there's something he's not saying.

"What?"

He smiles. "What do you mean, *what*?"

"That look on your face. What are you not telling me?"

"Priscilla, it may come as a shock to you, but I'm not about to tell you everything I'm thinkin'. That goes against man-code."

I start to make a comment about how ridiculous that sounds, but I stop myself. Tim has always been the most open guy I've known, so if he wants to keep something to himself, I'm sure he has a valid reason.

We pull up in front of Mother's house and stop, but I don't get out of the car right away. It feels good to just sit here in silence with Tim—something I wouldn't be able to do with just anyone.

"You okay, Priscilla?" he asks after several minutes.

I nod. "Tim, you're an amazing man."

"Thank you. I think you're pretty special, too."

He places his hand on mine, and I feel a sizzle travel up my arm. My mouth instantly goes dry.

"You okay, Priscilla?" He laces his fingers through mine.

"Um . . . yeah." I pull my hand away from him and open the car door. Whatever is happening between Tim and me feels good, but I don't know what to do with it. I've known him for thirteen years, and until this week, I've only seen him as a very good friend who is always there for me. I hop out of the car, bend over, and look him in the eye. "Thanks for everything, Tim."

His gaze locks with mine, and he slowly nods. "You're always welcome, Priscilla."

I slam the car door shut, turn, and walk as quickly as I can to the front door without looking back. After I open the front door to the house, I hear the sound of Tim's car pulling away from the curb.

"Is that you, Priscilla?" Mother comes out from the back of the house to the foyer. "Where did y'all go for dinner?"

I'm glad she's asking a question with an easy answer and one that I can talk about because it prevents me from facing something that is frightening to me at the moment—my new attraction to Tim.

Mother seems preoccupied, which is just fine with me. I tell her all about taking the Moss kids out to eat, and she pretends to listen. I pour myself a glass of water, down it, and put the glass in the dishwasher. "I think I'll go to my room now. I have a big day tomorrow."

I'm up early the next morning, but not early enough to catch Mother before she left for work. There's a note on the counter in front of the coffeepot letting me know she'll be home late. I eat a bowl of cereal and down a cup of coffee then head to work for a full day. My mind is racing with so many things—from what Laura's going through to my strange new feelings for Tim—so I crank up the music to excise the thoughts from my head.

There's a crowd outside the salon and day spa when I arrive in the parking lot. That's odd. I pull into my spot and get out, hoping to make it into the building without incident. I'm half-way up the sidewalk when some woman thrusts a microphone in front of me. "Is it true that you've been commissioned to travel with the First Lady?"

I stop in my tracks and stare at her, thinking this must be a joke. She's serious. "What are you talking about?"

"Priscilla!"

I glance up at the door of the salon and see Sheila gesturing wildly for me to go inside. "Excuse me," I say to the woman with the mic. "I have work to do."

"Just say yes or no."

"No." I tip my head down and forge ahead as cameras click around me.

When I'm close enough to the front door, Sheila grabs hold of my arm and pulls me inside. "I tried to call and warn you, but you didn't answer your cell phone."

I had the music up so loud I obviously didn't hear my phone. "What is going on?"

Chester peeks around the partition but quickly darts back when he catches me looking at him. "C'mere, Chester," Sheila says in her mom-voice. "Tell her what you done."

He slinks around the partition and gives me a long look of remorse. "I sorta gave them folks the wrong idea."

"Does it have something to do with the First Lady?"

Chester shrugs and looks at Sheila for support. She nods and motions for him to tell me.

"I got a call from one of the magazine reporters askin' questions about what you're doin' here, and I got a little carried away. I said . . . " He casts a pitiful look toward Sheila before putting his hand over his face. "I am so embarrassed."

"Okay, I'll tell her. He told the reporter that you were here for your class reunion, but you're leavin' the day after to work with a very important dignitary."

"Where did the reporter get the impression you were talking about the First Lady?" I ask.

Chester holds out his hands. "She kept askin' who the dignitary was, and I kept on sayin' *no* when she mentioned names, until she asked if it was the First Lady. I didn't answer her that time." He scrunches his forehead into a pitiful expression. "I never actually came right out and said you were travelin' with the First Lady."

Sheila rolls her eyes. "But you didn't deny it either."

I put my purse down on the reception desk and walk around behind the counter to reschedule Laura Moss "Why did you even say I'm working with an important dignitary?"

"I don't know. This is the first time anyone has called me for information, and it made me feel . . . well, it made me feel—"

Sheila steps up to help him out. "It made him feel important. Some people just can't help themselves."

Chester folds his hands and places them under his chin as he looks at me with pleading eyes. "I'm really sorry, Priscilla. I'll do anything you want to make up for it."

I glance over at Sheila, who winks and gives me the go-ahead to tease Chester. "I'll think of something really good. In the meantime, I need to let a few people know I'm changing Saturday's schedule."

Sheila leans over and looks at the computer. "Don't tell me Laura talked you into givin' her a Saturday appointment."

"She didn't. I'm the one who offered it. After what she's been through, it's time she had a little extra pampering."

"Want me to give her a free facial?" Chester asks.

I lift my eyebrows and look back and forth between him and Sheila, who nods before I smile at him. "What a great idea! She'll get extra special treatment, and you'll make up for what you said to the reporter."

"One more thing, Chester," Sheila adds. "March right out there and let the folks know you were mistaken—that Priscilla isn't goin' anywhere with the First Lady."

"But—" He looks at me for support.

I grin at him. "You heard her. Go tell them."

It takes every ounce of self-restraint I have to keep a straight face until he's gone. Sheila and I both crack up laughing at the same time.

"He's lovin' your fame a bit too much," Sheila says between snorts of giggles. "You shoulda seen him last time you were on air. You'da thought he had somethin' to do with it."

I quickly pull a straight face. "I have to admit I agree with him."

"What?" She gives me a questioning look.

"If it weren't for you, Chester, and the rest of the folks who work for the Cut 'n Curl, none of my success would be possible."

She flicks her hand from the wrist. "Get out. It's all you, Priscilla. There are thousands of hair salons with good hairdressers all over the country, but you don't see their owners on TV."

"I'm just sayin' . . . " I smile at her as I pick up the phone to start making my scheduling calls.

The noise out in front of the salon dies down quickly after Chester comes back inside, his face red and glistening with nervous sweat. "You'd think I done somethin' really bad the way they took the news."

"They'll get over it." I point to the schedule. "Looks like you have an opening on Friday, so why don't you give Laura a call and let her know you're gifting her with a free facial."

His shoulders hunch, and he hangs his head, looking an awful lot like one of Laura and Pete's kids when they're being punished. But I don't feel bad since the free facial was his idea. Tim's comment about his mother saying he's never grown up pops into my head. If I didn't think I'd get called out for being sexist, I might comment about all men having a hard time growing up. No doubt Sheila would agree with me, but there's no point in starting a discussion that has the potential to get out of control while I'm here such a short time.

I'm asked to do some of my favorite cuts—the quintessential long shag and a short razor cut. Most people love the movement those two styles give them, and I get to fall back on my creativity as I layer according to facial shapes. They're the easiest ways to flatter a face, either by making the client appear thinner or taking attention away from something they're not happy with.

"How about some highlights?" I ask my last appointment of the morning.

"I don't know." She studies herself in the mirror. "What kind of highlights were you thinkin'?"

"Something subtle . . . like a hint of butterscotch here and here." The association with food generally grabs folks.

"Ooh, yeah, that sounds delicious."

She leaves right at noon looking like a butterscotch sundae. On her way out, she gets all kinds of compliments from all the hairdressers and some of the clients. We do that for one another to reinforce people's confidence.

Sheila motions for me to join her in the break room, so I follow her back. "I brought enough food for both of us so you wouldn't have to go out." She opens the fridge and announces, "Lasagna."

"Thanks."

She sticks the containers of lasagna in the microwave, while I pour both of us glasses of iced tea. Sheila and I have always worked well together, and at times like this I miss working in the salon.

Almost as though we'd rehearsed it, we're finished with the meal preparation, and we sit down together. Sheila says, "You wanna say the blessin', or do you want me to?"

I nod toward her. "You."

We bow our heads, and she thanks the Lord for the beautiful day, our food, and simply being together. After she says, "Amen," I echo her and open my eyes to see her grinning widely.

"What are you smiling about?"

She giggles. "After all these years, I think you're startin' to come to your senses with Tim."

33
Celeste

Wanna call Pete 'n Laura?" Jimmy gently lifts my legs and shoves one of the pillows beneath them. "How's that? Comfy?"

"Yeah, thanks. I don't know about callin' the Mosses. They might put us to work."

Jimmy cackles. "That's okay, sweetie. I don't mind workin'. In fact, I think it'll be fun to run around town doin' stuff for the reunion."

I point to the hotel room phone. "Okay, go ahead and call 'em then, but don't tell 'em nothin' about the baby."

"Why not?"

"I wanna surprise 'em." I'm still in my first trimester, but I couldn't wait to buy maternity clothes and wear 'em. And now that I'm pregnant, I don't hold my stomach in, so that little bit of a tummy-pooch shows from all the cookin' I been doin' since me and Jimmy got married.

Jimmy lifts the receiver and punches in their phone number that he obviously still remembers. He exchanges a polite greeting with Laura, but I can tell the instant Pete gets on the line because his language turns salty.

"Jimmy!" I whisper.

He cups the phone and whispers back, "Sorry, hon." Then he goes back to his conversation with Pete and makes arrangements for us to go over to their house tomorrow evenin'. Jimmy even offers to bring dinner. After he's off the phone, he plops down on the bed next to me and takes off his shoes and socks. "I'm not used to watchin' ever'thing I say around my buddies."

"You need to break that habit on account of I don't want our baby to learn that kinda trashy talk."

"He'll hear it in the locker room."

"Or maybe *she* won't."

Jimmy laughs as he bends over and drops a kiss on my not-quite-so-new-but-improved nose. "If it's a she, I hope she's as purty as you."

How can I fuss at a man who says such sweet things? "I want my babies to be as happy as I am."

"Babies? As in more 'n one?" He gets right up in my face and grabs both my hands. "Celeste, do you know somethin' you ain't told me?"

I pull my hands free and swat at him with a pillow. "No, silly, I'm just talkin' about the babies we'll have in the future."

He gives me one of them vacant grins that lets me know he ain't so sure what to say. I s'pect he's thinkin' we might not wanna have another kid, but he don't wanna say that on account of my condition.

We watch TV for about an hour when one of my cravings hits me hard. "Jimmy, I want some hush puppies."

He looks at the clock and frowns. "Where am I gonna get hush puppies at this hour?"

"Joe-Bob's Fish Fry."

"Celeste, Joe-Bob's is clear on the other side of Hattiesburg."

"Please, Jimmy. I don't think I'll be able to go to sleep if I don't get some hush puppies."

He lets out a breath, closes his eyes, and shakes his head before he gets up and slides his bare feet into his shoes. "Okay, I'll go get 'em. Want anything else while I'm out?"

"A tub of slaw would be good."

"Do me a favor and give 'em a call so the order will be ready when I get there."

I smile and nod. "Okay, sweetie."

As soon as he leaves, I call in the order and switch the channel from the news to my favorite sitcom that Jimmy thinks is stupid. I figure it'll take at least forty-five minutes for him to go to Joe-Bob's, pick up the order, and come back.

Almost exactly forty-five minutes later, he comes walkin' into the room with a humongous brown sack that looks like it's filled to the top. "Today's their fried catfish special, and I figgered while I was there . . . "

I inhale the aroma of fresh-fried catfish, something I haven't smelled since I left Piney Point. Biloxi has some good seafood restaurants, but nothin' like Joe-Bob's. Me and Jimmy done ate supper, but one thing about this pregnancy is I'm always up for another meal.

Jimmy lays everything out on the little round table and pulls a coupla chairs over. "Where you wanna sit?"

I point to the chair by the window. "I'll take that one."

"I'll go get us a coupla cold drinks."

By the time Jimmy gets back from the vending machine, I've already eaten two hush puppies. Them things'll melt in your mouth they're so good.

Jimmy laughs as he watches me stuff a bit of catfish into my mouth. "Celeste, your eyes is rollin' back in your head."

"This is a taste of heaven."

He nibbles a tail off one of the catfish on his plate and nods. "Don't I know it."

After we finish our second supper, I stuff everything in the bag so Jimmy can take it to the garbage can down the hall. We don't want our room stinkin' more'n it already does.

Me and Jimmy both sleep great with our bellies full, but when I wake up, I have a hard time gettin' up. Jimmy stands over me, his eyes wide as saucers. "Man, Celeste, your cheeks is so puffy you look like one of them Cabbage Patch dolls."

I wanna smack him, but then I remember how sweet he was for goin' over to Joe-Bob's last night. As I slowly sit up, the stench from the fish fills my nostrils. "This place reeks."

"It'd be worse if I didn't take the bags down the hall. Let's get dressed and go for a walk."

Walkin' is the last thing I wanna do, but I know it'll be good for me. So I get outta bed, take a shower, and do my best to cover my puffy face with makeup like Priscilla taught me.

Jimmy grins when I come outta the bathroom. "Lookin' good, hon. I got me the purtiest wife in Miss'ippi."

Me and Jimmy's been married five years, but since I got pregnant, he's gotten sweeter. Somethin' happened when I started carryin' his baby—and I like it. If it takes bein' pregnant to get the kinda compliments he's dishin' out, we just might wind up with a houseful of young'uns.

We hold hands as we walk through the lobby of the hotel, toward the front door that Jimmy opens for me. It's still early mornin', but the heat from the sun beatin' down on the sidewalk and the front of the buildin' near 'bout takes my breath away.

"Wanna have breakfast at Olson's?"

I nod. In spite of how much I ate last night, I'm starvin' half to death. "Pancakes sound good to me."

"Me too. I think I'll order a double stack."

I smile as we walk into Olson's Diner, knowin' me and Jimmy have both been blessed with genes that allow us to eat near 'bout as much as we want without havin' to worry about gettin' fat. Back in school, I was made fun of for bein' so gangly, but now them same girls is havin' to go on diets. The only reason I'll be gainin' any weight is 'cause I'm carryin' a baby, but once it's born, I know the weight'll come right off. At least I think it will, except maybe a little bit of tummy.

We stuff ourselves before walkin' around downtown, hopin' to see folks we know. But we don't. Piney Point has grown, partly from people who work at the University of Southern Miss'ippi in Hattiesburg wantin' small-town life when they go home and partly from Piney Point and Hattiesburg city limits gettin' closer and closer to each other. One of these days you won't know when you leave Hattiesburg and arrive in Piney Point if things keep headin' this-a-way.

"Wanna stop off at the Cut 'n Curl on the way back to the hotel?" Jimmy asks.

"Sure."

"Seems weird not to see 'em on Main Street. I wonder how that knitting shop is doin' in the old Cut 'n Curl location."

I glance over at the store and see all kinds of stuff in the window—from scarves and sweaters to blankets in all colors. "Looks like they're busy knittin'."

"Yeah, I reckon that's good."

"Maybe I should take up knittin'."

Jimmy glances down at me, but he don't say nothin'. Good thing 'cause it don't look like he'd have somethin' nice to say.

Since the new Cut 'n Curl and spa are a few blocks from downtown, we drive over there, instead of walking. Jimmy looks up at the buildin' and then back at me. "Don't look that much different than how it did before the old place burnt down."

"It's called a replica."

"Whatever it's called, I don't get why she didn't go for somethin' more modern. This place looks just downright old."

We get outta the car and go inside where some young girl is standin' at the desk starin' at somethin' on the computer screen. She looks up at me and Jimmy and grins. "Y'all got an appointment?"

"Nah," Jimmy says. "We just stopped by to see how Priscilla's makin' out with her new digs."

The girl makes a confused face. "I beg your pardon?"

"This place. It's new." Jimmy speaks slowly, like he's talkin' to someone who don't speak English.

"I don't think so," the girl says. "It's been in Piney Point for, like, ever—at least a couple years."

"Three years," I say as I step up beside my husband. "Is Priscilla here?"

"Yes, but she's with a client right now."

"Can you go tell her Celeste and Jimmy's here to see her?"

She tightens her lips as she looks back and forth between me and Jimmy, tryin' to decide what to do. I'm about to tell her we'll come back later when she nods and says she'll be right back.

After she disappears behind the wall, Jimmy shakes his head. "This place is weird. I don't get why women wanna come here when they can go to that place over by the Interstate, where they don't make folks have appointments, and they send out coupons for ten-dollar haircuts."

"That's why," I say. "We like to feel important, and if we have an appointment, we know that time has been set aside for us."

Jimmy opens his mouth to tell me what else is on his mind when I hear Priscilla comin' from behind the wall. Her voice is distinctive and accent-free, sorta like a newscaster's.

"Hey, there, Celeste," she says as she approaches. Her gaze travels up and down me, and she breaks into the widest grin I ever seen on her. "Are congratulations in order?"

"They are if you like to congratulate new mamas and daddies," Jimmy says. "Me and my wife is gonna be parents in about six months."

"Oh." Priscilla's eyebrows is still raised high. "You look . . . very nice."

We chat about this and that for a few minutes, until she looks at her watch. "I need to go back and wash out the color, but it sure was good to see both of you."

"Don't tell Laura you seen us," I say. "We're goin' to her house now to see if she needs any help."

She gets a strange look on her face. "Oh, you might want—"

The girl behind the desk interrupts and says she has a call on line three. Priscilla waves, picks up the phone, and walks around behind the short wall.

On our way out the door, I wonder what Priscilla was about to tell us. Oh well, I reckon if it's important, she'll let us know later.

34
Priscilla

I hang up after talking to Mother and ask Alicia where Celeste and Jimmy are. "I wanted to tell them something before they see Laura."

"They left."

"Maybe I can catch them. Do me a favor and get me Celeste's number. I think I still have it listed under Boudreaux."

Alicia approaches my station after I finish washing the color out of my client's hair. "I think the number you have listed for Celeste Boudreaux is old. I tried calling it, and some guy answered. He says he doesn't have a clue who Celeste is."

"I really need to talk to her." I pause and think for a moment. "Maybe Laura or Pete has it. Do me a favor and call Laura Moss and try to get either Jimmy or Celeste's cell phone number."

Alicia nods. "I'll try."

After she leaves, I put the finishing touches on my client's hair and spin her around to get her approval. "So how do you like what I did with your hair?"

She studies her hair from the front and side angles. "It looks real nice, Priscilla. I wish you'd think about stayin' here in

Piney Point, but I don't reckon you'd ever wanna do that, now that you're famous and all."

I smile down at her. "It has nothing to do with fame. It's just that I have so many salons and my products on TVNS, I don't have time to stay in one place very long."

As she stands, I can feel her hesitation. When she turns to face me, I see a completely different kind of expression—a more motherly look—on her face. "If I can offer one piece of advice, Priscilla, that would be to find yourself a nice man, settle down, and have yourself some kids before it's too late." She touches my arm. "I know how important a career is to some women, but just remember that your career won't come visit you in the nursing home when you're an old woman."

I smile back at her and refrain from telling her what I'm thinking—that in the future, I'll only take appointments for people going to the class reunion. After she leaves, I sweep the floor around my station and try not to think about her advice, but her words keep playing over and over in my head. Having children has never been high on my priority list, but it's actually starting to play in my mind.

The sound of snapping fingers brings me back to where I am. Sheila hands me a slip of paper. "Celeste's number. Alicia said you need it."

"Thanks. I need to give her a quick call. Be right back." Without another word, I run toward the back room so I can speak to Celeste in peace.

I punch in her number, and the call goes straight to voice mail—with her voice. At least I know I have the correct number. I leave a message for her to call me back immediately.

When I return to my station, Tim is sitting in the styling chair. "Hey, Priscilla. I know you're busy as all get-out, so I thought I'd just drop by and say hey."

"Hey." I pick up one of my hair volumizing combs. "Have time for me to style your hair?"

He points to the comb. "Not with one of them. I got me too much hair as it is."

"I can thin it out."

Tim laughs. "You just wanna get your hands on my hair."

I lift my hand in mock surrender. "Busted. So what's on your agenda today? Laura got you hopping?"

"Not really. I expected to have a bunch of loose ends to tie up, but looks like Pete and Laura done it all."

"You sound sad about that."

He shrugs. "I reckon I am. I like to feel needed." He looks at himself in the mirror as I snip the ends of his hair. "I coulda waited 'til Friday night to come to town, and I don't think anyone woulda missed me."

"I would've." The instant I say those words, I know they're true. But Tim's expression lets me know he doesn't believe me.

"Thanks, Priscilla." He smiles as he stands. "I better get outta here so you can get back to work. No point in me hangin' around makin' a nuisance of myself."

"You're not—"

"Priscilla, your next appointment is here." Alicia gestures for the woman to have a seat at my station.

Tim gives me a long look before he leaves. I have to stifle an overwhelming urge to run after him.

"He seems to be such a nice young man. Your mother told me he's been chasing you for years, and you never let him catch you."

I turn toward the woman who sounds very familiar. "Mrs. Graham?"

She grins. "I was worried you wouldn't recognize me, Priscilla."

Whew. I haven't seen Virginia Graham since I left Piney Point to open my Jackson salon. Not long after I moved away, she retired from being the receptionist in the English department at the Piney Point Community College where both of my parents are still professors. "Of course, I recognize you. So what can I do for you today?"

"I'm thinking about changing to a more youthful hairstyle. You don't think people would think I'm silly for that, do you?"

"Absolutely not." I lift my volumizing comb again. "How would you feel about letting me try out the Ms. Prissy Big Hair system on you?"

She giggles. "If that's the one you use on TVNS, I'd love it. Your products look so lovely on all those TV models."

"What's nice about them is that they're real people, just like you and me."

"Oh, Priscilla honey, I know you're trying to be nice, but you're nothing like me or anyone else around here."

"What are you talking about?"

"You're bigger than life—the one claim to fame Piney Point has and probably the only one we ever will have. You're a TV star."

As I work the comb through Mrs. Graham's hair, I talk about how I'm still the same girl who used to come sit on her desk while Mother counseled students in her office. "Remember that time I got all that chocolate on my dress, and you managed to get it out before Mother saw it?"

Mrs. Graham laughs. "Yes, I do remember that. Your mother couldn't—and still can't—stand food messes. That's why she never liked anyone to eat at their desks. I was worried sick she'd find out I kept chocolate in my file drawer after you wiped it on your dress."

I pretend to zip my lips. "I never said a word."

"That makes us coconspirators, doesn't it?" Mrs. Graham points to a *Famous People News* magazine teetering on the edge of the counter. "So is it true what they're saying about you and that boy?"

"Mrs. Graham, I'm sure you know that's just a tabloid with a bunch of made-up stories."

"Maybe so, but according to your mother, this one might be closer to the truth than you want people to know."

So now my mother is part of the gossip chain? Ever since she joined the Classy Lassies Red Hat group, she's been different. Dad even blames them for breaking up their marriage. I've reminded him that if his and mother's marriage had been strong enough, no social club would be able to come between them. Besides, according to Mother, the reason she joined the group in the first place was because Dad had already lost interest in doing things with her.

After she leaves, I try to call Celeste again, and I still go straight to voice mail. She must not have her phone on. I call Tim to see if he'll try to track them down.

"I'll do what I can." Tim chuckles. "Want me to lasso 'em and bring 'em in?"

"Very funny, cowboy."

"Seriously, what's the big deal? You'll see Celeste when she comes in for her appointment, right?"

"I don't think she's scheduled one this time."

"Okay, this sounds serious. Ever since you made her over ten years ago, she swore she'd never attend another reunion without having you work on her."

"Maybe you can lure her in here with an offer for a free service," I suggest. "I don't think she's ever turned down something free."

"Gotcha. I'll see what I can do."

If anyone can find Celeste in Piney Point, Tim can. That man is relentless in his pursuit of whatever he's after, including me . . . until now. Something has changed in our relationship, and I sense that Tim's feelings for me might have faded. And that really bugs me.

35
Tim

The first place I go is the hotel on Main Street, where I suspect Jimmy and Celeste are prob'ly stayin' since they're old Piney Pointers. I've noticed that folks from this town are loyal to their own, and they only accept change when there's no other choice. I amble right on up to the registration counter and grin at the girl standin' there. She looks at me, flashes a flirty smile, then her eyes get all huge.

"You're the guy in the magazine . . . the one with Priscilla Slater . . . I . . . uh . . . Can I help you?"

Now havin' to force myself to hold the smile, I nod. "Would you mind connectin' me to Jimmy and Celeste Shackleford's room?"

She points to the house phone on the wall next to the desk. "Pick that up and dial zero."

I do what she says. She looks directly at me as she answers and offers assistance. I repeat my request, and she says, "Hold please."

The phone rings a half-dozen times, until I finally hang up. I glance over at the girl who is still starin' at me and shrug. "I reckon they're not in their room."

"Um . . . they might be at Bubba Moss's parents' house. I heard them talking about going there when they left about an hour ago."

I stop and stare at her. Why didn't she tell me that to begin with? "Okay, thanks."

"Have a nice evening."

On my way to the Mosses' house, I call Priscilla at the salon, hopin' she's between customers and can talk. Sheila answers, and as soon as she learns it's me, she tells me to hold on 'cause Priscilla really wants to talk to me. I tell her I'll wait.

"Hey, Tim." Priscilla sounds outta breath. "Did you find Celeste?"

"A little birdy told me they were headin' over to the Mosses' house."

Priscilla groans. "I was hoping we'd catch them before they went."

"Is there a problem?"

"Yes. It's supposed to be a secret, but I think you need to know that Celeste and Jimmy are going to have a baby. I probably shouldn't worry about this, but I'm afraid Celeste will say the wrong thing, and Laura will sink into one of her moods."

"You're right, Priscilla. You shouldn't worry about it. Women get pregnant all the time, and I'm sure they'll deal with it. Things have a way of workin' out."

She sighs. "I know."

"If I see Celeste at the Mosses' house, do you want me to have her call you?"

"It'll probably be too late." She pauses. "Thanks for trying, Tim. I have to get back to my client."

After I disconnect the call, I try to think about all the different possibilities of how things might go between Celeste and Laura. Them two women have the strangest relationship I ever seen. They act like they can't stand each other, but when they're workin' on a project together, you'd never know where one left off and the other began. It's almost like they're workin' off the same battery.

When I arrive at the Mosses' house, I see a real expensive, brand-new, sparklin' white SUV parked in the driveway. That don't look like nothin' I ever seen Jimmy or Celeste drivin' before. Maybe they haven't made it here yet.

My hopes are dashed when Laura flings the door open and I see Celeste sittin' on the sofa with Jimmy right there next to her. "Don't just stand there starin'," Laura says as she takes a step back. "Come on in. We were about to eat the supper Jimmy and Celeste picked up on the way here."

Jimmy hops up, strides right over to me, and shakes my hand. "How ya been, Tim? It sure is good to see ya."

"I've been just fine." I'm so stunned by the way Jimmy's actin', all sure of himself and confident. I lean over and smile at his wife. "Hey, there, Celeste."

She lifts a hand and wiggles her fingers. "Hi, Tim."

"We brung enough food for an army, so why don't you join us?" Jimmy glances over his shoulder at Pete. "Y'all don't mind, do ya?"

"No, of course not." Pete turns to his daughter who's sittin' on the loveseat with some scroungy-lookin' boy who looks like somethin' a cat might've thrown up. "Why don't you young'uns fill your plates first and come on back in here to eat so us adults can have a decent conversation? Renee, you and Wilson need to behave."

The ratty boy—obviously named Wilson—stands up, and without even lookin' at the Moss girl, heads straight for the kitchen. I glance over at Celeste, and she frowns, but neither of us says nothin'.

Jimmy joins his wife and offers to help her up off the sofa. "Ever since we found out we was havin' a baby, I wanna make sure Celeste is comfy. Sure does worry me when she gets sick." He pulls her to her feet and gently places his arm around her. "You feelin' all right, sugar?"

She nods and smiles like she's the happiest woman on earth. I feel a tiny twinge of jealousy, but I shake it off. I always thought I'd be a daddy by now, but I'm not, so I need to accept it. I don't go to church every Sunday, but when I do, I keep hearin' about the Lord's will and how He makes things happen when they're s'posed to. I don't see any argument against that, so I figure my time ain't come yet.

When we get to the kitchen, where Laura has lined the food up on the counter, buffet style, Jimmy pulls up a chair for Celeste. "Take a seat, honey, and I'll fill your plate." He glances up at the Moss children and Wilson. "Y'all don't mind if I fix my beautiful baby mama her food first, do you? She's eatin' for two, ya know."

Wilson ignores Jimmy and starts heapin' piles of food on his plate, while Renee glares at him with only an occasional glance over at Celeste. Is that longing I see on her face? There's something I can't explain about what's happenin' here, and it ain't all good either. Wilson and Renee still aren't speakin' or even lookin' at each other as she follows him into the family room with her half-filled plate.

Jimmy places the plate of food down in front of Celeste and then gets in line behind Laura and Pete. I feel awkward since I wasn't invited. "I don't wanna crash y'all's party."

"Don't be silly." Jimmy looks around and settles his gaze on me. "Why don't you call Priscilla and have her join us? I'm sure you can see we have plenty."

That would make things less uncomfortable, so I pull out my cell phone and punch in Priscilla's salon number. "She just left," Sheila says. "But if you call her cell phone real quick, I bet you can catch her on her way home."

I try her cell phone, and she answers before the end of the first ring. "Did you find them?"

"Yup, and we're all standin' here in the Mosses' kitchen, about to eat supper."

"Can't you get away?"

"Um . . . no." I glance around and see several pairs of eyes focused on me. "Guess what."

I hear her sigh. "What?"

"You're invited. Why don't you swing by for a bite to eat? I'm sure everyone would love to see you."

"Did Celeste—?"

I interrupt her before she starts askin' questions I can't answer in front of all these folks. "It was Jimmy's idea to call you, and everyone misses you."

"Okay, I get it. I'll be right over."

Priscilla is a smart woman. I'm glad she picked up on the vibes.

I know I stretched things a bit 'cause not everyone is as crazy about Priscilla as I have been since the moment I laid eyes on her. But this is one of those times I think it's important for her to see why I haven't been able to capture Celeste and Jimmy and take them to her. Once she gets here, it'll be obvious.

"So is she comin'?" Laura asks.

I nod. "She said she'll be right over."

Laura frowns as she glances around. "We're not gonna wait for her."

"I don't think she expects us to." I look down at Laura who obviously can't stand Priscilla, or anyone else for that matter. She's one of those people my uncle used to call "joy stealers." When everything is goin' good, she's the one who points out anything bad that can possibly happen.

Pete goes out to the garage and returns with a couple folding chairs. "Laura always said the best thing about havin' a round kitchen table is you can always fit one more person."

Laura's lips is smilin', but her eyes is shooting daggers at her husband. Hoo-boy, I sure don't wanna be around after ever'one leaves. I can only imagine the chewin' out Pete's gonna get.

Folks take so much time gettin' their food, Priscilla arrives before everyone's seated. "Bonnie Sue let me in and told me to come on back to the kitchen."

Pete gestures toward the food. "Get yourself a plate and fill it. We have plenty of chairs."

36
Priscilla

The dynamics in the Mosses' kitchen are sizzling with a combination of hostility, one-upsmanship, and cluelessness. Laura obviously wishes we weren't here. Celeste is walking around, flaunting her pregnant belly that isn't even big enough to be donned in maternity clothes. And Pete acts like he's having the time of his life, entertaining all his old pals, except when he gives that Wilson boy a look that could kill.

Tim and I exchange a glance, and I can tell he sees it too. He might not have the best vocabulary in the world, but he's a very smart man.

"So what do you think you're havin', Celeste?" Pete asks. "A girl or boy?"

Celeste shrugs. "I don't have no way of knowin'."

"One of the ladies who answers the phones where I work says you can tie a weddin' ring to a string and dangle it over your belly." Pete pretends to hold an invisible string as he explains. "If it's a girl, it swings sideways, and if it's a boy, it swings longways."

"No," Laura says. "I believe it's the other way around." She makes a face. "But that's just a silly wives' tale."

"Way I see it," Jimmy says, "is we have a fifty-fifty shot at havin' a boy."

"That'll be good." Laura rolls her eyes. "'Cause girls will give you nothin' but grief."

Jimmy glances over at Celeste before responding. "We don't care what we have, but I have to admit I'm kinda hopin' we have twins."

Celeste sputters, and food comes flying out of the corners of her mouth. "Twins? Jimmy, if we have twins, I'll—"

Jimmy puts his arm around her and squeezes. "Honey, there's prob'ly no chance on God's green earth we'll have twins, so don't get all worked up." He gives Pete and Tim a conspiratorial glance. "But if we do have twins, you know I'll be right there helpin'."

Pete says, "Just like I did with our young'uns."

"Really, Pete?" Laura has her hand on her hip as she glares at her husband.

I lift my hands to stop this conversation from escalating. "Okay, I think we get the picture. It's not easy raising children, but I'm sure we all agree that they're blessings."

Laura drops her biscuit, gives me a look that sends a chill down my spine, jumps up, and runs from the room. Pete looks at me and shakes his head. "You really done it this time, Priscilla." Before I have a chance to say another word, he's up from the table, running after his wife.

Okay, I'm obviously missing something because as far as I know, I haven't said anything everyone didn't already know. I've stated the fact that it's not easy raising children, and I've voiced the opinion I think most decent people have: that children are blessings. That sounds supportive to me. What did I do wrong? I look at Tim and see that he's just as stunned as I am.

Jimmy stands and hooks his thumbs in his belt loops. "Maybe I better go see what's goin' on. Even for Laura, that's an overreaction. Even if she's had nothin' but trouble from them young'uns, I don't think she'd wanna trade any of 'em in." He takes a step toward the door and glances over his shoulder at Celeste.

"I don't know if it's such a good idea to go out there," Celeste says. "There's no tellin' what they'll do to you."

Tim nods. "Let's give 'em just a few minutes alone. Maybe Pete'll come back in here and tell us what this is all about."

"Oh, okay." Jimmy lifts his hands in surrender before walking back over to the counter. He lifts the unopened bag. "Who wants dessert? We brung chocolate chip cookies, pecan pie, and pound cake."

"I'll have a little of each." Celeste tilts her head down and giggles, something I don't think I've ever heard her do. "This baby is makin' me hungry nonstop."

Jimmy laughs and tells us about how she craved hush puppies last night, and I wonder if they've completely forgotten about Laura and Pete. Tim glances at the door and then at me, shaking his head, letting me know he's thinking the same thing.

I turn down dessert, but Tim brings me a cookie anyway, so I nibble on it, while Jimmy and Celeste talk about some of her pregnancy issues. When she turns, her maternity top clings to her still-small waist.

We're all finished with our desserts when Pete returns and sits down at the table. He folds his hands and looks around at the rest of us. I hold my breath until he finally opens his mouth to speak.

"Ever since we found out Renee was pregnant, me and Laura's been on edge." He turns his attention to me. "I wanna apologize to you, Priscilla. You didn't say nothin' wrong. We're just bein' a tad too sensitive these days."

"I didn't know Renee was pregnant," Celeste says.

Pete shakes his head. "She's not anymore. Renee lost the baby."

"I'm so sorry." Celeste's voice cracks. "I wish I knew."

"It's our fault we didn't tell you." Pete stands back up. "Her sorry, good-for-nothin' boyfriend took off as soon as he found out she was pregnant."

Celeste points toward the family room. "Ain't that her boyfriend out there right now?"

Pete nods. "Yup. He came back right after she had the miscarriage." The strain on his face shows as he continues. "When I told Renee he couldn't come back here, she said she'd go somewhere else to see him." The sound of his shaky voice breaks my heart.

"What a dawg." Jimmy cracks his knuckles. "You didn't have to let him back in."

"It's not that easy," Pete says. "We tell him that, and we might never see Renee again. She mighta gone astray, but she's one of our babies, and we love her no matter what."

"Of course you do." I can't just sit back and say nothing. "But she's also smart, and I think she'll eventually come to her senses."

"You'd think . . . " Celeste stands up. "C'mon, folks, I wanna go out there and get more comfortable. This chair is hurtin' my back."

She leads the way to the family room, with Jimmy scurrying right behind her. I watch as Celeste plops down on the loveseat, right beside Renee, who scoots over even closer to her shaggy boyfriend. Jimmy grabs a pillow from the sofa and gently places it behind her before sitting on the arm of the loveseat.

Celeste turns to Renee. "Ain't it sweet how Jimmy is so concerned about me now that I'm carryin' his baby? He's such a wonderful man."

Renee scowls at Celeste but doesn't say a word.

That doesn't deter Celeste. "Good men are hard to find, but they're worth waitin' for."

Now it's obvious to me and most likely everyone else in the room what Celeste is doing. I have to admit she has more audacity than I ever gave her credit for.

"Just last night, when I had a teeny little cravin' for somethin', Jimmy didn't waste a single solitary minute. He took off and got me what I wanted . . . " She leans over and looks Renee in the face. " . . . and now look at him. What a wonderful man."

Jimmy has a stunned look on his face. Laura and Pete are sitting there staring at Celeste, their mouths open, obviously dumbfounded. I turn to Tim and see the look of shock that we're all feeling.

"You two are obviously in love, so I bet he'll be just as good to you as my Jimmy is to me." Celeste settles back against the pillow and sighs. "I bet he don't make you want for nothin' very long before he gets it for you."

The room grows still and silent for what seems like forever, until Renee jumps off the loveseat and turns to face the boy. "You are nothing but a jerk. Get outta my house. Right. Now." She takes off running upstairs.

The boy shrugs but doesn't move, until Pete stands up and takes a step in his direction. "You heard my daughter. Out. Now."

Laura walks up behind Pete and folds her arms as she glares down at the boy. "Wilson, if you don't leave right this minute, there's no tellin' what me or my husband will do to you."

Without wasting another second, Wilson hops up and makes a beeline for the door. Laura slams it behind him. "Good riddance." She brushes her hands together and turns to Celeste. "I never knew you were so smart."

37
Trudy

When I call Laura to let her know I'll be at the reunion after all and that I'm bringing a guest, she seems distracted. "Okay, fine."

Then I call Mama, who clearly isn't happy about the fact that I'm bringing Darryl to the reunion. "What if Tim Puckett shows an interest in you? I don't know this Darryl guy, but I do know Tim has the means to sup—"

"Stop it now, Mama. Darryl is not only sweet and cute, he has a solid direction in life."

"The question is, what direction?" Her tone is annoying, and I want nothing more than to let her have it with sarcasm.

But I don't. "Just trust me on this. You'll like him."

"You do realize he can't stay here, right?"

I sigh. I was hoping Mama would let him use one of the three guest rooms she has, now that my sisters and I no longer live with her and Daddy. "What do you suggest?"

"I've heard that all the hotels in Piney Point are already booked, since it's comin' up so soon. Maybe there's a room somewhere in Hattiesburg."

"I'm sure there is." After I get off the phone, I go online, find a hotel as close to Piney Point as possible, and book a room for Darryl. As annoyed with Mama as I am, I have never expected anything different from her. She's one of those conniving types who schemes to get her way. I shudder to think I might have been prone to that back in my younger days.

Darryl doesn't seem to mind that he'll be staying in the next town over. "It'll be fun to meet all your old classmates. I bet you were a load of fun to be with back in high school."

"I'm not so sure I was." I don't know if it's a good idea to warn him about Michael and how distant I was to my classmates, so I decide to wait a while to tell him. Once I've told him, I know there'll be no taking it back.

My job has become so demanding I've had to arrange for backup, in case something goes wrong. "Just go and have a good time, Trudy," my supervisor tells me. "You need a vacation."

"I know, but—"

"No *buts*. What's the worst thing that can happen? This is department-store fashion, not life or death."

"Okay."

It's Thursday, and the class reunion bonfire is tomorrow night, so I mentally tick off the items I'll need. Darryl calls me on my cell phone.

"Are you sure I won't need to wear a suit to the Saturday night party?"

"Positive. Most guys just wear polo shirts."

"Khaki or navy pants?"

I smile. Shortly after I started dating Darryl, I took him on a shopping spree to help him pick out some clothes that flatter him more than the high-waisted, high-waters and T-shirts with sayings he used to favor. Amazing how much better a man can look in the right clothes.

"Bring both."

"I don't want to embarrass you in front of all your friends, Trudy. I know how important the twentieth reunion is."

"There's no way you'll embarrass me, Darryl. So stop worrying. I'll pack as soon as I get home, and I'll call you when I'm ready."

After we hang up, I reflect on what he told me about his twentieth class reunion. I was right about him being on the geeky side when he was in school. He said that the very girls who never gave him the time of day were all over him at the reunion. I listened to him, all the while thinking I would have been one of those girls. I shudder to think I've ever been like that, but I've changed.

Since I laid everything out last night, it doesn't take me long to pack. I call Darryl and let him know I'm ready.

"I'll be right there," he says.

I stand by the door, and as soon as I hear his footsteps, I open it. He grins, opens his arms wide, and sweeps me into them. His hugs are the best.

"What's all that?" he asks, pointing to the pile of bags behind me.

"That's just my stuff. You do have room, don't you?"

He laughs. "Good thing I travel light." Without another word, he hoists one bag over his shoulders and lifts another one. "Grab my keys out of my pocket, okay? You can unlock the car."

Darryl is such a gentleman he wouldn't even think of asking me to carry my own bags, which makes me want to help. Having someone truly caring for me is so different from anything I've ever experienced before. What Darryl and I have is real and solid. I sure hope Mama can see that, but I'm not sure she will. After all, it's taken me years of being away from Piney Point to know what's really important, and I still struggle with some of the insignificant beauty issues that continue to nag me. Like aging. A woman's body changes so much as she approaches middle age it's a wonder anyone recognizes her after the age of thirty-five . . . or maybe even thirty. I always thought I was above the butt spread and squishy midsection, but I'm dealing with it just as much as the next woman. Well, maybe not quite as much. I've been selling fashion long enough to see that I'm still better off than most.

All the way to Piney Point, I fill Darryl in on what to expect. "Mama is rather unenlightened about a lot of things," I warn.

He casts a quick smile in my direction. "Trudy, honey, don't worry so much. I think I have a pretty good idea of what I'll see."

"I don't know, Darryl. Piney Point is rather unique."

"Maybe not as much as you think. Don't forget I grew up in a small town in Alabama. Based on what you've already told me, Piney Point sounds mighty similar to my hometown. Nothing will surprise me."

"Okay." I study his profile as he drives and ponder his comments. Maybe he's right.

The drive from Atlanta to Piney Point is long, but we finally pull into town around midnight. I wish I'd taken the whole day off so we could've left earlier, but at least we made it safely. I direct him to the house I grew up in. He pulls into the driveway, and without wasting a second he gets out, grabs my bags, and carries them to the front porch.

"I'll put these inside."

"You don't have to." I don't want to take a chance that Mama or Daddy will still be up.

He gives me a look of understanding and nods. "Okay, if you'd rather I didn't . . . "

The last thing I want to do is hurt his feelings, so I relent. "Well, maybe you can help me carry the bags to my room. We just need to be real quiet and not wake Mama or Daddy. They can be so grouchy when they don't have enough sleep."

"I promise I'll be quiet."

I slowly turn the key in the lock and open the door, cringing when it squeaks. Darryl follows behind me, carrying two of my bags. We're almost to my room, when I hear footsteps coming up the hall.

"I thought you'd be here earlier," Mama says. "What took you so long?" Even in the dim light from the bathroom night-light, she looks beautiful for a woman in her early sixties.

"We couldn't leave 'til I got off work." I glance back at Darryl, who is standing there, still holding onto my bags. "Mama, this is Darryl, my . . . date for the reunion."

"Oh?" Mama turns to him. "And where are you from, Darryl?"

I've already told Mama everything I thought she needed to know about Darryl, including the fact that he's from an Alabama town similar to Piney Point. But this is her way of getting under my skin, and there's nothing I can do about it.

He smiles at Mama as she stands there interrogating him. I want to stop this craziness, but knowing Mama, anything I say will only make her that much more determined to torture me.

"Why don't I finish carrying all of Trudy's bags inside so she can go to bed?" he finally says. "We can chat tomorrow after everyone is rested. Trudy's had a long day."

Mama looks back and forth between Darryl and me then nods. "Fine. Trudy, turn the porch light off after he leaves." She goes back to her room without another word.

"Sorry about that," I whisper.

He cups my face in his hands and gives me a long, tender look. "There's nothing to apologize for."

After he leaves, I get ready for bed. The room hasn't changed since I left home to marry Michael. The pinks and purples and sparkly silver accent that I used to love now seem overdone. Maybe I'll have a chat with Mama about redecorating my old room.

I awaken to the sound of someone knocking on my bedroom door. Mama doesn't wait more than a few seconds before opening the door and smiling at me. "Trudy, your guest is here. Why don't you get dressed and come on into the kitchen?" Her demeanor is different and throws me off.

"I have to take a shower." I toss back the covers and sit up. "But it won't take me long."

"Take your time. Darryl seems like a very sweet boy, and we're enjoying each other's company." She winks at me. "He just might be the one."

As she closes the door, I sit in stunned silence. Surely I'm hearing things. I never expected Mama to appreciate Darryl—at least not right away.

I don't waste any time showering, dressing, and putting on my makeup. Whatever good thing is going on in the kitchen can't last long.

They're laughing so hard when I join them they don't even see me right away, so I clear my throat. "What's so funny?"

"Trudy, why didn't you tell me Darryl was a Rhodes Scholar?"

I cross the kitchen, pull a mug from the cabinet, and pour myself a cup of coffee before turning around to face them. "What's a Rhodes Scholar?"

Mama lifts a hand to her mouth, obviously trying to stifle laughter, but Darryl gives me a thoughtful look as he speaks. "It's an academic scholarship."

"Come on, Darryl," Mama says as she looks at him in awe. "It's the most prestigious scholarship that's ever been awarded."

"I'm not so sure about that." Darryl looks embarrassed but pleased by the fact that Mama is so impressed.

"Trudy, this young man is not only brilliant, he's modest to a fault. He's definitely a keeper."

Now I'm the one who's embarrassed, so I change the subject. "Are you hungry, Darryl? I'm starving."

"Your mother made me some pancakes." He turns to Mama. "And they were delicious."

"I'd like some pancakes too." I glance back and see that all the dishes have been washed and put away. "I'll make 'em."

"Trudy, honey, you're putting on some extra pounds. I think you might want to pass on the pancakes." She looks me up and down with obvious disapproval. "How about a poached egg and piece of dry toast?"

Tears of embarrassment sting the back of my eyes. I can't look at Darryl for the shame I feel.

"I think Trudy is beautiful." Darryl gets up from the table and walks straight over to me before turning around to face Mama. "And now I know where she gets her looks."

"Why, thank you, Darryl." Mama is actually blushing. "It's not easy maintaining a decent figure, though. I have to work at it."

"Trudy and I like to go for long walks every chance we get, so I don't think an occasional pancake or two will hurt."

Mama ponders his comment and finally nods. "You're probably right. Denying yourself of everything will only make you binge later. Isn't that right, Trudy?" She laughs. "Did you tell Darryl about that time—?"

I glare at her, stopping her midsentence. "Mama, stop it right now. I can't continue living up to your expectations and worrying about my weight all the time."

A pained expression flickers across Mama's face. "I'm just trying to help."

"But you're not helping. I'm a professional woman with a good life, and the last thing I need to worry about is my . . . middle-age spread."

Mama holds my gaze for a few seconds before shrugging. "Then suit yourself. If you want pancakes, you know how to make 'em. I have to get going, or I'll be late for my pedicure."

After she leaves, Darryl pulls me into his arms. "Want me to make you some pancakes?"

I shake my head. "I don't really want breakfast. I've lost my appetite."

"You need to eat something." His voice is firm but loving. "Sit down, and I'll fix whatever you want."

38
Priscilla

I'm impressed that Celeste has managed to maintain a beauty regimen as long as she has. "Your hair color is perfect," I tell her.

"It took me a while after we moved to the coast, but I finally found a hairdresser who knew what he was doing."

I lift a section of her highlighted hair. "What would you like me to do then?"

She shrugs. "Just wash, trim, and blow dry."

That's exactly what I would have advised. As I work on her hair, we chat about her life on the coast and how Jimmy's managed to build a business with a small loan from her mother's estate.

"He's all worried people will think he's freeloading off my inheritance," Celeste says.

"Who cares what other people think? As long as you and Jimmy are happy, that's all that really matters."

Celeste narrows her eyes as she looks at me in the mirror. "Do you think he's a freeloader?" The challenge behind her question makes me nervous.

"No, I don't think that at all. In fact, I'm impressed by how the two of you have grown as a couple."

Her shoulders relax, and I let out a breath of relief. "Yes, we have grown . . . in a lot of ways. Jimmy has turned out to be a wonderful provider. He never had the chance to show his abilities as long as we were in Piney Point and he stayed at the resin plant. It took movin' to the coast where nobody knew him to prove he's smart."

"I'm glad y'all had that opportunity."

"Yeah, me too. By the way, that incident at the Mosses' house was quite a spectacle, wasn't it?"

I was hoping to avoid that subject. "Um . . . yeah."

"Laura called me later and said after Renee watched how good Jimmy treated me she knew that Wilson boy was a scuzz-bucket. Can you believe he abandoned her when she found out she was pregnant and then came back after she lost the baby?" She rolls her eyes. "Jimmy says he wouldn't let Wilson back in the house after that, but I know Laura and Pete were afraid of what she'd do if they banned him."

"I'm glad she came to her senses." I don't know what else to say, and I wish I didn't have to say anything.

"Yeah, Renee is a smart girl, but she let her hormones get the best of her. I promised Laura I'd have a talk with her after she calms down a bit."

"That's probably a good idea." I rack my brain for a new topic to discuss. "What are you wearing to the bonfire tonight?"

"I'm gonna have to swing by Olson's Department Store for some maternity jeans."

I glance down at her maternity top that clings to her still-slim waistline, but I don't mention that she probably doesn't need maternity jeans yet. "It's been a while since I've been to Olson's."

"Me too."

We've run out of things to talk about, so I work in silence, while she watches the progress in the mirror. When I'm finished, she stands, brushes herself off, and walks straight to the counter to pay.

Tim drops in a couple times during the afternoon to let me know what's going on. "We have the bonfire set up and ready to light." His eyes flicker with a playful twinkle. "I just hope that's the only thing that's lit."

I chuckle. "Now that Pete's sober, we might not have to worry about that."

"Laura wanted to have a dry party, but some of the fellas squawked and insisted on havin' a keg. I'll do what I can to keep Pete away from it, but he's pretty wily."

"Some things are out of our control." Did I just say that? Even I know I'm a control freak.

Tim grins and nods. "You got that right."

"I'm glad to know I finally got something right. So what time do you need to be there?"

"I promised Laura I'd be the first one there. If you can't leave that early, I'm sure you can prob'ly hitch a ride with Celeste and Jimmy."

"I can drive."

"I know." Tim shoves his hands in his pockets and gives me one of his charming smiles. "But I was hopin' to take you home later, and if you drive . . . well, that might not work out."

"I'll call Celeste."

His smile brightens as he backs toward the door. "I best be gettin' on outta here. There's a ton of work that still needs to be done, and I promised to pick up the meat for the barbecue."

"See you around seven?"

"Yup. Call me if you're runnin' late or you can't get hold of Celeste."

After Tim leaves, I turn around and see an audience. "How long have y'all been standing there?"

Sheila smiles at Chester and Alicia before turning back to me. "Long enough to know that boy is amazin'. Isn't that right, Chester?" Before he has a chance to respond, she adds, "Priscilla, when will you come to your senses and marry Tim?"

I let out a laugh that's a little too loud and way too high-pitched. "I don't think marriage has ever come up between Tim and me."

"It's not for his lack of tryin'." Chester shakes his head and glances at the clock. "I have a facial in five minutes, so I better get the room ready."

Alicia silently walks away, leaving Sheila and me alone. "So are you ready to face another class reunion?"

"I guess."

She laughs. "After the last two, I wasn't sure you'd ever wanna come back. But I reckon curiosity is a mighty powerful force."

"You're so right."

"Everyone in town is curious about you, now that you're such a big star."

"It's not just me." At least I hope it's not. "I think everyone is curious about anyone they haven't seen in a while."

"Could be, but I know you've been a big draw for this year's reunion. From what I hear, it has the highest expected attendance in the history of Piney Point High. Some folks from other graduating classes wanted to come just so they could rub elbows with the TV star, and Laura had to tell a bunch of 'em no."

"I don't think—"

Chester joins us. "I just happen to know Laura had Tim hire a couple off-duty cops to keep intruders away."

"I thought you had an appointment," Sheila says.

"She's not here yet."

I lean toward Chester. "So what's this about Tim hiring off-duty cops?"

He slaps his forehead. "I reckon I shouldn't have spilled the beans, but now that I have, I might as well tell you what I know."

"Yes." I widen my eyes and fold my arms. "You better."

Sheila rolls her eyes. "Big mouth."

"So tell me."

Chester avoids looking at Sheila as he fills me in. "According to the scuttlebutt, the press has offered big bucks to some folks to get them into the reunion . . . or at least take pictures for them."

"Folks who went to school with me?"

"It started with the paparazzi goin' to people in your graduatin' class, but they couldn't get any takers. That's why they turned to some of the younger, more entrepreneurial types."

"You're kidding."

Sheila shakes her head. "I wish he was, but that's the truth, Priscilla."

"Why didn't y'all tell me before?"

Chester places his hand on my shoulder. "Because, Priscilla, my dear woman, Sheila was afraid if we told you, you might decide not to grace us with your presence, and that would be just awful."

His sing-song tone makes me chuckle. "You were afraid the paparazzi would scare me away?"

"That's exactly what we thought." Sheila nudges Chester away and puts her arm around my shoulders. "We were tryin' to protect you."

"I appreciate that, but I'll be fine." My employees have obviously underestimated my ability to deal with my fame. "So, will the off-duty cops be at the bonfire and the party tomorrow?"

"Yep." Chester offers a clipped nod before he waves at someone behind me. "My appointment is here. Too-da-loo, ladies."

Once he's gone, I turn to Sheila. "Who is paying for this?"

Sheila shrugs. "I'm not a hundred percent sure, but I think that's why Laura had to charge folks more this year."

"That's not good. I mean, it's not their fault the paparazzi are after me. I need to talk to Laura."

A panicked look crosses her face. "No, don't. I mean, we weren't supposed to discuss this with you."

"Oh." That does pose a problem. "I have to do something to make it up to everyone."

"Trust me, if anyone didn't wanna pay, they wouldn't come."

"Still . . . " My mind starts whirring with all sorts of ideas. "Maybe I can buy gift cards and hand them out."

Sheila makes a face and shakes her head. "I don't think that's such a good idea. What will you tell them?"

"It's a party favor?"

"Let me see if I can come up with a better idea." Sheila nods toward the reception desk. "I think both of our appointments have arrived."

Trudy's mother makes her way to my chair, chattering nonstop about how happy she is her daughter finally met a decent man. "I think she's met Mr. Right . . . finally. I mean, I thought Michael was perfect for her, but she wasn't able to hold onto him because of some silly notion that she didn't have to keep working at her appearance once she got married—"

"Trudy has always looked beautiful."

"Thanks to me, she did for a while. Anyway, as I was sayin', she met this man in Atlanta, and can you believe this, he's a Rhodes Scholar. He's such an intelligent man, which more than makes up for his . . . well, dowdy looks, and you and I both know that can be fixed if the right woman gets hold of him . . . "

She rambles on and on about such insignificant stuff I want to run from the salon screaming. But of course I don't. I continue working on her hair until I have it just like she wants it.

"How's this?" I hand her a mirror and twirl her chair around.

She inspects the back and gives me a smile of approval. "Perfect as usual. If you ever decide to come back to Piney Point for good, I want a weekly standin' appointment with you."

"Sure." No way will I return to Piney Point for good. If I ever go back to doing hair full-time, it'll most likely be in the Jackson salon.

"Make sure you get to know Trudy's new guy." She stands and twirls around to face me. "He's a Rhodes Scholar, ya know."

"Yes, you've already mentioned that."

"It is quite impressive, isn't it?"

"I have another appointment now, so Alicia will take care of you."

She smiles without crinkling her eyes before turning to leave. She's barely gone when Sheila walks up. "I never knew nobody so caught up with tryin' to impress folks as that woman."

"Sh." I glance over my shoulder to make sure no one else can hear. "At least this time it sounds like she has a reason to be impressed."

"Yeah, I heard. Rhodes Scholar, huh? Not bad for a ditz like Trudy."

"Sheila! Trudy is absolutely not a ditz. In fact, she's quite smart."

"Yeah, I s'pose you're right. I hear she's doin' quite well at her job. Accordin' to what folks is sayin', she's movin' on up the corporate ladder real quick."

39
Tim

As promised, I'm the first person to arrive at the bonfire location. Pete's cousin knew someone who worked with someone else who had a connection who said his farm was available. I expected to see a farmhouse and a barn, but when I got here to build the fire pit, I realized all we had was a chunk of hilly land with a few trees and nothin' else. Not even an outhouse . . . and that can be a problem when you got a bunch of folks eatin' and drinkin'. So I called Laura who called around and found someone to bring portable potties. Now they're here, about ten feet from the fire pit.

I call Laura again. "Whatcha want, Tim?" Her testy tone throws me a curve.

"Can you call them potty folks and tell them I need 'em to come back?"

She grunts and pauses. "They said they delivered 'em."

"They did, but they're too close to the fire pit."

"What do you want from me, Tim?"

I'd like to ask her the same question, but I'm not about to with her in this kinda mood. "All I want you to do is ask them folks to come move the potties."

"Why can't you just move the fire pit?"

"'Cause there's trees ever'where, and we can't have the fire too close to the trees."

She grunts again. And then she don't say nothin'.

"Laura, do you wanna give me their number, and I'll call 'em?"

"No, I'll do it. Just don't go anywhere."

"Call me back and let me know what they say, okay?"

She hangs up on me without givin' me an answer. If anyone else did that, I'd be hoppin' mad, but I know that's just how Laura deals with stress, and I've learned that organizin' a class reunion is about the most stressful thing a person can do.

I'm not about to light the fire 'til the potties are moved, so I walk on over to my car, open the door, and sit down sideways on the seat, my legs stretched out. This farm is peaceful—the kinda place I might like to have for my own one of these days. I lean back and fold my hands behind my head to ponder what life might be like years from now. Until the last Piney Point reunion, I imagined I'd be with Priscilla, but now that I think about it, that was nothin' but a pipe dream. What would a woman like her ever see in a man like me? Don't get me wrong. I know she likes me . . . and maybe even loves me in her own way, but not how a woman would love a man she would wanna marry.

I hear the sound of a vehicle approachin', so I hop up with the hope it's the potty folks. But it's not. It's the catering van.

A middle-aged woman approaches, while a man goes around behind the van and opens the doors. "Where you want the tables?" the woman asks.

I originally thought the food should be where the potties are now, but even after they're moved, that don't seem right, so I point to the other side of the fire pit. "How's about over there?"

"You got it."

I start to help them, but the woman gives me a dirty look and says they'll go faster without me, so I back off. "Just let me know if you need somethin'."

"Any running water around here?"

I shake my head. "Not that I know of."

They exchange a glance and continue about their business. I turn and stare in the direction of the highway, hopin' to see the potty folks, but the next vehicle I see is Laura's old mini-van—same one she had five years ago.

She don't waste a minute gettin' out to look things over. "Why'd you have them set the food out over there?"

I look down at the five-foot-nothin' woman who scares me more 'n anyone else ever has and take a step back. "It makes the most sense. Where would you have put it?"

Laura turns around, surveys the layout, and shakes her head. "The portable potties need to be moved."

"I know. That's why I called you."

Without another word, she whips out her cell phone, punches in a number, and immediately starts ragin' to some unfortunate person on the other end of the line. With an exaggerated motion, she punches the phone off, plants her fists on her hips, and announces, "You stay here and wait for 'em, while I go see about the music. Zeke and the Geeks were s'posed to be here already."

I wonder why she hired them again, but I'm not about to say nothin' for fear of her wrath smackin' me in the face. "Would you like me to have the food tables moved?"

"Where else ya gonna put 'em with the potties right there?"

That's exactly what I was sayin'. I just shrug and don't say a word.

Laura lifts her hand to shield her eyes from the settin' sun as she looks toward the highway. "I hafta get back home, so ya think you can hang out here for a while?"

I nod. "I'm here all night if you need me."

"Okay, good." She don't say another word as she takes off toward her minivan and zooms away in a cloud of dust. I reckon that must mean she trusts me to take care of things.

She's barely gone when Zeke arrives, without the Geeks. He parks next to my rental car, jumps out of his truck, and heads straight over to me. "Hey, my band was s'posed to be here already."

"I'm sure they'll be here soon."

Zeke laughs and glances around. "You don't know some of those dudes. They have to ask directions—" He scrunches his nose and turns to me. "Are those portable potties, right there by the fire pit?"

I nod. "Yep."

"Weird." He shrugs. "I wouldn't have put 'em there, but I guess you know what you're doing."

"I wouldn't have put 'em there either, and that's why I'm expectin' the potty people to come move 'em."

Zeke gives me a curious look and smiles. I chuckle, and within seconds me and him are both laughin' real hard, lettin' out some of the steam built by all the stress. And we don't stop 'til we hear the sound of a truck makin' its way over the bumpy grass.

"Oh, good. They're here."

Zeke lets out one more snort before leavin' me to deal with the potty folks. He walks over toward the food tables, pulls out his cell phone, and starts punchin' in some numbers.

The man gets outta the truck and walks straight toward me. "Ms. Moss says you wanna see us?"

"Yeah, we need those moved."

He looks over his shoulders at the two aluminum structures. "What's wrong with where we put 'em?"

I stare at him for a few seconds and decide not to explain nothin'. I mean, after all, if he can't see for himself, he won't understand nothin' I say. "I just want 'em moved, okay?"

He shrugs. "Sure thang. Where you want 'em?"

I point toward some trees. "How 'bout over yonder by them pine trees?"

"Okie doke. Will do."

Good thing the potty folks came when they did 'cause folks start arrivin' to help light the fire and finish settin' up minutes after they're gone. Some security guys man their posts between the designated parking area and the bonfire pit. For the next hour and a half, I'm directin' parkin' and tellin' people where to put stuff. The rest of Zeke's band finally arrives, and they get all their equipment set up. I'm relieved they knew enough to bring a generator. Too bad they don't sound no better than they did last time I heard 'em. A couple of the band members have changed, but I can't tell the difference.

No one tells me when Priscilla arrives, but everyone gets real quiet and turns to look at her as she slams the car door shut and struts toward us. Jimmy and Celeste take a little more time gettin' outta the car.

Priscilla's wearin' a pair of skin-tight jeans, a pink tank top, and some sneakers. Even from a distance, I can tell she looks more refined in her casual get-up than any of the rest of these folks prob'ly look on Sunday mornin'.

I'm on my way to greet Priscilla when Celeste darts past me. "I gotta get to the potty and fast," she says. "Why'd you have 'em put them things all the way over there?"

"Sorry."

Jimmy comes up from behind. "Ever since my wife found out she's pregnant she spends half her time runnin' to the bathroom."

"Oh." I turn around toward Priscilla, who is less than two feet away from me, a smile playin' on her pretty lips. I swallow hard. "Hey, there, Priscilla. You're lookin' mighty fine."

"Thank you, Tim." She glances around at the crowd. "Looks like the party is in full swing."

"I reckon' you could say that."

She turns to Jimmy. "Pregnancy becomes Celeste. She practically glows."

Jimmy puffs his chest up and gets one of them full-of-himself looks on his face. "My wife is the purtiest girl here."

Priscilla smiles and pats him on the arm. "I agree."

Trudy and some guy I never seen before walk up. "Hi, Tim . . . Priscilla . . . I'd like you to meet Darryl."

I shake the guy's hand and see the way he hangs on to Trudy with the other hand. Trudy looks around, actin' all nervous. No doubt she's lookin' for Michael, who is here—alone. I heard one of the guys say Michael don't like hangin' out at home with his naggin' wife. Just goes to prove that the high school class hero don't always turn out to have the best character.

When I spot Maurice comin' toward Priscilla, I hafta force myself to take a deep breath and unclench my teeth . . . and my fist. He's the guy she always fancied herself bein' with, 'til he tried to take advantage of her after the tenth reunion. Priscilla wised up and told him to hit the road when she saw him for what he was. I still wanna punch his lights out, but I know better.

"Hey, there," Maurice says as he cuts a narrow-eyed glance in my direction. "How about—"

Before he has a chance to continue, Priscilla cuts him off. "How about nothing, Maurice. I think your *fiancée* wants to see you." She points toward Didi who looks like she's ready to pull someone's hair. "You better go see what she wants." Then she smiles at me.

He looks surprised, but he nods. "Okay." Then he walks off without another word. Trudy does her best to hide her amusement, but I can see the smile playin' on her shiny red lips.

After Trudy and her guy take off to get some food, Priscilla gets real close. "I appreciate all you've done, Tim." Her breath tickles my face as she speaks softly into my ear.

"You know I like doin' it." Her smile makes my heart thump hard, but I force myself to play it cool.

Pete and Laura walk around, hand in hand, and that just looks weird. After all, in the past, I don't think they even spoke two words to each other at either of the reunion parties, and now they're here as a couple. I look real close at Pete's face and see it's a strain for him to be at a party without a beer or somethin' to loosen him up, but I hafta hand it to him. He's behavin', even though I'm sure he knows there's a keg over by the food tables. A few of the guys are imbibin', but there's not a whole lotta action over there, and the party is tame . . . so tame it's finished two hours after it started.

40
Priscilla

Throughout the night, I've been watching Tim in action. Not only has he singlehandedly set everything up for the bonfire, he's turned into the go-to person for everyone from my class. On top of that, he has the ability to make me feel as though he's doing all this for me. And maybe he is, but after all these years, I suspect there might be something else.

Now that the party is winding down, I look around and see that most of the people in attendance didn't bother using the trash receptacles to dispose of their plates, cans, napkins, and marshmallow roasting sticks. Tim somehow manages to follow after them, picking up trash, and telling them he'll see them tomorrow night—all the while smiling and acting as though he's enjoying himself.

I walk up to him and place my elbow on his shoulder. "How do you do it?"

"What are you talkin' about, Priscilla?"

"All this. You're like a one-man show. If it weren't for you, none of this would have happened."

Tim chuckles. "And that might not be a bad thing. Don't look to me like the bonfire was all that successful."

"Oh, I think it was. People seemed to be having a good time."

"Didn't last long, though." He glances around at the half dozen people still lingering. "We had to shut the other two parties down."

I take a step back and tilt my head toward him. "People have grown up."

Tim shrugs. "Maybe."

Laura approaches, with Pete right on her heels. "Let's get everything cleaned up so we can leave. I'm glad this thing's over. Now all we have to deal with is tomorrow night."

She makes it sound like such a chore I wonder why she continues being in charge. Tim nods. "Okie dokie. I'll go tell the caterers they can shut down."

By now, everyone else has left, so the four of us finish picking up trash and getting it ready to be carried away by the cleanup people Laura has hired to come in the morning. An hour and a half later, Tim and I are on our way back to town.

As he drives, I study his profile. Tim is a nice-looking man who is aging quite well. The strength of his jaw shows a rugged determination, and his deep-set eyes appear to notice everything.

I'm compelled to touch him . . . to connect with some invisible force that's making me want to get closer to him. He gives me a quick glance and smiles as I place my hand on his shoulder.

"What's that all about?"

I sigh. "I don't know. I just wanted to touch you."

"That's nice." His shoulder relaxes.

We ride in silence for a few minutes before we come to our first turn. "Wanna hear some music?"

"No, not really," I say. "I'm really enjoying the silence."

He chuckles. "I bet you don't get much of that."

"You're right. Sometimes it seems as though my life is way too noisy."

"Ya know, I think there might be a country song in that."

"There probably is." I pull my hand to my lap but continue looking at Tim. "So how do you like living in New York?"

He shrugs. "It's okay."

"Do you ever feel like life's living you rather than the other way around?"

Tim frowns for a moment then nods. "Yes, that's exactly how I feel sometimes, but I don't see any other way."

I scooch down as far as the seatbelt will allow, lean my head back, and close my eyes. "I always thought my life would be perfect once I had a successful run on TVNS."

"Are you saying it's not?"

"Yes, that's exactly what I'm saying. Tim, I don't know what's happening to me, but I feel restless—like there's something I've been missing. Every once in a while, I get a flicker of what it might be . . . then it disappears before I can identify it."

"That's real deep, Priscilla . . . real deep."

"Sorry, Tim. I didn't mean to end the night on a down note. You did a fabulous job with the bonfire."

He smiles. "Do you think folks had fun?"

"Absolutely. Even Trudy. And I don't think she even gave Michael a second thought after he tried to talk to her."

"She seems to be into that Darryl guy."

I agree. "I hope so. It's so hard to let go of who we were back in high school, but I think she's finally managed to do that."

Tim clears his throat. "Have you done that?"

"What? Let go of the old Priscilla?"

"Yeah."

"Ya know, I thought I already had, but now I realize that's always been my driving force. And now that I see it, I want to move on and stop holding myself back."

Tim gives me a look of disbelief and shakes his head. "I don't see nothin' holdin' you back, Priscilla."

"That's just it. Appearances are so deceiving, no one would know that everything I've done has been to prove myself to everyone else." This thought has been playing in my head, ever since I realized how unfulfilling reaching my goal has been, but it's the first time I've ever verbalized it. And now, I need to do something about it. But what?

As if he could read my mind, Tim nods. "It's never too late to fix what's broken."

Now I'm ready for some music, so I turn on the radio. Tim cuts a glance at me, and he gives me one of his eye-crinkling smiles. We ride the rest of the way to my mother's house with only our thoughts and the sound of music between us.

He pulls into the driveway and gets out. I know better than to open my own door because Tim, being the consummate southern gentleman, likes doing it for me.

On our way to the front door, I take his hand in mine and hear a quick whoosh of his breath. But he doesn't say anything until we reach the doorstep.

"I . . . " He looks down at me, and I feel something stir in my heart. "What's going on?"

I swallow hard and let go of his hand. "I'm not sure." And that's exactly why I need to tread carefully. I want to kiss Tim, but doing that will change the dynamics of our relationship, and I don't want to risk losing something wonderful that we already have.

"Good night, Priscilla." He touches my cheek but quickly draws back his hand. "I'll stop by the salon sometime tomorrow while I'm out runnin' errands for Laura."

He waits for me to unlock the front door and step inside before going back to his car. I stand by the window, watching his taillights disappear as he turns toward town.

Mother isn't home, so I have the house to myself. It still irks me that she's dating Mr. Barrymore, but I'm not the one living her life, and she seems to be happier than ever. I know Dad has dated a few people who work at Piney Point Community College, but he says he's too set in his ways to be in a long-term relationship. I wonder why I never noticed how little attention Dad gave Mom before. And when I come to town, he doesn't go out of his way to see me, and that hurts.

My thoughts wander to all the years I've been away from home and how my life has seemed to be gilded. Now I know that's only perception. In reality, I'm still the same insecure, lonely person I always was. I've had occasional dates when time has allowed, but no man has hung in there with me . . . except Tim.

41
Laura

I'm barely in the house Saturday mornin' after gettin' my hair done when Renee walks right up to me. "Where you been?"

"I had to get my hair done for the reunion."

She looks at my hair and does a double take. "Looks nice."

"Thanks." She continues to look at me, so I know something's up. "What?"

"Mama, I've decided it's time I get a job so I can move out on my own."

I stare at my daughter and wonder why I let her graduate early since she still has so much growin' up to do. "You can't move out, Renee. It's expensive livin' on your own."

"I'll get a roommate." She frowns. "And I'll need a car, but maybe Grandma will get Randy to help me find a good deal."

"He better." I grab a bowl and start mixin' the batter for some muffins. "What kinda job you plannin' on gettin'?"

"One of my friends just got a job at the bank. Maybe I can do that."

"You're only seventeen, Renee. What makes you think they'd hire someone your age?"

"I don't know. Maybe I'll do somethin' else, like work at the Dairy Curl."

The last thing I wanna do is tromp on my daughter's ambition, so I change my tune. "The bank might hire you after you turn eighteen next month. If that's what you really wanna do, I think you should walk right in there and fill out an application."

"That's not how it works, Mama. They only take applications online these days."

"Then start gettin' your résumé together so you can apply the day you turn eighteen."

She gives me a puzzled look. I grin, and she smiles back. "Okay."

Life has taken so many turns lately I don't always know which way is up. Ten years ago, if someone had said my husband would be sober, my firstborn would be fightin' for our country, and my second-born child would want to be a banker, I woulda told 'em they were crazy. Now I know anything's possible, *thank ya, Lord*. I mean, folks kept sayin' they were prayin' for us, and I believed them, but now I see how the impossible can actually happen. I need to stop missin' church so much, with all these miracles happenin'. It just doesn't seem right not to give credit to God when he's blessin' my socks off.

I go to the bottom of the stairs and holler up. "Breakfast is ready. If you're hungry, y'all better come on down, or there won't be anything left."

You'd think a herd of elephants lived here by the sound of feet scramblin' to get to the kitchen. With a family like ours, though, if you're the last one at the table, you're likely not to get one of my hot, delicious blueberry muffins I like to fix on Saturday mornin'.

Pete starts to stab a sausage, when I cut him a look. "Why don't you say the blessin', Pete?"

"Oh . . . yeah." Pete puts down his fork, looks around at everyone, and bows his head. "Lord, we come before you with thanks for our family and for this food . . . "

He pauses, so I take up the slack and finish the blessin'. As soon as I say *Amen*, everyone echoes me.

The sound of forks clinkin' on the plates lets me know everything is okay and somewhat normal in my life . . . at least at ten o'clock on Saturday mornin'. I've decided to turn over a new leaf, and instead of fussin' at someone, I'll start a pleasant conversation and hope it stays that way.

"So Renee, why don't you tell everyone what you been thinkin' about doin'?"

She pauses, her fork halfway to her mouth, and gives me a strange look, like I done lost my mind or somethin'. I nod to encourage her to talk.

"Okay." Renee puts down her fork and folds her arms on the table in front of her plate. "I think I'd like to be a bank teller."

Bonnie Sue snorts and rolls her eyes. "Why would any bank hire you?"

Renee scowls at her younger sister, and I can tell she's ready for a fight. I hold up my hands and get everyone's attention. "I think Renee would make a fine bank teller, and I plan to support her on this."

I turn to Pete, hoping for his encouragement, and he doesn't let me down. "I'd be mighty proud for my daughter to become a bank teller."

Jack nods. "Yeah, that'll be cool. Maybe I can stop by every now and then for some samples."

Bonnie Sue gives her little brother one of her bratty looks. "You're such a dweeb."

I smile as my children do their normal Saturday mornin' bickerin'. Pete and I exchange a look, and his lips twitch as he tries hard not to laugh. All is right in our world . . . at least at this moment. That is likely to change at any moment.

Pete sticks around the kitchen and nibbles off the plates as I clean up. Ever since he stopped drinkin', he's done stuff like this. I'm not so sure I would've appreciated havin' him underfoot all the time when we first got married, but now, even though he's in the way more than he's not, I'm happy to have him sober. So I don't even fuss at him about droppin' crumbs all over the place.

"Whatcha got on your agenda this afternoon?" I ask as I close the dishwasher door.

"I thought I'd go over to the Community Center and make sure all the equipment works."

"Did you get the extension cords from the guy at work?"

"Yeah. And I promised Zeke I'd help him set up the band's equipment."

"They sounded pretty bad last night." I lean against the counter and fold my arms. "I wish we had a backup plan."

"I think it might've been the acoustics. Music don't sound the same outdoors as it does inside."

"It'll just be louder." I stop myself before getting too negative. "But that's okay. We have a full program, so there won't be as much time for the music."

"Have you told Priscilla what you got planned?"

I shake my head. "No, and I don't want you to either. It's s'posed to be a surprise."

"I hope it don't tick her off."

"Why would it?"

Pete shakes his head. "Ya never know about women. Sometimes the very thing I think they'll like gets me in all kinda trouble."

"You're just bein' silly, Pete. Now run along and make sure everything is workin' at the Community Center, and don't forget to check for the screen. We'll need it for the PowerPoint presentation. I'll be over there shortly."

Pete leaves, and I holler up for Jack. "What?" he yells.

"C'mere."

He comes to the top of the stairs and looks down at me. "Whatcha want, Mama?"

"Don't forget you're runnin' the PowerPoint show for the reunion tonight."

"I know."

"I want you to do a trial run for me in a few minutes."

"We don't hafta do that. It's just fine."

I fold my arms and give him my "mama look." "It very well may be just fine, but I still wanna see it."

He lifts both hands in surrender. "Okay, okay, just give me a few minutes to get it ready."

I sweep the kitchen and mop up the spots to give him time to do whatever he needs to do. When I arrive at the door of his bedroom, I notice the worried look on his face.

"What's wrong?" I walk up behind him and see that everything is out of order. "That's not the way it's s'posed to go."

"Okay." The tension in his voice catches me off guard, letting me know that somewhere along the way my happy-go-lucky child has started to care about somethin'. Even though the PowerPoint presentation is a hot mess, I'm happy he cares enough to be worried.

It takes him the better part of the day to get things like I want 'em. He lost a coupla the pictures, but it still looks good. I'm most impressed by the music he matched to the show.

"You're pretty good at this, Jack. Maybe you can think about doin' presentations for a livin' when you grow up."

"Nah, I still wanna be a game tester."

"Then that's exactly what you should do, as long as you go to college." Of all my children, Jack is the most scholarly. I would've thought Renee would go to college, until her combination junior-senior year of high school. The last good grade she made was in her summer-school English class that enabled her to graduate early. After she met Wilson, she forgot how to study.

"Can I go over to Bryce's house?"

Normally, I'd be happy to have Jack outta the house on a Saturday, but too many things can go wrong . . . like he'll take off without tellin' me and lose track of time. This reunion is important, and I'm countin' on him.

"Not today, sweetie."

He scowls. "Stop callin' me *sweetie*."

"Okay, Jack. Tell you what. I know this is a sacrifice for you, so I'll even pay you for your time on this PowerPoint presentation."

His eyes light up, lettin' me know I hit the jackpot to his heart. "Cool. My first payin' gig."

"Maybe you can have your pals over here tomorrow afternoon . . . after church."

"Church? We just went last month."

I nod. "Yes, church. I've decided that we need to get in the habit of goin' every Sunday and not just once in a while."

"Can Bryce spend the night and go with us?"

Normally, I don't encourage the young'uns to have overnight guests, but how can I say no to invitin' a friend to church? "Sure, that sounds fine."

"That means he'll be goin' to your party with us."

"I know, and I think it'll be good for you to have someone your age to talk to."

Jack grins. "Thanks, Mama."

42
Priscilla

I'm between two of my morning appointments when Sheila tells me Mandy needs to talk. I take the phone from her. "Hey, Mandy, what's up?"

"Beth Fay did really well in her print ads . . . at least after we got her to calm down and quit being such a ham."

I laugh. "Why am I not surprised?"

"She actually came right out and asked if she'd ever be able to go on air with you."

"What did you tell her?"

"I said she needs to talk to you about it. So brace yourself. I won't be surprised if she pounces on you as soon as you return to Jackson. But she looks awesome in the ads."

"Is she still in Jackson?"

"No, I sent her back to Raleigh. That woman drives me crazy."

I laugh and get off the phone. Sheila gives me a questioning look, and I just shrug. No point in talking too much about something I'm not sure of.

Trudy is my last appointment for the day before I go to Mother's house to get ready. She walks in and smiles directly at me. "Hey, there, Priscilla. You're lookin' really good these days."

"Why, thank you. So are you." And I mean that. Now that Trudy has given up on trying to recapture her beauty-pageant looks, she has a more natural, approachable quality that I find very pretty.

"I think it must be love." She sits down in my chair and lifts her head while I fasten the cape around her neck. "I used to think I was in love with Michael, but now that I've met Darryl, I know what I used to feel was something different . . . more like desperation."

"Perhaps it was wanting to live up to expectations?" I challenge.

She narrows her eyes and actually allows her forehead to crinkle, something I've never seen her do before. Then slowly she nods. "Yes, totally."

I brush her hair back from her face. "I think a lot of us have had to deal with that."

"Oh, I can imagine you did. But you've far exceeded what anyone thought you'd do."

"In some ways you're right." I motion toward the sink area. "Let's go wash your hair so I can cut it wet."

Once we're back in the chair at my station, Trudy picks right up where we left off. "Mama still doesn't know what to think about me working so many hours and moving up with the store, but I've decided it's not about her."

"You're right." I section off the sides of her hair and clip them. "I've heard you're doing quite well at your job."

"Oh, I am, but that's because I love what I do." She sighs and smiles. "And Darryl thinks it's cool that I have a career. He and I have such a great relationship, and I never feel like he's looking over my shoulder for something . . . or someone better. For the first time in my life, I'm very happy." She holds my gaze in the mirror and pats her chest over hear heart. "I mean truly happy, deep down."

"Good for you, Trudy. Every woman deserves a chance at happiness."

"How about you?" She levels me with another reflected gaze in the mirror. "Are you happy?"

I shift from one foot to the other. "Well . . . I suppose I am . . . most of the time anyway."

"But other times?"

I laugh. "You're the first person who has asked me so many questions."

"That's too bad." She purses her lips. "Ya know, Priscilla, I think you and I are more alike than we ever knew."

"Why's that?"

"I was always the beauty queen, and you were the brainiac. People had in their minds what we were supposed to do with those gifts, and we tried as hard as we could to meet their expectations."

"But I didn't—" I stop when I see her raised eyebrows. She's absolutely right.

"Think about it. You didn't want to finish college because you wanted to do hair, but once you started working here, you felt like you let folks down. So what did you do then?" She lifts her hands out from beneath the cape and gestures around to make her point.

"True."

"Just because I've always been beautiful doesn't mean I don't have smarts. And I've gotten pretty good at reading people, which is why I think I'm so successful at my job. Back when I was still on the sales floor, my customers used to call ahead to make sure I was working before coming in to shop for clothes. They knew I would level with them and send them home with outfits that really did flatter their figures . . . not just a bunch of pieces I could sell just to make my quota."

As Trudy talks, I ponder what she's saying. I really enjoy doing hair, but hearing Mother go on and on about not fulfilling my potential altered my thinking. I'm pleased with my accomplishments, but now I have no doubt they're not making me happy.

"So do you think you and Darryl might . . . well, you know . . . get married?"

Her eyes twinkle. "Don't tell anyone, but I think we might be headed in that direction."

"That's awesome." I start snipping small sections of her hair to add texture. "How about I try out my newest products in your hair?"

"Are you talkin' about the Ms. Prissy Big Hair everyone's ravin' about on TVNS?"

I laugh at how quickly she falls right back into her old accent. "That's exactly what I'm talking about."

Her smile gets even bigger. "I would absolutely love it!"

"Good! I can't think of a better model than you, Trudy."

When Trudy gets up from my chair, her hair is layered on the sides, with height at the crown, and it looks natural. "Wow! You really are gifted at making a woman look utterly feminine and glamorous." She leans toward me and gives me a gentle hug. "Let's keep in touch and maybe get together sometime. I know you have some salons in Atlanta, so maybe you can let me know when you're in town, and I can have you over."

"Sounds wonderful."

She starts walking toward the front then stops and turns to face me. "One more thing, Priscilla. If you like Tim as much as I think you do, don't wait around forever, or you might lose him. And if you don't think there's any hope for the relationship, let him know so he can move on." She gives me a softer smile. "How much do I owe you?"

After Trudy leaves, I'm emotionally drained. In the hour she spent in my station, I spent more time examining my deepest thoughts and feelings than I have in my entire life with anyone else. If Trudy ever decides to get out of retail, she might want to consider counseling.

Sheila tilts her head as she joins me in the back room. "Something seems different."

I nod. "You're right. I'm not quite sure what it is, but I think there'll be some changes coming down the pike soon."

A look of concern flashes in her eyes. "Don't make it too drastic."

"Don't worry, Sheila. I don't think you'll be affected in a bad way."

"I certainly hope not 'cause I'm real happy right now, and that hasn't always been the case."

I wrap my arm around her shoulders and squeeze. "I want what you have, and I'm going to get it as soon as I figure out what it is."

"Other folks might say you're not makin' a lick of sense, Priscilla"—she looks at me for a few seconds before she grins. —"but I know exactly what you're sayin'."

43
Tim

I walk into the Community Center multipurpose room and spot Laura and her youngest kid over in the corner, hunched over a laptop computer. And they don't seem to be arguin'. *Do wonders never cease?*

"Hey, there." Their heads pop up, and I wave.

"Oh, hi, Tim." Laura flips the computer shut. "What're you doin' here so early?"

She's obviously hidin' somethin' from me. "Settin' up. I thought that's what you wanted me to do."

"I do, but not now. Me and Jack are busy. Can you come back in about an hour?"

"I reckon I can." I turn to leave but stop when I get to the door. "If you need help with whatever you're doin', I might can do that. I know my way around computers pretty good."

"No." Now I know how her young'uns feel.

"All righty then. I'm outta here."

My next stop is the Cut 'n Curl. "Hey, Tim. If you're lookin' for Priscilla, she's not here. She wanted more time to get ready for tonight." Sheila looks me up and down. "Lookin' good, Tim. You wearin' that?"

"No, I'm just tyin' up loose ends before I get ready for the big party."

Sheila continues lookin' at me with a curious expression, makin' me mighty uncomfortable. "Tim, have you noticed Priscilla's been actin' a little different lately?"

She's right, but I don't wanna get into a discussion with no one about Priscilla on account of I might say somethin' I'll regret later. "I dunno."

"Takes a smart man to admit he don't know somethin'." She gestures for me to get closer, so I do. "Let me give you a little advice. Pay real close attention to Priscilla. I sense change comin' with her, and you might pick up on some clues that you need to be aware of."

"Okie dokie." I back toward the door. "I better get goin'. The party's comin' up in a few hours, and there's things to do."

Actually, since Laura ran me off, I don't know what to do with myself, since I'd planned to wrap everything up at the community center before headin' back to the hotel to get ready. I glance at my watch and see that almost an hour has passed. Maybe Laura and her kid are done now.

Her minivan is still in the parkin' lot, but I go ahead and pull up alongside it. With the time bein' what it is, I s'pect she's prob'ly about to go home. As I round the corner, I glance in the window and see Priscilla's face on a big screen at the front of the room, above the stage. *What is goin' on here?*

I have to resist the urge to bust in on whatever Laura's doin' and ask her that very question. But I don't. I know I have to do somethin', though, so I figure I'll just warn Priscilla that she might be the center of attention in the program.

As I enter the humongous room, I make as much racket as I can to warn Laura. She looks up, and her boy shuts the computer down. Both have guilty looks on their faces, but I pretend not to notice. This worries me 'cause I know Laura don't treat some folks so good, and Priscilla just might be one of them folks tonight.

"I gotta set everything up and make sure it all works before I go to the hotel and get dressed."

"Go right ahead," Laura says as she guides her young'un toward the door. "We're all done here 'til tonight. See ya in a coupla hours."

As soon as they're gone, I look around for signs of what they been doin', but I don't find a single solitary thing. So I pull out my list and check everything off as I do it. Looks like all the cords are here and in place, the tables are set up for the food, and the sound system works just fine. I walk around once more, and this time, I spot a table sittin' off to the side of the stage. There's a black piece of material coverin' a real tall lump. I look over my shoulder to make sure ain't no one watchin', and then I lift the corner of the cloth. It looks sorta like a trophy, so I turn it toward the light to see what the printin' on the bottom says. Then I drop the cloth and smile. Priscilla's gonna be real pleased tonight. Her classmates is finally gonna give her some credit for all she's done.

Now that I know what Laura has up her sleeve, I'm not so worried about Priscilla. Yeah, I know I should never worry about Priscilla on account of she's always been good at takin' care of herself, but I can't help myself.

Showered, shaved, feelin' all fresh and manly, I amble up to the front door of Priscilla's mama's house. Right about this point when I first came here, my nerves near 'bout got the best of me. But now, I'm feelin' all confident and know I'm just as good as anyone—even a college professor. Ms. Slater might know her way around the grammar rules, but I think I understand human nature a bunch more. That woman turns more folks away with her persnickety ways than she attracts, and I s'pect that's what's turned her into a sourpuss. She used to have her nose stuck up in the air, but now her face looks like she's been suckin' on a lemon all the time.

I ring the doorbell, expectin' Priscilla to answer, but that don't happen. Instead, Ms. Slater flings it open, and I'm dumbstruck by her big ol' honkin' smile.

"Hi there, Tim. Come on in. Priscilla will be out shortly, but I'd like you to meet someone."

Her niceness has completely and utterly caught me so off guard I open my mouth and nothin' comes out. So I follow her into the family room like a puppy dog with a new kid.

Sittin' on a couch is a man who looks like a bigger version of Mr. Slater. Priscilla's mama turns to him. "Stand up, Barry. This is my daughter's friend, Tim."

The man stands and sticks out his hand. "Good to meet you, Tim. I'm Barry Barrymore."

I have to stifle a snicker. "Nice to meet ya, Mr. Barrymore."

"Call me Barry."

"Okay, and you call me Tim." How lame is that, I think. He done called me Tim. I wanna kick myself in the behind for bein' such a doofus.

"Would you like some sweet tea, Tim?"

I know my eyes must look like they's about to pop outta my head, but who is this woman and what did she do to Priscilla's mama? "Um . . . no, thank you, ma'am. As soon as Priscilla's ready, we best be gettin' on over to the party on account of I gotta help out with the signin'-in."

Barry nods and smiles. "I remember my last reunion." He hikes his britches up by the belt loops and shakes his head. "Next one's gonna be a biggy. It's the fiftieth."

Priscilla saves the moment by appearin' in the doorway. "My, don't you look lovely, sweetheart?" Ms. Slater goes up to her daughter and gives her a smooch on the cheek. Priscilla's eyebrows shoot up fast as mine done a few minutes ago. "You two run along and have a wonderful time."

On our way down the sidewalk to my car, Priscilla shakes her head. "She's totally different around Mr. Barrymore."

"So do you like this guy?" I ask as I slide into the car beside Priscilla.

"He was okay. Most of the time we never gave him a second thought, but when he left and Rottweiler came—"

"Rottweiler? As in the big dog?"

She laughs. "His name was Rotteler, but he was so mean we called him Rottweiler."

"My cousin used to have a Rottweiler, and he was a nice dog."

"Well, this one wasn't. I think he was trained to kill."

All the way to the Community Center, we laugh and kid around about some of our meanest teachers. There's only a coupla cars in the parkin' lot when we arrive—Laura's minivan and Jimmy and Celeste's SUV. Before I get out, I turn to face Priscilla. "I'm not sure if I should do this . . . I mean, I'm kinda torn, but . . . "

"Spit it out, Tim."

"Expect anything tonight."

"What do you mean by that?"

"Just don't be surprised by anything that happens, okay?" I hold up my hands. "That's all I'm sayin'."

"Tim, come on. We've known each other how long? You know you can trust me."

"I done said too much already. Come on, let's go in and see what Laura wants us to do."

She opens her mouth, but I shake my head, and she laughs. "Okay, whatever."

44
Priscilla

The moment I spotted Tim talking to Mother and Mr. Barrymore, I wanted to grab Tim by the hand and run away as fast as I could. And I might have if seeing him hadn't made me so weak in the knees. He's been having a strange effect on me lately. It's almost as though I've been seeing him with different eyes. I know he's pursued me as a romantic interest in the past, but sometimes I wonder if I've become more of a habit to him now than someone he wants a love relationship with. And that really bothers me way more than I ever thought it would.

And now he's telling me that something's going to happen, but he's not about to tell me what it is. My mind races with all sorts of possibilities. When we get to the door, I stop and tug on his sleeve. "Tim, please tell me what you were alluding to back in the car."

"What I was what?"

"You know, when you said to expect anything." I look up at him, hoping he'll at least give me more of a hint. "Please tell me what's going to happen."

"Priscilla . . ." He takes a step back. "I'm afraid I said too much. To be honest, I'm not a hundred percent sure something's gonna happen. I just want you to brace yourself, in case it does."

"How do I know what to brace myself against? Is it . . . good or bad?"

He cups my chin and holds my gaze. "In my book, it'll be good."

At that very moment, I know what I want to happen. All this time I've been taking Tim for granted I've missed the most important thing in my life. Tim is a loving, caring man who has always been there for me. He's smart, even though his grammar can still use some work. But seriously, that's the only thing I've ever been able to find wrong with him.

I want to start a romantic relationship with Tim and see where it takes us. In the past, my fear was having my focus diverted away from my goals, which unfortunately turned out to be so much less satisfying than I imagined. Without fulfillment in my personal life, everything else seems insignificant.

"Nickel for your thoughts?" he asks.

I stick out my hand. He fishes in his pocket and comes up empty. "Sorry, I left my change on the dresser back at the hotel."

"Okay, you owe me. I was just thinking that tonight just might be one of the best nights of my life."

He nods and gives me a serene smile. "I think it just might be."

Maybe . . . and that's just my wishful thinking . . . Tim is hinting that he wants the same thing I want. He's actually given me enough clues in the past, but it's been awhile. Not once during our current visit to Piney Point has he even brought up the subject of something more between us than friendship.

"Hey, Priscilla . . . Tim." Trudy and Darryl come up from behind. "We thought we'd get here a little early and see if y'all needed some extra hands." She gives Darryl a loving look.

"Actually that was Darryl's idea, and I thought it was a good one."

Before I have a chance to say a word, Laura darts around from behind the pillar. "Why don't y'all sit here at the sign-in table 'til Celeste and Jimmy get here?"

As Trudy and Darryl take their places, Tim pulls Laura off to the side and says something that causes her to look at me and frown. I wonder if it has something to do with whatever he's being mysterious about.

I'm given the assignment of being a greeter. Since we've never had a greeter at our other reunions, I know it's something Laura and Tim manufactured just to keep me out of the way. But I do it, hoping that I'm making it easy for whatever Tim has in store for me.

The second Celeste walks through the double doors, she marches right up to Trudy and scowls. "Get up. It's always been my job to sign people in."

Trudy laughs. "That's fine. I wouldn't wanna take your job away from you. I was just helping out 'til you arrived."

Celeste rearranges all the name tags, and from the way it appears, the only reason she's doing it is to let Trudy know who's in charge of the sign-in table. Trudy obviously couldn't care less as she walks around, holding onto Darryl's arm, chatting and laughing in a way I've never seen her do before. This guy must be special to bring out the likable side of Trudy.

Then Trudy's ex-husband, Michael, walks in and struts right past the sign-in table, over toward me. "Where's my ex-wife?"

Before I have a chance to say a word, Laura appears. "Which one?" That woman seems to be everywhere.

"Which one?" Michael folds his arms and gives her a condescending glare. "Which one do you think, Lorraine?"

"My name's not Lorraine, and you know that, Michael . . . and just for that, I'm not helping you find anyone."

I stifle laughter. Looks like not everyone got the message that it's okay to change. Michael obviously hasn't. And speaking of folks not changing, here comes Maurice, with Didi right behind him. Or should I say Dr. Didi Holcomb, ear, nose, and throat specialist—the woman who has always felt slighted by the fact that I edged her out of being class valedictorian and voted Most Likely to Succeed by a very slim margin.

"Hey, Maurice," Laura says much louder than necessary. "I thought you weren't comin', Didi."

Didi narrows her eyes and glares at me then grabs Maurice's arm. "I changed my mind."

"Well, good. Get yourself a name tag, grab some food, and find a seat. Zeke and his band are playin' 'til the program starts, which should be in"—Laura glances at her watch then at me before turning back to Didi—"about an hour or so."

Tim appears and takes me by the hand. "Let's get our food and grab a decent spot before everyone else gets here."

After we fill our plates with chicken wings, mini crustless sandwiches, veggies, and dip, we make our way back toward the tables, all clustered around a dance floor in front of the stage. A hand waving about in the air gets our attention.

"Hey, Priscilla! Over here." It's Trudy, her face lit up as though she's really excited about having us sit with her.

I glance at Tim, and he shrugs. "Whatever you wanna do, Priscilla, is fine by me."

"We might as well sit with them." And deep down, I'm looking forward to getting to know Trudy's guy, Darryl, a little better. He must really be special to have had this effect on her.

As soon as we join them, Darryl strikes up a conversation with Tim. They have quite a bit in common, and within minutes they have plans to play a round of golf next time Tim goes to Atlanta.

Tim leans toward me and whispers. "I like this guy. Maybe the four of us can get together sometime."

I nod. "Sounds good." Now my hopes are higher than ever that Tim's little secret might be what I want.

Every now and then, he touches my arm, or he looks at me in a way that makes me tingle. I want to say something about how I feel, but this doesn't seem like the best place to do that.

Zeke and the Geeks entertain us with their own style of music—including some we actually recognize. I know that our reunion budget is slim, but I would think Laura could find a better band. However, I also know that Zeke is one of Pete's former drinking buddies, and he feels an allegiance to the guy.

After a slow song that was popular back when I was in school, Zeke calls Laura up to the microphone. Tim stiffens and gives me a strange look.

"What's wrong?"

He folds his hands on the table, stares up at the stage, and shakes his head. "Nothing's wrong. Just look up there."

Next thing I know, I see my picture on the screen behind Laura. I cast a curious look at Tim, who nods toward the stage.

"So you knew about this?"

"Actually, I wasn't sure until I cornered Laura and asked her about something I seen earlier. She told me you was gettin' the award this year."

"Was this the secret you couldn't tell me?" I bite my bottom lip to keep the tears from forming. This award is nice, but it's nothing compared to what I really wanted . . . and now I want that more than ever.

"What's the matter, Priscilla? You look like you're about to cry."

Now I can't stop the flood of tears and flow of words letting Tim know what's been on my mind. "I was hoping you would . . . tell me you . . ." I pull my lips between my teeth, sniffle, and take a deep breath. "Tim, I know this is a weird time to say this, but I can't help myself. I love you, and none of this matters if we can't be together."

His face goes blank, and I want to crawl beneath the table. But then Laura says something that has everyone looking at me, so I have to pretend. Again.

45
Laura

The lights are low, with the glow from the PowerPoint presentation flickerin' at the front of the room. Most of the folks have quit blabbin', so the sound of my recorded voice screechin' through the speakers in the corners of the room comes through loud 'n clear. I cringe as I hear my country twang. I've always prided myself in tryin' to have good grammar, but now I think I might should put some effort into my accent. I mean, a southern accent is soothin', but not when it sounds like it comes from the sticks.

"Good job, hon." Pete winks at me.

"I shoulda had someone else talk."

He crinkles his forehead. "What're you talkin' about? It sounds just like you."

"That's exactly what I'm talkin' about. I sound like a hick."

He puts his arms around me and squeezes. "You're my hick, though, and I love ya."

I cut him a look lettin' him know I don't like bein' called a hick. He tilts his head back and laughs out loud.

"Sh!" And that doesn't come from me. Apparently, folks like what Jack and I put together.

I look over at Priscilla and see the tears tricklin' down her cheeks . . . and not a single bit of her makeup is runnin'. That just beats all. If I'd been in her shoes, I'd have streaks of mascara and eyeliner runnin' down my face.

But I can't let her cry-happy moment irritate me so much. I got my own personal joy to smile . . . and cry about. My oldest young'un is doin' great in the Army. I mean, he's only called home cryin' twice, and that's just 'cause he misses my casseroles that I'm not makin' anymore. Renee finally kicked that Wilson boy to the curb, and even though I got my doubts about her gettin' a job at a bank, she knows what she wants to do. Bonnie Sue is prob'ly gonna not only finish high school, she's lookin' at colleges. If someone had told me when my young'uns were little that Bonnie Sue would turn out to be the academic one, I woulda laughed my butt off on account of she's so into boys and hair and makeup and fashion . . . and celebrity magazines. I actually thought she might wind up doin' hair and workin' for Priscilla, but fickle as she is, she's decided she might wanna learn business instead.

And then there's little Jack, the youngest of my four kids. That boy has always been determined to do whatever he wanted to do, which most of the time isn't what Pete and I want. Before he started talkin' about gettin' his learner's permit, I never saw him actually study a book more than a coupla minutes at a time. But that child is determined to do it on the first round, and he's already memorized most of the book.

Jack's sittin' at the table in the back of the room runnin' the PowerPoint presentation about Priscilla's life. This mornin', I started doubtin' he could pull it off, but once again, he's pulled a rabbit outta the hat and made me proud. He still doesn't know what he wants to do, but I realize now that doesn't matter. Whatever he gets into he'll do well 'cause that's just who Jack is.

Everyone in the room gazes up at the screen . . . well, everyone but Didi, who keeps cuttin' looks over at Priscilla. I have no doubt that if murder was legal, there would be no Priscilla Slater. But Didi doesn't wanna go to jail, so the only killin' she does is in her mind and with her eyes.

"Hey, look at Tim." Pete nudges me in the side. "He looks like he done seen a ghost."

I pull myself from my own thoughts and turn to see Tim starin' down at Priscilla, no longer payin' a bit of attention to the presentation. "Must be somethin' Priscilla said. That's just like her to turn a happy moment into somethin' awful."

"I'm not so sure it's awful." Pete points to Tim, and I swat at his hand, so he lowers it. "But he's clearly surprised about somethin'."

I shake my head and cluck my tongue but stop when I remember that's somethin' my mama does. Seems like ever'day, I get more and more like her. "I hope she lets him down easy. That boy puts up with a lot from her."

Pete grins. "He puts up with a lot from all of us. I wonder why he does that."

"You can't be blind. He's so in love with Priscilla he doesn't know what to do with himself."

46
Priscilla

My heart practically stops as Tim stares at me without speaking then looks down. "Priscilla . . ."

"What?" I wish I'd kept my big fat mouth shut. It's so not me to share my feelings, and the one time I do it, I wish I hadn't.

He gives me a glance of something that resembles sympathy before turning back to the screen with a still shot of one of my TVNS presentations. "You look mighty good up there."

I bite my bottom lip to keep from crying. Finally, my classmates have recognized me for all the hard work I've put into my career. I try to focus on the fact that this is what I've always wanted, but it's hard to override the empty feeling in the pit of my stomach . . . and my heart.

Occasionally, someone will turn around and smile at me. I force myself to smile back, even though it takes every ounce of energy I have.

"I don't know for sure, but they're prob'ly gonna want you to make a speech when this show is over," Tim whispers. "You might wanna start thinkin' of somethin' to say."

Yes, that'll give me something to think about besides Tim's rejection. Ironic how I've been putting him off for thirteen years, while he pursued me with kindness, and now that I'm ready to be in love, he wants . . . well, I'm not sure what, but it's obviously not what I want.

Years of thinking on my feet for TVNS presentations give me what I need to stand up in front of my graduating class. It's the feelings I'm having a problem with.

The show about my life finally comes to an end, and Laura goes right up on the stage, clapping her hands and encouraging everyone else in the room to stand. I'm used to attention, but when the man sitting next to me smiles my knees grow weak, and my heart wants to reach out and grab him.

Laura finally quits clapping and lifts her hands as she leans toward the microphone. "I'd like y'all's attention, please. This reunion is very special because we have someone here who has made a name for herself and put Piney Point on the map. I think we all agree that Priscilla Slater is one of a kind, and we have the honor of knowing someone like her. She makes women beautiful . . . I mean, look around, y'all. Most of us ladies are stylin' with Ms. Prissy Big Hair. Thanks to Priscilla, we know how to make our hair big without losing softness." A few people chuckle. "And women all over the TVNS viewing area can be almost as beautiful as us women from Piney Point."

Some guy I can't see hollers, "No way! We got the most beautiful women in the world!"

Laura laughs. "Honey, I said *almost*." More laughter erupts until she gestures to quiet down. "I'm tickled pink to have Priscilla among us."

I've known Laura most of my life, and I've never heard anything even remotely like this coming from her. She's either had a change of heart, or she's the best actress I've ever seen.

Laura points toward the back of the room. "Now I want to give credit to someone who has worked hard for y'all tonight. The person who is most likely to be the *next* celebrity from

Piney Point is Pete's and my son Jack. He brilliantly put this presentation together, and I don't think anyone will disagree that he did a real bang-up job. Stand up, Jack." She starts clapping again, so everyone in the room—including me—follows suit. Jack stands up and sits down very quickly. "Now it's time for me to bring Priscilla Slater up to the stage to give her our coveted award, the statue for bein' *Most Successful*. This is fittin' on account of she was voted most likely to succeed our senior year. Come on up here, Priscilla."

As I walk up to the stage to accept my award, my knees start to weaken, and a flutter of nerves courses through my body. After dozens of aired Ms. Prissy Big Hair shows on TVNS, even I'm surprised at my case of nerves.

"Speech! Speech!" I'm not positive, but I think Tim might have started the chant that now echoes through the room.

I step up to the microphone and smile, a trick I learned when I first started speaking in public. After the chanting ends, I look around the room. "I'm honored and privileged to accept this award." Then I turn to Laura and wink. "In fact, like you, Laura, I'm tickled pink. You must be very proud of your son Jack. I know I would be. He made me look much better than I really am. Thank you, Jack." I clap, but only a few people join me, so I stop and continue speaking. "Now I want to thank all my classmates from Piney Point High School, particularly you, Laura, for all the hard work you've put into bringing our group together every five years. I know this has been a monumental task, but you've risen to the occasion every time. Thank you, Pete, Celeste, Jimmy, and Tim"—I lock gazes with him before continuing—"Tim, who went to a different school at a different time but has managed to join our class and make us forget he didn't go to school with us. And I thank all of you for coming."

Laura steps back up to the microphone and chatters about some things I don't pay attention to as I walk back toward my spot with Tim. He winks and leans forward. "Good job, Priscilla, but you didn't have to say nothin' about me. I'm just happy to be here."

"I meant every word I said."

His hand brushes my shoulder as he places his arm around my chair, and I tingle at his touch. For the first time in my life, I feel as though I'm free-falling.

Zeke and the Geeks return to the stage after Laura finishes her speech. Tim and I sit there and chat with people who come up to congratulate me. The rest of the night goes by in a blur as I realize how Tim is trying to avoid discussing my revelation.

Since Tim is here to help, we wait until all but the reunion committee has left the Community Center. Tim immediately springs to action, folding chairs, putting them into the racks at the back of the room, and doing whatever else Laura tells him to do. I fold tablecloths, pick up trash, and try hard not to berate myself for blurting my feelings. So what if I told Tim I love him? Is that so bad, or should it even be a surprise? After all, he's been in my life for thirteen years—with me from my earliest days in the salon to my current celebrity status. I've never doubted his motives either. Sure, Tim met me when he was trying to sell me products from his uncle's company, but there's no doubt in my mind that he'd be right there beside me, even if I stopped purchasing anything. At least, he would have been there *before*. I'm not so sure about the future. I might have ruined everything.

Once the last chair is stacked and all the crumbs have been swept, Tim turns to me. "Ready to go now?"

We ride to my mother's house in silence, but once he parks at the curb, he doesn't make a move to get out. "Priscilla . . ." He looks down, sighs, and then meets my gaze. "About what you said earlier. It's not that I . . . well, you know how I've always felt about you—at least before—"

I can't stand to listen to any more. In fact, he's already said enough to let me know it's too late for us. "Stop." I clear my throat. "Tim, I really shouldn't have said what I did. I mean, this whole experience has been such a roller-coaster ride, and my emotions have really gotten the best of me."

He blinks and stares into my eyes for a few seconds. "So you were just talkin' out of emotion."

I nod. "Yes, pretty much."

"I never seen you do that before."

"A lot of things have happened that are new to me, so I'm sure I've been acting out of character quite a bit lately. Besides, you're in New York now running your uncle's company, and I have to spend quite a bit of time in Jackson, so it wouldn't work out anyway."

"Yeah, you got a good point."

"So . . ." I reach for his hand and hold it in both of mine. "Are we still friends?"

"If that's what you want, I reckon I can't see any reason why we shouldn't be."

My heart is starting to ache so badly I can't go on any longer. "I need to go in, or Mother will worry."

"Hang tight, Priscilla." He opens his car door, takes one more glance in my direction and smiles. "I'll be right there."

He gives me a hand to help me out of the car. "Whatcha doin' after church tomorrow?"

"I got a call from Beth Fay. Felicity at TVNS contacted her and said one of the other vendors canceled at the last minute. We need to clear some of the Ms. Prissy Big Hair kits out of the warehouse, so she wanted to know if I was free to go on air first thing Monday morning. I'm flying out of Jackson late

Sunday, so I have to leave in the morning. Beth Fay's meeting me in New York Sunday night."

"Oh. I reckon we can't get together then."

We stand there in my mother's front yard gazing into each other's eyes, until I slowly shake my head. "I'm afraid not."

He walks me to the door and places both hands on my shoulders. "Priscilla, I'm sure once upon a time, me and you woulda made a—"

I place my finger on his lips to shush him. "Thank you for all the wonderful things you've done for me, Tim. You're the best friend a girl can have."

47
Tim

I wanna kick myself all the way to New York and back after tonight. My timin' couldn't be worse, and there's not a single solitary thing I can do about it.

Or maybe there is and I can't figure it out. One person who can, though, is my uncle. No matter what kinda fool I make of myself in front of him, he's proved many times over he'll still be there for me. It's past ten o'clock, but they've lived up in New York long enough to think it's still early.

Uncle Hugh answers his cell phone. As he listens to me talk about what happened this evenin', I hear him gaspin', but he don't say nothin' right away. Finally, when I run outta steam, he clears his throat. "I was afraid something like this might happen."

"So what do I do about it?"

"Timothy, you know good 'n well I don't know much about women. If Tammy didn't come right out and tell me what she's thinkin', she and I would never have gotten together. I'm the most clueless man on the planet." He laughs softly. "So why don't you give Tammy a call?"

"Isn't she there with you?"

"Nah, she went back to Vancleave early. I told her I'd join her as soon as you got back to run the office."

"Think she'll still be up?"

"Even if she's not, she'll wanna talk to you about this. Timothy, one thing I will tell you is that when it comes to matters of the heart, you hafta speak your mind and not leave anything unsaid. Women might like the strong silent type, but they still want us to tell them the important stuff."

"Okay, I'll call Aunt Tammy now." After we hang up, I pause to ponder how to tell her what's going on. Before I have a chance to punch in her number, my phone rings.

"Hey, Timothy, this is Aunt Tammy. Hugh just called and said you need me. So tell me all about your problems."

I give her a quick rundown about my feelings for Priscilla. "Tonight she told me she loves me, but later on she said it was on account of all the emotion. Things has been crazy for her lately."

"Timothy, are you listening to yourself?"

"Uh—"

"Things have been *crazy* for *both* of you."

"So what're you sayin', Aunt Tammy?"

"Bless your heart, Timothy, you take after your uncle on matters of the heart, so I'll spell it out for you. You need to put a stop to all this silliness and get a commitment from her. You've gone on long enough without one."

"So how do I get this . . . commitment? She ain't exactly easy to hold still."

Aunt Tammy laughs. "You've known her long enough, so why don't you propose?"

I 'bout near choke. "Propose?"

"That's what I said. You love her, and she said she loves you, so why not?" The tone of her voice dips lower. "Unless you just want to let things continue as they have and risk her finding someone else to marry."

"She wouldn't do that."

Aunt Tammy makes a tsking sound. "She might. When a girl's emotions get the best of her, no matter how smart or successful she is, she's likely to react when the opportunity shows itself."

I can't think of anything worse than Priscilla marryin' someone else. "I reckon she'd be a might surprised."

"Good. Catch her off guard."

"I can't do that. Me and Priscilla . . . well, it just won't work out. She even said that. If we'd done it five years ago, maybe, but not now."

"And why not?"

"Well, for one thing, we're both set in our ways."

Aunt Tammy laughs. "Bad reason."

"Bad or not, it's still a reason." I stop and try to remember what she told me, and then I remember. "Oh, and don't forget that I live in New York City now, and she don't."

"How do you feel about moving back to Mississippi?"

"Huh?"

Aunt Tammy laughs. "Don't tell Hugh I told you this, but he's missin' New York City somethin' awful. Said the crickets are near 'bout driving him batty."

"So . . . are you demotin' or firin' me?"

"I'm not firin' or demotin' you, Timothy, honey. I'm just tryin' to save you from a lifetime of loneliness."

"Well . . ." I have no idea what to say to that.

"What are you doing tomorrow afternoon?"

"Nothin'. I booked my flight back to New York on Tuesday, thinkin' I'd need to help clean up after the reunion and return some of the things we borrowed, but Laura told me she don't need me."

"Good. Why don't I come up to Hattiesburg, and we can have a nice little chat. I might even book a hotel room and stay overnight so we can watch Priscilla on TVNS."

48
Priscilla

Mother gives me a good-bye hug on my way out the door. I have to hurry to catch a plane to New York. I'm coming out with a new Ms. Prissy Big Hair line with some additional products in the fall, so this is the perfect opportunity—at least for business.

As I drive to the airport, I reflect on what has happened over the past week. All my friends whose lives were way more messed up than mine have found their grooves, and here I am, wishing I could have a piece of what they have. I want to be in love and know that someone will always be there for me. I want someone to share my thoughts with at the end of the day. I want a man who will look at me first thing in the morning and not mention the fact that one side of my face is smashed with wrinkles from my pillowcase and that my hair is lopsided. I want a man I can laugh and cry with. And I don't want just anyone. I want Tim.

My flight is uneventful, so my thoughts go back to what I'm missing in life by getting everything I've worked for. The irony of success is that it's the price we sometimes have to pay that can lead to failure in every other aspect of life. And I'm paying that price.

Beth Fay's flight arrived an hour before mine, but she said she'd wait for me at baggage claim. And she's right there, shifting her weight from one foot to the other, checking her watch, and looking around. When she spots me, she smiles and waves.

"An hour seems like forever," she says. "Let's get to the hotel so we can have some dinner and go over your itinerary."

Even though Beth Fay drives me a bit batty when she travels with me, she handles enough of the minute details that I can kick back and simply do my job. And I know better than to even try to share a room with her. At first she balked when I said to book two rooms, but when I reminded her she'd have her own bathroom, she said she thought that would be an excellent idea.

"I hope you don't mind staying at the Marriott this time." Beth Fay looks at me and waits for a response. When I just shrug, she continues. "I called the Waldorf, and all they had vacant were their two smallest rooms, which won't be big enough for all our stuff."

That would've been okay with me, but I know how persnickety Beth Fay can be. "The Marriott's fine."

She breaks into a smile. "I love the Marriott. It's so close to the theaters."

"Beth Fay, we're not going to have time to go to the theater. This is all work for me, and I want to get back to Jackson as soon as possible."

She raises her eyebrows and pulls her chin in. "My, my, my. You sure are testy today. What happened to you?"

I let out a sigh. "Sorry, Beth Fay. It's been a long week."

After staring at me for several very uncomfortable seconds, she turns away and looks out the cab window. I'm happy for the silence, and not at all disappointed that she doesn't strike up another conversation until we arrive at the Marriott.

We check into our rooms and get situated before dinner. Then it takes us the better part of the night to go over all the things I need to talk about on air.

"Don't forget to mention that the volumizing system not only adds body to a woman's hair, it moisturizes it." Beth Fay jots some notes down on my card. "Last time you left that out, and I just happen to know that most women associate a lot of body with dry, fly-away hair."

"Is that so?" I look at her in disbelief. Until I came along, Beth Fay had no experience in the hair business, and now look at her.

She tilts her head. "Well, isn't it?"

"I suppose."

"Oh, and I hope you remembered to bring a solid-color top. That print blouse you wore last time didn't do a thing for you."

"I remembered." I'm glad I'll be alone in my room in just a few minutes. I stand up and start stacking papers. "I'm exhausted, so I think it's time to wrap this up for the night. We can pick up anything we left off in the morning."

"I'll call you at six sharp."

"Fine." I walk her to the door and close it the second she's out of my room. It takes me about ten minutes to get ready for bed and turn off the light. And then it takes me more than an hour to stop thinking about all the mistakes I've made with Tim before I'm able to fall asleep.

We eat a light breakfast at the hotel before getting a cab to the TVNS studios. Felicity meets us and takes us to a room to get ready. She smiles at Beth Fay. "We were only able to get two hair models on such short notice, so how would you like to be one of the models today?"

Beth Fay's reaction is no surprise, but it is rather startling. She bolts out of her chair, pumping her fist, shouting, "I've finally made the big time!"

Felicity fights a giggle as she turns to me. "Looks like the answer is yes."

One of the producers comes to the door and motions for Felicity to go see about something, leaving me with my assistant who is currently floating several inches above the floor. "Can you believe this? I'm actually gonna be on TV. And I owe it all to you, Priscilla. If you hadn't hired me, I'd never be—"

Felicity returns. "C'mon, let's go get the two of you into makeup."

After Beth Fay goes off with her stylist, Felicity whispers, "I hope you don't mind that I asked her, but you did say you'd like to see how she does on air."

"I think this is perfect. After she calms down, I think she'll be just fine."

"So tell me about Tim."

I lean toward her. "What are you talking about, Felicity?"

"How do you feel about him?"

"Where did that come from?"

She shrugs and glances away. "I don't know. I just wondered after our talk and the picture and all . . ."

"Pictures can lie, you know."

Felicity turns back to me and lifts an eyebrow. "Can they really?"

It's time to take our places on the studio set. Beth Fay listens attentively as the producer gives her instructions, and the assistant attaches my microphone. The second we're live, Beth Fay's expression freezes, and I can't allow myself to look at her at first or risk cracking up with laughter at her fear. I can tell Felicity is dealing with the same thing.

"So let's go over all the benefits of the Ms. Prissy Big Hair system," Felicity tells our viewing audience. "The shampoo and conditioner are designed to work synergistically to add body and texture, while leaving your hair hydrated and silky soft." She turns to me.

"That's right," I add. "And now we use this special volumizing comb to lift the hair—"

"Excuse me, but we have a call from someone with a question." Felicity smiles into the camera. "Good morning, Eve from Tennessee. Have you ever used the Ms. Prissy Big Hair before?"

"Oh yes, and I've been tellin' all my friends how fabulous it is. All the other big hair products make your hair crunchy and stiff, but Prissy's products leave my hair so soft and feminine feelin'. My boyfriend told me just the other day he not only loves the way my hair looks but how it feels and smells."

"That's wonderful, Eve. So what's your question?"

She asks if the products work for all hair types, and I assure her they do. Satisfied, she hangs up, and we take our next call. Everyone who has tried the products loves them, and those who haven't tried them are excited.

"We have another call, this one from a man." Felicity picks up a volumizing comb and starts fidgeting with it, avoiding eye contact with me. "Good morning, Tim from Mississippi."

My mouth immediately goes dry. Tim from Mississippi? Then I let out a nervous laugh. It has to be a coincidence.

And then Tim speaks. "Hi, there, Felicity. I'm calling with a testimonial and a question for Priscilla."

Felicity holds up a finger letting me know something is going on. "Let's hear your testimonial first."

"My Aunt Tammy's sittin' right here, and she said to let your customers know the Ms. Prissy Big Hair system works just fine on processed hair. Can I ask Priscilla my question now?"

Felicity turns to me and nods. My face is now so hot I can only imagine how red it must be. I clear my throat. "What can I help you with, Tim?"

"You can start by agreeing to become my wife."

I glance around the studio and see the producers and camera crew laughing and nudging each other, letting me know they're in on whatever sick joke is being played. My body feels as though someone has turned it inside out. I want to run, but we're live on air, so I can't do much of anything.

"Tim, we're talking about the Ms. Prissy Big Hair."

"Yeah, I know you are, but I'm talkin' about us. Priscilla, I love you with all my heart, and I want to marry you. All I'm askin' for is an answer. Will you please make me the happiest man on earth and marry me?"

I open my mouth, but nothing will come out. Felicity gives the producer the sign to cut to the B-roll. We made the film clip about how my conditioner goes deep into the hair shaft and hydrates it, making it bouncy and soft. And that's exactly how my insides feel at the moment.

The producer walks over shaking his head. "The phones are ringing off the hook. Your fans want to know your answer. Is it yes or no?"

I take a sip of water one of the production assistants brings and nod. "Okay, I'm ready to go back on air."

Felicity narrows her eyes. "Are you sure?"

Beth Fay is sitting stone-still, watching me. I smile at her, and her lips quiver into a slight grin.

"Positive."

As soon as the cameras are rolling again, I take a deep breath and smile into the camera. "Tim, I think this is something we should discuss privately, but for now, the answer will have to be"—I pause until everyone in the room looks like they're ready to pounce on me—"maybe. Call me later after the show, okay?" Before anyone else has a chance to speak . . . or even breathe, I pick up the can of volumizing hairspray. "And ladies, for those of you who experience limp locks by mid-afternoon, this spray will perk your hair right up." I spray some into my own hair and scrunch it between my fingers. "See? My once sad, lifeless hair is happy again."

The sound of Tim chuckling in my earpiece makes me smile. Felicity grins, gives me the thumbs-up, and starts sharing her own testimonial about the Ms. Prissy Big Hair system, giving me a moment to regroup.

The entire mood of the show has changed, but I'm fine with that. Instead of callers asking about my product, they ask questions about my relationship with Tim. I answer as noncommittally as I can, and when I get stumped, Felicity helps me out. She's a pro and a very good friend.

We sell out in record time, so my show ends early. As soon as my microphone is removed, Felicity lets out a breath. "All I can say is *wow*."

I laugh. "Yeah, me too."

After I'm off air, I head straight to the coffee shop at the corner. My cell phone rings, and I see that it's Tim. With a smile and a shaky hand, I answer.

"Hey, I hope you're not ticked about what I did."

"No, Tim. In fact I'm very happy."

"You are?" His voice catches, so he clears his throat. "I mean, that's good."

"Yes, it's very good."

An awkward silence falls between us, and we both start to speak. We laugh.

"You go first," he says.

I suck in a breath and close my eyes as I blow it out. "Okay, how soon can you be in New York?"

"That's what I was about to say. Aunt Tammy didn't waste no time—I mean *any* time—booking me a flight, so I should be there by suppertime. How about me and you—or you and me—gettin' together?"

"Absolutely."

"Put on your prettiest dress 'cause I'm takin' you someplace special."

As soon as we hang up, I head back to my hotel to rest and start getting ready for the big date. I have more than half a day, but I want to look my best for Tim.

The afternoon drags, but when Tim finally calls from the lobby letting me know he's here, I lose all sense of time. I grab my clutch and go to the elevator. All the way down, I feel as though everyone is looking at me, but I don't really care. The only thing that matters to me at the moment is what is about to happen with Tim.

We reach the lobby, and the elevator doors open. As the other people step off, they make a path for me, which is strange. Then I see what's happening. Tim is standing about ten feet from the elevator, down on one knee, with a ring box in his hand.

"Priscilla Slater, will you make me the happiest man in the whole entire world and . . ." He looks me in the eye and winks. "And—"

Without waiting for him to finish, I close the distance between us, wrap my arms around him, and say, "Absolutely, yes!"

He slips the ring on my finger, and that's when I realize how much I'm shaking. But he seems calm, which relaxes me.

Everyone applauds before scattering. Tim offers me his hand, and I take it. "Sorry it took me so long," I say.

"That's okay. This was all worth waiting for." He gestures toward the door. "Let's go eat. I'm starvin'."

I laugh. "Just like a man."

"Yup. I reckon there's somethin' to that sayin' that we're all alike."

"Trust me, Tim, you are totally different from any other man I've ever met." I squeeze him. "And that's what I love about you."

Discussion Questions

1. Which character in the book do you relate to the most—Priscilla, Laura, Trudy, Tim, or Celeste? Why?
2. Why do you think Priscilla isn't happy, even though she's reached her career goals. In what ways could she be more content?
3. How have you seen Priscilla's relationship with her mother change? Can you see yourself in either of them?
4. How would you describe the relationship between Laura and Priscilla? Laura and Celeste?
5. Laura had issues with both of her stepparents, but one of them gained favor during this story. What does this say about Laura and her family values?
6. Why do you think Tim came back to help with the twentieth reunion, other than his relationship with Priscilla?
7. What is the biggest change you saw in Trudy? Do you think she's really over Michael? If so, what helped her see the light?
8. Have you ever had a makeover at a salon? Did you feel different afterward? Did you keep up the routine, or did you go back to how you looked before?
9. What do you think was the catalyst that changed Laura's husband, Pete?
10. Priscilla obviously had to make quite a few choices throughout the Class Reunion series. Were you ever faced with having to make a decision between family and career? Are you happy with your decision? What would you change?
11. Have you been disappointed after you got what you thought you wanted? What did you do about it?
12. Did anything surprise you in *Tickled Pink?* If so, what?

We hope you enjoyed *Tickled Pink*, the final book in Debby Mayne's Class Reunion series. If you haven't read the first two books, *Pretty Is as Pretty Does* and *Bless Her Heart*, here's the first chapter of the series, which introduces us to Priscilla and her classmates as they prepare for their ten-year reunion.

Pretty Is as Pretty Does

1
Priscilla Slater

We are thrilled to announce
Piney Point High School's
10-year reunion
on June 7, 2003, at 7:30 PM
in Piney Point High's
newly renovated gymnasium.
Attire: Sunday best
RSVP: Laura Moss 601-555-1515
PS: There will be a preparty
at Shenanigan's in Hattiesburg
starting at about 5:00 PM.

Wow. Ten years. As I read my high school reunion invitation a second time, I can't help smiling. Although I own one of the most successful businesses in my hometown of Piney Point, Mississippi, I've lost track of most of the people I graduated with.

Knowing the people I went to high school with, this is going to be one crazy event—that is, if everyone attends. I'm not surprised Laura added a preparty to the invitation. Her husband has never attended any social event before prepar-tying his face off—even in high school. Pete Moss graduated with the distinct honor of high school lush, and as far as I know, he continues to hold that honor, which is ironic since I don't remember ever seeing Laura touching a drop of anything stronger than her mama's two-day-old sweet tea.

Poor Laura.

I pin the invitation to the bulletin board beside the fridge. And for extra measure, I jot the date on my calendar. In pencil, just in case . . . well, in case something comes up.

As I kick off my killer high-heels, I wonder if Maurice will be there. I sigh as I remember the guy who, in my mind, almost became my boyfriend. I used to stand in front of my bedroom mirror, practicing "looks." I think back and realize things weren't as they seemed, but I still wonder if he'll see me differently now that I've made something of myself. Not that I'm trying to impress anyone.

And I sure haven't impressed my parents. Quite the opposite. Still, I've taken a small-town beauty shop and turned it into a fabulous business—one of the most successful in Piney Point. And I'm not ready to stop there. I already have three shops—the original, which used to be called Dolly's Cut 'n Curl, one in Hattiesburg that formerly held the title Goldy's Locks, and the salon where my current office is located in Jackson. In honor of the first, they are all called Prissy's Cut 'n Curl, although I'm seriously considering changing the name to something a little trendier since I'm planning to expand. I mean, really, can you imagine anyone in New York City telling her friends she gets her hair done at the Cut 'n Curl? Besides, I hate being called Prissy.

I'll never forget Mother's reaction when she found out I'd dropped out of my first semester of college and enrolled at the Pretty and Proud School of Cosmetology. You'd have thought I announced I wanted to pledge Phi Mu or something. No offense to anyone in Phi Mu. It's just that Mother was a Chi Omega, and that makes me a legacy, which carries even more clout than being Miss Piney Point, something I never was. Mother would have had a fit if I'd even suggested entering a beauty contest. So when I met some of the Chi Omegas at Ole Miss, I was surprised by how many of them were beauty queens—something Mother never mentioned. Makes me wonder what happened to her between her Chi O heydays and now.

My parents are academics and proud of it. Mother is a professor of English, and Dad is head of the history department at the Piney Point Community College, but you'd think they had tenure at an Ivy League school the way they carry on.

I missed lunch today and my stomach's grumbling. But when the noise turns to hissing, I relent and pull a Lean Cuisine from the freezer. I know how to cook, but it seems pointless to do that for one. I also know that one Lean Cuisine isn't enough, so while it heats in the microwave, I grab a bag of salad and dump the contents into a bowl. Then I chop a tomato, grab a few olives, and pour a tablespoon of ranch dressing on top. I step back and study the salad before I squirt another tablespoon or two. The salad's full of fiber and the Lean Cuisine is low-fat, so I figure that balances out the extra calories.

Just as I'm about to sit down and enjoy dinner, the phone rings. *It has to be Mother,* I think. She's the only one who ever calls my house phone. I hesitate, but my daughterly duties overcome me. What if she needs something? I'd never be able to live with the guilt if I didn't answer an important call from the woman who gave birth to me after twenty hours of labor—or so she tells folks when they ask why I'm an only child.

"Did you get your invitation yet?" she asks without letting me finish my *hello.* "Are you planning on going?"

Leave it to Mother to know about the reunion before me. "Yes . . . well, probably."

"There's really no point, Priscilla. After all, it's all about showing off all your accomplishments, and it's not like you've made all that much of your life."

I bite my tongue, as I always have. I want to let Mother know how I really feel, but talking back has never gotten me anywhere with her, so I somehow manage to keep my yap shut. She takes that as encouragement to keep going.

"That silly-frilly little job of yours will get old one of these days, and then what will you do?"

"Mother, you know it's more than a job to me."

She laughs. "All you do is decorate the outside of women—"

"Some of our clients are men," I remind her.

"Okay, so you work on the outer appearance of women . . . and men. How does that really make any difference in the world? You could have been so much more than that, Priscilla. Your father and I—"

"My business makes a huge difference in a lot of people's lives. Our clients feel better about themselves, and I keep a couple dozen people employed so they can feed their families."

"Well, there is that." Mother pauses as she reloads. "At any rate, why would you even want to go?"

"Because I want to?" I can't help the fact that I'm starting to sound like an adolescent.

"That's a shock. Your father and I were wondering why you haven't shown your face in town in the past year. Then it dawned on me that you didn't want folks to see you wearing braces. I'm surprised you even have a salon left. You know what the mice do when the cat's away."

"I hire people I can trust," I tell her through gritted teeth.

"So are you going to the reunion or not?"

"Like I said, I'm not sure."

"Do you want your old classmates to see you in braces? After all, since you're so into appearances, I would think—"

"I'm getting them off soon, so that's not an issue." I suspect she's annoyed that I got braces for cosmetic reasons. I begged Mother to let me have braces when I was a kid, but after the dentist assured her it wasn't necessary for good dental care, she told me I was just being shallow. Throughout high school, I smiled with my mouth closed so people wouldn't notice my overlapping front teeth.

Mother lets out one of her long-suffering sighs. "Okay, well, if you do decide to go, give us plenty of notice so we can clear our schedule for your visit. Your father and I have social obligations, since he's the head of his department."

"Yes, I know." Ever since Dad's promotion, Mother likes to remind me of his position. And it's been at least three years. "Whatever I decide, there's no need to clear your schedule."

"You know you're always welcome to stay here at the house," she adds.

I wish I really did feel welcome. "Thank you, Mother." But I've learned to live with the tension.

"And don't forget to bring your church clothes. We're not like your church in the city. We still show our respect by dressing nicely."

"Yes, I know."

I hear Dad calling out to her, so I'm relieved when she tells me she needs to run. After I hang up, I lean against the wall and slide to the floor. Talking to my mother is exhausting.

On my way to the office the next morning, Mother's voice rings through my head. "Someday you'll thank me for this," she'd said when she dropped me off on the steps of my dorm at Ole Miss, her alma mater. She reminded me it's always good to start out away from home to get a taste of being on my own but with a safety net—as if I was arguing about where I was going to college. The real argument happened when I dropped out.

See, ever since I entered my teenage years, I dreamed of doing something with clothes and hair and eventually turn it into my own business. I never minded studying in high school if it meant making my parents happy, but college wasn't the path that would lead me to where I wanted the rest of my life to go. Just *do* it, right? Some of the most successful young entrepreneurs either skipped or dropped out of college. Look at Steve Jobs and Mark Zuckerberg.

I pull into the parking lot of my Jackson shop and open the car door. And pause. I sit there and stare at the two-story, red-brick building with an upscale salon on the ground level and my office upstairs. This is the first salon I built from the ground up, and I'm mighty proud of its success in the two short years since I've been there. The Jackson newspaper did a story on me once and claimed I'm lucky in business. I might not have finished my first semester of college, but I'm a logical thinker and planner. I did a year-long study and determined this location had the most potential for growth. The old mansions in the neighborhood are being bought for a song, divided up and renovated into apartments, and sold for a fortune. Then there's all the twenty-something, fresh-out-of-college hipsters moving into those apartments. My success isn't luck—it's knowing what I want and being willing to work hard for it.

Finally, I get out of the car, grab my briefcase, and head up the side staircase to my office. Before I open the door, I know Tim is here by the fresh scent of Abercrombie and Fitch's latest cologne for men.

"Looky what the cat drug in."

"What are you doing here so early?" I toss my briefcase into the tiny office behind my assistant, Mandy, who is too busy opening mail and acting like she's minding her own business for me to think she's not getting a kick out of my annoyance. "Any messages?"

"Just got here, Prissy. You got a ton of mail from yesterday."

"I need to talk to the mailman. It's just not right for all our mail to get here after we leave."

"I know, right?" Mandy cuts a glance over at Tim then rolls her eyes toward me.

"So are you here for my order?" I ask Tim. He's still in one of the three chairs across from Mandy's desk.

Tim is a sales rep for his uncle's beauty supply company, and he covers most of the center of the state. If he gave all his customers the attention he gives me, he'd never have time to sleep. Even Mandy has noticed.

"I thought I'd take you to breakfast."

I fold my arms and arch an eyebrow as I study him. "What's the occasion?"

He shrugs. "I dunno. I thought maybe we could talk about your reunion."

"Are you kidding me?" I shriek. "*You* know about the reunion?"

"Um . . . " He glances over at Mandy who shrugs and busies herself with some paperwork that's been sitting on her desk for a week. Finally, he turns to me and meets my gaze with challenge. "Yeah. I talked to Sheila last week when I stopped by your salon in Piney Point."

Sheila's the hairdresser I put in charge of the Piney Point salon when I left to open the Jackson office. "Why did you stop by there? I do all my ordering here."

If Tim doesn't stop shrugging so much, his shoulders will get stuck. "Old time's sake, and all that." He stands. "So if you don't have a date, I'm available."

Tim has a crush on me. We dated for a while, but after he started getting serious, I resisted all his advances. I have a business to run, and I don't have time for romantic distractions. Besides, the chemistry isn't there for me. "It's almost two months away. I have no idea what I'm doing that night."

He follows me into my office. "At least think about it. We've been friends for a long time, and you can totally be yourself with me." He holds both hands out to his sides and makes one of his goofy faces. "My mama taught me good manners, so I won't embarrass you. I know which fork to use for the salad, and I even have my own tux."

I can't help laughing. "You're kidding, right?"

"Yeah, you start with the outside silverware and work your way toward the plate."

"No, Tim," I say slowly. "I'm talking about the tux. You seriously own one?"

He nods.

"But why?" I leave out the part about how he has always fancied himself a redneck, and even if he hadn't come out and said that, I would've known the instant he told me he owns every single book Lewis Grizzard and Jeff Foxworthy ever wrote.

All satisfied and full of himself, he replies, "It's from my stand-up comic days, back before I came to work for Uncle Hugh."

That explains a lot. "That might be rather ostentatious."

"Osten-what?"

Oops. "Showy." He looks so eager to please, I can't tell him no right now. "I'll have to let you know, but first, tell me why my last hair color order is taking so long."

"I take it you don't want to go to breakfast?"

Want to learn more about author
Debby Mayne and check out other great
fiction from Abingdon Press?

Sign up for our fiction newsletter at
www.AbingdonPress.com
to read interviews with your favorite authors, find tips
for starting a reading group, and stay posted on what
new titles are on the horizon. It's a place to connect
with other fiction readers or post a
comment about this book.

Be sure to visit Debby online!

www.debbymayne.com
http://debbymayne.blogspot.com

Abingdon fiction™

Every Quilt Has A Story

Enjoy the Quilts of Love novels from Abingdon Fiction

Visit us Online
www.AbingdonFiction.com

Find us on Facebook
Abingdon Press | Fiction

Follow us on Twitter
@AbingdonFiction